I0780596

E.J. ASHMORE

FOR THIS VERY PURPOSE

By E.J. Ashmore

ISBN:978-1-968792-38-1

Endorsement

EJ's unique perspective brings the Exodus to life on a deeply personal level, revealing how God woos His people into relationship, proving His jealousy for them, and entering into a dramatic courtship to win their hearts. By focusing not only on God's pursuit of His people as a whole but also each individual—Hebrew and Egyptian alike—EJ beautifully showcases the redemptive power of God's love."
—Joel Richardson, NYT Bestselling author, internationally recognized Bible teacher.

Acknowledgements

First and foremost, I'd like to thank my dad, Greg, and my son, Adam, for believing in me, and along with Melissa, and Alison from church, and Rachel, for being my first readers and pushing me to publish. Thank you, Jed, from Scribophile for teaching me all about "telling" and going through each of my books line by line *twice* to sharpen and improve my writing and believing in my story. Thank you, Lynne from ACFW Scribes, for teaching me about close third person vs distant third person, for your great recommendations, and for cheering me on. Thank you, Doug from ACFW Scribes, for being my cheerleader and encourager. Thank you to my editor, Sarah, for your meticulous work on both books. Thank you Cynthia Hickey, for giving my beloved books a chance. And thank you, Joel Richardson, for showing me the big picture of God's beautiful love story and redemption plan, all your teachings, and your patience with me as I hounded you for publishing advise.

To my precious sons,

Adam and Zackary.

Book One

But for this very purpose I have raised you up, to show you My power, so that My name may be proclaimed in all the earth.

Exodus 9:16

Terms

Avaris: small town of Hebrews at the bottom of Goshen
Goshen: Top part of Egypt designated for the Hebrews and their sheep
On: Egyptian name for Heliopolis
Memf: Egyptian name for Memphis
Jt: Ancient Egyptian for father
Mwt: Ancient Egyptian for mother
Abba: Hebrew for father
Ima: Hebrew for mother

Main Characters:

Hebrews
Eliza: 16 years old Hebrew slave
Miera: Eliza's 11-year-old sister
Adam: Eliza's 17-year-old brother
Zechariah: Eliza's 15 years old brother
Sarah: Eliza's mother
Jeremiah: Eliza's father
Toddler twin girls: Eliza's 3 year-old sisters
Rahel: Eliza's 16-year-old best friend, Hebrew slave
Moshe: Moses
Aharon: Aaron
Hoshea: 40-year-old pyramid slave

Egyptians
Seti: 18 years old Egyptian. Son of Ameneten
Sabu: Seti's 18-year-old friend
Huya: Seti's mother
Ameneten: Seti's father and Egyptian priest
Kabelo: Seti's 15-year-old brother
Nala: Sabu's wife
Lumeri: Seti's 17-year-old betrothed

Egyptian Priests
Kipuri
Amoshe
Sebeki
Asmuri
Ipuur

Chewy: Seti's horse
Nimrod: Sabu's horse

Chapter 1

"I hope you didn't slop that on my new floor." Huya's harping voice jolted Eliza from her daydreaming on the door stoop.

A cat scurried out the wooden door, and it smacked her backside. Dirty dishwater splashed from the clay basin she held. After scanning the area, Eliza found the woman glaring at her from the rooftop patio. "No, my lady. I was careful."

Looming near the ledge, Huya braided the long locks of a black wig with amethyst beads, though a bobbed, blonde wig topped her head. The nightly routine of preparing the next day's hairstyle and jewelry had a calming effect on the usually temperamental woman. She pointed her finger. "I know what you did the other day. You can't hide anything from me."

Eliza cringed. She had dragged the basin across Huya's new floor, leaving a scuff mark on the orange mosaic tiles two nights before. Buffing it out with a rag only made it worse, and covering it with a mat was conspicuous enough. Gazing toward the stable at the end of the steps, Eliza swallowed the words at the edge of her tongue.

She reminded herself to be grateful to have been assigned to such a prominent Egyptian family. It could have been much worse—she could be making bricks or gathering straw like her brothers and parents. At sixteen years of age, she could easily be swapped out to the mills or fields. Her mother's words echoed in her mind: "Don't mess this up, Eliza. Very few Hebrews have it as good as you. God's protecting you two beneath their roof."

The truth of those words settled deep. Not only were her tasks minimal compared to what the majority of her people endured, but her younger sister worked alongside her—providence at its finest. Plus, having a fly-on-the-wall view of the handsome Seti wasn't bad either.

Nevertheless, servitude would be easier if her masters didn't hover over her every move. The mistress was a thorn in her flesh.

Eliza suppressed a sigh and dipped her head. "I'm deeply sorry for my clumsiness, my lady, and I promise to scrub it clean." The basin jabbed into her hip. She set it on the ground, then proceeded to fully bow. Up until the evening, the day had been uneventful, thanks to Eliza keeping a low profile in anticipation of her next question. But now her fate hung on the scuffed mosaic. "May we leave after I dump this?"

"No. You should be whipped. Scalded. My Amene' will bring home buffing oil tonight, and you'd better hope it gets those marks out. Stay up all night if need be."

Eliza's head shot up. "It's the seventh day, and the contract says we can return to Goshen each week—"

"I know what the contract says, you rat. It's a suggestion, not an obligation. You don't deserve it this week."

"Oh, please! I must go." The nagging premonition that this could be the last sabbath she'd see her family had weighed on her all week. While wealthy Egyptians spent their seventh days in the luxuries of concrete baths fenced off along the Nile, their domestic slaves returned home for one free day and night.

"I beg of you," Eliza pleaded. "I'll scrub it upon my return. It's not going anywhere. I'll do extra tasks. Paint your toes. Fix the hole in the stable door. Anything. I must go home this week." Tears welled in her eyes. She folded her hands and planted her face to the ground. If bystanders saw, and Huya was aware, all the better.

After a moment of reveling in Eliza's groveling, Huya scoffed and narrowed her kohl-rimmed eyes. "You're not touching my feet. But you will fix the hole in the door and polish the scuff marks when you return. And don't ask for help, either. Now scat, before I change my mind."

"Thank you! Thank you, my lady. I promise I will work hard and not ask for help." Eliza jumped to her feet and grabbed the basin.

With a flick of a hand and a click of her tongue, Huya turned back to her work on the wig.

Eliza hurried down the stone steps toward the stable. After dumping the dishwater behind it, she dried her hands on her tunic and checked the area for her younger sister. Miera was last seen sweeping, but she wasn't there now. Perfect. Her absence bought time to wait for Seti's imminent arrival.

Pacing at the rear of the stable where Huya wouldn't see her, Eliza filled her lungs with the scent of livestock and horses—refreshing compared to the stickiness inside the Ameneten home. Though structurally sound to withstand a sandstorm, it didn't allow for much breathability. Soon, she'd make the three-hour trek home under a cool night of stars, a tranquil prelude to the elation of seeing her family. She couldn't wait. But for now, she paused at the rear entrance of the stable to admire the bright, orange sky fading into deep shades of red.

She'd bet a full plate of gazelle and a warm slice of honey-bread that Seti savored the same sunset somewhere. The older son of Master Ameneten unknowingly brought joy to her work week. His presence sent her into an imaginary world of engaging conversations, adventures in undiscovered places, painted skies, and star-filled nights.

She'd fit nicely under his arm at the end of the day, nestled in his warmth as he related his latest studies. A couple of years older than Eliza, Seti spent his days studying for the priesthood. His flawlessly toned physique, thick black hair, and deep almond eyes set her heart aflutter. Yet who was she but a dirty Hebrew, invisible but for the occasional scolding or teasing? Of all the boys she could have admired back in Goshen, she had to fall for a betrothed Egyptian.

The sun had barely skimmed the horizon when the thunder of sprinting horses and chariot wheels reached her ears. Seti. Lumeri's screams rose above the din as always. Eliza dove behind a horse, sending cats scampering in every direction.

Seti's horse skidded to a halt outside the door, his painted wooden chariot barely missing the support pole. He roared with laughter while his betrothed, Lumeri, desperately clung to him.

A second chariot burst through Seti's dust cloud, smashing into the stable door and tilting sideways before coming to a rest on both wheels. Seti's best friend, Sabu, regained his balance, while his wife, Nala, hunkered at his feet.

The rat-sized hole Eliza had promised to fix now encompassed half of the door. Jagged pieces of wood stuck out at every angle. She drew in a breath and kept low. Nothing worked in her favor.

Seti leaped from his chariot with a fancy step-dance in the sand beside his friend. He twirled around Sabu on his toes, slapped him on the shoulder, and laughed before finishing with a kick of the washbasin as the grand finale.

"Just wait." Sabu helped Nala from his chariot. "Every victor has a fall."

The dirt cloud filling the stable didn't bother the boys but sent Nala into a coughing fit. She hunched over, her wig sliding off-kilter.

Seti smoothed Lumeri's jet-black hair with his hand and tucked a strand behind her ear with the sensitivity of handling a glass figurine. Eliza raked her own thick, knotty locks back into a bun, tying it with a scrap of cloth from her pocket. Curls sprang out around her face. She licked her hands and ran them over the frizz.

"Are you well?" Seti's voice was quiet and gentle—a voice he only used for Lumeri.

Eliza held her breath, not willing to miss a thing.

With a forced smile, Lumeri nodded, avoiding his eyes. Instead, she straightened the silver sequins trimming her pink tunic. Unlike most Egyptians who could barely afford dyed cotton, she wore a different color every day. If this counted as her daywear, Eliza could only imagine what Lumeri donned for special occasions.

"I asked if it was all right to race," Seti said.

"I'll be fine, Seti."

His concerned gaze remained on her as he removed the woven bag from his shoulder. Though reckless and haughty at times, he was a man of sensitivity and tenderness toward those he loved. A flutter broke forth in Eliza's heart as she pondered what it'd be like to be at the center of such devotion. While Lumeri worked on her tunic and Sabu tended to his hacking wife, Seti pulled a lump of cake from his bag and passed a piece to each of his friends.

The aroma of cinnamon tickled Eliza's nose, competing with the dusty stable air and rank body odor. Her mouth watered, but she'd have to wait and eat her mother's cakes in Goshen.

"I'm the only one who can make it around the S-Turn without slowing. In fact, Chewy speeds up." Seti rubbed Chewy's nose and peered at Sabu from the corner of his eye. "You might as well not even bother."

"Hmmph. It'll soon be called the Sabu Turn. I've got to have at least one thing in this city named after me," Sabu said, crumbs spraying from his lips.

Their gloating and stories had grown predictable each weekend after their races around the Seti-Turn (or S-Turn for short), a sharp curve Seti had named after himself that was located on the high ledge of the villa neighborhood. And every weekend, Seti boasted and heckled whichever friend endured his dust cloud, usually Sabu.

Seti barked a laugh. "Then give me a challenge or find a new place. Or maybe a new horse."

The girls giggled, and a slight smile etched his face.

Such arrogance. He didn't have the slightest clue how he came off or the damage he left in his wake. He didn't even scold Sabu for wrecking the door. But the good in him outweighed the bad.

Lumeri bit into her cake with such delicacy that Eliza gagged. She'd have at least half of that treat in her mouth by now. But Lumeri was beautiful and graceful, never dirty. Tiny nose, flawless skin, youthful glow. All the markings of Egyptian beauty. Not a single callus marked her hands. She exemplified how Seti liked his girls.

With his mouth full, Seti released the harness from his horse and set it aside.

His gaze fell on Eliza at once. "Look." He nodded toward her.

Caught again, her cheeks grew hot, and her heart hammered as she stepped out from behind the horse, wishing she'd at least washed her face before dumping the water.

"She's spying on us," Lumeri exclaimed loud enough that Sabu and his wife stopped their quiet chatter and turned.

The pile of manure behind the haughty girl looked inviting. Did Miera leave it there for such an occasion? The corner of Eliza's mouth quirked at the thought of Lumeri squirming in it, pink tunic stained brown. But Seti would run to her rescue, then scold Eliza. Maybe whip her. He might not let her go to Goshen. She folded her hands and dropped her head.

"Sneaking away?" he asked.

She itched to run from his demeaning stare but forced herself still, unable to form a reply.

Miera's voice shattered the lingering silence. "What happened to the door?"

All eyes turned to the eleven-year-old, dirty-faced girl peeking through the hole in the door. Though it swung open, Miera climbed through it. Her foot caught, and she flopped to the ground.

Laughter erupted at her expense. Miera's impulsiveness had a habit of coming at the right time, and Eliza let out the breath she'd been holding.

Unfazed, Miera straightened, dusted herself off, and caught sight of her sister. "Come on, Eliza. It's time to go."

"No, not yet." Seti faced Eliza. "Our horses are thirsty. And the chariots need polishing. I have important people to meet tomorrow and can't be seen on a dirty chariot."

"I have important people to meet," Sabu mimicked, rolling his eyes.

"I can do it," Miera said, her gaze darting between Seti and Eliza. "It's my job anyway."

Eliza lifted her face to Seti in time to catch the dimpled smile she loved so much. She rarely got to see it so close.

His brown eyes sparkled beneath his thick, expressive brows. "I want Eliza to do it." The smile fell, and his eyes narrowed. "Then you can leave. And make sure you bathe before coming back. You reek of moldy rags."

With a sharp inhale through her nose, Eliza pressed her lips together and dipped her head, fighting to hide the rage burning inside her.

Lumeri and Nala snickered behind their hands, but Sabu crossed his arms and shook his head.

With a flick of his hand, Seti dismissed her. The four of them whispered as they headed toward the house. He walked with an arrogant bounce, not once giving her another look.

Unable to move, Eliza waited, shaking with fury. What did she see in him?

Miera hurried to Eliza. "What did you do?"

"He thought I was hiding…"

"Were you?"

"What do you think?"

Eliza and Miera traveled with only a sliver of moon to guide the way to the town of Avaris, nestled in the southern corner of Goshen. Three hours on foot led to blistered feet and cramping calves. Once home, the girls heaved themselves up the steps to the single bedroom on the second floor, where they were greeted by the squeals of their toddler twin sisters. The tots pummeled into Eliza's arms, and she squeezed them tight.

"You're late." Eliza's mother retrieved the twins, kissed their foreheads, and lay them on the mat. She grabbed hold of Miera and gave the girl a quick inspection for new bruises or wounds.

"I'm fine, Ima, but Eliza got herself extra work again." Miera wiggled out of her mother's grasp and plopped on the floor beside her older brothers, Adam and Zechariah, dunking her blistered feet into their basin of warm water.

Their mother turned to Eliza with a mixture of relief and disappointment on her face.

Eliza lowered her gaze and wrapped herself in a warm blanket, pretending not to notice. Not once in all these years had Miera received a whipping. Eliza made sure of it. Every sabbath, she brought her sister home safe and blemish-free but still endured her mother's looks and jabs. Eliza sighed. She'd take those disapproving looks for the rest of her life if it meant her mother could feel like a mother once a week.

Her mother had arrived home first, as usual, gathered the twins from the elderly women next door, and prepared water and bread for the older children, a task she cherished.

Adam tugged on Eliza's bun, and she swatted him away while flashing him an endearing smile. She missed his teasing and Zechariah's antics. Her brothers rarely made it home since being stationed at the brick farms. With no contracts, brick workers were subject to the government, and the decision to release them on the sabbath rested solely on the mood of the Egyptian foremen.

After the children had settled in, their mother came near with a candle and sat at the girls' feet. All eyes rested on her, waiting for the words she had spoken every sabbath for the past six months. "Not this week."

The Egyptian foremen came down hard on the men of the brick farms. Adam and Zechariah were fortunate they were so young; their father, not so much. Eliza hadn't seen him in six months, and before that, a year.

"Is he ever coming home?" Miera whimpered.

"I can't answer that, my dove." Her mother placed a hand on Miera's knee. "But things are going to change, starting tomorrow. I have news for you all."

A heaviness descended on the dusty room. The uneasy feeling Eliza had carried all week churned in her gut.

"Remember when you were little, and I told you the story of Moshe the prince, and how he was a Hebrew like us?"

Eliza shared a confused look with the boys before turning back to her mother.

"Well." Her mother's eyes lit up, and she leaned in and whispered, "He's returned."

"What?" Adam asked. "He's alive?"

"Yes. It's been forty years. He's an old man with a family of his own from the Midianites in the east. He has brought news for us all." She smoothed out her tunic. "He and his family arrived in Goshen a few days ago and reunited with his siblings. He and his brother, Aharon, went to the palace to confront Pharaoh."

Zechariah shifted on his elbow. "Didn't he grow up in the palace?"

"Wait." Adam never missed a beat. "What do you mean, 'confront Pharaoh'? What's the news?"

"It was said that El Shaddai had spoken to Moshe. The Lord heard our prayers and appointed him to free us from bondage and bring us to the promised land."

"What?" All four drew near.

"Unfortunately, Pharaoh didn't take too kindly to the proposal and sent them away. He then ordered that no more straw be given to the brick-makers, so now we have to gather it ourselves before starting work."

"Why?" Adam asked. "Where did Moshe go?"

"Nobody knows." Their mother shook her head, her hopeful smile gone. "But you boys will stay at the brick farms while I gather straw. We won't be returning for any more sabbaths until the orders are lifted. Eliza and Miera, pray that things don't get so bad that your master gives you back to the fields."

"What? No!" Miera cried. "I'll die out there!"

"This is ridiculous," Zechariah scoffed. "Is this a joke?"

Their mother shook her head. "I don't know, my dove. I don't know if he came just to stir trouble or what. But you must not say a word. I don't want any of you getting hurt or taken away. I want you all back as soon as possible next sabbath. Return, even if I don't, so the neighbors can give me word that you're well. You must obey and not cause trouble."

Adam's feet left the basin, but Zechariah grabbed it before he could kick it over. "So Pharaoh's angry with Moshe, and now he's punishing us?"

Their mother pointed to each of them. "Do not say a word to the officials. Don't argue or push back. Nothing. Do you understand?"

They nodded.

She left the room, and Miera softly cried beneath her blanket. The boys grumbled quietly on their side of the room until their soft snores took over.

Eliza's mind reeled as she gazed out the window at the stars. What could this mean? Was it a joke like Zechariah said? Moshe had murdered an Egyptian guard and then fled. So why come back, unless God told him to?

Her body ached for sleep, but thoughts of Moshe and Seti swirled in her head, keeping sleep at bay.

Seti had said her name. She smiled, wrapping her arms around her midsection and pretending they were his. Extra work was nothing compared to her brothers' daily workload. But why, even after Seti's jabs and jokes, did she care for him? She held no value and meant nothing to him. Besides, he'd marry Lumeri come fall harvest. Marriage was out of the question for Eliza—unless one was arranged. Then, like many Hebrew families, their number of children would attest to the number of times the couple saw each other. Though her family was fortunate to reunite more often, her parents were still robbed of their children and each other.

The cool wind soothed her face, offering relief from the oppressive heat.

If El Shaddai, the God of Avraham, Yitzhaq, and Yaakov, heard the Israelites' prayers, then He might hear Eliza's as well. "Oh God, if you're listening, please release us from this bondage. I pray that the promises of a new land are real. I don't want to be a slave forever."

She paused and bit her lip. "And God? Maybe you can make Seti love me. But he's an Egyptian, and he worships gods of his own. I wouldn't want that. He'd be perfect if he knew You and loved me. But I barely even know You."

She winced at her words. Who was she to talk to this ancient God? She had nothing with which to sacrifice or gain His favor. Nothing but herself.

Eliza woke late, refreshed. She hadn't slept that long in a week. The sun was high and the room empty. She threw on her tunic and ran downstairs, finding the place empty. She dashed outside and sighed with relief at the sight of the twins and her mother sitting at a table with the neighbors.

Her mother handed her a roll when Eliza approached. "Miera and your brothers went to the gate with the others. Moshe and Aharon are in Avaris, and everybody's going to meet them."

Eliza snapped to attention midbite. "You're not?"

"Later. I'm watching the children. When Sheri gets back, I can join you. But if you want to see him, you'd better go now."

"What about Rahel?" She meant to see her best friend at least once before returning to work.

"Yes, she stopped by earlier and said she'd wait for you there. I let you sleep in."

Eliza turned to run when her mother stopped her with a hand. "Take some rolls with you and a couple of pigeons."

After filling her arms with rolls, Eliza ran to the pigeon cage in the house and snatched two younglings. She shut them in a basket, stuffed the rolls in a leather sack, and dashed out the door toward the town gate.

The Avaris gate swarmed with more Hebrews than Eliza had ever seen in one place, yet no one looked familiar. All of Avaris must have come. While elderly men and women congregated around the tribal leaders or in groups along the road, children played on the outskirts with chickens and goats.

Chest heaving, Eliza scanned the crowd for her brothers. She climbed on a table and shielded her eyes from the sunlight. Maybe she'd catch a glimpse of Moshe.

"Eliza!" A freckle-faced, lanky girl bounded out of the crowd toward her. Eliza jumped off the table and ran into Rahel's arms.

"Did you meet him?" Eliza asked.

"Yes. Yes, I did."

"What's he like?"

"Like any other old man. Looks kind of like Aharon, I guess."

Eliza laughed. "I want to see!"

"They're getting ready to eat. Don't worry, you'll get to meet him."

As the girls filled each other in on their work week, the crowd dispersed in an organized frenzy, preparing for the midday meal. Children cleared the area of animals, men dragged tables and benches from nearby houses, and women brought what the elderly and maimed had prepared.

It was a feast unlike any Eliza had ever seen. Her family shared a meal with neighbors on the sabbath, but nothing like this. She left the rolls on a table laden with bread and cakes. Other tables contained bowls of fruits, broiled fish, teas, and beers. A separate table provided a basin for handwashing.

Eliza joined Rahel's family on a mat surrounded by the Yehudah clan. She waved to her brothers and Miera, who sat with their kin, the Levites.

Tribal leaders sat in a place of honor at the head tables. Moshe and his family joined the Levite leaders.

"Oh, by the way, you can take the pigeons back home. There won't be any offerings," Rahel said, a carrot sticking out of her mouth.

Eliza glanced at the pigeon basket in the dirt. "How can I talk to him if he's not accepting offerings?"

"Silly. He's a man, not a god. Just go up to him and introduce yourself."

But her mother had told her to bring the pigeons. She'd never gather up the courage to talk to Moshe. Rahel was right—he looked like any other old man. Though serious, he smiled as he conversed with friends and family.

"Look at his sons." Rahel pointed. "Next to his wife, there, to the left. Aren't they handsome?"

Eliza swatted her hand down. The two young men sitting beside Moshe were indeed handsome. They both sported mops of black curls, high cheekbones, and wore simple tunics. Moshe's wife had lighter skin than theirs, but still dark enough to contrast the white hair peeking from under her scarf. Beautiful.

After the meal, the chatter quieted in anticipation of Moshe to speak. Instead, Aharon stood on his chair and assessed the crowd. The place went silent.

"We have cried out to the Lord in response to the increased affliction since last week's meeting with Pharaoh." He paused, almost hesitant. "These are the words of El Shaddai: 'I am Yahweh, who will bring you out from under the yoke of the Egyptians and deliver you from their bondage. I will redeem you with an outstretched arm and mighty acts of judgment. I will take you as my own people, and I will be your God. I will bring you into the land that I swore to give to Avraham, Yitzhaq, and Yaakov.'"

No one moved. Eliza's heart thumped against her chest. The stories her mother told were true. He even said the name.

"Why isn't Moshe speaking?" Eliza whispered.

Rahel shrugged, unraveling and re-braiding the long braid that hung over her shoulder.

After a nod from Moshe, Aharon continued. "After the meal, Moshe and I will speak again with Pharaoh."

"No!" a man yelled. "If you go back there, Pharaoh's anger will burn hotter still."

"You must trust us," Aharon said. "The Lord has heard our cries."

"You tell us one thing, but Pharaoh's actions tell another. You deceive!"

"You make us out to be fools!" another shouted.

"We came here for a solution when we should be gathering straw, but all you've given us is more trouble," another added.

Others shouted in agreement. Several jumped to their feet in protest. They blocked Eliza's view of Aharon and muffled his response.

Rahel sprang after her father when he raced to join a group of men pushing forward, airing their heated opinions. They surrounded the tribal leaders, angry and yelling, while others looked on. The women and children slowly dispersed.

Eliza sighed, picked up the basket, and headed toward the main road leading away from the gate. Hopefully her mother didn't start this way; it would be a waste of time—except for the food. That was a treat. She couldn't remember the last time her belly ached from fullness.

Eventually, Rahel's bounding footsteps crunched in the gravel behind her. She slowed to a walk, panting. "It's no use."

"Did Moshe change his mind?"

"Nothing could change that man's mind." Rahel kicked a stone as they strolled.

"I don't understand. It's only going to make things worse." Eliza found a stone of her own to kick.

They walked in silence. Children dragged their feet as their mothers pulled them along. A small child leading several sheep scurried past them.

When they reached Rahel's street, she stopped. "I have to go to the brick farms."

Eliza's mouth dropped open. "No, Rahel. I'm so sorry."

"You don't?"

"Not yet. As far as I know, Miera and I are still working at the Ameneten household."

"Just wait. They need everybody on the brick farms or fields to gather straw. That takes priority over domestic service."

Eliza and Miera were due back at the Ameneten home later that night. She hoped to bathe and cover her hair with a scarf like Moshe's wife before Seti would see her again. A list of extra work awaited her return. It was going to be a long night.

Chapter 2

The marmalade sky trickled into a deep purple above Seti's head. He smoothed Chewy's silky mane and whispered into the horse's ear the remnant of an old thanksgiving prayer of Horus. He and Sabu stood on a rocky cliff overlooking the west side of On. Four small pyramids belonging to the Menf and On priests rose on the outskirts of the city.

One day, Seti would rest under the protection of the gods, having carried on the Ameneten heritage begun by his ancient Father-of-Old years ago. Only priests of highly regarded lineages and who had earned Pharaoh's favor were granted pyramids. The Ameneten family was one of four. Seti puffed his chest and inhaled the lustrous scent of frankincense drifting from the nearby shrubs.

The cliff overlooked much of the city. Seti had named it "My Mesa," as it appeared to be a sinking mesa from a distance, with only one side sticking out, forming the cliff, and no one ventured there but him and Sabu. It had become their meeting place in the evenings, after Seti's daily studies and Sabu's work in the pastures.

The view of the city, the pyramids, and beyond never failed to take Seti's breath away. At night, the endless sky was magical, dusted with stars—the souls of pharaohs and heroes of old. It was quiet, breezy, and serene. Seti could stare all night, imagining what Ra or Osiris, his favorite gods, discussed as they journeyed through the land of the dead before returning at dawn. Now and then, a star would streak through the vast sky, signaling someone's safe arrival in the afterlife.

"You know Moshe is back at the palace tonight." Sabu's deep voice shattered the mesmerizing silence. He chewed a reed and nodded toward the east.

Seti gazed eastward toward the palace, smiling at the mischief in Sabu's tone. He mounted his chariot. If the horses ran at full gallop, they'd get there before dark. "Hmm?"

"We'd make it before sunset. Maybe catch him before he leaves. I want to see him with my own eyes."

Seti gave a commending nod and spun his horse around.

Sabu chuckled and followed. They crossed the open field and let their horses run before turning toward the city.

With Sabu in the lead, they plunged through the streets of On toward the palace. Seti recalled the stories of the Hebrew prince who ruled Egypt years ago. As fortune would have it, the fool ran away. A Hebrew cannot lead a nation containing Hebrew slaves. It wouldn't work. If Moshe ruled Egypt, he'd set his people free and make the Egyptians their slaves. Hebrews would take over the pyramids, the projects, everything, and make them their own. But the gods wouldn't allow that, would they? Egypt belonged to Ra, as did the Egyptians. Not the Hebrews.

Rumor had it that upon his return, Moshe demanded that Pharaoh set the slaves free. As much as Seti liked having slaves, it might be a good thing. Their numbers were too great, and they didn't belong. It didn't matter either way what Pharaoh decided, but without question, the slaves were hard workers and skilled with their hands. Useful.

Seti and Sabu reached the palace gate at dusk. Their horses lathered as they slowed to a stop. His muscles ached from such an exhilarating ride, but it was a good ache—it bolstered his strength and ability. A group of teenage girls giggled nearby, pointing at him and Sabu. Seti stepped from the chariot, his legs wobbly after the half-hour ride.

With a sheepish grin, he turned to the girls. "How about some water for our horses?"

Squealing, they ran for the nearest well.

Seti raised his brow at Sabu, then led him up a small hill which rimmed the entire outer courtyard of the palace, topped with a granite fence, leaving the horses on the road. The outer courtyard housed hundreds of courtiers, scribes, coffers, and other palace attendants, as well as the training grounds for the army and their horses. A colonnade shaded the main thoroughfare, crossing the entire courtyard to the heavily guarded gate on the inner wall. The six-foot-thick stone wall stood eighteen feet high, preventing even a glimpse of the palace grounds, which housed the treasury, armory, and Pharaoh's many wives, concubines, and extended family.

All Seti wanted was a glimpse of the old man. No need to get inside. He wasn't there for trouble. He huddled against the fence with Sabu, eyes on the colonnade below, the very colonnade he traversed five years earlier for his ordination into scribal school. Now, at eighteen, he was well-versed in both Egyptian and Hebrew script. He credited his quick wit and memorization skills to the gods. They shone their faces on him, a sign of their approval. In three more years, he'd be a full-fledged temple priest. The honor of carrying the Ameneten priestly heritage filled Seti with pride.

Distant yelling behind the wall snapped him to attention. Two shadowy figures emerged from the colonnade, headed toward the outer gates.

Moshe and his brother. The long Hebrew robes and beards gave them away.

But which one was Moshe? The two walked hastily, one carrying a staff. Just a couple of old men. Who would think they'd possibly have influence over Pharaoh? Seti smiled, as their pace and stiff posture suggested they hadn't prevailed.

"Do you think Pharaoh freed the Hebrews?" Sabu asked, eyes on the men. He and Seti crawled along the edge of the fence, keeping pace.

"I don't know. They look disappointed. I don't think Pharaoh would be that easy to sway."

"You never know," Sabu said.

Seti stole a surprised glance at his friend, then turned again to the strangers.

"Hey!" he yelled through the fence. So much for just catching a glimpse.

Sabu ducked, stifling laughter with his hand.

Seti gave him a confident nod then stuck his face through a decorative opening in the fence. "Hey you! Moshe! Prince of Egypt!"

The Hebrews stopped and faced them.

Seti smiled, and Sabu laughed behind him. "So, is he letting your people go?"

They looked at each other, then continued walking.

"Don't ignore me! I am a future temple priest. Tell me, is Pharaoh letting your people go?"

But the men paid him no heed. Seti and Sabu hurried along, matching strides with them.

"Don't you think it useful to let us know? I have Hebrew slaves. I could spread the word!" Seti yelled.

Nothing.

Seti ran ahead. "Come on, what did Pharaoh say?"

Sabu grabbed a stone and tossed it over the fence. It bounced on the ground near the men, and they halted and looked up. Sabu giggled and sent another stone cracking across the road near their feet.

As Sabu pulled his arm back to hurl a third, Seti pounced on him. Laughing, they tumbled down the hill, away from the fence, and came to a rest on the sandy plain below, near the edge of the road. They lay on their backs, out of breath.

"You're going to get me in trouble," Seti gasped. "My Jt has a good rapport with the guards, and I'll need it too."

Sabu sat up and nodded toward the palace. "Fools. Who do they think they are? How dare they walk up to Pharaoh and demand anything."

Seti gazed at Sabu. "They do have some guts though, don't they?"

"No, stupidity is more like it."

By the time they reached the horses, the girls were long gone, and most of the residents had retired to their homes for the night. The domestic slaves would have already returned from Goshen to begin their work at dawn.

When Seti arrived home, the city was asleep. The place was pitch-dark, save for the moon. He left Chewy in the stable and nearly ascended the walkway but instead, ducked around the rear of the stable to the outhouse where the two Hebrew slave girls slept. He had to make sure, just in case a secret message hadn't been sent to all the slaves to pack up and leave.

He pushed open the door, and a sliver of moonlight illuminated the inside of the outhouse. The younger of the two slaves lay sleeping in the hay near the wall. Where was the other? Eliza? He pulled the door shut, turned, and bumped into her.

Eliza stumbled back with a gasp. "What are you doing out here?" She covered her mouth and dropped into a bow.

Seti masked his surprise with a smirk. "Just making sure we still have our slaves." Yet, his facade vanished at the flash of her piercing glare before she looked downward in submission again. He swallowed that image of her shocking, moonlit eyes and gestured for her to stand. Then, a thought occurred. She could be in contact with Moshe.

He straightened and blocked the door. "Where were you?"

Her mouth opened, but no words came out.

"Where were you? With other Hebrews? Are you in contact with Moshe?"

"No." Her eyes rounded at his accusation.

"You are not to leave the premises except to do your duties. It is well past curfew. Where did you go? If you weren't with Moshe or the others, what were you doing?"

"Praying. I—I was praying." She spoke so softly he had barely heard her.

He leaned forward. "Praying for your release?" What did he care what she prayed for, who she prayed to, or where she prayed? "Where did you go?"

She pointed up the road where no houses had yet been built—a quiet open area. Seti glanced in the direction then back at her.

"Look at me," he said.

He studied her from her brown, curly hair to her dusty, bare feet, waiting. Her gaze slowly lifted to meet his. The fear in her eyes sent a wave of compassion over him, and he caught himself staring. A strange warmth rippled through his chest.

"You are not to leave past curfew. You know that. Don't let me catch you out again."

She looked away.

Seti stepped aside. "You may go."

She hurried past him into the outhouse and shut the door.

What had come over him? He never paid the slave girls any attention or cared where they went or what they did. But now, after seeing Moshe, he interrogated her. He had every right to demand her whereabouts.

Chapter 3

Eliza buried her head beneath the hay in the outhouse and groaned in frustration. Of the few times she'd dared to sneak out, Seti had to catch her in the act. He knew Moshe had spoken with Pharaoh. His questioning indicated he took Moshe's presence seriously. What would he think of her leaving?

Only when Miera shook her awake did Eliza realize she had fallen asleep, if even for a short while. Sleepless nights were common, and she never quite got used to waking so early.

While she slouched on a bench in the stable with her eyes closed, Miera bounced about, her morning wake-up song to the animals on her lips. She filled the wagon with empty buckets and pails. Each of the oxen received a kiss on the nose before Miera slipped the harness on one. She owned the mornings like a lone rooster on a chicken farm. Except she had a better voice.

While she rode in the wagon, resting her blistered feet, Eliza led the ox by the reins. Every morning began the same way: wake up before sunrise to beat the morning rush to fill the buckets with water.

The sun nearly breached the horizon when the girls arrived at one of the many man-made pools branching off the Nile, each protected from the likes of crocodiles by a copper wire fence. But today, something was off. Slaves mingled near the water's edge in groups, buckets and pails sitting at their feet. Oxen and mules stood near empty wagons. Three Egyptian women dashed by, barely dressed. The sight stopped Eliza in her tracks.

She waved down a pair of young boys headed back. "What's happening?"

They lifted their buckets for her to see. Nothing.

She raised her brow.

"It's blood," one of them told her.

"What's blood?"

"The water. Real blood."

That didn't make sense. "Did something die?"

"No, the water itself is blood!" The one boy nudged the other, and they moved on.

The water is blood?

A chill shot through her. She dropped the reins and ran to the pool, leaving Miera and the ox on the road. Heart pounding, Eliza shoved through the group of onlookers and came out to the edge of the bank too fast, losing her footing. She slid down toward the thick flowing blood. Grasping for roots, she struggled to catch herself. Her feet went under before she came to a stop. The blood's unexpected warmth churned her stomach, and bile surged into her throat. A putrid smell overcame her. She clamped a hand over her mouth, but it was too late. Her stomach heaved, and the contents spurted between her fingers. No food chunks, thankfully, since slaves didn't get breakfast. Once she regained control of her trembling and wiped her chin with her arm, she tried to lift herself on the soft sand, but it gave way, and her feet sank deeper. The more she struggled, the deeper she sank.

Stop struggling. Deep breaths.

The stench rose from the surface of the thick river of blood like a steam cloud. Eliza leaned back and heard a crunch beneath her. Fish. Dead fish everywhere. Fresh, warm, and soft. Holding her breath, she used the carcasses for traction and climbed up the bank.

Miera emerged from the crowd and gasped at the sight. "Is it really blood?"

Eliza nodded with a shudder, unable to speak.

The noise of the crowd increased as more people converged along the edges and banks. Eliza wrung out the hem of her tunic and peered down at the canal at the far end of the pool. The blood continued as far as she could see. Several Hebrews walked the banks, searching. Some dug into the dirt for fresh water. Egyptians joined the commotion on both sides of the canal. Eliza scurried to Miera, sand clumping and turning pink on her wet feet. Unable to sneak in a bath like other days, she'd have to work all day like this, and she wouldn't even get the chance to rinse out her mouth. Better stay far away from Seti.

"Get a bucket," she told Miera. "We'll have to prove it, in case Huya doesn't believe us."

By the time they returned to the Ameneten home, all of Egypt already knew.

Eliza showed Huya the blood, and the woman shrieked, springing backward. "Get that away from me!" Huya plugged her nose and waved Eliza off. "Dump it somewhere away from the house. Behind the outhouse."

While Ameneten worked at the Ptah temple in Menf, Seti, his brother Kabelo, and two other students buried their brows in the *Heka,* deep in the temple library. They copied the text word for word onto slate slabs by candlelight, overseen by the senior scribe.

Further advanced than the others, Seti rested his head on his palm and listened to the choir. Because of the layout of the caves beneath the temple, their voices reverberated to the library. Each morning, he spent the Heka session enamored by the pleasant voices bouncing off the stone walls. With the sunrise to behold on his way in, and the ensemble of choir voices tickling his ears, each morning awakened his senses to a world of beauty.

The choir stopped. It wasn't time for them to stop. Then, a distant cacophony of male voices sounded from the doorway. He glanced at Kabelo and the others. They concentrated hard on their penmanship, unaffected.

Seti rose from his mat and peeked into the hall. Except for the flickering of candlelight every few paces, only a dark emptiness stretched before him. The cool air refreshed his face after sitting in the musty library. The voices grew closer, one of them his father's.

"Young man?" The head scribe lifted an eyebrow. "It's not time yet."

"Something's happening." Seti left the library.

Ameneten appeared around the corner, deep in discussion with two priests, candles in hand. Upon seeing Seti, all three paused.

He locked eyes with Seti. "Moshe turned the Nile to blood. There's panic in the land."

"What?" Did Seti hear him right?

The men hurried past him, his father motioning him to follow. "Moshe was here last night again. This time, he turned the Nile to blood. Even the streams and the ponds. Everything! He's using some sort of power from the Hebrew gods. The magicians can't even counter it."

Seti hurried along behind them. "I don't understand. Blood?"

"Listen, boy!" one of the priests, Kipuri, snapped, shooting Seti a fiery glare. "Did you not hear what your jt said? The man is evil! He's using his magic to scare us. As if his god has power over Hapi."

Seti stepped back, eyes wide. He'd never seen a priest lose composure before.

"Get Lumeri and the other dancers." Kipuri waved a hand. "We need the favor of Hapi."

"Ye-yes, my lord." Seti glanced at his father, still not sure what to do. "Where are you going?"

The four stood silent.

"Now!" Kipuri yelled.

With a quick bow, Seti broke into a mad dash down the hall. If this was true, he had to see it for himself. Blood? The Nile? The whole Nile? Whose blood?

Osiris and Hapi oversaw the Nile. Without its predictable rising, flooding, and undulation, Egypt would be nothing but an arid desert. Lack of rain wasn't a concern. The people were well cared for, as long as they upheld the Maat and kept the gods happy. The Maat had never been disturbed in all of history.

As Seti darted across the empty foyer, his footsteps echoed off the marble walls. The choir had gone. The god-statues stood alone against the wall. He came into the open, squinting in the morning sunlight. A sense of foreboding lingered in the still, humid air. Shouts and cries sounded throughout the city. Off-duty priests climbed the steps to the foyer, followed by several dancers.

He halted on the steps to scan the young dancers for Lumeri, thankfully not finding her. Besides dancing before the god-statues, pleasing the priests translated to pleasing the gods. Lumeri's devotion to such an act of worship unsettled Seti, though he couldn't understand why. If it pleased the gods, it should have pleased him.

The girls, clothed only in loincloths, colorful gems, and bright head scarves, ran up the steps toward the foyer entrance, ready to save the world with their provocative dancing. He hurried past them. At the bottom of the steps, he turned and gazed up at the temple. This must have just happened. Catastrophes drove the residents to the temples to beseech the gods. At least, that's what he'd been told. Nothing of note had ever happened in his lifetime. After hopping on his chariot, he headed for Lumeri's house.

He found her standing in the road with her friends, asking others for a ride. His chariot slid to a roaring halt beside them, kicking up a cloud of sand that made the girls cough and swat the air.

"Get on."

She waved to her friends, climbed aboard, wrapped her arms around him, and held tight as he turned the chariot around.

"The river is blood?" he asked as he whipped his horse into a run.

"That's what I heard. That Moshe man cast a spell on the Nile or something." She buried her face into his shoulder, away from the blowing sand.

"Did you see it?"

"No."

The closer they got to the temple, the denser the crowds on the streets became, making it hard to maneuver. Seti pulled back on the reins as they neared a group of litters carrying courtiers and coffers from the palace. His wheels dug deep into the gravel and kicked up dust onto a team of oxen pulling a cart of dirtied miners.

"Why are we stopping?" Lumeri asked, eyes darting in every direction.

"I can't go around—" He scanned the chaos for an opening. "It's our Nile. We are the crown of the Earth." How could the gods of the Hebrews have command over their Nile? His heart pounded as he watched an argument flare between the courtiers and a group of street workers.

"I know, Seti. We shouldn't tarry, though." Lumeri said, irritation in her voice.

He turned to her. "I don't really want you to go."

Lumeri scowled.

"They have plenty of dancers already."

"We need as many as possible. Priests too. You're almost a priest. You should know."

"They don't need me. Or you. Let the professionals handle it." Normally, Seti would jump at the chance for extra worship, but an odd urge to get away from Menf and On simmered deep in his core.

"Ugh, I *am* a professional, Seti! The gods hear me." She shook her head and stepped off the chariot. "If you won't take me, I'll walk. They need me."

It was either please the gods or keep Lumeri to himself, betraying his calling. He hesitated. "Something's not right."

"Well, you're right about that." She spun and stomped away.

"Lumeri, wait. Listen to me!"

She ignored him and pushed through a group of men.

Seti forced his horse through the crowd. He brought the chariot to a halt in front of her. "Get in. I'll take you the rest of the way."

She sighed and climbed in.

Unable to get to the temple steps because of the congestion, they dismounted in the street. Lumeri handed him her sandals and her wrap. When she reached the top of the stairs, a slew of anxious priests encircled her before disappearing inside as if being swallowed by the temple itself. The irony hit Seti like a slap in the face—the Hebrews were the slaves of the Egyptians, but the Egyptians were the slaves of the gods.

There was no returning home that night. Seti joined Sabu on the riverbank, overlooking the bloody Nile. The sun had set. The city quieted. Everyone but the priests and the dancers retreated to their homes. No reflection of the stars shimmered on the river. Instead, it moved in a slow, blackish swirl, clotting and gathering around dead fish, stones, and twigs. The smell of old blood and rotten fish wafted on the breeze over the neighborhoods.

Seti's muscles screamed for rest after a day of tension, yet he couldn't relax. Pharaoh had not let the Hebrews go, which meant Moshe must be retaliating. The Egyptians had carefully and diligently worshipped their gods, year after year, in fear. The land was sacred, the Nile even more so, yet the gods were silent. Seti shuddered.

"How long is this going to last?" Sabu asked, yawning.

Seti shook his head.

Sabu rested his elbows on his knees. "Surely, Osiris must be more powerful than the Hebrew gods. Can't they fight?"

Lying on his back, Seti stared at the sky. He let out an aggravated sigh. A sliver of the moon continued to shine, untouched by the events below. At least Khonsue, the moon-god, hadn't betrayed them. An unfamiliar feeling of helplessness trickled through Seti's veins. There had always been something he could do, some control he had, but while the temple workers and priests toiled, Seti proved useless. Worry set in. Did they work in vain? Never in his life, nor in all the histories that he knew, had the gods been challenged in such a way. As the night progressed, his optimism withered.

"Maybe it's not about power. Maybe they're angry at us. Or we're being tested," he hypothesized.

"It seems like they would make it known so we can repent. You're almost a priest. Shouldn't you sacrifice something and ask them?" Sabu asked.

"What do you think my jt's been doing? Every priest in the nation, even. They'll offer more sacrifices tomorrow."

A breeze rushed over them, sending a chill through Seti. He turned on his side to face Sabu. "The moon's still shining, at least. So not all the gods are angry."

He glanced at the sky in time to see a falling star. "I wonder who the Hebrew gods are, that they have such power over the Nile. Or how they could persuade Osiris and Hapi to comply.”

“They don’t teach you that in your training?”

“No. I mean, until now, I didn’t even know they had gods. But I guess everyone has at least one.”

“Well.” Sabu lifted his eyes skyward. “It appears the Hebrews have gained favor with theirs.”

Chapter 4

"I call this 'My Mesa', because I found it." Seti spread a woven blanket on the ground. Lumeri stood at the ledge, gazing into the sunset. He turned to look at her, admiring how the evening sun rimmed her profile with a red aura. Her delicate, sheer tunic did little to hide her form. *Ra is good.*

"How could you have found it? I'm sure other people know about this."

"You know what I mean. Nobody else comes here but Sabu and me. So, I guess, if you want to be specific, you could call it 'Seti and Sabu's Mesa.'"

He poured wine into two silver cups. Water would have been better, but there was still none in Egypt. It had been four days since the Nile had turned to blood. The wineskins came from the temple kitchen, as did the rolls and grape jam. Seti sat cross-legged on the blanket with his cup, pleased with his idea of a sandwich-and-wine picnic on the mesa with Lumeri.

Lumeri joined him, picking up her cup. "I'm so tired." She took a sip, the cup delicately held in both hands. She'd danced at the temple all day in front of the god-statues. The third round of dancers had taken over in the early evening, giving Lumeri's group a much-needed break.

Seti tilted his head to the side. "Are you making any progress with Osiris and Hapi?"

"I think so. When I'm dancing, I feel their presence. It's like the inside of my head fills with smoke, and they're reading my thoughts. So, then I start thinking about the Nile, you know, and all the water. I feel like I make a connection with them, especially when the flutists are playing. Like I'm in a trance with the gods. I love it when they invade my mind."

Squinting, he hoped something intelligent would come out of her mouth. "Did they say anything to you?"

"Only what they have said before. Same thing over and over again. Osiris wants me to be the *Gods' Wife*."

Sometimes, he questioned whether such words came from the gods or her own confused thoughts. The Gods' Wife would dedicate her very soul for Pharaoh's pleasure. "But if you were to become the Gods' Wife, you couldn't marry me. You couldn't marry anyone. You'd become one with Osiris and at the mercy of Pharaoh's pleasure."

"Exactly. That's why I haven't responded yet. He knows I'm planning to marry you."

Seti shifted on his elbow. "This doesn't bother you?"

Lumeri rolled her eyes and tilted her head back, stretching her long neck. Mind turning to mush, Seti's gaze traced her profile from her chest, up her throat, and stopped at her gold-dusted eyelashes. She tossed her hair back and flashed him a sultry gaze.

Enchanted by her seductive posture, he listened as she filled him in on the drama between her and the other dancers over the past four days.

Her family had moved to Menf from Upper Egypt a year ago, her father transferring to the Giza complex in the mortuary. When not in Giza, he served at the On and Menf temples. After meeting Ameneten, he offered his daughter to marry Seti. Ameneten jumped on it, seeing it as his ticket into the Giza complex. Dancing since toddlerhood, Lumeri and her sisters joined the Menf temple dance crew. She had her eye on becoming a priestess, ministering to the female gods. She was beautiful, funny, and sometimes fun. He admired her devotion.

Lumeri immediately latched on to him, spreading the news that she would be an Ameneten wife. They set the betrothal for the wheat harvest, only a couple of months away.

She rambled on about the girls in the temple, specifically the ugly one who kept fumbling their dances. The wine, more potent than Seti was used to, sent his thoughts in a swirl, and his gaze roamed the hazy horizon in the distance.

When Lumeri's ramblings paused, Seti snapped out of it. "Kabelo and I will be going to Giza soon. Jt has it all lined up. We'll go inside the pyramids and maybe even explore the Sphinx. I've been waiting for this for years. Maybe you could have your jt take you, and we can tour the place together."

"I've been there already."

Seti sat up, his voice rising a notch. "Good! You can show me around, be my guide."

"I don't want to go there again. It's kind of boring."

"But the hieroglyphs are ancient. I'm dying to read them. I could interpret them for you. And we can visit the mortuary and see how they build the coffins. It will be kind of romantic. We can explore together."

"But they stink inside. And they're so dusty."

"Not the inner chambers. The priests keep those especially clean. That's where the god-statues are, so they have to be clean."

"I can't breathe in those places. Seti, I've been there before and have no interest in going back. Please don't make me go."

Seti sighed. He wasn't making her go. "What if you get some deep connection with the gods while you're there?"

"I won't. I already know. It doesn't work that way."

It would've been the perfect adventure. "Will you at

least go to Giza? We could go wherever you want. You can lead the way. I will follow."

"I don't know," she said, her voice whiny. She played with a stick on the ground.

"Did something happen while you were there to make you not like it?"

"No, nothing happened. It's just, you know, boring."

Disappointed, he lay on his back and stared at the first two stars that appeared. The sun had set, leaving a red and purple glow on the western horizon. Lumeri didn't touch her sandwich. He grabbed it, crammed it in his mouth, then refilled their cups.

"This is a nice little picnic." She lay on her back. Her blonde wig fanned out around her head. The dusk shadows and kohl made the whites of her eyes glow.

Seti swallowed the butterflies fighting to break loose from his insides and lay beside her. "The view of the stars from here is brilliant. It's the main reason I brought you here. Seeing it from the city or the temple doesn't even compare."

"That's nice."

His hand found hers. He smiled.

"I like to imagine the stars are the gods in the New Life—divine souls after they leave the pyramids." His head spun, making the stars dance. "I mean, I know there's more to it than that. It's just something I like to entertain. Just like there's the Heka maintaining the Maat. The true gods, complete deities, would be the brightest of the stars. And the ascended, like Osiris and Isis, would be the next. Then the pharaohs and the other demigods. And then the nature deities. They are the dimmest." He paused to still his vision. "Do you ever find yourself getting lost in such vastness?"

Her hand relaxed in his.

Entranced, his dreams spilled from his mouth in one long breath. "I think I'm going to build my house right here, on this very spot, so I'd come home to this view when not traveling as an Hour Priest. Did I tell you about being an

Hour Priest? It'd require more schooling, of course, to study the path of the gods, dead and alive, and the constellations. I'd map the stars and direct the building of the pyramids. And I'd be able to predict catastrophes such as what's happening now."

He paused and took a breath, gazing past the shadowy silhouette of the pyramids that appeared like mountains on the otherwise flat horizon. One day, on his travels, he hoped to set foot on a mountain. The mesa was the highest landform he had ever experienced. Only in scrolls did he glimpse other landscapes: a single mountain plopped down in random spots in the deserts of the unknown, or a series of jagged ridges and spikes like the pokey points of bread dough after touching it.

He pressed his lips together and glanced at Lumeri. She lay beside him, head turned, eyes closed, and mouth half open. Asleep.

Seti sat up in disbelief, the magic of the wine gone. When did she fall asleep? Did she hear any of his plans? Was he that boring? He'd listened to her ramblings; she couldn't do the same for him? Disappointed, he downed his wine and hers also.

It had been a week before the water returned. Hebrews and Egyptians alike would make the trek to the river each morning to see whose god prevailed. Ships had remained docked, trade at a halt. Fish and other aquatic creatures washed up on the banks and the marshes. The day their victory became evident, the somber quiet broke into fervent celebration. Egyptian cheers rang across the land.

The Ameneten family joined the priests in the sanctuary waters—a fenced-off designated dugout of the

Nile for prominent families to bathe. After that, Pharaoh threw a ceremonial feast for the gods in the palace courtyard. All Egyptians were invited, prominent or not, a first since the coronation of Pharaoh. The only Hebrews allowed past the gates were personal servants and those who worked on the palace grounds.

With Huya gone, Eliza could do her chores in peace—no enduring critical jabs and taunts or looking over her shoulder. After washing a week's worth of pots and plates, she moved on to the linen.

Miera burst into the main room, where Eliza sat on the floor beside a large water basin and a pile of linen. "Look what I found!"

She dropped to the floor beside her sister and held up a pair of leather sandals laced with red jasper and onyx stones on their straps. Lumeri's sandals.

Eliza gasped. "Where'd you find them?"

"They were in Seti's chariot. Look, they fit." Miera slipped her foot into one, tied the straps snug, and stood to examine her foot.

Eliza nodded with approval. "They look nice on you." Her stomach knotted at the thought of Miera getting caught with them, but then again, the Amenetens wouldn't be home until evening.

She pressed a finger to her lips and smiled with a mischievous glance at Miera, then rose and dashed to Huya's vanity room. Since outgrowing her last pair of sandals years ago, calluses had covered her feet. She sifted through a large basket of jeweled sandals near a rack of exotic wigs. Would the calluses go away if she wore sandals again? Could she ever have pretty feet like Lumeri's? Unlike the sandals most women wore that sported painted glass baubles, Huya's had real gems.

Miera donned a long blonde wig laced with tiny seashells and a bead-net cape that skimmed the floor with trinkets to announce the wearer's arrival. She braided Eliza's hair and set the braids on top of her head with shiny pins. They both adorned their ears with earrings and piled on necklaces. Eliza draped herself in a deep purple wrap and a shawl of carnelian and amethyst beads, cinched at her waist with a turquoise pendant. With a kohl brush in hand, she posed in front of the polished bronze mirror against the wall when Miera glided in front of her.

"If Ima could see us now." Miera posed with a hand on her hip. "She'd faint at so much color."

"And Rahel."

Miera clenched her fist around a turquoise necklace and turned to Eliza. "What if I…"

"No, don't you dare," Eliza said, grinning.

"Well, at least the sandals. Lumeri has been gone all week. She must have hundreds. She can't miss them." The sandals transformed Miera's blistered feet into those of a queen.

"I know, it's tempting. But if they catch us, they might send us to the bricks. You don't want that, do you?"

Miera sighed. "That's only if they catch us."

The sound of chariot wheels and laughter sailed by the window.

The girls turned to each other. "Quick!"

They dashed around the room, returning everything to its rightful place, then hurried to the main room as the Ameneten family entered the front door. Seti and Kabelo immediately went to their rooms to change, but Huya and Ameneten stopped in their tracks. The girls kept their heads down, folding linen, Miera's sandaled feet tucked coyly under a wrap.

She tossed a kilt at Eliza's head with a muffled giggle.

"I want meat. Get some water boiling," Huya said before marching into the den, Ameneten at her heels.

"Shhh," Miera whispered as soon as the room cleared. "You still have her earrings in and your hair up. You'd better get out of here. I'll do dinner."

Seti and his family gathered around the table for the first time in a week. Pride and relief replaced uncertainty and tension. The Egyptian gods had come through, though absurdly late. It had been a long week, but it was over. Seti guzzled a large jug of water.

Between bites of a delicate crocodile dish and warm bread, Ameneten informed the family of the happenings at the Ptah temple. "We sacrificed eight hundred cattle. Eight hundred!"

"Wow, I bet that was bloody," Kabelo replied, eyes hungry for details.

Huya raised an eyebrow. "It took that many to finally convince the gods to look upon us with favor?"

"Well, combine that with the sacrifices at Giza and the Ra temples."

"Imagine the amount of blood. Think for a moment." Kabelo set down a skewer of crocodile thigh. "You were literally competing to see who could produce more blood—the Nile, or us. Land or water."

"That's absurd." Huya wrinkled her long nose.

"The Nile didn't produce its own blood, you dung-rot. Moshe did it," Seti said.

Kabelo smiled and pointed a finger in the air. "Fine. A blood competition between gods. How do you like that?"

With an eye roll, Seti turned to his father and asked the one question burning in his heart, "So what was it, Jt? A test? Were our gods upset with us?"

"I don't know, son."

"You don't know?"

"All I know is that what we had done must have been enough. I don't know if we will ever know what that was all about." Ameneten filled his mouth with a mixture of bread and water.

"So who knows how many cattle it took to convince the gods that we're worth fighting for?" Huya asked again.

"It wasn't only cattle. We sacrificed hundreds of chickens and crocodiles, too. But I think the turning point was the women."

Seti spat a mouthful of water across the table. His mother jumped up, yelling in disgust, and Kabelo broke out laughing.

"You sacrificed the women?" Seti yelled between coughs.

Ameneten dabbed the corners of his mouth with a flax napkin. "No. We didn't sacrifice them. They went willingly."

"That's the same thing!"

"No, Seti. They weren't sacrificed. They are alive. But they gave themselves over to the gods."

"What do you mean they gave themselves over to the gods?" Seti demanded.

Ameneten sighed, put his roll on the plate, and looked at Seti.

"It means they are naked temple slaves," Kabelo answered for him.

Seti shoved his brother off his cushion, yelling curses from the heavens. He gave him a sharp smack on the head. Huya pointed her copper tongs, demanding they stop, and Ameneten's voice rose above the commotion. "It's true, Seti. I think that's what saved us. You should be thankful. You can get another wife."

"It's not supposed to work that way! We are the people of this world. We own it!" He narrowed his eyes. "We own the slaves, not become the slaves." Throwing his napkin on the table, Seti stood.

"Servants. We do it willfully. That's how we've kept the gods' favor for so long. And the Maat, of course." Huya sat again, smoothing out her yellow gown.

"No!" Seti stormed out of the house.

How dare Lumeri leave him for a god! He ignored his mother's calls as she followed him.

"You're going to be a priest, Seti. Get that through your head. You must learn how we appease the gods."

"You're not helping, Mwt." He hitched his chariot to Chewy. One of the slave girls had polished off yesterday's dirt.

"Listen to me!" Huya stopped at the entrance to the stable. "You can marry anybody you want. There are plenty of pretty girls out there. Be proud. You don't often see that kind of ambition in a girl these days. I will find you another one."

Seti adjusted Chewy's reins but paused as Eliza ducked behind Kabelo's horse, hiding again. Only this time, she had a pile of braids on her head and his mother's turquoise earrings dangling from her ears. He turned to Huya, caught off guard, and forgot his words.

Huya planted her feet, crossed her arms, and glared her kohl-rimmed eyes.

He collected his thoughts. "Then find me another one. But I must speak with Lumeri."

With an exaggerated huff, she stormed back up the walkway to the house, fists swinging at her sides. He turned to Eliza, but she was gone. If his mother had seen her, she'd have the girl whipped.

"I saw you," he said into the dark, "and you better take out those earrings before my mwt catches you." Not surprised by the lack of response, he led Chewy out and headed to the temple.

The sight of the temple back to normal hit Seti's gut like the water he guzzled at dinner— refreshing, but a little shocking. No congested crowds or endless lines of desperate people looking to beseech the gods. No menagerie of animals waiting to be slaughtered. A new appreciation for the mundane settled on him. He shot one last "thank you" to the sky before dismounting the chariot. As he climbed the empty steps to the entrance, the image of the dancers running up the very same steps a week ago came to mind.

Lumeri appeared at the top with her hands on her hips. He smiled when he saw her, but his smile faded at the lack of anything but jewelry she wore.

"Don't look at me like that." She rolled her eyes. "Quit acting like a little boy."

He stepped up to her, standing tall to make a point he was not little. "What did you do?" he asked gently. "My father told me..." He reached out for her, but she stepped away.

"And you didn't see this coming? I've been hinting for months now." She turned away, the strings of onyx dung beetles dangling against her back. Her lotus perfume did nothing to hide the wine on her breath.

"Hinting?"

"I've become the Gods' Wife as of yesterday. I now belong to Ra and Osiris. They will provide for me forever. And I can have whatever man I want for pleasure, as long as he's willing to cede to the spirit."

Seti shook his head in disbelief. "You already have the priests..."

"Yes, but I want the kings, the pharaohs, the gods. Now they're all mine. I have whatever Osiris has. And dancing keeps me youthful. You should see the way the priests look at me when I move for them. They love it."

He had seen, and he regretted it.

"They know how effective I am. They practically fight over me. The other girls look up to me. What will I be if I quit? What do you want me to do? Get fat and make babies? Typical. You knew what I wanted, Seti."

"I never said you had to stop working." He inched

toward her. "It doesn't matter, you can still serve the gods, just not—" he glanced around—"Isn't my attention enough?"

"See, you're not listening. I want the gods and the kings. Osiris. I want the priests. I don't want to be like your mother. I know you just want a younger version of her—"

"You're far from right about that," he snapped.

"—and to live like Sabu and Nala. If that's so, then why even be a priest?"

Seti straightened. "I was born to be a priest. An Hour Priest. I am the first born."

Lumeri scoffed, throwing a hand in the air. "And I can't stand the way you look at me when I dress for dancing."

"Dress?"

She raised a brow. "Everyone else looks at me with envy, lust, and pride. The priests hold me in high regard. But you, you look at me with pity."

"You know that's not true."

"Then you're not attracted to me?"

"Lumeri!"

Lumeri rolled her eyes. "What you want from me, Seti, I can't give you. I won't give you. I suggest you take some time and reconsider your path, because priests don't act like that. They share the dancers—"

"I know!" Seti's stomach threatened to hurl his dinner. "You could have told me this a long time ago."

"It was Osiris. He designated me for more than you could ever offer. This will place me in Pharaoh's pyramid and secure my soul, unlike your jt's pitiful little tomb. While you rot under the watch of weak gods and cheap perfumes, I will be preserved for eternity and guided to the heavens. My decision saved the world."

"You mean the Nile?"

"The world. We all did." She spread her hands toward the temple. "But they definitely couldn't have done it without me."

Seti stared in disbelief. He shouldn't have come here. This was a mistake. He stepped away from her.

"You don't want to share me with a god?" she taunted, her face blank. She fanned herself with her hands. "I thought you'd be proud, that you'd love Osiris as much as I. I made up my mind, and it saved Egypt."

"You," he pointed at the steps. "You waited here for me—to tell me this?"

She turned away again, swinging the beads in his face. "Goodbye, Seti. When you're a priest, you can come back to me for a little while."

She sauntered to the foyer, as if achieving something she had worked hard for.

No, even if I am a priest, I will never come back to you.

Seti balled his fists and fought the urge to run after her. He turned and descended the steps two at a time, swallowing the pain burning in his chest. She was right—he should have seen it coming. His blood boiled. Past conversations surged to the front of his mind with a vengeance. What a fool he'd been.

He whipped his horse with fury and rode full speed to the mesa cliff. There was no way he'd return home. Not this night. On the cliff, under the stars, Seti screamed curses at Osiris and Ra with all his might. From the gods' silence toward their people, to the women submitting like animals, to the utter betrayal from both Lumeri and Osiris—he let out his fury until his voice gave out. Finally, he fell to his knees and curled into a ball beneath his cloak and fell asleep.

Chapter 5

Seti woke the next morning, smacking a frog from his face. He sat in a daze, squinting in the morning sun. How early was it? Something leaped into his lap. Another frog. Frogs everywhere. He jumped to his feet in disbelief. They were on Chewy, too. They covered the ground, filled the chariot, and climbed the cliffside. The air reeked of swamp fumes.

Oh no! It's because I cursed the gods!

Huya placed her chair on top of the food table, climbed onto it, tucked her feet beneath her, and cried.

"It was finally a good day yesterday. What happened?" she whimpered.

Eliza cleared frogs from the countertops and away from the bread, while Kabelo frantically swept them into piles, only for them to disperse just as quickly.

"Just stomp on them!" Huya screamed.

"I can't, there are too many!"

A sinking feeling settled in Eliza's stomach. She grabbed a broom and rushed outside. Just as she feared, frogs covered the ground like a filthy, woven blanket, moving in waves between the houses. She paused on the steps, staring wide-eyed, as they jumped on her ankles. Slaves and Egyptians alike huddled on their rooftops, swatting frogs over the edges. The horses jumped about in the stable, the cattle squirmed in the corner, and the oxen had run away with the wagon. Miera was nowhere in sight. She must be searching for the oxen. Eliza turned and hurried inside.

"Get on the roof. That's where everyone else is!" she yelled to Kabelo and Huya.

"The roof, the roof," Huya mumbled as she gingerly climbed off the table. Kabelo dropped the broom and ran up the stairs before Huya reached the floor. She scowled at Eliza. "Don't just stand there, grab the food!"

Eliza scurried around the room, grabbing whatever food sat out. She dashed up the steps, not waiting for Huya, and snatched Kabelo's broom on the way. The roof wasn't as bad as inside. After she set the food down, she took to sweeping while Kabelo kicked the frogs from where he stood. Huya arrived, breathless, with her chair. She set it down and climbed onto it, staring forward as if in a daze.

Eliza paused to take in the scene. The same chaos ensued on each house. Up and down the street, townspeople gathered atop their homes and cried out to one another. Children sought refuge in trees, and panicked livestock were even led up the stairs. Hammocks were strung up on the villas. She couldn't believe the week they were having.

Seti pulled up on his chariot. He peered at them from below, leaped from the chariot before it stopped, and dashed into the house. His hurried footsteps pounded on the stairs.

He ran to his mother. "It's my fault. I cursed the gods."

"Oh, you imbecile, shut up! It was Moshe again."

He froze. Eliza's eyes widened. He cursed the gods? It was Moshe? Seti glanced at Eliza, who turned away and continued to sweep. "Moshe?"

"He's at it again," Kabelo answered. "He went to Pharaoh again to release the Hebrews, and Pharaoh must have denied him. Then all these frogs started coming from the Nile. Jt came back to check on us and told us."

Seti's eyes darted between Kabelo and Eliza. "Where's Jt now?"

"Back at the temple again, begging Osiris."

"But he needs to appease Heket, right? Not necessarily Osiris? Heket is still around, right? I mean, frogs answer to her." Seti paused to catch his breath.

"I don't care who they answer to. I want them gone." Huya pointed to a flat green splotch on her chair.

"They're sacred!" Seti yelled.

"Oh no, they aren't sacred anymore." Kabelo stomped on something moving under the rug.

Seti gasped at the flattened amphibian. Kabelo challenged him with a scowl.

Ignoring Kabelo, Seti looked around frantically. "I need to go to the Nile."

Huya's face shot up. "We need your help here."

"You're not going to appease Heket by going to the Nile, Seti, you know that!" Kabelo yelled.

"Why not? I go there to talk to Osiris all the time."

Kabelo glared across the roof. "You're not a priest yet. Get over yourself."

"Will you two shut your mouths? Seti, help me!" Huya wrung her hands in the air.

Seti cleared the frogs from around her. Eliza watched him, still curious about what he meant regarding cursing the gods. He had been gone all night. His hands shook as he swatted at the frogs around his mother, careful not to hurt them, yet with a ferocity Eliza had never seen in him before.

"I've never seen so many frogs in my life. This is way more than flood season," Huya exclaimed.

Sabu's chariot roared to a halt in front of the house beside Chewy. He called up to Seti, who snapped to attention and flew down the steps to meet his friend. He was gone as fast as he had come.

Pushing his horse into a full sprint, Seti followed Sabu through the streets. There was no end to the infestation. Everywhere they turned, a sea of green greeted them. A tinge of guilt nagged at him for leaving his mother and brother behind. If his father found out he left them the way he had, Seti wouldn't hear the end of it. As he followed Sabu, it became apparent they weren't headed toward the Nile.

"Sabu!" Seti hollered over the commotion of the chariots. "Where are we going?"

Sabu bore ahead, full speed, splattering many a frog beneath his chariot wheels.

He slowed his horse to a trot near the courtyard gate, and Seti caught up. "Why are we here? I thought we were going to the Nile."

"No. Moshe's talking to Pharaoh. I want you to use your influence and get us in."

Seti looked at the gate. Moshe was in there? Now? And probably his brother Aharon, too. Maybe Pharaoh would put an end to this madness. If Moshe had anything to do with this frog business, Seti wanted to know more. If only he could speak with Moshe.

"I don't know if I can," he said, patting Chewy's rear.

"Try. This is why I came to get you. We have to do something. Just tell Pharaoh's priest or the vizier or at least see how far in you can get—"

"We? What are we going to do? My jt's at the temple right now, and Lumeri…I'm not a priest yet."

Sabu nodded toward the guards at the gate. "You can get the guards to let us in."

"I don't know."

When they reached the gate, they dismounted from the chariots. The palace guards relaxed their stance as their eyes landed on Seti.

One stepped forward. "We cannot let you in."

Seti eyed the two men who stood on either side of the gate. Normally, there were six guards, dressed in full military kilts with shields and spears. He neared the iron gate and peered through the bars to the colonnade on the other side. Mayhem unfolded with frogs invading the homes of palace personnel and guarded buildings, covering the grass courtyard and granite streets, making no distinction between elite and commoner.

"We cannot let anyone in at this time," the guard stated, hands tightening around his spear.

What kind of influence did Sabu think Seti had? "It's not dusk yet."

"Extenuating circumstances."

Seti peered through the bars again, Sabu stepping beside him.

"You let Moshe and Aharon through," Seti said. "What gives them more privilege than me?"

"Moshe's privilege, Seti, is because Pharaoh summoned him. He did not come here demanding to enter. When Pharaoh summons you, I'll let you in."

Seti's eyes widened. "Pharaoh summoned him?"

"Leave, Seti. You know the rules."

The second guard stepped beside the first.

Sabu nudged Seti, but Seti grabbed his arm and spun him toward the horses.

"What are you doing?" Sabu whispered as Seti led him away.

When out of earshot of the guards, he let go of Sabu. "Moshe was here in the morning, and that's when the frogs started, right? Then Pharaoh obviously couldn't take it anymore, so he summoned Moshe to come back. They must be negotiating. Or maybe the magicians are doing something. But do you know what this means? Moshe is still here, and he's staying nearby, not in Goshen. We can follow him."

Sabu stopped in his tracks.

"Let's wait and hide, then follow him. We can find out where they're staying. It's got to be close."

If Seti could corner Moshe, he'd apologize for the stone-throwing and try to get answers from him. He tied their horses near the market down the road then led Sabu up the hill along the same stone fence as the week before. This time, they climbed into a tree near the gate, but out of sight of the guards. He chose a thick branch to rest on and watched the pandemonium below, waiting for two straggly, robed old men to appear.

"I heard about Lumeri," Sabu stated after settling on his branch.

Seti stared ahead and crossed his arms over his chest. He would never admit the emotion that overcame him last night, nor the cloud that marked his soul.

Sabu kept his eye on the courtyard. "Maybe it's for the best. I mean, it saved the Nile, right?"

Seti flashed a fierce look at Sabu before returning his gaze to the view. "It's nothing worth talking about."

Sabu scoffed before continuing. "Well, I know you're going to want to rant about it sooner or later. That was partly why I came to get you. That and the frogs have taken over my farm, and I'm afraid they'll ruin my crops. They filled the house. The women were going mad. I had to get out of there. They wouldn't let me leave until I told them I'd get you to talk to somebody at the palace."

"Well," Seti chortled, "it was a good reason to leave my house as well."

"And you may actually make a difference if you get in."

"Like I said, I'm not a priest yet. And the priests are doing everything possible at the temple. There's nothing I can do. Pharaoh holds the power of the gods."

"Either way, I'm not stuck on the farm sweeping frogs with my sisters."

Likewise, Seti had left his brother to endure their mother. Eliza and her sister would tend to them. They were trustworthy.

Speaking of Eliza, what was that look she gave him on the roof? A look of concern or pity? How dare she look at him like that. How dare she look at him at all.

"Well, let's find out more about this Moshe tonight." Sabu's voice shook him from his thoughts.

With a heavy head, Seti closed his eyes. "Wake me when you see him." His stomach growled. When was the last time he ate? Yesterday? His body ached from sleeping on the limestone, the wild chariot ride through town, and now sitting on a hard tree branch.

He jerked awake with a reflexive grab of the branch above when he felt himself tilt sideways. He glanced at the ground and then at Sabu a couple of branches away. Sabu's arms crossed his lap, head hung forward, and eyes closed, leaning against the trunk. How long had they slept? It was dusk.

"Sabu!" he yelled. "Sabu!"

Lifting his head, Sabu blinked tired eyes toward Seti.

"I think we missed him."

The two turned toward the empty road. Only frogs lay before them.

"Yeah, let's go home. I'm tired." Sabu straightened.

Before Seti jumped from the branch, the two old men emerged from the shadows, coming down the road. Seti paused, raised his hand to Sabu, and motioned for him to stop.

Decked in robes and sporting long, graying beards, the men stood out starkly amid the Egyptian culture, as if from a different world. Even the Hebrews didn't dress like that. Aharon carried his staff like a walking stick, and he and Moshe walked swiftly, side by side, as if on a mission. The frogs scattered, clearing a path before them. Seti watched, amazed.

Seti and Sabu quietly dropped from the tree, landing on their feet. They hurried to the fence and followed along, crouching as they went. The two men appeared to be alone, but several palace personnel followed along in the shadows.

As Moshe and Aharon reached the gate, Seti and Sabu descended the hill toward the road. Careful not to attract the attention of the guards, Seti crept into the open but kept near the shrubs. His foot slipped on a frog, and he fell on his butt, sliding through more frogs. He lost control and rolled down the hill until coming to a stop at the side of the road, in front of the gate where the men had just emerged. Sabu ran to join him.

"You!" Moshe yelled.

Seti sat up, and Sabu skidded behind him. He gazed at the strange men in astonishment.

The gate slammed behind the men, and the guards locked it. Moshe walked around Seti, making a hmph noise as he did so.

Seti scrambled to his feet but couldn't find his voice.

"You! Stop!" Sabu ran after them.

The men stopped and turned. Moshe growled, "What do you want with us, boy?"

"What do you want with us?" Sabu snapped back.

A frog croaked in the silence. Then Moshe lifted his chin and said, "Tomorrow I will inquire of God, and He will kill the frogs."

Aharon gave a confirming nod. They turned their backs and continued on, Aharon thumping the end of his staff onto the ground.

Seti stood with mouth agape beside a stunned Sabu.

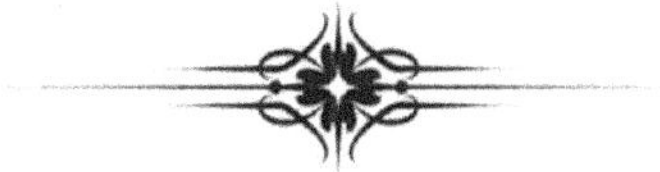

Eliza stepped gingerly into the soft mud, letting the waves of the East River Branch wash over her ankles. After the long trek from the Ameneten home on the gravel road, her feet welcomed the mud, even though it crunched with shards of fish bones. She blocked her face as Miera splashed by with a group of Hebrew boys.

A whip splat hard against the water's surface. "No playing!" an Egyptian woman squalled from a chair perched on the bank. She pulled the whip back as if to strike again but instead pointed at the boys. "Or back to the city you go!"

Murmurs filled the air as the children grabbed their nets from the shore and set out to fill them with fish carcasses. Eliza turned away from the woman and made a face.

"Be thankful, Eliza," Miera whispered, ahead of her, dragging her net through the water.

Eliza scoffed. "Be thankful."

"Behave a little while longer. Calev told me Pharaoh will set us free when we get this all cleaned up."

"It's true," a teenage girl whispered, dangling a large frog from her hand.

"No talking!"

The shrill of the woman's voice shot down Eliza's spine. Biting her tongue, Eliza turned away from her sister for fear Miera would keep talking. Miera was right, though; she should be thankful. They had spent the past three days shoveling dead frogs off the streets onto tarps. She could have been digging holes with the boys or trapped in the house with Huya, listening to that woman bellyache over scrubbing frog-slime from her new floor. Watching the mistress work was not as fun as Eliza imagined it would be.

Thankfully, each day the neighborhood slaves switched stations, and today Eliza stood in the cool water, a light breeze hitting her sweaty face. She had easily adapted to the stink of rotted flesh the day before, after it adhered to her tunic and hair. Huya wouldn't let her in the house with that stench, which was fine, as long as Eliza stayed far from Seti. He didn't need yet another reason to be disgusted with her. What if he'd seen her in the gown the other day? All decked in pearls and emeralds? He noticed the turquoise earrings in the split second he caught her in the stable. What did he think? Something pleasant must have crossed his mind, for he had shown mercy.

She skimmed her net across the surface of the water, scooping up floating fish in one big sweep. Such a shame they all died. Roasted tigerfish sounded exquisite. Even the foul-tasting tilapia would satisfy her grumbling stomach. The neighbors in Avaris always had tigerfish to share. Two sabbaths had passed since Eliza had last been home. The faces of her family and Rahel lingered in her mind as she worked, their features fading with each passing day. Did anybody make it home at all? Had they been slaving in the fields as long as she had been in On? The old sleeping mat in the upstairs room sounded inviting, as did her mother's rolls and playing with the twins.

Where did Calev hear about being set free? Eliza glanced at the boys wading toward the opposite bank, toward the croc den.

"Calev!" Eliza stepped forward, glancing at Miera, then back at the boys. "Calev, the croc den!"

The six-year-old waved her off, but another boy steered him and his friends away. Eliza sighed and exchanged a worried look with Miera before wading the opposite direction. Heaven forbid Miera say something and get whipped because of her. The woman on the shore was known for her lack of mercy, regardless of the age of her target. She slapped the hand of her fanbearer and barked at him when he got too close to her chair. Tension hung thick in the air lately, intensifying the ire of Egyptian masters. If Pharaoh freed the Hebrews, their masters might protest, or worse, beat their slaves before complying.

One day, all Hebrews would be free. But something gnawing at Eliza's insides told her not yet. She raised her gaze to the heavens. "Oh El-Shaddai, please let it be true."

Chapter 6

Seti slouched against his brother on the cloth bench of his chariot, rocking and bouncing along the stony road. He let out an exasperated sigh and pulled his turban over his eyes. After spending the previous day sanitizing the temple from the frog infestation, including draining and refilling the pools, the trip to Giza had lost its thrill. He'd scrubbed his skin raw, then reconsecrated himself to the gods by shaving off every last hair from his body and bathing in natron salt. His father could have at least arranged for canopies. Instead, the sun cooked Seti's bare skin, despite the turban. The caravan of eight four-person chariots crammed tight with students and scribes. It was supposed to be a half-day's ride, but it felt like a trek across the Sahara.

"Get off, Seti. We're almost there." Kabelo shook Seti off his shoulder.

Seti sat up and fixed his turban. After his eyes focused, the Great Pyramid of Giza came into view. A surge of energy shot through him. At last, they had arrived.

Standing at the exact center of the Earth, the Great Pyramid of Giza divided Lower and Upper Egypt. Built by the gods many centuries before and aligning perfectly with Orion's belt, it served as a link between them and those who dwelt on the earth. Not only did it function as a communication tower, but it also comprised a mortuary complex for the Great King Khufu and his family. Smaller, yet still great pyramids dotted the terrain, mirroring the constellation and guarded by the Sphinx.

Many different dialects of hieroglyphs from ages ago filled these pyramids—the whole purpose for the trip. Tasked with copying down as many as they could, Seti and the others would then take their copies home the next day for deciphering. Anyone who found something yet unrevealed by previous scribes would have their name engraved in the temple of On, complete with a procession through town. In years past, everyone chose to search the Great Pyramid. Not Seti. The south pyramid, the least touched, would hold the most secrets. Let the ancients be revealed.

Upon arrival at the small inn just outside the mortuary, the Giza priests supplied each student with a camel. Not as fast as a horse, but it would do. Seti had until supper to report back to the inn, and he had much to accomplish.

Just past the mastaba tombs surrounding the pyramids stood the ancient Giza library. It contained everything from biographies of kings resting in the Kings' Valley, to copies of every known hieroglyph in Giza and Saqqara, along with maps of not only every pyramid in Lower Egypt, but of the skies they spoke to.

Two massive Arabian slaves opened the towering doors for Seti, and he stepped inside the library. He inhaled the thick scent of aged leather, papyri, and incense. Such satisfaction. If only his room at home smelled like this. The gods obviously protected this sacred space, for it held no hint of frog rot nor natron. The other students had rushed off toward the taverns in uptown Giza. Clearly, they cared little about their names, placing the rare Rhumi beer above all else. All the better for Seti. He'd memorize the map of the south pyramid if he could get past his gawking at the endless aisles of knowledge. Scrolls, books, and compiled leaflets lined the walls from floor to ceiling, each calling his name, begging to be opened and searched. A labyrinth of towering shelves and ladders crammed the small space, even on the balcony near the priests' quarters. The place was too small for the hordes of records it kept. Seti craned his neck as he wandered each aisle, wishing he had all week to explore. The library itself needed a map.

If Seti couldn't be an Hour Priest, he'd be a library keeper. He'd commit every last fragment to memory and be the most sought-after historical priest in all of Egypt. He'd keep every surface meticulously clean, down to the last papyrus. Not a speck of dust would touch such caches of wisdom.

"Ahh, one of the scribal students from On, I presume." A clean-shaven priest called from his perch on a ladder. "No Rhumi beer?"

"No, my lord." Seti gave a slight bow. "I'm looking for pyramid maps. Specifically, for the south pyramid."

The priest crinkled his forehead as he studied Seti. "Not the Khufu Pyramid?"

"No, my lord. Maybe another day." All the days in the world wouldn't be enough. Giza was only one mortuary of many.

"Very well. Take a seat, and I'll have it delivered." The priest nodded toward a group of cushions arranged in a circle at the far end of the aisle.

Seti chose a tasseled cushion by the window overlooking the complex. What a view. Nothing could beat studying in the Giza library with the sun gleaming on the Sphinx in the distance—not even getting lost with Lumeri.

The next morning, Seti and the students gathered on the causeway on camelback, each armed with an oil lamp, pen, and several thin sheets of papyrus. They were to report back by supper. Seti tossed his leather bag over his shoulder and gripped the handle of his lamp. He glanced at the south pyramid, his heart pounding with excitement. Up close, it dwarfed those of the priests of On and Menf, but that even was dwarfed by the Great Pyramid to the east. Oh, if he had more time. He'd never been inside any other pyramid but his father's, and that wasn't even complete yet. On the rare occasion his father took him to Giza for work, they'd visit the temple or the library, but never the pyramids themselves. Such masterpieces of the gods called to Seti's restless soul.

"And where do you think you're going?" Kabelo asked as Seti studied the south pyramid, imagining the tunnels crisscrossing at three levels inside.

Seti shrugged, trying desperately to contain himself. If the others had an inkling of his plan, they might interfere.

Kabelo shot him a side-eye then shook his head. "We all know you want your name in On, Seti. If you weren't our father's son, you'd be Pharaoh's. Ra's, even. Only you'd obsess over such a matter."

"Then it fits you're not the firstborn," Seti scoffed. How had Kabelo or any other scribal student made it this far in their studies and not hold this privilege in the highest regard? Thankless buffoons. No god would regret shining his face upon Seti. He'd make sure of it.

The head scribe blew the shofar, and Seti nearly kicked his camel in the side.

Careful, it's not a horse.

As a large group of students broke off in excited chatter toward the Great Pyramid, a couple branched toward the north pyramid. No one headed south. Perfect! Seti swallowed the glee threatening to escape his lips. He shielded his eyes against the early noon sun and urged his camel to hurry.

Two beefy guards, decked in royal desert *thawbs* with gold-trimmed turbans covering shaven heads down to goat-skinned boots, stood watch at the entrance. Seti flashed them his pass—the head scribe's seal on a clay tablet—and they lowered their spears. One took the camel while the other gave a low bow as Seti entered. What prestige! One day, it would come so commonplace that Seti wouldn't blink an eye. His renowned name would be his pass, and he'd enter with a simple flick of a hand.

Once hidden by the shade of the entrance tunnel, he bolted. To his dismay, the slap of his sandals on the limestone betrayed his cool façade. So be it. Like his brother said, everyone knew Seti's ambitions anyway. He was top of the class and the talk of the priests. Even Pharaoh esteemed him, according to his father. Ahead lay the chambers, deep and hidden, where tombs of heroes of old resided, encrypted with legends and stories.

The flame of his lamp flickered out, and he was forced to slow to a hasty walk. Candles lined the walls of the tunnels every few paces. From one of these, he relit his own. Occasionally, a shaft of sunlight beamed from a vent, forming what looked like glowing white pillars in the corridor.

The place was a maze of tunnels. The map clear in his mind, Seti turned down the central aisle, beneath the pyramid.

Rarely, a flickering light appeared in the distance, only to reveal a Sem priest coming from an embalming, or a Ka priest leaving after his service to the coffins. The presence of these figures coming his way signified he headed in the right direction.

After some time passed, worry set in. If only he had copied the map, but that would have been cheating. If he succeeded, it would be proof of the gods' blessing.

Shafts of light illuminated the corridor. They were becoming fewer and farther between. The length of the vents creating these shafts suggested the depth he had ventured.

At the next shaft, a dim, orange glow beamed from near the floor. Could this be it? He followed the light beneath a low arc in the wall that opened to a large room. The vaulted ceiling, etched with intricate pictures, reached several cubits high. Beams of light from vents crisscrossed in every direction, the widest converging on a central coffin. Around it, other coffins sat evenly spaced throughout the room in a crescent shape.

Seti's heart leaped, and he rushed to the middle. The granite coffin, speckled with carnelian, was polished each morning by the Ka Priests, so much so that he could see his reflection as he examined the etchings across the top and sides. He pulled off his bag and took out the papyri, copying the symbols as fast as he could, the vents providing more than enough light.

Seti paused to shake his cramping hand and gazed around. Except for his breath and the pen scraping on the papyrus, the silence grew thick and eerie. The vastness of the room made him feel small and insignificant. Artwork of not only the gods associated with the afterlife but also of those entombed, decorated the walls and stone pillars, painted in beautiful colors he rarely saw in Menf. Statues of the gods of the dead were strategically placed to guard the coffins. Seti sat back on his heels, a sense of foreboding filling his chest.

A low humming joined the sound of his breath, slowly growing louder. Seti was the only one in here, right? He hadn't consecrated himself before entering. Was he supposed to? The scribe hadn't mentioned it, nor did he restrict the students from getting too close to the coffins.

The humming intensified, sounding more like buzzing. Seti glanced at the other coffins. None were opening. That was a good thing. Like a shade pulled over a window, the vents suddenly darkened, and the light beams vanished. Seti drew in a sharp gasp, grabbing the oil lamp. What happened to the sun? He didn't dare move. The dancing lamplight cast flickering shadows, bringing the paintings to life. The watchful eyes of the statues blackened.

He crammed his things into his bag and darted to the arched opening. Before reaching it, a curtain of gnats enveloped him. They buzzed in his ears and bit his face and arms. They flew up under his kilt. He draped his leather bag over his head, leaving his eyes and nose uncovered, and left the great room, sprinting down the corridor.

The vents in the tunnels dimmed, crammed full with gnats. They were everywhere. He was forced to slow down or lose the light of his lamp.

Preoccupied with swatting gnats, he lost track of his whereabouts. He stumbled through the winding tunnels, lamp barely holding light, one hand stretched out to feel for the walls. His feet tangled, and he fell, dropping the lamp. It rolled ahead with a tinkling sound on the rock, and the light went out.

Exhausted, he wanted to give up, but with each bite, he flinched and squirmed. Crawling across the floor, he felt for the lamp. His fingers closed around it. He scrambled to his feet, spotted a lit candle further down the corridor, and used it to relight his lamp. Thankfully, the flame repelled the gnats, at least a little.

The sky had dimmed to a dark gray by the time he emerged from the last tunnel. Though on the third level of the pyramid, he could make out nothing beyond his own hand. Hopeless and out of breath, he refused to let his mind resort to pure panic. Losing any train of thought would succumb him to insanity or worse: death.

Think. Think.

Someone in the distance yelled Seti's name, but the commotion of the gnats muffled the direction, and his swollen eyes obscured his vision. He tried to yell, but as soon as he opened his mouth, insects filled it. Spitting, Seti stumbled forward, hands outstretched. The head scribe appeared, took the lamp, and draped a woman's wrap over him, covering him head to toe. Seti nearly collapsed in the man's arms, but the scribe urged him forward. Clinging to him, Seti blindly followed, struggling to keep up. His legs grew heavy and swollen, his sandals lost in the pyramid.

The scribe led him to a sealed tent at the foot of the pyramid. Students and priests huddled inside. Seti dropped to his knees, finally giving in to the demands of his muscles. He panted for air, thankful to be able to safely open his mouth. A strong blow of his nose sent dead gnats into the wrap covering his face. He curled into a fetal position on the hard rock, not answering any of the questions directed at him.

Hours passed before a foreign slave made it to the tent with medical supplies. He ducked inside, closed the flaps with clamps, then handed the scribe his woven bag and a handful of head nets that had been quickly sewn together at the foot of the pyramid.

Seti sat on the floor against a crate, eyes only able to open a sliver due to the swelling. His leather bag sat in his lap. The scribe mixed potions into a jar of oil. With a soft brush, he painted his skin with the concoction, then passed it to the others.

As each of the students and priests applied it in turn, the scribe made his announcement. "I'm sorry, but we're going to have to remain in this tent until the gnats die down. There's no way we'd make it home. We can go over what you found while we wait. Was anyone able to write anything down worthwhile?"

Seti lifted his head. "I touched a coffin. Is that bad? Do you think that's why the gnats came? I wasn't consecrated."

"You made it all the way to the chamber?" Kabelo's eyes grew big.

"Just one," Seti mumbled, his swollen tongue stifling his words. He spat a copious amount of saliva to avoid the sting of swallowing.

"Though I'm impressed you made it that far, Seti, you

don't have to be consecrated to touch a coffin, just if you open it. You didn't open one, did you?"

Seti gave a slight shake of his head before thumping it against the crate behind him.

"Good. If I'm right, the gnats came from the same place as the frogs—and the blood. I believe this is another of Moshe's doings. I have received word that the gnats have invaded all of Egypt, not just here."

The students groaned and mumbled. Seti closed his eyes.

"We can go over what little we have, but I'm afraid this trip will have to be made up later this year or next year. You will not be tested, and we'll offer a make-up class free of charge."

Seti painted his skin with the potion, rewrapped himself, then curled up on the floor and fell asleep.

Chapter 7

Eliza knelt behind the cabinet of clay jars in the back room of the Ameneten house and unclenched her fists. She wrapped her arms around her knees and prayed once again for her freedom. *Is this a joke?* Zechariah's words about Moshe's return taunted her as she recalled the message Huya had received from Master Ameneten describing his drive to the temple two days ago: The city of On appeared devoid of life. Stables had been closed tight, tents sewn shut, and fabric of every kind blocked windows and plugged cracks in the walls and doors of homes. Even the staff at the temple took to closing off every possible entry for the gnats, just in case, but so far, Ptah had kept them out.

"Why hadn't Ptah kept the frogs out, then?" Huya snapped. "Do we have their favor or not?"

With the men of the house gone, it was up to Eliza to tend to Huya's emotional needs on top of protecting the household. Miera had only made it out to the stable once to feed the animals and cover them in thick blankets. Her presence in the house offered Eliza at least some comfort. After composing herself, Eliza returned to the den to find Huya curled on the couch, only her eyes peering out from inside the cocoon of her blanket.

"It's that Moshe again. I know it is." Huya repeated in a low mumble. "He did this."

Eliza made tea with yesterday's leftover water and gathered as many vegetables as she could find without going outside. She concocted a stew of olives, lentils, potatoes, and goose legs over a small fire in the middle of the main room. Despite the unbearable heat it created in an already stuffy house, the hearty smell distracted from the stench of rotting frogs and brought in a homey feeling that reminded Eliza of Avaris.

When the stew was finished, she poured it into three ceramic bowls. For the first time in weeks, she and Miera weren't eating cold scraps. The girls exchanged smiles as they raised the bowls to their noses, savoring the aroma. Eliza held the bowl in one hand and traced the light blue etchings of faience with her finger. Such a peculiar dish felt too beautiful in her dirty hands. She handed one to Huya.

Huya's arms scrambled out of the blanket, and she plucked the bowl from Eliza. She sat up on the couch and took one bite before spitting a potato piece onto the floor.

"This is awful! No garlic? No seasoning? What in Amun's name is this?"

Eliza and Miera paused, their bowls in their laps, sitting cross-legged at the hearth. Spoon halfway to her lips, Eliza's veins turned ice cold.

"Don't just stare at me. Make me something else. Preferably with seasoning that doesn't taste like frog!"

Neither moved.

"There isn't any seasoning left," Eliza finally said.

"Well, you're just going to have to find some, aren't you? Go ask a neighbor. I'm not eating this wretched filth. We are people of prominence. And while you're at it, get some mesh so you can make head coverings."

"My lady, the gnats," Eliza said.

"So?"

Eliza stared at her hands. Her breathing intensified as she struggled to keep from saying something she'd regret.

"Shall I tell my husband of your disloyalty?"

She scrambled to her feet, shoved her bowl into Miera's lap, and rushed from the room. She ripped down the curtain over the outer door and ran outside into the swarming gnats, not to the neighbor's house, but to the outhouse. After slamming the door behind her, she threw herself onto her mat, buried her face into a pile of hay, and cried openly and loudly. No one was outside to hear her wailing anyway. She couldn't stay with that woman one more day. They'd been locked up in that house for two days straight because of the gnats.

"I can't do this anymore, God," she cried into her dirty blanket. "I just want to run away. Make bricks. Something, anything else."

After some time, with a pounding headache and tired eyes, Eliza forced herself to surrender. She conjured the image of Seti peering out his window at a beautiful sunrise as he did each morning. That always lifted her spirits. She stood and dusted the hay blades from her tunic. "I can do this. I can do this."

She wrapped herself in a blanket, covered everything but her eyes, and stepped outside. The neighbor's house was tightly sealed, but she gathered her courage and headed over. She pounded on the door. No one answered. Who would dare open their door in this mess anyway? As she pounded again, the tears came roaring back.

"Open the door!" she screamed.

The door creaked open, and a pair of dark brown eyes peered out. Eliza quickly brushed the hair from her face, pulling the blanket down under her chin. "I need spices." Embarrassment flushed her cheeks. "You got any spices?"

The door opened a little more. Those brown eyes belonged to little Calev, the Hebrew slave for the household.

He wrinkled his brow. "You came here for spices?"

"Please, anything. Please," she begged.

He disappeared and returned with three jars. He silently handed them to her, slammed the door, and resealed the cracks. Eliza cradled the jars in her arms under the blanket and made her way down the stone walkway toward the Ameneten house. On the way, she passed a small pile of dead frogs.

"Taste like frogs, you say?"

She pulled one from the pile and shook a stray leg from it. After stuffing the frog in a jar, she returned to the house.

Inside, the couch was empty. Huya was nowhere to be seen. Miera remained at the fire with the two bowls still in her lap.

"You've been gone a while," Miera whispered as Eliza sealed the door.

"I know." Eliza grabbed Huya's bowl and dumped the stew back into the pot. She followed it with spices from each jar. Pulling the dead frog from the garlic jar, she squeezed it in her fist as hard as she could. Its putrid juices oozed into the stew. Miera's eyes widened with horror.

"Shhh."

After a satisfying amount of frog juice had dispersed into the pot, Eliza returned the carcass to the garlic jar and placed the jars on the counter. She'd repay the neighbors for the garlic later. She set the pot over the fire, reheating and stirring frequently.

Within minutes, Huya emerged with a fresh blanket wrapped around her. Seeing that Eliza had returned, she sighed. "It's about time. Where's the fabric?"

Eliza had forgotten about finding mesh fabric. She had been gone long enough. "I looked everywhere," she lied. "Nobody had any. Everyone in the city is looking for some."

"The linen will do for now. You did get the spices, though, right?"

"Yes, my lady."

Miera stared at the bowls in her lap, her face pale. Eliza snatched her bowl from Miera's lap and scarfed it down. It was cold but still delicious. When she finished, she refilled Huya's bowl from the pot. After handing it to Huya, she went to the back room. If she were to ever laugh in these last three weeks, it would be now, and she couldn't let anyone see it.

She pinned herself against the wall and listened. Nothing. Then, coughing. Eliza giggled, her hand covering her mouth. More coughing. Little footsteps slapped the mosaic as Miera scurried away.

"I don't care, Lord. If you smite me for this, I don't care," Eliza whispered. She had never dared rebel before, and it felt good.

After a moment, Eliza peeked around the corner. Huya hacked and coughed from the sitting room. The ceramic bowl hit the floor with a crash, and Huya screamed for Eliza. Eliza froze. Huya screamed again, this time with venom in her voice.

Eliza stepped into the hall and sauntered to the den as coolly as possible. Huya stood at the counter, the garlic jar in one hand and the frog in the other. Their eyes locked.

"I had to see what in Amun's name you put in my stew, and I found this," Huya stated calmly.

"I—I, how did that get in there?"

"My husband cannot leave the temple, my sons are stuck in Giza, and I'm trapped here with you two Hebrew rats, and this, this is what you do? You ungrateful piece of earthen scum. I am defiled now and have nowhere to cleanse myself. I provide you with a safe place to stay, an easy workload, and this is how you repay me? This is how you treat your master?" Huya stepped forward, pointing. "Oh no, little slave girl. You're done. Your time is finished. You had it good. Now you can go with the rest of your vermin. May the gods curse you in due manner. Get out of my sight! I will have your replacements here by morning."

Eliza ran from the house in tears. Why was she crying? She knew this would happen. It's what she wanted to happen, right? She threw herself into the hay in the outhouse and bawled with no restraint. She did have it good compared to most slaves. She could be gathering straw, making bricks, or working for a nastier family, if such a family existed. Did she just make the biggest mistake of her life?

"You!"

Miera slammed the outhouse door and stood in the dark. She dropped her wrap, exposing her bitten flesh. "Do you realize what you've done? Now we have to go to the bricks. Now we'll get eaten up by gnats. It's because of you—" She sobbed between words. "Because of you, I am being punished!" She dropped into the hay next to Eliza, sobbing.

In her anger, Eliza had forgotten about her sister. She couldn't bear the thought of leaving Miera here alone, or of Miera being whipped by burly men while she packed mud and straw.

Miera eventually fell asleep, curled into a ball under the blankets. Eliza lay awake, frozen in hopelessness, staring at the cobwebs above, hating herself. They stayed in the outhouse all the next day. No replacements arrived. No one came to chide them or send them away. No one came at all. With solemn fear, Eliza ventured into the gnats to fetch water, only to return to the outhouse. When awake, she and Miera reminisced about being home in Avaris with their mother. But most of the time, they slept. The humidity inside the outhouse only intensified its foul odor, reminding Eliza how vile her life had become.

Seti and Kabelo returned from Giza the next day, exhausted and covered in oil and potions. Seti had downed an entire wineskin to dull the pain and intended to sleep for a week. His skin burned even under the oil. His bedroom window had been sealed shut. He'd normally leave the flaps open to let the air in, but someone, probably Eliza—certainly not his mother— had sewn them shut. He didn't want to see the light anyway.

His mother stormed into his room and whipped the blankets off him. "We need to talk!"

He squinted up at her.

She pulled relentlessly on his arm. "Seti, we are having a family meeting."

He found Kabelo waiting in the den. Seti slumped over the side of the couch and rested his head in his hand, eyes barely open. Kabelo reclined on the opposite end. Unlike the familiar aroma of sweaty bodies in the house, the air smelled of a rich heartiness of spices and onions. Fresh ash and scraps blackened the usually empty hearth. Huya sat across from them in Ameneten's fur-lined chair.

"That slave girl, she poisoned me. I want new ones. New slaves."

"Poisoned you?" Seti's ears perked. Nothing evident of sickness characterized his mother—only vitriol.

"She put a frog in my stew. A dead frog. One she found outside. Mixed it into my stew and fed it to me."

"Frog stew?" Kabelo asked.

Seti sat up. "Why?"

"I don't know why!" Huya spat. "She's evil. She's always hated me. I bet she's been plotting this since those frogs came. Better yet, since Moshe came."

Despite the circumstances, frogs were still sacred in Egypt. Eating a frog was blasphemous. A dead one, even more so. His mother had been defiled and needed to be cleansed and consecrated before she could appeal to the gods for anything. Could the girl have planned such a scheme?

"Was it Eliza?" He knew the answer, though he couldn't pinpoint why.

"Whichever the older one is. I want her removed from this place. Her sister, too. Get rid of them both. Get me new ones. Ethiopian, Sidonian, I don't care. Just not Hebrews."

Since his father was held up in the temple for a month, Seti managed the household, and the ultimate decision fell on him. The punishment, the search for new slaves, and transactions were his to make. The process could take longer than the time their father would be away. Seti was in no mood for this.

"Do we have to talk about this now?" he asked.

"Seti! Do you realize how serious this is? I am a priest's wife. I won't have those girls come out of that outhouse until she's dealt with. She will never step foot in this house again. She tried to kill me."

Though he doubted the intent was murder, he understood the urgency. Why did she have to do that? She was so timid around him, but she must be different when he was away. The image of Eliza the night he confronted her two weeks ago returned. Those eyes. He pressed the memory away. He refused to be haunted by those eyes.

"She always looks at me with disdain. I never should have agreed to Hebrew slaves. They are evil filth poisoning our country. They need to go."

His father had chosen the girls in the market after being promoted. The family had just moved into the upscale neighborhood in On, and everyone around them had Hebrew slaves, which sent Huya on a quest for her own. She complained nonstop about the work required with the bigger house and how it kept her from enjoying the lavish lifestyle of the other priests' wives. Seti had been thirteen at the time, Kabelo ten. He wasn't sure of the girls' ages, but they must be close to Kabelo's.

They worked quietly and contently, stayed out of his hair, and never caused trouble. His father allowed them to visit Goshen on the seventh day as part of the transaction. Huya had shown no disdain toward them that Seti had noticed, though he wasn't home much. His father had chosen them deliberately: he wanted female slaves but not ones his sons might find attractive. The girls were plain, dirty, and skinny. Eliza walked like a boy. Nothing graceful about her. She was an easy target for jokes. The younger one was more girly and bubblier.

Having slaves freed Seti and his brother from chores, allowing them to focus on their education and training.

"What do you want me to do?" he asked, yawning.

"I want them gone. Tomorrow."

"It's a bit more complicated than that, Mwt. I can send them away, but it will be a while before we can get replacements, especially if you don't want Hebrews. The shipments only come once a month. If you want money for the girls, they'll need to be appraised, which could take some time." Was it worth his time if Moshe kept fighting to set them free?

The Egyptian government arranged and divided the Hebrews, selling them for domestic use to those who could afford them. The profits went to the realm and the temples. Other Hebrews worked directly under Pharaoh's oversight for his special projects. Only foreign slaves tended to the palace and its yards.

"How about something exotic this time? Pretty. Obedient." Kabelo wiggled his brows.

Seti glanced at his brother in disgust. Though Kabelo was young, he was all passion and no self-control. The whole purpose of his father choosing ugly slaves was to keep his sons pure, specifically Seti, since becoming a priest required purity. Once a priest, Seti had full rein over any priestess or dancer, even if he were to marry. Commitment to the pleasure of the gods took precedence over commitment to a wife. Kabelo had shown no desire for the priesthood, and he wasn't expected to. But Seti didn't want to subject any girl, slave or not, to his brother.

"What?" Kabelo asked. "For me."

Huya narrowed her eyes at Kabelo. "I wonder if we should stick with boys."

"Come on." Kabelo smacked the cushion. "That's no fun."

"Jt doesn't want boys," Seti reminded her.

His father didn't trust Huya. Though they'd start out young, they'd grow to be men. Foreign boys were considered owned for life, unlike Hebrew boys who'd transfer to harder labor at eighteen.

"Oh, give it up, Seti. Boys it is." She clapped her hands.

He didn't want to make that kind of decision without consulting his father. But acquiring foreign slaves would take a while anyway. He had access to the finances while his father was away, and they had plenty of money to spare.

"One or two?"

"Two. I don't want one being split between the animals and the house. What we have going now works. Except, make sure they aren't siblings this time." Her voice lifted.

His mother's mood changed with such abruptness that he raised his eyebrows. "You'd be without slaves for at least a month. Could you handle that?"

Huya slumped, head bowed in frustration. Seti's own head spun with annoyance.

"You sure you want to get rid of them so quickly?" he asked. "They have never caused trouble before."

She rested her chin on her palm, contemplating. He could see the anger Eliza had caused her, but she also couldn't go so long without slaves. And he worried about leaving his mother alone with Eliza again.

"How about we switch them," he suggested. "Make Eliza work outside with the animals and her sister do the indoor chores."

"She needs to be punished. Severely. She needs to know."

"Have her whipped," Kabelo piped in.

Huya's contorted face broke into a slow smile. "I will do the whipping."

Seti's eyebrows raised again. He'd never witnessed a whipping and couldn't imagine his mother doing such a thing, though he'd seen her whip the horse when his father let her drive the chariot. That was funny. No wonder women weren't permitted to drive. He cringed at the thought of his mother whipping Eliza. He'd be forced to watch, being the head of the family. What had set her off to do such a thing after all these years of no incident? Maybe Moshe's presence encouraged the girl to act out.

"I think I'd enjoy it." Huya smiled so big her wooden tooth shone.

"Give her a choice then," he said. "If she chooses the bricks then we get foreign boys. If she chooses to be whipped, then you can have your way with her."

Huya nodded, steepling her fingers with a malevolent gleam in her eye. Glad it was over, Seti retreated to his room. He covered himself with the blanket, laying his head on his pillow with the net still on his head. The fear in Eliza's eyes when he'd confronted her a few weeks ago resurfaced. Could she take a whipping? She carried herself with a tough demeanor but appeared frail and weak. He hoped—at least for her sake—she'd choose the bricks. Then, he'd never have to think of her again.

After two nights in the outhouse, the door creaked open, and a ray of sunlight burst through, blinding Eliza. She shielded her eyes as she sat up, surprised to see the sun after four days of gnat-filled skies. Huya stepped inside, followed by Seti and Kabelo. All three wore full- body nets.

"Reeks in here," Kabelo muttered, his nose buried in his elbow.

Miera sat up and inched beside her sister. None of the

Ameneten family had stepped foot inside the outhouse before.

"We had a family meeting." Huya crossed her arms and peered down her nose. "We decided to give you a choice."

Silence. The air thickened. Eliza wilted under the glare of Huya and her sons. She'd never felt so low.

Huya went on. "You can either receive twenty-five blows at the pole, or we send you both away to the brick farms and replace you."

More silence. Eliza glanced between Huya and Kabelo. She didn't dare look at Seti.

"Blows? What is that? A whip?" Her voice cracked.

"Precisely. By my hand, since it was me you dishonored."

"You defiled my mother with the god of fertility. You should be made infertile—"

Seti smacked Kabelo on the arm to quiet him.

More silence.

Miera whimpered. "We can't go to the bricks," she whispered to Eliza. "I won't last. I'll die." She clung to Eliza's arm.

Eliza looked away, embarrassed by her sister's unmasked fear. The choice was simple. "I'll take the twenty-five blows. Just me, not her." Anything to escape Seti's staring eyes.

"Just you," Huya said.

"No!" Miera flung herself onto Eliza.

Eliza bowed her head. She owed it to Miera, if nothing else.

"So be it." Huya showed no emotion at Miera's display. She turned and opened the door, leaving them. Her sons followed.

Miera sobbed in her lap, but Eliza remained unmoving, eyes fixed on the closed door. Rage ran hot through her veins as she suppressed the urge to scream. God wasn't setting them free. He was making everything worse.

Chapter 8

No one returned to the outhouse. Had they been replaced? No one came to give Eliza any blows either. When that would happen, she didn't know. But the buzzing of the gnats outside diminished to silence. In the dark, Eliza listened to her sister's rhythmic breathing, all sprawled out in the hay, asleep. Unsure how long it had been, Eliza sat, motionless, for hours.

Late in the night, she rose and stretched her stiff body. Wrapping her blanket around her, she ventured out the door and gently shut it behind her, careful not to wake Miera. Maybe they could run away together. She paused on the doorstep. A gentle breeze cooled her sweaty face. Fresh air. She inhaled deeply, letting it fill her lungs. Stray gnats fluttered here and there, but not enough to keep her inside. She might go for a walk.

Seti paused as the outhouse door creaked open and shut. He had been sitting in the stable, oiling Chewy with aloe, unable to sleep. He stood and peered over Chewy. Eliza. She was going out to pray again, even after he had specifically told her not to. He remained still, unsure whether to show himself.

The dark figure stood against the door, wrapped in a blanket, hair sticking out in bunches from underneath. Ire burned within him against her gods and against her, the one who poisoned his mother. After setting the oil brush next to the pail, Seti marched straight for her.

Her head lifted, and she stepped back, her big brown eyes widening in the moonlight.

"Oh, quit with the scared little kitten act! I know you're nothing like that." He stopped close enough to strangle her. But he didn't, though the thought crossed his mind.

She bowed her head. "Shhh." She touched her lips with a trembling finger. "Don't wake my sister."

The image of that little girl crying and clinging to Eliza earlier flashed through his mind, and a sliver of compassion overcame him.

Then a thought occurred. He straightened and cocked his head. "Tell me, who is the Hebrew god of the Nile?"

Why hadn't he thought of this before? The priests would revere him for relaying information on the enemy. Just how much of a threat was this Hebrew God?

Her head remained bowed as she stammered for a moment. "We don't have a god of the Nile."

That didn't make sense. He was about to ask again when a gnat flew in front of his face inside the net. He swatted at it, but the net got in the way. Irritated by the interruption, he grabbed her elbow and propelled her to the stable where they could sit in the light, away from the gnats. He brushed off a bench for her to sit but found her looking at him oddly. Her brow furrowed, and she scrunched her eyes, studying him. He must look hideous from the gnat bites and the sheen of oil. At least the swelling had subsided. He had returned from Giza like this, the whole trip botched.

"What happened to you?" She spoke to him like a lost sheep, and it embarrassed him.

He scoffed and motioned her to sit. "Tell me about your gods. I want to know everything. I want to confront them."

She sat, hands awkwardly on her knees. "We, we worship only one God, El Shaddai. He's the creator of everything, not just the Nile. The one true God. I don't know much about Him, but I know He keeps His promises. And He defends us—"

Seti raised an eyebrow at her abrupt cut off, sure she questioned her own words. He sat beside her. "What promises?"

Her face was expressionless. Then she shook her head. "The promise to our Father Avraham. That after four hundred years of living in a strange land, He would bring us to our own land, and there He will raise us up to be His witness to the world."

Seti's eyes widened, and he drew in a breath. He wasn't expecting that. He expected a petty promise of sustaining the Hebrews under the care of the Egyptians. They were a gift to the Egyptians as slaves, so his people could focus on the higher-minded things of life. No god ever made promises, especially to humanity.

"You're kidding, right?" He laughed. "I hate to break it to you, but He's not keeping His promises. Open your eyes. You are slaves. You are not protected or defended."

She looked away longingly, as if wanting to run. If she believed in these stories, then she was as much a fool as she was a slave.

A quiet breeze blew between them. Movement sounded in the stalls as the horses rearranged themselves. Was this all it was? No challenge? No declaration of war between the gods over the Nile? Just hopeful slave fantasies.

"I'm sorry, that's just not how the world works." He expected her to cry, but she didn't.

Sadness clouded her face as she gazed at the moon just above the roof of the neighbor's house.

"What god makes promises to mere man?"

She turned as if surprised at his question. "Well, um, He treasures us. Since the fall of man, He has set out a plan to bring us back to Him. He wants to draw humanity to Him, not force anyone against their will."

Her hands fidgeted in her lap as she talked. She paused, and her eyes slowly rose to meet his gaze as if for approval, a daring move on her part. He caught the moment and held on to it for a split second before she looked away. He had looked into those eyes once before, and now he wanted more.

More curious about her now than her god, he filled the silence. "Fall of man?"

She inhaled and exhaled deeply, staring at her hands.

He quirked a slight smile, reveling in the way she squirmed under his stare. Accustomed to being followed by girls in fits of giggles and questions to the point of annoyance, her behavior amused him. "Go on, quit holding back. Make me understand."

After a moment, she answered, "When God created man and woman, He made them perfect. He gave them freedom to choose to obey Him or not. He wanted man to freely love Him, but man chose to disobey. The relationship between God and man was severed, just how man wanted it. But He still loves us and wants to reclaim that fellowship without forcing us against our will. He promised a way to bridge the gap between us, to bring us back to Him. God is not like man and cannot lie or break his promises."

God created man? The Hebrew God? Man was created purely for the service of the gods, not for love. Every culture knew this. Seti nearly bit his tongue holding the laughter in. The way she explained it suggested there was more to it than what she'd explained. It was either more complicated, and she was trying to simplify it, or she didn't fully understand it herself.

He sighed. A heart-lifting tale was all it was. If only

gods were like that. But they weren't. It was nothing but false hope for the Hebrews to cling to. She believed what she said, despite the obvious flaws.

"And what does that have to do with this promise to give you land? What does that have to do with Egypt?"

"It's part of His plan to win the love of humanity. Through us."

None of this made sense. Her gaze found the moon again, as if asking it for help. Seti furrowed his brow. She didn't know what she was talking about. She let out a small sigh in surrender, as if realizing how defeated she was.

"Through you Hebrews?" He chuckled. "Then why has He allowed you to be our slaves if He loves you so much? Better yet, why must humanity suffer the way it does if He loves us so much?" He hoped she'd see the foolishness of her theory.

"All I know," she said softly, looking at him, "is that He allows suffering and affliction to draw man back to Him."

The seriousness of her deep eyes held him captive. But when his laughter burst forth, she looked away, and he immediately regretted it. "Umm…that's not love."

"How else will man come back to Him?" she fired. "If man fares well on his own, he feels no need for God. It's our nature. How many people flooded the temple when the Nile turned to blood? How many sacrifices were made? How much pleading and meditating, how many offerings were given during that time? And it's done wholeheartedly, but how much heart is put into a sacrifice when all is good?"

He straightened at her boldness. She was more perceptive than he thought. As if she had heard their conversation at the dinner table after the blood cleared from the Nile. The slave girls were in the stable when his family ate, or so he thought. He clearly underestimated this girl.

"But what kind of relationship is that?" he fired back, more to hide his surprise than anything. "That your God must make something bad happen to get your attention, so you crawl back to him?"

"What kind of relationship is it that you must manipulate the gods to give you what you need to survive?" The words had rushed from her lips on a sharp exhale. She winced and bowed her head, as if waiting to be slapped.

He blinked in astonishment. Did she speak like this often when he wasn't home? She rarely spoke a word in his presence. The realization that he could make her do whatever he wanted burst forth in his mind. He could easily put her in her place. Then shame flooded him. But why? He had every right to do so.

"Forgive me," she mumbled, head still bowed.

"So, your God grasps onto whatever kind of relationship with man He can get, regardless of how cheap it is?" He almost wanted her to fire back again.

But she spoke carefully. "There's nothing cheap about it. Even if it were, as you say, it still wouldn't be offered freely. It wouldn't last. If we give Him the chance, He will prove Himself faithful. But we must obey, too, because how can He use anyone if they don't obey? Love is so much more than that."

"Love?" Seti laughed. "What do you know about love?"

She shot him a piercing glare.

He had hurt her. "You have my apologies." Surprised that he apologized to a slave, he let the words hang.

"You mock me."

"You are more bold than you can handle," he told her. "You forget your place."

She looked down again. "You said, 'make me understand.'"

That much was true.

"May I be excused?"

"No." He was just getting started.

She continued to look down, her hair hiding her eyes,

but the disappointment was evident.

"Take me to where you were praying," Seti commanded.

Her head shot up at once, eyes wide behind the strands of hair, and he couldn't help but smirk.

"Take me to where you were praying," he said again, standing.

She stood with obedience, wrapped in her dirty blanket, while he stood in his net.

"Lead the way." He motioned to the door.

She stepped out of the stable into the open air. He left his oil lamp behind and strode quietly beside her as she led him to the street. The hill was not far, just a couple of houses away. His sandals scraped the stones on the road, her bare feet as quiet as a mouse.

"What is man that your God should care for him, if He's such a God of gods?"

Eliza lifted her head skyward and nearly skipped a step. "What is God that He should not care for man? We are made in His image. He didn't just make us, He created us, to love and tend to us. To be loved by us."

"We are made in His image?" Seti glanced up. What did she think when she saw the stars? "We are made in His image? He looks like us? Not an animal?"

A giggle escaped her, catching Seti by surprise. He looked straight ahead, pretending not to notice, suppressing a smile. She had let down her guard. He had never heard her laugh or giggle or even seen her smile, at least that he could remember.

"No. We are made in His image, not Him in our image. But He did create the animals too. He made everything—the heavens, the earth, the sky and the mountains. Even the seas." She shot him a look of wonder. "Even Sheol."

Keep her talking. She might say something he could use. Even if she didn't, the way she talked of her God stirred something in him that he didn't want to end. "And the gods?"

"Everything. But He loves us. Haven't you ever made something with your hands and loved it?" The question was odd, yet he was more taken aback by the thought that this might be the first meaningful, non-slave question she had ever asked him.

Instead of answering, he searched his memories for any other such questions from her.

"Or like a child," she went on. "The love you have for them is so perfect, so unconditional. You created them, yet they are their own being. And when you look into their eyes, there is nothing they can do to make your love go away."

The things this girl spoke of were deep and complicated, more than a simple give-and-take relationship between the gods and man. It was as if she were from a world he never knew.

He watched her out of the corner of his eye and wondered how often she sneaked here in the middle of the night. Could she literally speak to her God without the aid of a priest? What else did she do in secret? He was so busy with his life that he never imagined the lives of slaves or what ran through their heads.

Seti searched the wonders of the heavens, and his silly theory of the stars came to mind. Walking ahead and turning so he walked backward, he held his hands to the sky and asked, "All that? If He created all that, where is He?"

A second little giggle escaped her. This one lasted longer, if only for a second—music to his ears.

She lifted her hands to the heavens. "God set His glory in the heavens, laying them out like a scroll to behold and for tracking the days, months, and seasons. They are for us. We are the central tile in the mosaic. He sees the whole picture and tends to each and every individual piece, but it's all for us. As far as where He is, it's as though He pitched a tent with His own hands and then inhabited it and cared for it. He is on the outside, but on the inside too. And sometimes, He appears to us in ways that allow us to see Him, embodied, if He so chooses." She grinned at the peculiar expression on his face. "What?"

Seti's mouth dropped, stunned to silence. Her adoration for her God rivaled even the priests', capturing his soul. He half-smiled in return, a sinking feeling in the pit of his stomach. Gazing at her beaming face in the moonlight, a longing for her swept through him. The sight of her filled him with warmth, as if a dark veil had been ripped from his eyes. This was a foreign feeling, something he hadn't experienced before. Turning from her, a sadness took over. She was a slave. Off limits. Forbidden. The joy he saw in her as she spoke of her God was unlike anything he could reciprocate when speaking of his own gods.

What had she said that disappointed him? Eliza had never seen that look on his face before. He continued to walk ahead, leading the way up the road, ignoring her. Reaching the top of the hill first, he veered off into the weeds.

He faced her, standing with his arms stretched, the weeds so tall they reached his waist. His white kilt glowed in the moonlight beneath the mesh netting. "Is this it?"

This was her spot. If she lay down here in the weeds, she would not be seen. Now, if he discovered she was gone from the outhouse, he would know where to find her. He dropped to the ground and lay on his back, just as she had done weeks before. A pang of sadness touched her heart. He had taken over her one safe spot.

He gazed up at her. "A slave should never stand above her master."

She timidly eased herself down in the dirt beside him, stiff as a board, aware of his closeness. Why was he doing this? She used to dream of him out here with her, talking about God together. And here they were. Yet, there was nothing romantic about it.

"And the sun and the moon?" he asked, a wistfulness in his tone.

She couldn't speak.

He asked again, "The sun and the moon? They give us life, though, right?"

Collecting herself, she answered, "Another creation. He's bigger than the sun and the moon. He gave those to us to make the earth habitable and to count days and seasons." Her words were short.

The bobbing tension in her voice sank Seti's heart. He had ruined the moment somehow. Folding his sweaty palms under his head, he pondered how inappropriate it was to take a slave to a secret spot and talk about such things. The feelings and thoughts that crossed his mind earlier shamed him. He had to be careful. Here he was, lying next to a slave girl in the field, mostly against her will. Were these feelings due to missing Lumeri? Eliza's words revealed that there was much more to her, so much more than he could even begin to know. And more to her God.

He no longer cared or was curious enough to ask questions. The tall weeds stood over them, concealing them from the road and houses. This was her hiding spot. Her mesa. What was he doing? A cool chill sent shivers through his body despite the heat radiating from her. He fought the temptation to apologize again, this time for intruding on such an intimate spot. How much of a jerk could he be? He should have excused her when she asked. Her breathing slowed, and he peeked over to see if she was asleep. Nope. Wide awake.

He looked away in shame. How many times had he

hurt her?

"Why did you choose the lashes instead of the bricks?" Seti asked.

She turned to him, eyes sparkling, though she quickly looked away. Why did he ask that? Wasn't he furious with her not too long ago?

She ripped a reed from the ground and wound it around her fingers. "My sister, she won't last on the brick farms. It's not her fault I did what I did. She shouldn't be punished. But I can take the whipping."

Laughter burst from him before he could stop himself. "I don't think so. I take it you've never been whipped before?"

"No. Have you?"

"Uh, no." He had never even seen one.

"Your mwt's a weakling. I can live with her strikes more than I could live with myself if my sister was whipped by grown men." She backtracked. "I mean, I'll be fine…"

Seti, unfazed by her comment about his mother, didn't know how to respond. She was doing this for her sister? He wouldn't do that for his own brother. Maybe she thought her God would come to her rescue. He couldn't remember learning of any god coming to the rescue of a human, not even an Egyptian.

Maybe he could help her. He leaned on his elbow. "I have some stuff that you can take to help you through it."

"What do you mean?"

"You know, to help with the pain."

"Like, get me drunk?" she asked, her voice kicking up a notch.

"No, like a potion. I got some from the temple for myself. It will help get you through the worst of it."

"Oh no." She shook her head. "I'm not taking anything from your temple. Nothing from your gods. Nothing from you."

"You're crazy. You have no idea how bad it's going to

be." What was he doing? She deserved all twenty-five lashes and all the pain they'd cause.

"I would rather suffer than have your gods help me."

He opened his mouth to protest, but she turned away. Still, the inexplicable urgency he felt for her compelled him to try again. "But what if your God doesn't help you?"

"It's temporary pain. Besides, I deserve it. I'll just take the punishment and get it over with."

He stared at her in disbelief. All for her sister? Any normal person would beg for mercy. But no, she was taking it head-on. She hadn't once sought the opportunity in their conversation to weasel out of it. And she seemed offended by his offer to help. Brave? Yes. Stupid? Maybe.

They lay side by side in silence, staring in opposite directions. A cool breeze came upon Seti and sent shivers through his body. Or were the shivers because he had permitted his mother to whip this girl?

Finally, he stood, and without thinking, Seti reached out, grabbed her hand, and pulled her to her feet. Eliza's eyes widened, and he realized what he'd done. He looked away, embarrassed. It was instinct. He knew how to treat a girl, but not a slave. He was crossing boundaries. He marched ahead, suddenly wanting to get away from her, but her footsteps padded behind him, keeping pace. It would have been better to sell the girls. His blood boiled. He was being weak.

The words Kabelo spoke at the family meeting flooded his mind. He could make Eliza do anything he wanted and still be in the right. A powerful god could do the same with humanity, but it wouldn't be love. This must be what she meant regarding her God's pursuit of their love. Eliza said that human characteristics couldn't be attributed to such a god, but the desire for love is a human characteristic. Wasn't that proof that they had invented this god out of their own hearts?

He held his tongue until they reached the stable.

"You may be excused," he said coldly.

After she hurried past him to the outhouse, he returned to his house, shaken.

Seti tossed and turned in his bed, the feelings that had risen in him earlier angering him. How could he let himself sink so low? Not only did such feelings perplex him, but so did the things that came out of her mouth. In the five years of her working for his family, why hadn't he ever spoken with her? It wasn't that bad. It was quite fascinating, the mind of a Hebrew. The silly things they believed. Did they really think that after all these years they'd be rescued and given land of their own? After all the gods had done with them in Egypt?

When did a god converse with humanity and make a promise to them? How would a god even do that? And this was, supposedly, the God of all gods. He came down and made a promise to mere humans, as if He owed them something. Well, He's a weak god. What god chases after humans like a desperate girl chasing after boys? And to the point that He has to cause man pain to get a response? Moshe, who believes the same thing, thinks this would work in the Hebrews' favor. But the gods keep prevailing. And in the end, the Hebrews will lose.

Seti couldn't stop thinking about their conversation. Or her. He was intrigued and amused and curious, and he couldn't help himself. She was like a book he hadn't yet read, a history he didn't know.

Eliza could not calm her racing heart. Did she upset him? He was awfully abrupt at the end. She curled up beneath her blanket. Did she believe her own words about God? Seti was right: it was not reality. God's rescue was not happening. Her people were only suffering more and more.

She had recited what her mother told her long ago. Four hundred years—that would be now. The tribal leaders kept track. It made sense, right? Her mother would tuck her and her brothers in at night, repeating the same stories. Did her mother believe all that? Could Eliza recount the stories to him without sounding like an utter fool?

He said tomorrow she'd get the blows. When tomorrow? All she wanted to do was sleep in her bed, safe and sound.

Chapter 9

Shortly after dawn, Huya pounded on the door of the outhouse. "Get up. It's time."

Eliza had tossed and turned all night, dreading her impending punishment. She slowly stood, wrapped herself in her blanket, and stepped outside. Crisp morning air chased the gnats away, yet Huya stood wrapped in a blanket and head net. She grabbed Eliza's arm, pulling her forward.

"The other girl, too," she scowled and nodded toward the outhouse.

"No! You said it would just be me!" Eliza cried.

"Oh, calm down. It's just you, but she needs to see. You will be an example." Huya tied a rope around Eliza's wrists.

Miera stumbled out with her blanket. She remained silent as Huya led Eliza away like a donkey. Seti and Kabelo emerged on the stone steps, yawning as they followed along. Shame shot through Eliza. After last night, she couldn't bear Seti seeing her dragged like a fool. She should have chosen the bricks.

The scene playing out was not new to Eliza. She'd seen it before. Lead the accused across the neighborhood for all to see. Word would spread, eventually drawing a crowd. Every neighborhood had a pole where the accused would be tied and whipped.

Huya marched faster than Eliza could keep up. The rope tugged at her wrists, and her bare feet scraped across stones, prickly plants, and dead frogs.

Eliza kept her eyes downcast as children paused and gasped before running to tell others. Thankfully, not many were out yet. Maybe it would be a small crowd. Faint whispers surrounded her, and curious stares willed her to look up and explain herself. They must wonder how it could be Eliza from the Ameneten home. Eliza, who was always careful to stay hidden. Eliza, who admonished younger slaves when they got into trouble.

Miera followed silently, with Seti and Kabelo behind her. They crossed one street and then another. Huya led the group confidently, a perpetual smile on her face.

The short, stocky wooden post stuck out from the ground at the end of a house-lined street two blocks from the Ameneten home. The sight of it halted Eliza. It stood alone, an abandoned eyesore, surrounded by blood-stained dirt. Huya yanked her forward. Several slaves from nearby houses came near, each wearing handsewn head coverings. Huya wrenched off Eliza's blanket, tossed it aside, then tied Eliza's hands around the pole. Splinters stuck into her bare arms. Old blood spatter speckled the front. Eliza stood against it, stoic and unfeeling. She muttered a silent prayer and kept her eyes shut.

Huya backed away toward the others and pulled a whip out from beneath her blanket—one from the chariots in the stable—then took her place beside her sons and Miera.

"Tell us why you are here, girl," Huya yelled.

The statement drew Eliza from her trance. Huya didn't even know her name. She lifted her head toward Seti and Kabelo, who stood behind Miera. Surely, this validated Seti's stance that all she believed was a lie.

"Why are you here?" Huya yelled again. "Come on! You can speak."

"I put frog guts in your stew," Eliza said, her voice low.

The whispers around them intensified.

"What was that? I don't think they heard you." Huya slapped the whip against the ground, and Eliza flinched.

She gazed at the sky, cheeks hot. "I squeezed frog guts into your stew. The stew I made you, when we had nothing else to eat, but you didn't like it and sent me into the gnats to get something else!" Everyone would know what enticed her.

"You did that to dishonor me and Heket! You almost killed me!"

"It wasn't going to kill you." Anger pulsed through Eliza's veins, obliterating the shame.

"It dishonored and defiled me, you ungrateful Hebrew scab!"

"I'm a scab, and you're an insufferable woman!" Eliza screamed.

With that, the whip snapped across her face. She recoiled and turned her face toward the pole. Her eyes clenched shut, the sting of the whip running deep in her head. It took all she had to not cry out. She could not show weakness to Huya or her sons. She hugged the pole, her fingers clenching the wood, her whole body trembling. The air left her lungs, and she struggled to refill them. The children gasped in shock. Miera cried out. It wasn't supposed to go like this, not on the face.

That was one; twenty-four more to go. I can do this.

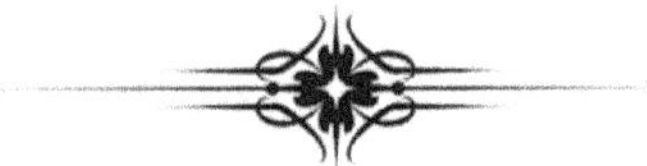

Seti's heart leaped in his chest at that first strike. Eliza was supposed to have her back to them. His mother whipped her again, this time across the back, ripping her tunic. But she didn't scream. Miera whimpered at the sound of each slap against Eliza's skin, while Kabelo held on to her.

Come on, Seti pleaded. *Where's your defender God now?*

He turned to the crowd. The audience had grown. It was clearly entertainment for them, something to spice up their mundane workday. But the younger children watched wide-eyed, clinging to the older ones. He'd imagined it all morning, but nothing could have prepared him for this. Did no one care? Was it so routine that all their hearts had hardened? Slave or not, no child should be whipped. His breathing intensified with each strike. Three. Four. She wasn't going to make it to twenty-five. Her legs quivered beneath her. *Come on, God, aren't you going to do something?* His hands clenched his tunic, and he stared at his mother in horror. She put her whole body into each thrust.

Huya paused to catch her breath. Unable to watch any more, Seti darted toward Eliza. Just as he reached her, the next strike wrapped around his arm as he shielded her with his body. He spun around, yanking the leather, pulling his mother off her feet. She flopped onto the hard ground in a cloud of dust. His eyes widened, not expecting that, but he refrained from rushing to her. The crowd gasped.

"Seti!" Huya screamed, scrambling to her feet. She snatched the whip from the ground and tried to pull it from Seti's grasp with no success.

"That's enough, Mwt. This is preposterous." He freed the whip from his arm but kept a firm grip on it, holding his stance in front of Eliza.

"Get out of there!" Huya tugged at the whip.

"No, that's enough. Go home." His mother could easily be cleansed, but Eliza would forever bear the scars.

The air stilled. The whispers stopped. Silence. All eyes darted between the wife of the famed Ameneten and his firstborn. It seemed even the animals paused to watch.

Huya stared, eyes aflame. Out of breath, she released the whip. Miera broke free from Kabelo's grasp and plummeted toward Eliza, but Seti and Huya remained still.

Keeping his eyes locked on his mother's, he pulled a small dagger from his pocket and handed it to Miera, who immediately began sawing the rope. Kabelo shifted his feet, eyes darting from Huya to Seti, then back to Huya again.

Finally, Huya lowered her voice. "You disgrace me, Seti. You better not come home. Stay away." She pointed her finger. "You are an embarrassment to our family."

His heart broke as she spun and stomped away, fists at her sides. Kabelo looked at Seti, face pale, and Seti nodded toward their mother. As Kabelo ran after her, Seti closed his eyes and slowly took a deep breath. Heart pounding, he turned to Eliza. She knelt on the ground, waiting for Miera to finish.

Seti snatched the dagger from Miera and sliced the rope. Once it broke, Eliza fell backward off her heels, landing on her rear. Her body trembled, and her chest heaved as she struggled to catch her breath. The sight of her face took his breath away. He grabbed her blanket and gently draped it over her shoulders to conceal her wounds from prying eyes and hungry gnats. He used a corner to dab the blood on her face. His gaze met hers and softened as he inspected the dark red gash stretching from her forehead down her cheek toward her jaw. Her bloodshot eyes brimmed with unshed tears as though waiting for permission to fall.

"Your God failed you," he said, unable to hide the pity in his voice.

"No, He didn't," she whispered.

His heart stopped.

He looked away to let himself breathe. A storm of anger and bewilderment raged through him. Her God had used him. How dare He? Seti shook the thoughts away and focused on Eliza's stunning gaze. "You shouldn't go back. It's not safe. Find somewhere else to go." He helped her to her feet, removed the net from his head, and placed it on hers.

"Thank you." The corner of her mouth lifted, as if she

tried to smile but couldn't.

"Eliza, let's get out of here." Miera took her sister's hand and pulled her away from him.

Seti pressed his lips together and nervously glanced around them. He nodded toward her as she reluctantly followed Miera, peering over her shoulder at him. As soon as Eliza was a good distance away, the children encircled her, concealing her. He stood alone next to the pole, hands shaking, dread and regret overwhelming him. Did he just make the biggest mistake of his life? He had come here thinking he was strong enough not to intervene, but he had caved.

Seti sat on the mesa's ledge, legs dangling, body and head wrapped in a blanket. No one would know to look for him here, except Sabu, who would show up eventually—especially once word spread. The Ameneten scandal would soon be on the tip of every tongue in the city. Seti cringed.

Sabu arrived within the hour, dismounted his chariot, and took a seat beside him. They sat in silence, staring at the city below. A warm breeze hit Seti's face. Ra shone his brilliance as usual, but it seemed to laugh at him. The beauty of the city concealed unspoken cruelties and suffering.

Seti broke the silence. "Have you ever watched a whipping before?"

Sabu sighed. "Only of adults. But it's pretty common to whip disobedient slave children. You just don't see it because you have your head buried in the temple all the time."

Was he so naïve? "We are more civilized than that."

"Yeah, but they aren't."

Was that how it was justified? "It doesn't bother you?"

"What? You were fine with it before. She was just a slave girl then, and now all of a sudden you care about her? What's gotten into you, Seti? Slaves get whipped. It's part of life."

Seti wanted to argue but kept his mouth shut. What had gotten into him? He picked at a loose thread from his blanket. He may have agreed with Sabu a week ago, but now?

"You know what she told me last night?" Not waiting for Sabu to answer, he continued. "She said that they, the Hebrews, only believe in one God. And He makes promises to them and defends them. How can they believe that? After all this time?"

"Only thing I can think of is they are delusional. Remember, they don't think like Egyptians, Seti. They couldn't even if they tried."

The answer didn't satisfy him. Delusional didn't explain the look in her eyes. It didn't explain Moshe. If only Seti could see Moshe, talk to him, ask him all his questions. He had his chance last week but failed.

"Even if it were any other animal besides something as sacred as a frog, she deserved every last stripe. I've never heard you speak of her before. Why now?" Sabu asked.

"She'd never done anything worth speaking of before."

"Do you think Moshe being back had anything to do with this?"

"I don't know. I caught her sneaking out a couple weeks ago, back when Moshe first arrived. She said she had gone to pray to her God. I don't know if that was the whole truth or not." She could have made it all up and led him to that spot up the hill just to expound on the lie. But her eyes, they told the truth, right? Would he have stepped in and rescued her if he hadn't spoken with her the night before? He didn't dare tell Sabu any more. Realizing there was no talking to his friend about this, he made up his mind. Sabu meant his best.

"Can you get Chewy and my bag? I need to go to the temple."

"Is that where you're going to stay?"

"It's the only place I can go." Plus, his father was there.

Eliza glimpsed the commotion on the river outside the wooden doors to her right. When she blinked, tears poured down her cheeks over the ointment slathered on her face. She sat on a table, legs dangling, leaning forward as an Egyptian woman worked to sew one of the open gashes on her back. A small group of Hebrew children had led her to this large brick building, telling her it was a linen shop behind the marketplace.

She gasped when the woman dabbed alcohol into her wounds. The cool air blowing in prolonged the sting. The strong wine they had given her wasn't strong enough. Tears cascaded down her cheeks, and she struggled to keep quiet.

Ships flanked the Nile, loading and unloading, making up for lost time once the river had reopened to commerce. Eliza concentrated on the activity on the dock to keep her mind distracted. Strange, light-haired men pushed bins on rollers up the gravel path and into the building where the contents were dumped onto the rock floor in front of her. Women sifted through the piles of cotton and wool linen from the north and silk from the east. Flax from Egyptian farms came in through another door. They worked in silence, sorting each kind into piles to be moved elsewhere in the building. No one batted an eye at Eliza, and she preferred to keep it that way. She didn't dare speak, afraid she might get turned in or someone may go after Seti.

Seti.

He was banished from his home. All because of her.

The thought of his life being ruined was too much to bear. God may be just, but He is also merciful. She only received five lashes. That was mercy. She deserved them all, especially after her inflammatory retort in front of the crowd at the pole. If she had kept her mouth shut, she would have at least saved her face. How much of a scar was this going to leave?

Miera bounced in with a plate of crackers and almonds as the woman tied off the last stitch.

"Look!" Miera held up the plate.

"Where'd you get these? We don't have money." Eliza's voice cracked after staying silent so long.

"I bought them," another Egyptian woman spoke from behind Miera. Eliza lifted her head but couldn't see through the tears. She grabbed a cracker and bit into it, not having tasted one since she'd been home.

"My name is Hiru. You can trust me." The woman watched the girls eat.

Eliza nodded before wiping her eyes with the back of her hand. Her mind swirled from the wine. Someone draped a blanket gently over her back and tucked it around her shoulders. Miera hopped onto the table beside her and pulled strands of Eliza's hair from the ointment on her face. Her head bobbed as Miera braided her hair, rambling on about something, but Eliza paid no attention. She closed her eyes and pictured Seti laughing. *What do you know about love?*

The question etched her mind. Oh, those sweet dimples that only showed when he smiled. She wanted to touch them. *What do you know about—*

"Eliza!" Miera gasped.

Eliza's eyes shot open. Two familiar men stepped in through the back entrance. Moshe? Was she dreaming? Delusional from the wine? Aharon set his staff against the doorframe, and both men dropped their woven sacks on the floor, heading straight to the plate of crackers.

Miera hopped off the table and ran to them. "You're

Moshe and Aharon!"

It wasn't a dream.

The men smiled. "Yes, you're right. And who might you be?"

"I'm Miera, and that's my sister, Eliza. We worked for the Ameneten family, but they whipped her for putting a dead frog in Huya's stew. But then Seti, their son, saved her and set us free. The other slaves brought us here. We don't know where else to go."

Eliza cringed. They didn't need to know all that.

Aharon glanced at Eliza, observing the shiny gash. "Ahhh," he said, nodding, eyebrows raised.

She wanted nothing more than to cover her face with the blanket but couldn't move. Hebrew and Egyptian women alike rushed into the room at the announcement of their arrival. They gathered around Moshe and Aharon, eagerly asking questions in their native tongue. Why were Egyptians speaking to him? And why were they so nice?

When Moshe spoke, the women quieted. "He refused. Again. And tomorrow the Lord will send flies over Egypt."

The room filled with gasps.

"Flies? We just got over gnats!"

"Swarms. He said swarms." Moshe popped a handful of almonds in his mouth. "It will begin tomorrow morning. The Lord is giving us a warning this time. Also, He is preserving the Land of Goshen. Whoever believes the Lord shall take shelter there, for He will protect it."

Aharon motioned to each of the women. "We must warn the Hebrews. If they can get to Goshen, they should go. Perhaps their masters will let them."

"Yes!" A few women scurried about, filling their sacks with what belongings they had.

"This will show the people," Moshe's commanding voice halted the flurry of packing and movement, "that the Lord makes a distinction between those who are His people and those who are not. And it'll be obvious to all that this is from the hand of Yahweh."

"Perhaps Pharaoh will finally understand and let us go. He'd be blind not to see it," Hiru said.

"He is blind," Moshe said, "and he won't let us go until the last plague. The Lord must first demonstrate His power over the gods, including Pharaoh. He wants us to be without a doubt when we leave here. He wants our undivided attention."

"But He has our attention."

"Does He? And He doesn't want only us to know. The Egyptians will also know who the one true God is. Pharaoh's heart may be hardened, but the people's are not. They will see that Pharaoh is no more a god than any of us. All of Egypt will know that Yahweh is God."

Moshe released a tired sigh before biting into a cracker, face downcast. Aharon hurried out of the room with several of the women to spread the word.

"Where's my Tzipporah?" Moshe asked quietly.

"She's in the market. She'll be back soon." Hiru gathered the empty dishes.

Eliza stared, awestruck. He seemed so... so human. So tired.

The room emptied. Only he, the girls, and a couple of women remained. Moshe turned his attention to Eliza. "You best be getting home. The flies will make you sick."

"Are...are you returning to Goshen?" Eliza choked out, her voice shaking.

"No, not yet. God wants me here, for Pharaoh won't last long before he summons me again. I will be safe here in On."

"Moshe?" Miera asked, tugging on his robe. "Can you ask God to heal my sister?"

His smile creased beneath his beard.

"No, Miera," Eliza said. "The Lord had great mercy on me already."

Miera frowned. "But now's your chance."

"Miera, we are not going back to the Ameneten house. We can go home. And better yet, everyone will be free soon. Isn't that right, Moshe?"

"Yes, you are right. But more plagues will come before Pharaoh finally lets us go. The Lord has promised that it will be done."

"The plagues really are from God," Eliza said, amazed. Of course, they were from God. It wasn't magic.

"You didn't think so?" Moshe's voice broke her thoughts.

"I wasn't sure. The Egyptians believe you cast spells on them, or their gods are punishing them for something. They can't accept that our God is stronger. They find reasons for everything."

"Well, they will understand. Then they will urge us to leave and give us their things. They will see that their gods…"

The effects of the wine sent her head spinning, and Eliza struggled to pay attention as he went into a monologue about God's plan. Something about gold and the firstborn. His voice trailed off after her eyes closed. She fought to open them, not wanting to disappoint this man of God.

She sensed him watching her and opened her eyes in time to see him head for the door.

"Where are you going?" Miera called after him.

"My wife will return soon, and I need to eat and take a nap. We must prepare everyone for the plague tomorrow."

Eliza didn't want Moshe and Aharon to leave. Listening to them speak was like hearing the voice of God. But the need for sleep took over. She was useless like this anyway. Maybe a nap would dispel the effects of the wine.

Someone placed a pillow on the table beside her and encouraged her to sleep. After Miera covered her with one of the new linens brought in, Eliza laid her head on the pillow and closed her eyes.

Seti crept into the temple early that afternoon, careful to avoid Lumeri, wherever she was. While his father busied himself with the god-statues, Seti made his way to the living quarters. He tore the sheet from his father's window, releasing dust and dead gnats into rays of light, then he climbed into the sill to wait.

He hadn't seen the temple's response to the gnats until today. Though they had died down, the linen still hung in the windows. Surely, the gods protected their temple. Yet the coffins in Giza hadn't been protected. How had the gnats gotten into the heart of the pyramid? The vents stretched hundreds of cubits, and the corridors had openings only at the ends.

The door opened, and Ameneten paused mid-step upon seeing Seti. He stood, freshly cleansed from the pools, wrapped in a white towel. Their eyes locked.

"I know what happened, Seti. I heard all about it," his father said and continued into the room.

Seti gulped and climbed from the windowsill. Of course his father would have already heard. "Now what happens? What are you going to do?"

"Seti." Ameneten sighed and sat on the bed, a raised mattress made specifically for priests. He motioned for his son to sit beside him.

Seti sat, emotions flooding over him.

"You are my firstborn. It would take a lot to lose your heritage and even more for me to disown you. I love you. You don't have to worry about that."

Seti kept his eyes on his hands, away from his father's gaze.

"But you dishonored your mwt. Since I wasn't there,

you were in charge. You permitted the whipping to proceed only to reverse your decision in the middle of it, in front of the whole town. What does that say to our people? What does that say to the Hebrews? To your mwt? You humiliated her."

Seti nodded, not fully agreeing, but remained silent.

"I'm worried about you, Seti," his father continued. "Ever since the plagues started, you seem to be doubting."

"I'm not doubting," Seti countered.

"I've seen it before in young men. They drop out or fail after doing so well."

"What are you saying?"

"What I'm saying is, I'm worried about you. I heard you had told your mwt that you cursed the gods?"

"I was angry. Because of Lumeri. It was only emotion. It isn't how I feel now."

"And then you defend a slave girl?"

"Well, come on, Jt. What would you have done?" Stupid question.

"She deserved it. It's part of being a slave. Part of their heritage. We have ours, they have theirs."

Seti picked at his fingernails. He should have known that would be the answer.

"I'm probably the only Egyptian to ever do that, huh?" he muttered.

"Well, not exactly," his father responded.

Seti locked eyes with him.

"The queen rescued Moshe."

That's right! The queen, rest her soul, an Egyptian—a prominent one at that—rescued a lowly Hebrew slave baby. Then she raised him as her own in front of the whole world. Seti wasn't so strange after all.

"And Moshe defended a slave being whipped by an Egyptian guard. Only Moshe killed the guard."

"And then he was banished," Seti finished, the weight of his actions settling on him. If they could banish a prince for that, what would happen to Seti?

"We don't know if he was banished or if he fled. But you didn't kill your mwt. You dishonored her. You won't be banished."

His father's words weren't exactly a relief, though they opened his eyes. Now Moshe had returned. The next question burned in his heart.

"Do you know what they believe, Jt? The slaves? They believe their God is rescuing them through Moshe. That it's a promise their God made and is now fulfilling. All this time, all these years, they have been waiting for this, and they believe Moshe is the one. They think their God loves them. But he keeps failing. That should tell them he's not the one. The dancers appeased Osiris and fixed the Nile, the frogs died, and the gnats are going away. Moshe is losing."

"Who killed the frogs?" Ameneten asked.

Seti paused and thought back to when he'd met Moshe and Aharon at the palace gate. He and Sabu had caught them on the road, and Moshe said: *I have inquired of God and tomorrow He will kill the frogs.* The Egyptian gods wouldn't have just killed the frogs, they'd have gotten rid of them altogether, and Moshe wouldn't have known when or how.

"Moshe?"

"Moshe knew what was going to happen. The Hebrew God told him and killed them."

"But the blood in the river. You sacrificed all those oxen. The women—they gave themselves to the gods. You were certain it was because of them."

"I was, yes. But that was then. What is the Nile, Seti?"
Seti stared. "What is it? It's a river."
"And?"
"And it's the source of life for the world. A gift from Osiris—"

"A source of life for Egypt," his father interrupted. "What is it to the Hebrews?"

Seti shook his head. It would be the source of life for

them, too. Neither they nor the Egyptians could survive without its water. What was his father getting at?

When Seti didn't answer, his father did. "It's a river of blood to them. An entire generation of males was thrown into that river."

Seti knew his history well, though it never resonated with him until now. It made sense. The previous Pharaoh had an entire generation of baby boys tossed into the river. But why didn't their God save those babies? He saved one. Just one. Seti looked at his father. "So, is Moshe going to win?"

"You mean is his God going to win? I don't think so." His father shifted to face Seti. "But let me tell you what happened this morning while you were dishonoring your mwt."

Seti waited.

"I was at the palace with Kipuri and Amoshe. We spoke with Pharaoh. He's not going to give in to Moshe. He believes it's a power struggle. But Jannes and Jambres even said the gnats were from the hand of the Hebrew God. They couldn't do anything to stop them. They could replicate the frogs but not kill or eliminate them." He looked deep into Seti's eyes. "When we were there, Moshe and Aharon came in. They demanded that Pharaoh let the Hebrews go, and Pharaoh refused. And so they announced what will happen next."

Seti's mouth dropped open. "What?"

"He's going to unleash swarms of bugs all over Egypt. But this time, they said Goshen will not be affected. It will only affect our people. They said their God will show a distinction between His people and Pharaoh's, and everyone will know that He is God."

How is that possible? He can direct the insects where to go, who to go after? The gods Kepri and Ra commanded the insects. If this happens, the truth of the strongest god would be known. Unless the Egyptian gods conspired with the Hebrew God, working together to prove a point. And what point would that be?

"What do you believe will happen?" Seti asked.

His father faced forward again. "I-I'm not sure. I guess we'll see."

They sat, both staring at the floor. What if Eliza was right, and she wasn't crazy, stupid, or naïve?

"Next time you go to the palace," Seti said, "take me with you."

His father stood and smiled. "I knew you'd want to go. We'll see what happens tomorrow. I plan on going with Amoshe and Kipuri to confront the magicians again if this plays out the way Moshe and Aharon say it will."

Seti stood and hugged his father. A sense of relief at his father's kind words rushed over him. After letting him go, he asked, "May I continue with school?"

"Yes. I will come get you when I plan to leave."

Seti blinked. His father said "when," not "if", as if anticipating Moshe's warning coming true. Did he question the gods' strength? Knowing that his father had to rise early in the morning to consecrate himself before waking the gods, Seti headed for the door. He planned on sleeping in one of the empty living quarters.

He halted in the doorway and turned to his father. "You know what she said to me? Eliza?"

His father shook his head.

"After she was released, I told Eliza that her God had failed her. And she said that He didn't. What do you think she meant?" Hopefully, Seti had been wrong about being used by her God.

His father puffed his cheeks and blew out a stream of air, looking at his feet. Seti was about to turn and leave when his father answered, "It means it was you. Her God rescued her through you, like He rescued Moshe through the queen."

It was true! "But," Seti stuttered, anger rising again, "that was my decision."

"Would you have done that any other time?"

"I don't know," Seti said. "I've never been in a situation like that before."

"Her God softened your heart to her, if even just for that moment."

He saved Eliza, not her God. Her God let her get whipped in the face. Seti's heart was softened toward Eliza the night before when he offered her that potion. He could think of no other time in the five years she had worked for them that he felt anything toward her other than curiosity, but not enough to compel him to talk to her. How dare such a god manipulate him. This could only mean that he had been weak, an easy target. Seti hadn't been guarding his heart. But then, if his heart had remained hardened toward her, he would have stood there and watched, like everyone else. And he wouldn't be in trouble; he could have gone home and lived his life like normal, like nothing had happened.

But what was normal now? The world all around him was falling apart.

Chapter 10

An eerie silence saturated the library the next morning. Seti and three others sat on cushions at their tables, slates in their laps, and deciphered the few hieroglyphs they had copied from Giza. Normally, he'd immerse himself in such studies, but instead, going to the palace with his father and seeing Moshe took precedence over everything else. He almost hoped the swarms of flies would come as predicted, just so he would go. He could decipher hieroglyphs any time, but witnessing Moshe confront Pharaoh? That would be life-changing.

Then it dawned on him—the choir. The choir wasn't singing, which was odd, since they never took a day off. When did they stop? The morning melody to the gods was as much expected as the birds' song or the rooster's crow. Several choirs rotated shifts to ensure one was always available.

Maybe the bugs had come. What kind of bug? Father had said swarms of flies. Thank goodness the temple was sealed shut. Would the gods let their temple be invaded by such uncleanliness?

The other students buried themselves in their studies, unbothered by the silence. The scribal master had left the library some time ago. He'd stated he'd be back but had yet to return.

"I don't hear the choir," Seti said, breaking the silence. The others looked at him. They listened as if to confirm his statement. "Something's amiss, don't you think? Master has been gone for a while."

"Where'd he go?"

Seti stood and crept to the door, peering into the dark corridor. The air was still, silent, and cool, as it should be. "Someone want to go look for him?"

They stared at him. He'd go, but his father might come looking for him while he was gone, then go to the palace without him. The temptation to see what was happening pulled at him, but he turned and took his seat.

"Why don't you go, Seti?" one of the boys asked.

"I have to stay here." He looked at his slate.

"Why? You've already missed yesterday and all last week."

"I'm waiting for my jt."

The boy took the hint that Seti wasn't going to elaborate and left him alone. Seti tapped his chalk pen impatiently. If only the library had a window.

A dog fly landed near his right hand on his slate. Seti held his breath and kept his hand still so as not to scare it off, watching as it scurried in circles. His heart sped up. This was it. The swarms were dog flies—chunky flies known for their determination and bite. A swat would only send it to a different spot on the body. These flies were common in the deep woods near the mouth of the Nile and in barns around the animals. Unless it was killed, it would not give up.

Another one joined its buddy on the slate, and the two circled each other. They must be coming from the corridor. Seti jumped from his cushion, startling the others. "Flies!"

"Flies?" The three asked in unison.

He peered down the corridor again but saw nothing. He quickly shut the door and stood with his back against it. Flashbacks of the gnats in the pyramid flooded his mind.

"What's going on?" a student asked.

"Remember the gnats? My jt said Moshe said there would be swarms of bugs today. See those dog flies on my slate?"

They looked, but the flies were gone.

"We have to seal the door," Seti said, heart pounding.

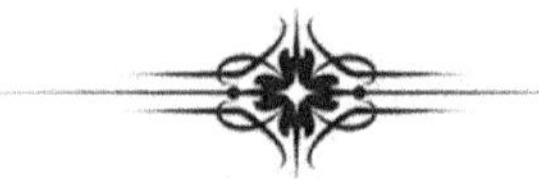

Eliza jolted awake as the wooden cart she lay in swayed and jerked beneath her. Two oxen pulled it over the gravel. Her head spun as she braced herself on a thin layer of straw covered with a sheet of white linen. A lamb rested on either side of her. Miera was nowhere in sight. Several slaves and cattle walked beside the cart, which bounced over rocks and gravel, setting her head and back ablaze with pain. Her stomach turned. She lurched over the side, splattering bile in the dirt. The back wheels of the cart rolled through the mess, spreading it further.

"Frog girl's awake," a voice announced.

Frog girl?

Eyes turned to her, then back to the road. The cool air and dark skies gave the impression of rain. She couldn't remember the last time it rained, maybe a stray cloud here and there but only the blazing sun and endless blue sky day after day. She clung to the wooden rail, knuckles white. Her body heaved, and she threw up again, splattering sandaled feet nearby.

"Hey!"

Slumping in the cart, she shivered and rested her head against one of the lambs. Questions jumbled in her mind. Exhausted, she let the tears spill down her cheeks.

The cart jolted to a stop, waking her. "This is your stop, Eliza," a woman's voice said.

She opened her eyes and recognized the small houses on the edge of the street. Avaris. They had brought her home.

"Come on." The woman climbed into the cart and grabbed Eliza's arm, helping her to her feet. Her head spun again but not as badly as before. How much time had passed since seeing Moshe? Eliza leaned on the woman and stepped to the ground.

Several others in their party veered off the road toward the neighborhood. Behind the cart, slaves and animals crowded the main road as far as Eliza could see. Men, women, and children plodded among the cattle, goats, and sheep. Most were covered in mud, wearing only loincloths, as if they came straight from the brick farms without stopping at the outhouses to change. Were they free? Had Moshe won?

"I believe this is yours." The woman handed Eliza the head net.

It was Seti's. He had placed it on her head at the pole just before she left him. She took it in her hands, treasuring it. Oh, Seti. She looked back. Would she ever see him again? Besides the net, she had only escaped with her blanket and torn tunic, neither of which had come with her to Avaris. Wearing a new tunic, she traced the edge of the head net with her finger, thankful to have it.

"Take the lambs, too. Both of them." The woman led the lambs from the cart and handed Eliza the twine tied to their leather collars.

"What for?" she asked.

"They need a home." The woman went to the oxen and led them back to the road.

Eliza stood in the dirt, the net in one hand and twine in the other. The lambs huddled beside her. She had never owned a lamb before. No one in her family had. They couldn't afford any. What was she to do with them?

She followed the others who had branched off for Avaris.

When her house came into view, Eliza's heart leaped. Her feet skipped into a run, but pain shot through her body, stopping her. Cries and shouts sounded on all sides as families poured from their homes to welcome their loved ones. It was a city-wide reunion. Her mother saw her first, squealed, and darted toward her, arms outstretched. Miera followed. How did Miera make it back before her? Then her father! Eliza broke into a run despite the pain. Dropping the twine, she plunged into her parents' arms.

Her father cupped her face in his hands and examined the gash. He touched it, making her flinch.

"It's still fresh." Eliza turned her face out of his hand, her chest heaving from the sobs pouring through. She gazed at the man standing before her, his face worn and leathery beneath a thick, curly beard, but his eyes as young and vibrant as she remembered. For a moment, she was a little girl again.

"You have lambs?" Her mother nodded toward them.

"They were given to me. I don't know why or by who."

Her father's eyes sparkled. "Perhaps a blessing from God. You're a blessing from God. Our freedom. God's blessings abound!"

Fresh bread, berries, and a bowl of eggs waited on the table, courtesy of Eliza's mother going overboard. The entire family would be under one roof. The aroma filled the house. Eliza's mouth watered despite the lingering nausea. The twins sat on their cushions at the table, and Eliza squeezed them both as tightly as she could. She straightened and gazed at them in wonder. What if they never had to know a life of slavery?

"The boys are on their way," her mother gushed, wiping her hands on her tunic. "They were in Menf, so it's taking them a little longer. Then we will eat."

Once everyone made it home and praised the God of

their fathers, they filled their bellies before retreating outside to a small fire. Except for the flicker of flames scattered around town, the night was dark and starless, but the air filled with chatter and laughter. Children bounced between families with arms full of cakes and treats.

Eliza drew her knees to her chest and gingerly leaned against the rock on which she normally sat, imagining the same scenario but in a different place. A land of their own, far away, with trees and grass. Fields of produce they'd reap for themselves. The twins could run freely. Her father would build furniture for their house, not statues for Pharaoh.

The joy on each of their faces swelled Eliza's heart, and she relished it, in case it was only a dream. The smoky scent of burning wood, the sounds of excited chatter, the sight of energetic smiles, and the taste of her mother's bread. Would she wake again to find herself in the back of the linen building? Or the outhouse?

Each of her family told their versions of the bloody water, the frogs, and the gnats. She and Miera fared well, having been spared the worst of it compared to the rest of her family. Her brothers and father were never given nets. They only had the linens they wore. And they had to sleep outside, buried under the hay. Blisters and marks covered their exposed skin. They almost looked as bad as Seti. But Seti had oil and potions.

She took in their laughter, the orange glow on their faces, and how none seemed bothered by their blisters, scabs, or slashes. They compared them in the light of the fire. While her father had the worst gashes on his back, Adam had the most bites. Eliza heard herself laughing for the first time in a long time. Real laughter. Belly laughter. It hurt, but she didn't care. When she was with them, she didn't even care about the gash on her face. She was one of them, not a dirty scab of a girl among the flawless Egyptians. She was finally home.

The laughter quieted when Miera relayed how they met

Moshe and Aharon in the linen building. Eliza added that Moshe said there would be swarms of flies in Egypt but not in Goshen, and that God would make a distinction between Pharaoh's people and His own. Her father confirmed it by saying the flies had appeared yesterday morning, meaning Eliza had slept for two days straight. The flies drove the slaves and Egyptians to abandon their work and seek shelter. By that time, Eliza and Miera had traveled far from On.

Adam and Zechariah chimed in, describing how the sky had darkened with great swarms of flies. Their bites left angry welts, forcing the slaves from the fields. By then, word had spread that Goshen was spared. In the chaos, the Egyptians lost control of their slaves. Scaffoldings fell, and at least one of the large rock statues collapsed when its supports were dropped. The terrified Hebrews took their animals and fled to Goshen.

"And when we reached Goshen," Adam said, "it was like stepping out of a dark cave. Instant relief and sunlight."

"Indeed," Zechariah agreed.

Eliza watched wide-eyed as Adam stepped over an invisible line and shielded his eyes as if blinded by a bright light. He caught an imaginary fly with his hands. "And if any flies made it in, they flew in circles like they were drunk. They couldn't land or bite. They piled on the ground near the edges of Goshen. It was quite staggering to see."

They talked late into the night, their voices quieting as they grew tired. Eventually, each retreated to their mats inside the house. Eliza claimed her spot by the window. She smiled at the sighs and snores of her family. No more sleeping in the outhouse. Ever. For the first time she could remember, Eliza didn't lay awake in the night. Instead, she fell fast asleep.

The large acacia door creaked when Seti eased it open, and a swarm of dog flies attacked his face, forcing him to slam it shut. He and the others had then melted candle wax and sealed the cracks in the door. This had left one candle and one lamp for light with very little oil. They sat against the wall or laid on the floor with nothing to do but sleep the time away.

Seti's father never came. What if it was too much for him? How foolish of Seti to hope for the flies just so he could go to the palace. Even the few that managed to get in made him miserable. The temple was not protected. What were the gods doing? Could they not see it was an attack on their own people? Were the gods angry? If the swarms came, it was from the Hebrew God. And He would divide the Egyptians from the Hebrews, sparing those in the land of Goshen. Hopefully, Eliza made it there. Otherwise, the flies would fill her wounds. Would her God have used him to save her only to let her die of pestilence?

To pass the time, Seti took the candle and roamed the library in search of anything on the Hebrew God or the "God of gods." He pulled out books, scrolls, and tablets. Nothing. Nothing on either one. At least not in a language he could decipher. If anyone needed information on religion, philosophy, or the earth, they would find it in Egypt, but Seti couldn't find anything. This would normally indicate that the Hebrews' God was a figment of their imagination, but the flies told him otherwise. If this God was real, could He be negotiated with?

The candle burned out, and Seti was forced to quit his search. The library at Giza would have more information. He crawled to the others where their lamp flickered in the diminishing oil.

His mind wandered back to Eliza. Her curly, brown hair hung wild, the signature look of a Hebrew woman. She often had it tied back in a bun, except for the morning his mother whipped her. Her small round face and big dark eyes, that little laugh on the roadway, and her smile in the dark. Seti caught himself smiling and scoffed out loud, pushing the image from his mind. But her words echoed in the dark. What was it she had said that was so beautiful? *"The heavens are laid out like a scroll, the moon and stars for His glory."* He never asked her what that meant. *"God's quest to bring man back to Him."* Hopeful slave fantasies. *"He keeps His promises. He defends us."* Was He defending them now? Seti sank to the floor and lay flat on his back, his stomach tightening in knots as the answer settled on him like the blackness of the room.

The heavy door opened with a pop when the wax seal broke, waking the boys. They sat up at the sight of an oil lamp entering the library.

"Seti? You in here?" It was his father. Finally.

Seti pushed himself from the floor.

"The flies?" one of the boys asked.

"The flies are gone. You boys better be getting home."

They scrambled to their feet and squeezed past Seti's father through the door. His father examined the wax on the door frame.

"Looks like you were safe." He touched the dry wax.

Seti sighed and stretched his achy bones.

His father smirked. "What? Are you getting too old for the floor?"

"What happened to going to the palace?"

His father motioned him through the door, then followed with the lamp. They walked side by side in the corridor.

"Pharaoh's letting them go."

"He is?"

"Yes, but I'm not sure of the circumstances. This was yesterday. The flies were still bad, and I wasn't able to make it out. But Amoshe made it. He told me Pharaoh begged Moshe to get rid of the flies, and he'd let the Hebrews worship their God outside of Egypt. I'm not sure what that means. Moshe said the flies would be gone by this morning, and they were."

"Wait, it's been two days?" Seti asked, counting back the time in his head. With no light, there was no telling how much time had passed.

"Yes, it's been two days. Are you well, Seti?"

"Just… just tired."

"You need nourishment."

"Did they leave already? The Hebrews?" he asked as they hurried up the steps to the main corridor. Sunlight beamed down the stairs, forcing him to shield his eyes. When he saw his father's face in the light, red sores glared back at him. Some had scabbed over, some still bled, reflecting the light. Seti dared not say a word and turned his face forward to avoid staring.

"They left for Goshen when the flies came. Every last one of them. I think word got out that Goshen was spared."

"Was it?"

"Pharaoh sent officers to see. They haven't yet returned. I assume that means Goshen was spared, and the officers sought shelter there. I'd bet they'll come back today."

"So, when are they leaving? Where are they going?"

"He said just outside Egypt. I'm not sure how long or if they'll return. I heard it was just so they could sacrifice to their God, but I doubt that's all they want to do."

A sense of urgency washed over Seti to go after them, to see the mass exodus with his own eyes, to find Eliza and see her one more time. Maybe…if even to make sure she got out safely. That's all, right? He was only being the good humanitarian that he claimed to be.

Instead, he grabbed a jar of water and a loaf of barley bread and took them to his room, navigating the back hall to avoid the dancers.

Chapter 11

"Wait, you didn't let me finish!" Moshe's voice could barely be heard above the commotion. Eliza fought to lay eyes on him but couldn't push through the mob that had met him at the Avaris gate. Word had spread that he was on his way to Avaris with a grand announcement.

"We're free! It's finally happening!" Somebody yelled, and the whole crowd broke into cheers. One woman fainted.

"It's not happening yet. Don't—" Again, the noise drowned out Moshe's voice.

Several men and women broke away from the melee in a mad dash to spread the news, giving Eliza a glimpse of Moshe.

"Moshe!" She shoved forward, her hand outstretched for his attention, when a large man bumped into her and knocked her to the ground. Several others tripped over her, creating a cascade of bodies. The gashes in her back screamed in agony. After rolling to her side, she struggled to her feet. Anger and cheers surrounded her in a cacophony of shouting. She had to get out of this mess before being trampled.

Leaving Moshe to fend for himself, Eliza scrambled from the chaos to an open space. She winced with each movement, worried the sutures had torn. How reckless of her to attempt such a feat in her condition. The town had erupted into a complete frenzy. Children left their sheep as they ran to tell their parents. Parents dropped their goods as they ran to tell their children. Others went into the fields to tell the shepherds. Old men skipped in the dirt, and old ladies leaped with joy, clapping their hands.

Eliza stood on the outskirts, gazing at the pandemonium. Didn't Moshe say there would be more plagues? Maybe Pharaoh had an early change of heart. Did the flies leave Egypt? This wasn't adding up.

Rahel emerged from the crowd, breathless. When the girls locked eyes, Rahel shook her head as if to answer Eliza's questions. Eliza sighed. She knew it. Her back stung, forcing her to sit in the dirt, hunched over.

In response to the upheaval, Moshe called for a meeting at supper, allowing time for those in upper Goshen to arrive. Tribal leaders traveled to Avaris from all over. Eliza and Rahel stayed to assist those at the gate with preparations.

In anticipation of an announcement of freedom, the people turned the occasion into a grand feast. Women prepared tea, wine, jam, breads, and cakes. Men grilled fish over fires. Vegetables from the fields filled bowls and baskets.

Women and children alike dressed in their native robes and gowns passed down from generations of old. A group of men and boys pulled their stringed instruments, lyres, flutes, and tambourines from storage and hauled them to the gate.

Eliza's heart soared. A surge of energy bubbled up inside her, and she greeted every arrival, chatting about anything and everything under the sun. Was this the new Eliza? The free Eliza?

She sniffed the air and closed her eyes, inhaling the sweet aroma of charbroiled fish and fresh bread. Slowly exhaling, she thanked God for bringing her here for such a time as this. If she'd been born a hundred years earlier, she'd have spent her entire life as a slave. Or she could have been stuck at the Ameneten house, missing out on the joy that filled Avaris. But she was here, with friends and family. Everyone was safe and sound. With her arms stretched wide, she twirled on her toes and laughed.

After the newfound energy depleted, Eliza perched on the dirt in front of the musicians, spinning a dandelion in her fingers and listening as they tuned their instruments.

"So you're the frog girl?" one of the men asked as he polished his lute.

"Yes, yes, I am." Eliza nodded, taken aback.

"We heard about you on the way up here. The Hebrew girl who cooked a frog over the fire and gave it to her master."

"Well, not quite." More than happy to set the story straight, she corrected him. "I just squeezed it into the stew. It had long been dead."

"That's even worse!" a teenage boy said, laughing.

Their laughter brought a smile to her face. She introduced herself and recounted the story. They paused their tuning and quieted, as if it were the most entertaining thing they had ever heard, though she left out the long night with Seti and the twenty-five lashes.

"So that's how you got that nasty mark on your face?"

She smiled, but the words stung. Was it that bad?

"How many lashes?"

"Five." Seti came to mind, but she pushed the thought away.

"Only five? That's it? You should see how many I got in just the past two months." The teenage boy turned and dropped his tunic to his waist. Scars in various stages of healing crisscrossed his back. The others dropped their tunics as well. The lines across their torsos and backs told the tales of slavery. The boys pointed and laughed, comparing stories. But none had any on their faces.

Their contagious enthusiasm quickly dissolved her insecurity. She had never witnessed such happiness among her people. It felt dreamlike, as if it could vanish in a heartbeat. How could it be possible for a Hebrew to experience such joy?

Moshe and Aharon sat at the head table, as they had weeks earlier, with the heads of the tribes on either side of them. The people of Avaris let those from out of town sit on benches and cushions, while they either reclined on the ground, stood in back, or climbed on rooftops. Children filled the trees, and the elderly filled cushioned wagons. As they hushed, Aharon stood to address the crowd.

He began with a greeting and introduction, despite his fame. Cheers and music erupted, cutting him off mid-sentence. Using his hand, he signaled the crowd to quiet.

"You've heard the rumor that Pharaoh has released you," he announced.

Excited murmurs followed, and he waited for silence. "It will be true, but the time has not yet come."

Like a gray cloud suddenly blotting out the sun, a wave of silence swept from the front to the back. Then, the yelling started.

"You said Pharaoh was letting us go."

"That's not what we were told."

"You misled us!"

Aharon waved his hands to settle them, but it only fueled their anger, and the yelling grew louder.

Moshe arose beside Aharon, lifting his staff above his head. The silence returned.

"Pharaoh might say now that he will let you go, but he'll change his mind. I know this because the Lord told me. He has arranged a series of plagues, and Pharaoh will continue to harden his heart. The Lord will tell me when the last plague happens, and then I will tell you.

"The Lord has bigger plans than just setting us free." Moshe shifted his gaze as he spoke, spreading his hand to encompass the whole audience. "He wants to make clear to every Israeli and Egyptian—not just Pharaoh—that He is the Lord of lords and the God of gods. The gods of Egypt will bow to Yahweh. He does not leave us in the dark. From the very beginning, starting with our Father Avraham, God laid out His plans for His people. Father Avraham's descendants through YitZhaq and then Yaakov would become as numerous as the sands of the sea. But first, His people had to live four hundred years in a land not their own. Those in Canaan will usurp their right to live there. No matter what the Egyptians do, we will continue to flourish. We are becoming a great and numerous people. The Lord will lead us out of Egypt to the land of Canaan, a land we will call Israel. But it will not happen quickly. He wants to build our trust in Him as a dependable, loyal God who loves His people."

Moshe jabbed the bottom of the staff into the table. "Until then, I suggest we remain the good citizens of Egypt that we are and continue to work, serve, and wait on God. "

"I'm not going back there," someone interrupted. Several others shouted in agreement.

Aharon held up his hand, and Moshe continued. "As long as we are not free, we will serve. We won't give Pharaoh any excuse to keep us or hurt us any more than he already has. If Pharaoh demands we work, then we obey. If he doesn't, then we stay here. If your masters demand your return, then go. If not, then stay until they do. But I'll tell you this: the remaining plagues will not affect those in Goshen. I'll remain in On, close to the palace, as I have been, and Aharon will do the same. My family will stay here in Avaris."

"What happens if some of us leave Egypt early?" a man asked, as if he knew of others who had already left.

Moshe turned to him, and then to the crowd. "The Lord has appointed me to lead you out of Egypt. I will follow His direction, and He'll guard us on all sides as we travel. Anyone who leaves before us, or after, will not have the Lord's protection or provision, and they won't know the way. That is why we must travel together."

"The Lord is everywhere. He can be with everybody at once," another said.

"That is true, but we must obey Him. If He wants us traveling together, that is what we'll do. He won't have us scattered about in the wilderness. I have a feeling He has more planned for us once we leave Egypt.

"On another note, I suggest preparing the bodies of Yoseph and his family, for we are to bring them with us. And Pharaoh has been sending officers here to monitor us and confirm whether Goshen suffers from the plagues. We are to treat them with respect and dignity. If they wish to stay overnight, offer your houses, for they are working for Pharaoh as we are. Perhaps they'll see the Lord's work through us and acknowledge Him as the one true God."

A low grumble rippled through the crowd but simmered when Aharon signaled.

"One last thing before we bless the Lord and eat," Moshe announced. "If you hear that Pharaoh has decided to let us go, do not take it to heart but wait for my word. Even so, I'll let you know before God sends the last plague so you may prepare. I'll instruct you in what to do, because we'll all leave at once. There will be no more mornings like we had this morning. Whoever fails to listen will be alone and without the protection and provision of the Lord. You may even be captured by the Egyptians, imprisoned, or left behind."

Moshe paused, waiting for any naysayers to speak up. None did. He nodded as if taking the silence as agreement.

"Now, let's bless the food the Lord has provided."

All heads bowed as Aharon said a blessing, thanking

the Lord for all He had done so far, all He will do, and who He is. After the prayer, both Aharon and Moshe sat while everyone else rose.

The food came out, and the air filled with music, chatter, and laughter. Eliza joined her family and filled her stomach.

As the night wore to a close, Moshe announced he and Aharon would head back to On in the morning to prepare for the next plague. The two shut themselves in a nearby house before the sun had fully set.

Eliza had followed Moshe and Aharon at a distance, watching them enter the house of the Nun family, home to an old friend of Adam's. Hoshea had once worked alongside her family on a farm before her brother transferred to the bricks. In those early days, he had been a mentor and father-figure to Adam.

"What are you doing?" Rahel asked, startling Eliza.

Eliza crouched behind a shrub across the street from the house. She put her finger on her lips and motioned for Rahel to get down.

"Are you spying on them?"

"Shh!" Eliza waved her hand fanatically.

"You know that's Hoshea's house, right?" Rahel had fallen in love with the man, though he had to have been in his thirties when they had last seen him years ago.

"Of course you know where he lives." Eliza rolled her eyes.

Rahel stared at the house with a dreamy look in her eyes. "I bet he's home now. Haven't seen him in years."

"Right." Eliza sat in the dirt. "You've been on the brick farms. Haven't you found somebody younger to gawk at? Hoshea's probably married by now. Do you think he'd be interested in a sixteen-year-old? He's got to be nearing forty."

"That's nothing. Middle-aged men marry young girls all the time." Rahel might be one-of-a kind. She fawned over

Eliza's father when they first met in the fields. She was eight then.

"In arranged marriages. Do you think they actually find each other attractive?"

"JoAnnah and Michah and Hannah and Eliab do, and they weren't arranged. Besides, Hoshea's special. He looks like he could be a warrior in another world. And he loves God like no other. No young Hebrew man loves God like that. I want a man who can lead. A man who'd rear our children to be Godly like him." Unlike most girls their age, Rahel dreamed of having a family like Father Avraham's—one of complete devotion to God. It was one of the many things about her that Eliza admired.

Oh, to talk about love with her friend. It had been so long since Eliza enjoyed such conversations with Rahel, but now was not the time. "I want to leave with Moshe tomorrow. I can't return to the Ameneten house, and I can't protect Miera if we get sent to the bricks. I can't be separated from her."

"Hey, the bricks aren't so bad—if you stay low…except when you're working in ponds of frogs or attacked by flies or gnats. Now that's bad." Rahel flapped her hand.

"Moshe stays somewhere by the linen building in the marketplace. I've been there and want to go back. I can sew dresses and nets, make myself useful there."

"And what about me?" Rahel asked, raising a brow.

"Come with me. We can work together."

Moments of pondering passed before Eliza spoke again. "But I—I don't know how to make this happen."

Rahel perked up. "Hey, you spoke with Moshe face-to-face, right?"

"Yes."

"Just tell him the truth. He'll recognize you. Maybe he'll have pity on you."

Eliza smiled. "I don't think so."

Rahel placed her hand on Eliza's shoulder. "Let me do the talking." She stood and held out her hand. With hesitation, Eliza took it.

"What are you going to do?"

"Knock on the door. What else?"

"What? Now?"

"Yes, now. While they're still awake. Go!" Rahel nudged Eliza toward the house. Stumbling into the road, Eliza paused and glanced toward the windows. Oil lamps illuminated the rooms, indicating those inside were indeed awake. Rahel stepped ahead, grabbed Eliza's hand and pulled.

"What about Miera?" Eliza whispered.

"We get our answers first, then you can get Miera." Rahel marched up the doorstep and knocked loudly, while Eliza stood back.

The door swung open, and there stood Hoshea, wearing only his loincloth as if he had come straight from the projects. He gazed at Rahel. Her eyes traveled up his body to his face, gawking.

He glanced toward Eliza on the walkway, hand on her heart. She didn't remember him being so tall or his shoulders so broad. Had he always looked like that? Then again, the last time she had seen him, she was a little girl, and the beauty of the male physique had not then dawned on her like it had on Rahel.

"What do you two want?" he asked.

"Uh, well. Uh…." Rahel mumbled.

Eliza snapped out of it. "I must speak to Moshe." She stepped up beside her friend.

"He's done speaking and wants to be alone." He was about to shut the door when Eliza stuck her hand against it.

"He and I spoke before. He'll recognize me." There was no forgetting her face.

Hoshea furrowed his brow and studied the crusty scab on her face. "Wait."

The door shut, and Eliza let out a breath of defeat. Was that it? The door creaked open, and Moshe appeared, Hoshea behind him. Moshe's eyes scrutinized Eliza as if trying to remember her.

"Moshe, I—" she choked on her saliva. Why hadn't she rehearsed this? Didn't Rahel say she'd do the talking?

"Out with it, girl."

Thankfully, Rahel spoke up. "Moshe, my friend Eliza cannot return to her previous masters, for they whipped her and told her never to return. And she can't go to the brick farms or projects, because she has to care for her sister who's too young and weak. They would both end up being whipped more."

Eliza gathered the courage to speak. "Moshe, I can't go back there. You saw what they did to me. What if they do that to my sister?"

"Why don't you just remain here?" Moshe asked.

Eliza drew in her breath. She hadn't thought of that. But she wasn't ready to leave Seti. Not until knowing he'd be safe. "Take us to the marketplace with you. If my sister and I stay in the back of the shop, we won't be recognized. We can sew."

"So can I," Rahel added.

Moshe hesitated, relaxing his stance.

"Please, Moshe." It was one of the few times Eliza took advantage of her big brown eyes. Tears would help, but she couldn't muster them. Hoshea knitted his brow with curiosity.

"Who is at the door?" Aharon's voice called. He appeared between Moshe and Hoshea, eyes immediately falling on Eliza. "Ahhhh," he said, pointing. "I know you."

Moshe peered over his shoulder at his brother. "They want to come back with us and work in the shop so they won't be recognized by their previous masters."

"Very well. We only have the two camels, though."

"We can walk!" Eliza blurted. "We've always walked

before."

"When you get there, tell the women that I said you may help in the back with the linen and food," Aharon said. "If they give you trouble, send them to Moshe or me."

Eliza let out a sigh of relief.

Aharon continued. "Moshe and I will be leaving in the morning. You may go whenever you want, but we cannot wait for you."

"Oh, Aharon, thank you so much!" Eliza grabbed his hand in both of hers and kissed it. Rahel covered her mouth in shock.

"Good night now." Aharon and Moshe disappeared, leaving Hoshea at the door.

"You sneaky little girls," he said, shaking his head, then his demeanor softened. "Send my regards to Adam for me, will you?"

"There's nothing sneaky about it, Hoshea. And we aren't little," Eliza told him.

When the door shut, Rahel and Eliza faced each other, eyes wide. Rahel took Eliza's hand, and they ran into the street, squealing and cheering, until Eliza's back forced her to slow.

Chapter 12

"See? The gods are blessing my family. We deserve it." Seti spoke more to himself than to Sabu.

Sabu laughed, and the sound lifted Seti's heart. He hadn't heard anyone laugh since that night with Eliza.

They stared off the mesa-cliff toward the small pyramids in the west. Taller than the others, the Ameneten pyramid had taken years to build with stones hauled from quarries far to the south. As the walls filled in around the main chamber, coffins and statues had been placed inside, leaving one long, narrow corridor. If additional items were added afterward, they'd first have to be taken apart and then reassembled inside.

The prospect of the near-finished pyramid brought a smile to Seti's face. That human hands could erect such massive, symmetrical structures amazed him. The top architects of the day couldn't duplicate the oldest pyramids of Giza, but they drew inspiration from them. After completing the main structure, divinely chosen artists decorated the chambers with exotic dyes and precious metals, depicting the gods who guarded and transported the souls of the occupants to the New Life. It was the closest a human could get to the Egyptian gods, and Seti was about to head there with Sabu.

The flies had vanished days ago. Refreshed, Seti took

a deep breath of hot Egyptian air and thanked Ra for filling his lungs with life. Osiris shone directly above them. Seti shielded his eyes and tilted his head back in an attempt to see the deity. Ra, the sun god in his visible form as Osiris, drove his chariot across the sky.

Life was almost back to normal. Yesterday, Pharaoh had sent a considerable portion of his army to Goshen to round up the Hebrews and bring them back to work. With so much left undone, Seti wasn't surprised Pharaoh had changed his mind.

His father, held up with work in the temple and tending to his wounds, sent Seti to ensure that the Hebrews resumed their work on the pyramid respectfully. After nearly escaping Egypt, they might have returned with bitter and rebellious spirits. Such attitudes required harsh discipline, which itself required Seti to reset his mind. He set his face to Ra and steeled his spine. No foreign god would use him again. He steered his horse toward On, needing to first retrieve his chariot and shoulder bags from his house.

With Kabelo studying at the temple and his mother out shopping as usual, Seti could sneak into the house without being noticed. Stopping down the street, he left Chewy with Sabu and crept around the back to make sure no one was home. The place was empty. He signaled Sabu to meet him at the stable with Chewy while he ran inside to grab his shoulder bags.

He filled the bags with his parchment collection, writing utensils, and another kilt and tunic. In the stable, he tossed them in the bottom of his chariot and fastened it to Chewy. He took one last look around, half expecting to see the youngest slave girl who had always kept his chariot meticulously clean and polished. Instead, the dirt and grime from the previous ride remained splattered across the front.

Seti led Chewy to the road and mounted his chariot.

"Finally," Sabu muttered, coming up beside him.

The snap of the whip across Chewy's rear end sent a

flash of Eliza and her torn tunic through his mind, startling him. Chewy lurched forward, and Seti lost his footing, fell backward, and hit the gravel road hard, knocking the breath out of him. Sabu roared with laughter.

What had come over him? Seti stood, stunned at his sloppiness. He brushed the dust from his tunic. Chewy continued ahead, scattering the bags' contents along the road.

"Chewy!" Seti yelled.

Laughing, Sabu whipped his horse and took off after Chewy. After catching up, he grabbed the reins and pulled, bringing the horse to a stop. Seti left the whip behind as he picked up the mess in the road, ignoring Sabu's taunts.

"What happened?" Sabu asked when Seti reached him.

How could he explain it? He'd whipped Chewy without a second thought since he was a colt.

"What are you doing?" Sabu watched as Seti unhooked the chariot.

"I can't do that to Chewy anymore." He grabbed the arms of the chariot and dragged it toward the stable.

"Can't do what? What did you do?" Sabu followed. "What are you doing, Seti?"

Seti paused on the side of the road, released the chariot, and shook his arms to loosen his muscles. He had no problem moving it around in the stable, but hauling it down the street wore him out.

Sabu watched from the road, arms crossed.

"I—I can't whip Chewy after seeing Eliza—"

"Eliza?"

Sabu would never understand. Seti didn't even understand.

"Are you serious?" Sabu asked. "The slave?"

Sighing, Seti glanced at Chewy, who remained in the middle of the road where he had left him.

Sabu steered his chariot into Seti's line of vision. "What? You do know that you've been whipping your horse since you got him, right?"

"Right. Well, I'm done now." Irritated with the demands of his friend, Seti slung the leather bags over his shoulder and went for Chewy, abandoning the chariot while Sabu rode ahead, shaking his head.

Oh, the thrill of racing Chewy bareback! The wind against Seti's face, the adrenaline soaring through his veins, and the feel of Chewy's powerful muscles beneath him couldn't compare to even the fastest chariot ride. And despite the sense of ownership he felt over the city streets, he favored the vast openness of the desert. No longer having to swerve or slow around obstacles, Chewy was free to run with all he had.

With Sabu, it was an automatic competition—no declaration needed. Sabu had a head start when they left Seti's house, but Chewy carried less weight with no chariot.

Sabu glanced over his shoulder. "I don't think so!" He whipped his horse as Seti gained ground, laughing as he passed, kicking up a dust cloud in his wake.

Upon reaching the foot of the Ameneten pyramid, Chewy slowed to a trot. Seti spun around to see Sabu come up the rear. His legs trembled in exhaustion, but he forced them still, not willing to fuel Sabu's mockery.

"Less weight helps," Seti said, patting Chewy's flank.

"At least I can feel my legs."

They trotted up the path ascending the side of the pyramid.

Hundreds of shiny bodies grunted in the sun, clearing paths and adding steps and rails for those who hauled rocks. Carts were assembled at the base and dragged up the paths by mules, laden with bricks, mud, and buckets of water. Scaffoldings arose, only to be taken down and erected farther up.

While the speed and power of a horse in full gallop

beneath Seti's control exhilarated him, the power he wielded over so many slaves sobered him. He gazed upon the scene like a god overseeing his creation of humanity. But with adoration.

Wait. That was how Eliza described the Hebrew God. Seti shook his head at the thought. Each time he ventured out here, he'd been awestruck, but the adoration was new. These slaves were forced back to work after nearly fleeing the nation, yet they worked with dedication.

The tension he held in preparation for disciplining them, along with the wall he had erected around his heart, melted against his will. Should he be disappointed? Come to think of it, the slaves rarely, if ever, slacked. Fights among them were rare, and Seti had yet to encounter one himself. He'd not once witnessed his father whip one. But Seti forced his will upon his heart. He would not soften to a slave again.

Workers stepped aside as he and Sabu steered their horses up the winding path. Though unaware of the specifics, Seti knew the overall plans of the project. Most of the coffins and statues had already been placed inside. Butterflies fluttered in his stomach at the thought of seeing his own coffin in a pyramid.

They reached the entrance, and Seti dismounted. He gathered his strength and stood tall to exhibit a sense of authority. Sabu shook his head at Seti and stepped out of the chariot. A nervous laugh escaped him before he gathered his composure.

"You've never been inside a pyramid, have you?" Seti asked at Sabu's hesitancy.

Sabu raised an eyebrow, a slight grin growing on his rugged farmer's face.

"Follow me."

A slave at the entrance handed them each an oil lamp, and Seti led Sabu proudly through the tunnel, careful not to bump those they passed. The cool air inside refreshed him.

Inside the inner chamber, they set down their oil lamps and gazed in amazement. Unlike the chambers in the Giza pyramids, the ceiling here was low and unvaulted, and the statues and walls remained unpainted. Only the occupied coffins bore etchings and hieroglyphs. Seti wove between them, searching for his.

Four coffins in the back corner displayed nothing but the names of his father, brother, mother, and himself. A fifth coffin sat next to his. Lumeri. Couldn't the designer have waited to engrave her name on it?

Seti traced his name, kneeling beside the one he would one day occupy. "Seti, firstborn of Ameneten III". A picture of Set, brother of Osiris, scowled haughtily at him from below his name. He wiped his hand across the image, wishing it'd rub off. Being named after the killer of Osiris was nothing to be proud of.

The last time he got this close to a coffin, gnats swooped in from the vents. Seti gazed at the two vents in the ceiling. Sunlight beamed through them at an angle, landing on the center coffin of his great Father of Old, the first Ameneten priest. No buzzing this time, only the low mumble of Sabu's voice filled the room.

Seti stood and leaned against his coffin, watching Sabu sound out syllables from hieroglyphs on a coffin near the far wall.

"You know, Sabu," Seti began, "if you treat me well enough, you can have Lumeri's."

Sabu startled and straightened, hands on his hips. "You mean if I marry you?"

Seti laughed halfheartedly, tempted to destroy the thing. There was no way they'd get it out now that she'd become the Gods' Wife. Her replacement's name could be etched over it, yet just the thought of marriage put a bad taste in Seti's mouth.

A lightheadedness swept over him so suddenly he

stumbled against Lumeri's coffin. What was that? Gnats? The vents were clear, but his vision narrowed. A mustiness permeated the chamber. His chest tightened. He couldn't draw in enough air to breathe. Leaving Sabu and the oil lamp behind, he fled to the darkened tunnel.

Seti stumbled toward the outer end, chest heaving desperately. His legs felt heavy, like when they had swollen up at Giza. Halfway through the tunnel, he halted to breathe. With his hand against the wall, he took slow, deep breaths. Blackness surrounded him. The coolness filled his lungs and revived him. Kneeling, he leaned against the wall. It couldn't have been gnats again. Was it the reminder of Lumeri? Did the gods not want him to step foot in a pyramid? Whatever it was, it had gone. In the pitch dark, he felt safe. Hidden. He took in the silence, not wanting to move.

Something knocked against Seti's knee, making him jump. A quick shuffle of sandals in the dirt was followed by a thud and groan as someone hit the ground beside him.

Seti scurried away in surprise. "Who is it?"

"Hoshea. Who speaks?"

The name wasn't familiar, though it sounded Hebrew. A slave. Collecting his thoughts, Seti answered, "Uh, Ezekiel, I am Ezekiel." Though they had first spoken in Egyptian, he answered in Hebrew.

"What are you doing here? Resting? Napping? It's all right, I won't say a word," Hoshea said.

Curious, Seti relaxed his posture and sat up, taking a deep breath.

"Are you hurt?" Hoshea asked.

"No. No." Seti paused. "Say, Hoshea? Can…can you answer a question for me?"

"Anything to keep from getting up."

"Well, um, do you really think our God is going to come and save us from the Egyptians?"

There was a pause in the dark, and Seti questioned his sanity. Then Hoshea spoke. "I see. You're having a crisis of faith. Remember learning about the promise to Avraham?"

A crisis of faith? "Uh hmm, well, I don't remember much."

"'Know for certain that your descendants will be strangers in a land not their own, and they will be enslaved for four hundred years. But I will judge the nation they serve as slaves, and afterward, they will depart with many possessions. In the fourth generation, your descendants will return, for the iniquity of the Amorites is not yet complete.' Our God sealed the covenant with His life."

Seti sat, silent. The last half of that was gibberish to his ears. "And what about Ra?"

Hoshea chuckled. "You have been immersed in Egyptian culture. Ra, Osiris, and the lesser gods were placed over the nations by the one true God—seventy gods for seventy nations. But God formed His portion out of the heart of the east and raised them in the hidden shelter of Egypt. Now that we are a nation, God will bring us to our land. As He promised, the families of the Earth will be blessed because of us. Don't you see? The serpent thought he had won when he brought death into the world, and the people chose the lesser gods. God gave them what they wanted. But He will win the hearts of the lost through us, despite the rule of the nations and the curse. God always provides a way back to Him—even while being just and righteous—for He is merciful and full of grace, and He loves even the lost."

"So, what about Ra?" Seti asked again, confused.

If there was light, he was sure Hoshea would be staring at him like a fool. There was safety in the darkness.

"Ra will lose and bow down to El Shaddai," Hoshea answered, as if to simplify everything he previously explained.

Seti's heart skipped, and he pushed himself against the wall. Ra was the strongest god, the god of gods, the life giver.

"Don't be afraid," Hoshea said, his voice as gentle as a

cool breeze. "As El Shaddai said to Avraham, 'Do not be afraid, Avram. I am your shield, your very great reward.'"

"Well, good for Avraham," Seti spat.

"You do realize that when God said Avraham, He meant us?"

"Yeah, I realize that. I just don't understand why such a great God would do such things for mere humanity. I guess I've given too much attention to the Egyptian gods."

"You have, and it will be a struggle to rid Egypt from your heart. I wish all the best to you and must get back to work. Much has to be done before we abandon this place. I would be careful, though, if I were you. Hiding in the dark like this can lead you down some wrong spiritual paths, if you know what I mean. I have a feeling you're not resting but hiding. Careful what you surround yourself with."

"Wait." Seti didn't want this to end. Though nothing made sense, there was something serene about the conversation in the dark. Something about Hoshea.

"The son of Ameneten himself is here," Hoshea said. "We can't let him catch us sitting around."

"And what will he do if he does?"

"I don't know. His family whipped a young girl in the face. I'm getting back to work."

Seti froze, horrified. Hoshea scrambled to his feet.

"Ezekiel?" Hoshea's voice sounded a little more distant. "Whatever your doubts, don't stay in Egypt."

"I won't." Seti swallowed bile, repulsed by Hoshea's words.

He remembered Sabu in the chamber. "Hoshea?"

The footsteps paused.

"Don't go in there," Seti warned. "The son of Ameneten and his friend are in there. You might want to avoid the chamber until they come out."

"Oh, well, thank you. I'll come back later."

Seti pinned himself against the wall, allowing Hoshea to pass without tripping again. But Seti remained there, fingers clenching dirt from the rock floor, his heart pounding in his ears. Shame flooded his insides. His family was known among the slaves for whipping young girls in the face. He sank to the floor in horror. His family name was tarnished. To any other Egyptian, it wouldn't have mattered. After all, why would they care what slaves thought? Would it have mattered to him a month ago?

Chapter 13

Seti had been in a daze all day, fretting over Hoshea's words while he waited for Sabu to finish exploring the pyramid. After returning to the temple long after dark, Seti strolled through the long grass, leading Chewy down the hill around the side of the temple. Built on a hill, it faced east. The ground floor opened into a stable of sacred animals, where a narrow stream from the pastures flowed beneath the stable doors, providing a constant water supply.

Once inside the stable, Chewy stopped to drink from the stream, and Seti waited. The bull standing across from him met his gaze. The Api bull, the living embodiment of Ptah and famed for its prophetic powers. Its black body camouflaged with the night, but its eyes glowed white in the lamplight. The sun disk glittered on its forehead.

He had never seen a priest consult the bull, though the basic process was known. Speak to the bull—Ptah—and it would relay the message to Ra. The priest would then receive a response directly from Ra in his dreams. Forget inquiring of Moshe or Pharaoh, Seti had Ra at his fingertips. He set the lamp down and grabbed the bridle from the bull's stall, fastening it to the animal's massive head. Unafraid of the gentle beast, Seti let it out.

The stable priest saw to the care of the animals during the day, taking them into the pastures to gaze at Ra while feasting on the lush grass. After their daily bath, the animals would be adorned in jewelry and holy garments matching those of the god-statues. Various fabrics were dyed and embroidered with ancient hieroglyphs of blessings and prophecies copied from the Giza pyramids. Bells dangled from tassels on the garment edges, making a pleasing melody as the animals moved. Gemstones set in precious metals crowned their heads and pierced their noses and earlobes.

Seti wasn't about to dress it up. He didn't know where the items were kept, and he'd probably have to consecrate himself before touching them anyway. He left Chewy in the stable and led the bull into the night, closing the doors behind him.

In silence, Seti followed the stream into the pasture, taking long strides over the tall grass. The vast, star-filled sky spread above him all the way to the horizon. He let the bull drink, then continued further. Would Hathor, the sky goddess, mother of Pharaoh, have been a better choice? Manifested as a cow, she was stabled beside the bull. But the Api bull was prophetic.

Seti took a seat on the ground far enough away from the temple to avoid being heard or seen. The bull munched on grass, oblivious to Seti's presence.

"You know why we're out here, right?" Seti's voice carried away on the warm breeze. "Can you speak to Ra for me?"

The bull chewed a large wad of grass, giving no indication he heard Seti's words. Seti gazed into its eyes.

"Why doesn't Ra speak directly to me? He knows my loyalty and love. I am just worried. Who is the God of the Hebrews?" Seti asked into the wind. "Ra, do you love us? Will you defend us? We see that your every need is met. We adorn you with the best of what we have. You receive the first of all we prosper from, the best of it. The firstborn of man and beast are consecrated to you.

"I'm trying, Ra. Trying so hard. What's happening to me? Osiris? Hathor? Hecket? Are you conspiring with the God of the Hebrews? Is it our turn to be slaves? Tell me what to do. Anything. I'll do whatever you want if you save us."

"He keeps his promises. He defends us."

"Are you the Hebrew God by a different name? They don't treat you the same. They don't love you like we love you. They do nothing, just believe. They don't even keep records of their God."

Seti lay on his back. The bull gazed down his nose at him as it chewed, its head blocking Seti's view of the sky.

"Is there something we're missing? Are you one god of many that answers to the Hebrew God?"

Hoshea's words about his family stabbed at his heart. Seti curled up on his side and held himself tight. If only he could go back and step in before the whip fell on Eliza's face. If only he had freed her the night before.

"Do you love me?" he whispered into the grass. Eliza was so sure of herself but so completely wrong.

"Are you capable of love?"

What did it look like for a god to love a person? Eliza said his gods didn't do anything for humanity without first being bribed and pampered, as if humans had something they wanted.

He closed his eyes, hoping to get an answer in his dreams. Ra would not leave a faithful follower in this much turmoil, would he?

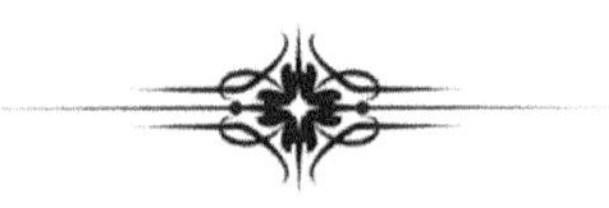

Seti's eyes popped open at the sound of men shouting in the distance. He lay still, staring at the tall grass that concealed him. A line of ants marched up a blade of grass, oblivious to the disasters befalling their world. Did Ra respond? Did Seti dream? Nothing. He remembered nothing. What if Ra responded, but Seti couldn't remember? He sat up, grass marks on his arms. The sun barely breached the horizon. Other than the sounds in the distance, an eerie quietness spread over the field. He was alone.

Alarmed, he spun around. The bull was gone! He jumped to his feet and shielded his eyes in the glare of the low morning sun. How far could it have gone? Seti darted through the field, wringing his hands. He'd yell for it but didn't know what to call it. A big black bull couldn't be too hard to find in an open grass field.

Then he saw it—lying on its side on the bank beside the stream. Seti's hands shot to his head in a panic. He jumped to the bank, splashed through the water, and knelt beside the bull, resting his hand on its cold, trembling body. Its shallow breaths were slow and ragged. *No, no! What did I do?* He turned toward the temple. The priests must be searching for it.

"Don't die. I'll get help."

Seti left the bull and sloshed across the stream, his legs weak with regret. He climbed up the bank and broke into a run across the field. *Please, Ptah, don't let it die. Osiris, keeper of the dead. Please.* The words circulated in his mind while he ran. He didn't remember wandering out so far. *Please, Ptah.*

The stable doors were still shut. Seti struggled up the hill toward the front of the temple and heaved himself up the steps. He had touched the bull without consecrating himself. Could that have harmed it? He darted across the empty foyer, the slap of his sandals on the marble floor echoing off the walls.

Ameneten and his colleagues slumped in the purification pools, nodding off, when Seti burst through the door, startling all six of them. His hands gripped his knees as he panted, a sharp pain piercing his side.

"The bull." He choked on saliva and pointed toward the west wall.

"What is it, son?" his father asked, alarmed.

"The bull. It's out there beside the creek. I think it's dying!"

His father's eyes widened with horror. The others gasped.

"The Api bull? Don't tell me it's the Api bull!"

"Yes." Seti was mortified. *Please, Horus, strike me with lightning.*

"Why's the Api bull outside the stable?"

All six priests scrambled from the pool.

"How did it get loose?" Kipuri yelled, scurrying for his towel.

Seti's father grabbed him by the shoulders. "Where, Seti? Where is it?"

"Out in the fields. In the creek. Way out there."

His father yelled over his shoulder, "Get the horses and the cart!" He shook Seti. "You stay here."

Seti, at a loss for words, nodded. He collapsed on the floor against the wall, while the priests rushed by, towels barely covering them.

A blood-curdling scream pierced the morning outside Eliza's window, waking her. Miera hunched beside her on the mat, wide awake, tears running down her cheeks. They locked eyes as another scream followed. Eliza winced at Miera's grip on her arm. The sound was unmistakable. God had struck the livestock. She didn't want to move. Not today.

"Miera, you don't have to cry about it," Eliza whispered, sitting.

"I know, but it sounds so sad, you know?"

Amazed at the empathy of such a young girl, Eliza embraced her. Rahel appeared in the doorway to their dormitory above the linen shop, a plate of cakes shaking in her hands. The tears on her freckled cheeks sparkled in the morning sun.

"I could handle the bugs and the frogs." Rahel's voice was faint. "But not death."

Moshe and Aharon had returned to the shop the day before with news of the coming plague. God intended to strike the animals in the pastures, except those in Goshen. That meant those in the fields, at the pyramids, and on the brick farms. Death would be severe and sudden but would not afflict the people. Instead, God was killing their livelihood.

"Seti." Ameneten's voice broke the silence in Seti's room. He stepped inside, gently shutting the door.

Seti lay flat on his bed, staring at the ceiling, hands under his head. He had shut himself in the room all day, dreading his father's return.

"Seti," his father said again. "The Api bull is dead." He sat on the foot of the bed, taking a deep breath.

"I didn't kill it." Seti's voice cracked.

"No. Not directly, no. It died from the plague infecting our livestock."

Seti looked at his father, confused.

His father continued. "The bull was safe in the stable, but you took him out. Furthermore, you took him without permission. You neither consecrated yourself nor the bull. You know the rules."

"I know," Seti whispered.

"What were you doing?" His father turned to him in anguish.

"I needed a revelation. I thought I could speak to Ra."

"You could have asked a priest—"

"I wanted to talk directly with Ra, not with a mediator. It was personal. I didn't plan it, Jt. I stopped in the stable with Chewy and saw the bull, and that's when I got the idea. I planned to have him back by morning."

"That's not how it works, Seti. You know that."

"Well, I got nothing anyway."

"Why didn't you come to me first?" his father asked.

"I didn't think you would let me."

"Well, you're right about that."

Seti sat up, eyes wet, gazing at his father. "What's going to happen?"

His father hesitated, looking anywhere but at Seti.

"What's going to happen?" Seti asked again.

"We haven't decided yet. There will be a meeting tomorrow. The bull is being embalmed as we speak. We'll have to find another one exactly like it without delay. I don't know where, but if we don't find one soon and consecrate it, Ptah will go elsewhere.

"Pharaoh will have to be notified. The bull holds great importance, especially considering Pharaoh's diplomacy in the East. I hope Pharaoh doesn't wish to consult it now in all this chaos. But regardless, we must present you to him along with what we deem to be a just punishment. Hopefully, he will leave the decision up to us and not take it upon himself. When we decide, we will set an appointed time with Pharaoh. After that, it will be out of my hands, Seti. I will no longer be able to help you."

Seti gulped. He picked at his fingernails.

"You realize this will have an effect on your future?"

Seti nodded.

"I don't know exactly what, but I'm pretty sure you will lose your heritage in the priestly lineage. We cannot have a priest with a controversial past. You didn't think of any of this when you took the bull out, did you?"

He shook his head.

"Why, Seti?"

Because doubts about the gods plagued him day and night. While it was the truth, trying to explain it to his father would cause further difficulties. But there was one thing he did want to say. "I overheard a slave yesterday, at the pyramid, say that our family likes to whip children's faces." Not repeating Hoshea's exact words, he stopped there and waited for his father's response.

"And?" Ameneten looked at Seti, as if waiting for more.

"Don't you see? It's shameful. We don't do that. It happened once, and I put a stop to it. That's not who we are."

His father's eyes narrowed.

"It bothers me. We are better than that. I'm ashamed, Jt. That was Mwt, and if Eliza's back had been turned, it wouldn't have happened."

"If she hadn't behaved the way she did, it wouldn't have happened."

"Maybe if she were an adult or something. Not a child. Not a girl. Now look at us." Seti clenched his fists. He should have known his father would respond this way.

Ameneten pulled his hand down his face. "This? This is why you took the Api bull out? Are you serious?"

Seti bit his tongue and faced the window. "Not exactly, but it contributed."

"You need to get over that, Seti."

"I thought I had, until I heard the slave."

His father sighed and tilted his head back, looking at the ceiling. Seti didn't take his eyes from the window. The sun had set, and the yelling and moaning outside quieted.

Thinking back to the bull, Seti asked, "What happened to the animals? What did you mean there was a plague?"

"Moshe's God sent a plague on the animals in the fields this morning. The horses, cattle, everything—except for Goshen again. Or that's what he said. We have yet to hear from the officers if that part was true. That's why we didn't take the sacred animals out this morning. We were warned by a messenger from the palace. It just makes your rash decision all the worse."

Chewy was safe in the stable. But the weight of Seti's idiocy pressed him into the bed. And he got nothing from the bull. Nothing from Ra.

"Why didn't Ra or Ptah protect the bull?" he asked.

Squinting his eyes, his father sighed. "I don't know."

"Was Ptah even in the bull? Or is that just a ploy?"

"Seti, it's not a ploy."

Seti rolled away from his father. He didn't know what to believe anymore. He clenched his fists again and held his breath.

"I have a big day tomorrow," his father said, breaking the silence. "You should stay in the temple. I'll look for you when we make our decision. If you run, you will be forbidden to return."

"I'm not going to run, Jt."

"I don't want to lose my son."

"I'm not going anywhere."

With a groan and popping joints, his father stood. He sighed as he neared the door. "Son."

Seti lifted his eyes to meet his father's.

"Please guard your heart. You're being pulled away."

"Jt, I am guarding my heart." But his father was right. "At least, I thought I was."

"Tell me, Seti," his father asked, "when is a heart most vulnerable to outside forces?"

Seti thought a moment. He should know the answer. But he didn't. "I don't know."

"When it's hurting." His father left the room and shut the door.

When the heart is hurting? His heart had hurt since Lumeri left him, whether he admitted it or not. The pain disguised itself as anger and bitterness. His future wife left him for a god. But was it really because of Lumeri? Or was it because the gods seemed to be rejecting him? And with no explanation. Were the gods leaving the Egyptians for the Hebrews? His mother's rejection compounded the betrayal. Rejection after rejection.

Eliza sat cross-legged on a mat on the floor of the main room in the linen shop. Unable to sleep as usual, she resigned herself to stitching a head wrap from one of the many scrap pieces scattered across the floor. All her life, she'd struggled to sleep at night, no matter how early she rose in the mornings. She yawned and peered out the window. A sky full of stars was too beautiful to miss anyway.

Candlelight flashed in the doorway of the loading room, followed by a thump and a frustrated groan. Aharon. Eliza jumped up and padded to the doorway. She stopped to watch Aharon rummage through a pile of scraps against the wall.

She broke the silence. "Why does Pharaoh keep hardening his heart? Can't he see his decisions are hurting his people?"

Neither startling nor looking up, Aharon answered, "God's hand is in this. Pharaoh is not acting alone."

When she didn't answer, Aaron stopped to look at her. "I don't think one consciously chooses to harden his heart. It's usually pride. There's a difference between hardening and guarding your heart."

"Yeah?"

"You want to guard your heart from ungodly things as well as ungodly patterns of behavior, speech, and thoughts. They become who you are otherwise. It's kind of like hardening your heart toward those ungodly things. But hardening your heart can manifest as stubbornness, an unwillingness to let God change you for the better and protect your soul."

Eliza leaned against the splintered door frame, candle in hand. Behind Aharon, the large wooden door on the back wall stood open a crack. He must have come in that way. But from where? A cool breeze swept off the river and sent her candle flame into a rapid dance, drawing her eyes from Aharon. The amplified flame bounced joyfully to an unheard beat, contrasting with the dark, silent room.

"That's my best explanation." He grabbed a large piece of cheap flax and wrapped it around himself.

Eliza snapped out of her trance and dashed to a nearby table for some copper pins. "Would you like me to sew that for you?" She went to Aharon and marked where to sew the linen. "I owe you."

After the pins were in, he took it off and handed it to her.

"So, the Lord knows when Pharaoh will give in?" she asked.

"Yes. But we don't know how many plagues Egypt will have to endure."

"I hope what we've seen will be enough."

Aharon grabbed his staff and headed to the door.

"Aharon?"

He stopped and met her gaze.

Something emboldened Eliza. Was it pinning the linen to him? His willingness to answer her questions? The strengthening of the flame in the breeze? "Next time you go to the palace, can I come with you?" She called this a 'Rahel-move'. Rahel had no fear.

"Ahhh." Aharon wagged his finger, smiling. "I see what you're doing."

"No, I just thought of it. Never mind." So much for her 'Rahel-move'. Her cheeks blazed hot with embarrassment, and she looked away. Boldness was not her strong suit.

"Let me discuss it with my brother," Aharon replied.

Her face lit up. "Thank you! Whatever he thinks is wise!"

Eliza muffled her squeal with her hand as she lay on her mat beside Miera. Elated at the possibility of meeting Pharaoh, she wouldn't sleep a wink tonight. What an experience that would be. And to watch Moshe do the work of God. To see Egypt's magicians stutter and fail. She had never been near the palace, and now she might go inside.

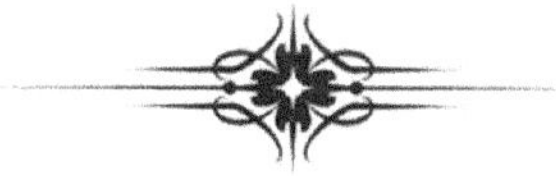

Unable to bear hiding in his room any longer, the next morning, Seti found a spot on the floor in the foyer to watch his father work. Ameneten hauled the large god-statues out of their private rooms one by one, his middle-aged bones cracking beneath him, yet he worked without so much as a grunt. Seti fought the urge to step in and help. He'd first have to be purified and consecrated, which he couldn't do until atoning for his sin. Would that even be possible? Tainted, he could never touch a god-statue again.

Once the statues were set for public worship, his father draped them in robes embroidered with their particular life stories. Then came the crowns and diadems. After finishing in the foyer, he went to prepare food for the gods.

The choir emerged once his father had left. Five men and three women, dressed in brilliant reds and magentas of sheer silk, formed two rows before the statues. They woke the gods with their soothing melodies. Not having heard the choir in person before, Seti remained where he sat, curious.

Commoners straggled in to pray. Some came in groups, but most on their own, men and women alike. It was busier than usual, probably because of the plagues. They approached the god-statues with eyes of fear, falling on their knees, foreheads touching the floor. Some cried in shaking silence, others wailed, begging the gods. A gift was left at the gods' feet in remembrance of each person's prayer.

A dirty old man staggered up the temple steps and fell to his knees. He crawled across the foyer in front of the choir on his knobby knees, leaving a trail of sand. His head hung low, and his body convulsed as he cried. The man remained near the choir, forehead to the floor, ignoring those coming and going around him. Seti sat forward, intrigued. Then it hit him like a splash of water. These were the farmers who'd lost their livestock. They had nothing but their own hands to reap their harvest.

He had to do something. But what? He had Chewy, but how much could he and Chewy do? There were too many farms. Montu, Khnum, Hathor, and Bat, the remaining sacred animals, were useless in the stable. Why couldn't they work? What if Pharaoh moved the domestic slaves to the farms? Seti didn't know much about farming, but the plight of this man and the others stirred his heart like never before.

"After giving it much thought and consideration, we have agreed on the punishment for your actions with the Api bull," Ameneten announced.

All six priests had entered Seti's room that evening. Seti jumped from the bed and waited for his father to continue, hands clasped behind him.

His father stood a step closer than the others, but still kept his distance, refusing to look Seti in the eye. The evening sun cast Seti's shadow at his father's feet in some symbolic mockery from Ra.

"You no longer qualify for priestly duties or roles. Instead, you will arrange a team to search for the next Api bull. This may take years. The team will be comprised of scribes and commoners. Travel essentials will be provided. You will no longer continue your schooling or scribal training. Access to the stable, the library, and the purification pools is forbidden.

"Tomorrow afternoon, Amoshe, Kipuri, and I will present you before Pharaoh and offer our proposal for punishment. If he agrees, and we pray that he does, your coffin will be updated promptly. But if he doesn't, you will be at his mercy. After sentencing, you'll make an announcement to the public. You are forbidden to join in the mourning ceremonies or any of the events that follow. Your authority and heritage will be transferred to Kabelo. If you run, you can never return, or you'll be killed." His father paused, voice trembling. "We consider this sentence light."

His father paused again before continuing in a shaky whisper, "Even I cannot touch the sacred animals, Seti. What made you think you could? He was out there naked. It's forbidden. How dare he look like the other animals. He's a god!"

His father's emotion was too much, but Seti somehow managed to hold his own in check, remaining still as his father collected himself.

"It is spoken."

The other priests nodded then turned in unison and filed out of the room.

As soon as the door shut, Seti collapsed on his bed. The weight of it all threatened to crush him. He had become a humiliation to the Ameneten family, and every generation would know because the inscription on his coffin would display his shame. His younger brother, who took the priestly duties half as seriously as Seti, would now inherit the role.

"It was a mistake," Seti whispered. If he hadn't

doubted or become emotionally caught up in the words of Eliza and Hoshea, it wouldn't have happened.

Would it? He had no one to blame but himself. Tears filled his eyes.

Chapter 14

Seti rose the next morning, snatched his woven bag, slipped on his sandals, and hurried to his father's room. Tonight was his meeting with Pharaoh. With the sun nudging against the horizon, Ameneten would be in the purification pool. Since the priests continued their daily routines, word couldn't have yet spread about the bull.

After grabbing a heavy, layered, jeweled collar from his father's bureau, he fastened it around his neck and gazed into the bronze mirror. The weight of the stones and gold pressing into his shoulders and collarbones was nothing compared to the heaviness of his heart. He sighed, staring at his reflection. Normally, he relished the aura of authority it gave him. Though his father had several, this was the one passed down to each new Ameneten priest upon graduation. It would have been Seti's in a couple of years.

Work now, sulk later. He spun from the mirror and hurried to the stable.

Seti hugged Chewy's neck. Let the plague have that useless bull, as long as Chewy was safe. Eyeing the remaining sacred animals with contempt, he led Chewy outside.

Unexpectedly, Sabu was already at the mesa when he arrived. Seti had planned to leave a message for him. As a farmer with morning chores, Sabu was never there this early.

This could only mean one thing.

Sabu sat on the ledge with his horse, Nimrod, standing nearby. At the sound of Chewy's hooves on the sandstone, he jumped to his feet. "I knew you'd come."

"You did?"

"Well, eventually, if I waited long enough."

Seti dismounted.

"Are you going to Pharaoh?" Sabu nodded at Seti's jeweled collar. "We have to speak with him."

"We do?"

"Your jt, someone has to talk to him. My family lost their oxen and cattle. Everyone lost their animals. The only reason I still have Nimrod is because he was stabled. He's all we have. We have an entire field to harvest before it rots. Pharaoh's ruining Egypt because he's too stubborn to give in to Moshe!"

"Well, that's why I came," Seti said.

"Look, Seti, I know you're rich, but those animals were a huge investment for us. We can't just replace them. Nothing was in the stables but Nimrod. Nobody else had anything in their stables either. They all just died. We can't hire more workers because there aren't any. Nala, my sisters, and my mwt are out there now trying to do it all by hand. You're the only one I know with any sort of influence."

Seti held up his hand. "I don't know if I have any influence with Pharaoh. I'm in a bit of trouble."

Sabu's stance changed from defensive to curious. "What kind of trouble?"

"I need your help," Seti said, "and I can help you too."

"What? What's going on? Why are you dressed up?"

"Come with me to the pyramids. I don't have much time. I'll explain everything."

Seti leaped onto Chewy. Sabu eyed Seti quizzically before fetching Nimrod and the chariot.

Dead cats and horses joined the livestock piled along the sides of the road. Whatever was exposed to the air that dreadful morning now rotted in the sun, which cooked their flesh into bloated heaps to the point of bursting. Buried frogs had been pulled from the ground as their graves were made deeper to accommodate larger animals. The stench of fresh death mixed with the old, rotting decay of the frogs.

Instead of racing, Seti and Sabu rode solemnly side by side while he recounted the events of the last two days. He included his conversation with Hoshea, but not how the Hebrew referred to the Ameneten family. Sabu couldn't possibly understand Seti's shame. The incident with the Api bull and impending punishment proposed by the priests was hard to get out. Seti's fate rested on his meeting with Pharaoh tonight.

"There's nothing I can do to convince Pharaoh. He'll be furious. He relied on that bull," Seti finished.

Sabu gaped at him. "Am I ever going to see you again?"

Seti had contemplated the various scenarios that could play out all night. "Well," he said with a sheepish grin, "if Pharaoh goes with what my jt suggests, I have to build a team and find the next Api bull. You can be my assistant."

Sabu scowled. He rode in silence, staring straight ahead. After a moment, he asked, "Earlier, you said you could help me. How?"

"I want to transfer the pyramid workers to the farms."

"The slaves?"

"Yes. They are under my command until Jt finishes in the temple. He has four days and then a day in the pools before he leaves. That gives us at least five days before he gets to the pyramid, and that's if he doesn't stop at home first. They should be back at the pyramid before my jt gets there, so he won't know any better. Even if he finds out, I have nothing to lose. At least we can harvest some of the fields."

"You think it will work? Can you start with mine?"

"Yes, but there are others I want done before it's too late."

"I don't know whether to be happy or sad. You're going to save our livelihood, but I will lose you."

"We don't know anything yet. But I'm serious about you being my assistant."

Sabu laughed. "I owe it to you!"

They reached the Ameneten pyramid by noon. Seti wasn't sure where to find the slaves his father had placed in charge or even who they were. He should have paid more attention in the past. Typically, Egyptian taskmasters oversaw the projects. The last Egyptians to set foot near the Ameneten pyramid had been Seti and Sabu, days before. For most of the month, when the slaves weren't in Goshen trying to flee, they worked with no oversight. There had to be some kind of hierarchy among them.

Perhaps if Seti rode to the entrance, they would see him, and the leader would approach. That made more sense than searching. Settling on that, he led Sabu up the path.

As they ascended, Seti studied the slaves nearest to them as they cleared the way ahead. Some bowed, and he acknowledged them with a nod, but none made eye contact. They all worked in silence as before, but now with no animals to assist. Several men dragged rocks that oxen could easily carry. Yet he and Sabu rode in on their horses, drawing attention to themselves—Seti with his jeweled collar. He shut his eyes tight with shame, wanting nothing more than to hide in the pitch-dark tunnel. Three days ago, he ran slaves off this very path, rejuvenated, thinking all his mistakes were behind him, and the world had returned to normal. *Fool.*

At the pyramid entrance, Seti motioned for Sabu to stay in his chariot. He stood tall, back straight, and chin up. Seti remained on his horse, scanning the hundreds of slaves.

They worked in rows, passing bricks and buckets from one to another.

He could never fully appreciate the complexity of building a pyramid, let alone leading a team of multitudes to do a job so perfectly. If Pharaoh were to have him killed, his embalmed body would be passed up the path like a brick and laid to rest in his coffin, unprotected until the gods inhabited the chamber. What god would protect his soul? Seti was a shame to his family and the gods.

"Can I help you?" a voice asked behind them.

Seti turned to a strong Hebrew standing tall at the entrance. Caught off guard, he fumbled for words. "Yes, uh, I'm just overseeing the project."

"Even with the plagues, we are still on schedule. Is everything to your satisfaction?"

"Beyond my satisfaction," Seti blurted without thinking.

He bowed and started down the tunnel.

"Wait!" Seti called, stopping him.

The slave paused and faced them.

"I'm looking for the team leader." Seti didn't know what to call it. He should have rehearsed this.

"That would be me, my lord, the task-master." The Hebrew bowed again.

Sabu's eyes went wide. Seti dismounted Chewy and stood head-to-head with the slave. The man held his stance, hands behind his back, but kept his gaze lowered.

Then he bowed again.

After an awkward glance at Sabu, Seti waited for the slave to straighten before speaking. "And what is your name?"

"Master, do you not know the name of those whom you trust? How do you lead a force if you can't even remember those who work in your name?"

Seti blinked. "What?"

"Forgive me," the slave retracted and bowed again. "I

am Hoshea."

Hoshea? The Hoshea? "Hoshea?"

"Yes?"

"I mean, you're forgiven, Hoshea. I've come with a request. Er, I mean, I've come with a change of plans." Putting his shock aside, Seti laid out his plan. "As you know, farmers in On, Menf, and the rest of Egypt lost their livestock. So, I need you to gather your men to help with the flax and barley harvest. There are certain fields where I'd like you to start."

"Master," Hoshea cut in, "we have no animals ourselves."

Seti scratched his arm and nodded. "You don't need animals if the entire team goes. The more men, the better. That's the point of sending you."

Hoshea stared. "You want us to abandon the pyramid and help the farmers?"

The air thickened as Seti struggled for words. He was going to have to change his tactic. "Well, you see..." He hesitated, feeling the eyes of both the slave and Sabu boring into him. "I was in the temple in Menf, worshipping, when the farmers arrived. All of them, from their farms. And they were crying out to the gods about their lost livestock and inability to harvest. I wanted to tell them that they were praying to the wrong god, for it's Moshe's God who did this, and they should be praying to Him. But I can't tell them that. So, if Pharaoh hears you are helping the farmers, perhaps his heart will soften, and he'll let you go with Moshe."

Hoshea stared in silence. Besides Eliza, no other slave dared look him in the eye.

"This is not a request." Seti straightened his shoulders.

With a deep inhale through his teeth, Hoshea bowed. Seti shot Sabu a glowing smile before Hoshea stood.

"You have my gratitude, Hoshea." Seti turned toward Sabu, scratching his chin. "I will leave my trustee with you. This is Sabu. He will be held with the highest authority in my name. Treat him as you would treat me. He will lead you to the desired fields. We're aiming to get as much done as possible within the next four days. After that, you are to report back here to continue your work."

"As you wish."

Elation bubbled in Seti's stomach, and he couldn't wipe the smile from his face. He suppressed the urge to shove Sabu playfully. Or hug Hoshea.

"My lord?" Hoshea asked.

"Yes?" Seti wiggled his brows at Sabu, unable to hold still.

"Something's happening to you."

Seti blinked. "What?"

Hoshea pointed to Seti's arms. Wet boils and blisters covered his hands and arms. Some oozed a yellow pus. He gasped, stumbling backward. Sabu yelled, staring wide-eyed at his own outstretched arms. They checked their legs and feet. Though clear, tingles trickled up Seti's legs. Seti locked eyes with Sabu, frozen in shock. The tingling turned to burning. Heat rose up Seti's shoulders and back, as if the sun was melting his skin. He shot Ra a look of betrayal.

Untouched, Hoshea backed away in horror, hands up.

"Seti!" Sabu yelled, pointing at Chewy. The horse wiggled, boils bubbling from under his coat. They turned to Nimrod. Boils covered his underside in a swollen bubbly mess of ooze.

"I will do as you wish, my lord, but you'd better leave," Hoshea told them.

"Sabu will return—" Seti choked as he struggled to mount Chewy.

"No. I'm not going anywhere until my farm is harvested," Sabu squeaked, digging fanatically at his arms.

"Sabu? Are you sure?"

Sabu groaned, scratching in agony.

Seti kicked Chewy into a run, leaving a cloud of dust on Hoshea, Sabu, and Nimrod. Chewy blazed down the pyramid, sending slaves diving in every direction. Burying his face in Chewy's neck, he clenched his eyes shut and clung to Chewy with all he had, trusting the horse to get him back to the temple. But Chewy ran with an anguished ferocity, his body pounding beneath Seti.

"Chewy, slow—" Seti struggled to maintain his grip. The horse paid him no regard.

"Chewy, I can't—" Blowing sand filled his mouth. He buried his face in Chewy's mane, his muscles straining to hang on. There was no calming this horse.

Chewy slowed as he neared the temple stable but wouldn't stop moving, squirming in circles near the door. Seti groaned as he forced his arms to release their grip, and he dropped to the ground. His legs crumpled upon landing, and he tumbled onto his side, the jeweled collar stabbing his skin. He rolled over and slid it over his head with what little strength remained, gritting his teeth against the pain of tearing blisters open. A soft cry escaped him, and he lay flat with eyes closed, too weak to care about the dirt stinging the pustules on his back.

The stable doors were locked. Already? He stood back, examining the doors through stinging eyes. They had crusted over with sand and tears, unable to open more than halfway. A scorching pain shot through his body, and he recoiled, stumbling backward. Giving up on the stable, he tied Chewy to a nearby tree.

The god-statues stood in the foyer, dressed and decorated with jewels. But there was no choir, no dancers. No worshippers or prayers. The statues stood alone, watching Seti limp across the floor, his legs covered in blisters and boils. It was spreading. This, too, must be from Moshe and his God, since the Hebrews at the pyramid had been unaffected.

Eliza tensed in the upper room of the shop, bone-needle suspended mid-stitch of a loincloth as screams erupted from the women on the floor below. Her gaze darted to the two Hebrew women beside her. The terror in their eyes confirmed she wasn't imagining it. Eliza jumped to her feet, dropped her work, and ran down the stairs to the main room. Halting on the bottom step, she grabbed the wooden rail to keep from plowing into a woman crouched on the floor before her. The woman hugged herself, crying into her knees. Others covered their faces with bubbling hands, running about aimlessly. Open blisters oozed with pus. Eliza examined her own hands and arms. Nothing.

"Is that leprosy?" Rahel spoke from behind her.

"I don't think so."

The crazed women streamed out the door into the street. Eliza, Rahel, and the two Hebrew women followed. The entire marketplace was in a frenzy. Egyptians screamed, grabbing at various body parts and covering their faces. Some rolled in the dirt and moaned. They made no attempt to move as animals pounded by, whipping carts against tables and crates, dispersing food and goods all over the road. Wet spots seeped through their wraps and tunics.

The Hebrew women squeezed past Eliza and dashed to a table with spilled fruit. They filled their aprons with grapes and pomegranates before running to the next table. Though tempted to join them, Eliza dared not. She'd probably get caught and whipped. Her hand covered her mouth in shock as she watched the spectacle in the street.

"What do we do?" Rahel asked.

"I don't know."

"Stay," Aharon's voice said from behind.

They both spun around. He gave a slight nod before turning toward the loading room. "If you want to go to the palace, don't go to Goshen. I don't think the Egyptians will let you anyway. Soon they will be even more desperate for your help."

"You mean we are going with you to see Pharaoh?" Eliza asked.

"Perhaps."

The girls clasped their hands in silent squeals, eyes wide. Aharon's words lifted Eliza's spirit even as her stomach twisted with the sorrow of watching the Egyptian's suffer.

That evening, Seti woke with a jolt, as if a rooster crowed in his head. He lay still, staring at the sheet covering his face. The palace. Pharaoh. Nobody had come to get him to meet with Pharaoh. As he sat, the sheet tore open the crusted boils on his back, and he winced as the air bit his raw flesh.

Holding his breath, he stood and wrapped himself with the white cotton bedsheet, careful not to tear any more blisters. A sour smell of sweat and rot assaulted his nostrils. Was that from him? Yellow spots with blood stained the mattress where he had been lying. Bile filled his mouth. His knees and ankles ached as he left the sleeping quarters.

He moved the curtain of the potion room aside. The overwhelming scent of myrrh and spikenard forced him a step back. Ameneten and the others sat on cushions in a circle in deep discussion. Sebeki lay on the floor, staring at the ceiling. Their oil-laden faces remained the only parts of their bodies not wrapped in linen strips.

When they didn't notice Seti's presence, he

interrupted, "Can I have some of that?"

They barely spared him a glance, then continued their conversation. His father shot him a warning look before motioning him to join them. Seti gingerly sat.

"Begin with this." His father passed him a jar of oil. "Then apply these." And a bowl of linen strips. "It's Kebset's latest concoction—blue lotus, myrrh, and spikenard with natron."

Seti grabbed the brush from the jar and started with his feet.

"Can't touch the statues like this," Kipuri said from the other side of Ameneten.

"Leave them out for now. They will be fine," Ameneten replied.

"All we can do is pray to Isis," Sebeki muttered, hand on his forehead.

"And Thoth, and Imhotep."

"I worry they will get angrier if we leave them in the foyer. They've already missed the music and choir," Ipuur, the quiet one, piped in.

"Wait, are you sure they're even mad at us?" Seti interrupted.

"Do you have any better ideas, Seti?" Sebeki's tone was anything but inquiring.

"No, but they aren't giving us a fair chance to repent or atone for anything. If this is punishment, we're unable to fulfill our priestly duties, which adds more punishment. Right?" Seti asked.

"Yes, we've covered this already. We don't know. It's the only thing we can think of," his father's words came with care.

"What if it's true that the Hebrew God is stronger?"

Silence stung the air. Seti looked from one to the other, hoping at least one priest might consider it.

"We will hear no adverse words against our gods," Sebeki answered after no one offered a reply.

His father pinned Seti with an anxious glare. He sighed and continued applying the oil. He believed the same thing a month ago. Could he blame them for being so thickheaded?

His father fixed his gaze on Sebeki. "I imagine Pharaoh and the magicians are also afflicted, but we need to have an emergency meeting with him. If this continues, Egypt will lose everything. Moshe won't let us recover before hitting us with another plague."

Eliza's voice quietly entered Seti's mind. *All I know, is that He allows suffering and affliction to draw man back to Him.* Were the Egyptian gods allowing this to draw their people back to them? But the people hadn't drifted away. They were crawling to their gods on their hands and knees, crying out to them, meditating, giving offerings, sacrificing animals. What more could their gods want?

"And the magicians?" Kipuri asked.

"Haven't heard from them since the gnats. They even attributed that to Moshe's God."

"And the Hebrews?"

"Goshen is spared, but the slaves remain here. They continue working. Isis knows, we need them now more than ever. They're the only ones who can get anything done. We're going to have to pull them from the four Menf pyramids and the statues, at least for the time being," a priest said.

"Absolutely not! The gods forbid we prolong those pyramids any longer!"

Ameneten nodded toward Kipuri. "Kipuri is right. We promised them that we'd finish the pyramids and Pharaoh's statue by the end of the harvest. Isis will provide."

Seti kept his head down but startled when Kipuri keeled forward, pressing his palm against his eyes with a murmur of some healing chant.

Handing Kipuri a damp cloth, Ameneten nodded toward the oil. "Careful around the eyes."

The others gave Kipuri little notice. "Isis has always

provided. Ra continues with his light, Osiris and Hathor sustain the Nile, and Isis and Set bless the crops. The slaves will not halt their work. Pharaoh's needs come before ours."

"Obviously," Seti muttered under his breath. Ameneten's nostrils flared.

Sebeki perked up. "I suggest we pray through the night. Call the dancers out and offer sacrifices."

Ameneten shook his head, eyes on the floor. "I don't think the dancers are in any condition to dance."

"They can and they will. The gods will see our affliction."

"I'll stay up and pray, but by no means can I make it to On like this, even in a chariot," Ipuur said.

"But should we entreat Pharaoh like this?" Asmuri asked, his fingers playing with the corner of a woven rug on which their cushions sat. "He has sent for a healer to deliver oil and strips tomorrow morning. We can send a message to him then."

"Good thinking," Ameneten said. "I'll send Asmuri with word. Perhaps if Pharaoh pleases Moshe, there will be some relief for us to recuperate."

Asmuri gave Ameneten an affirming nod.

Kipuri straightened with bloodshot eyes. "Send dancers too."

"I don't think Pharaoh's ready for that. And neither are the dancers."

Kipuri mumbled something and tossed the cloth.

"Perhaps soothing music?" another suggested.

"We could do that. Harps and string instruments," Ameneten said, nodding.

"Yes, good idea."

"May I ask something?" Seti interjected, brushing oil on his arms.

All eyes turned to him.

"Am I going to the palace tonight?"

"Are you serious?" Kipuri shot.

Seti nodded.

Kipuri shifted on his cushion. "Seti, if you can't contribute productively to the conversation, then leave us."

Without a word, Seti grabbed the oil jar and the linen strips and left the room.

The oil soothed Seti's skin. He had yet to apply the strips. Still draped in bed linen, Seti stepped outside to check on Chewy.

Chewy wiggled uncomfortably by the tree, the reins wrapped around his nose. His tail whipped about as if surrounded by flies, but he calmed at the sight of Seti. Though boils covered his underside and legs, the rest of him was spared.

"I'm sorry, Chewy." Seti rubbed his nose before untying the reins. "None of this is your fault. It's not fair to you."

Seti waddled to the stable gate and tried it again, but the crossbar wouldn't budge. He couldn't remember it ever being locked. Were they afraid he'd kill another sacred animal? Did they think he was that stupid? Or maybe they feared he'd do something in retaliation. Even with nothing to lose, he wasn't cruel. All his faithful service and dedication to the gods meant nothing.

Seti stared at the door. If the priests weren't safe from the boils inside the temple, then the sacred animals wouldn't be either. There seemed to be no discrimination between man and beast with this plague, except for ethnicity.

Giving up on the gate, Seti returned to Chewy. He had to find a safe place for him. Chewy had been protected from the livestock plague while in the stable. What if another plague like that came?

He glanced at the empty temple yard. Most Egyptians huddled in their homes in distress. The priests and dancers would gather in the foyer at the feet of the god-statues at any minute. And they'd be there all night long.

Seti limped alongside Chewy as he led him up the hill. At the top, they rounded to the front of the temple and ascended the steps. He made sure the coast was clear before taking Chewy into the foyer. Only the eerie, empty eyes of the god-statues watched them. Seti hid his face, hurrying to the back hall. They climbed the winding stone steps toward the living quarters on the third floor. Balancing the oil jar, bowl of linen strips, and Chewy's reins, Seti entered an empty room at the far end of the hall.

After shutting the door, Seti painted the horse's legs and underbelly with oil.

"You get your own room. You're going to have to stay quiet for me," he whispered. "No one can find out. No crazy horse tricks in here, okay? And don't be looking out the window either."

"Seti!"

Seti's eyes shot open under the water. His heart leaped at his father's scream, and he sat upright in the pool. Ameneten stood opposite him on the ledge with Sebeki. "Get out of there! What do you think you're doing?"

"It's a purification pool, Jt. It works wonders for the boils."

"No! Get out of there! You're defiling it." Ameneten's voice echoed off the porcelain walls but had no effect on Seti's rebellious spirit.

"Defiling it? Wasn't this pool just filled with dead frogs not too long ago? It's purifying my skin."

His father's face reddened with embarrassment before turning to anger.

Seti dipped his head under the surface while his father

paced on the edge before him. When he came up, Ameneten demanded, "Get out. Now. This is preposterous. You're not making any of this easy for me. Asmuri returned from the palace. Pharaoh's requesting the Api bull."

Seti wiped the water from his face with his fingers, blinking his eyes open. "Are we going to the palace then?"

"I don't know. I don't know, Seti. I cannot do this!" Ameneten gripped his head with both hands and bent over in a loud groan, his starched kilt barely moving.

Compassion swept over Seti, and he regretted the pain he had caused his father. He lifted himself from the pool onto the ledge and examined the open blisters and boils on his legs. Though clean and fleshy, they burned if touched. Maybe the water didn't purify anything, but it felt good on his wounds.

Sebeki remained near the door, eyeing the water.

Ameneten tossed Seti a robe. "We're having a meeting in the potion room. All of us. Get dressed." With that, his father stomped out, Sebeki at his heels.

Seti threw the robe around his shoulders and hurried after them, leaving a trail of water behind. His stomach knotted as his father's words sank in. Though he wanted to get this over with, he worried over Pharaoh's decision.

Like the day before, the six priests sat on their cushions in a circle. A table near the door contained oil jars and fresh linen strips brought in from the funerary. Seti grabbed a jar, a brush, and a bowl of strips and joined the men. They stared at him.

Ameneten fumbled with his hands in his lap. "Can we stall this?"

"I'm ready, Jt."

"Yes, but I don't know if Pharaoh's ready."

"He's never requested the bull before. He has always come here. We don't take the animals there." Asmuri wiped his brow with a scented cloth.

"Can we tell him the bull is sick?" Ameneten asked.

Kipuri sneered across the circle. "Really? Even Pharaoh knows the sacred animals don't get sick."

Returning the sneer, Seti said, "But that's exactly what happened. Sacred animal or not, he got the plague and died."

"No, Seti. That was no plague. That was from the Hebrew God!"

"Why didn't Ptah protect the bull?" Seti demanded. "Couldn't he defend himself from the Hebrew God?"

His father held up a hand. "Seti, please."

"I'm serious, Jt!" Seti slammed the brush on the floor. "How long are you going to pretend that's not what's happening here?"

"Know your place, son of Ameneten!" Kipuri's cheeks shook with fury.

Seti ignored him. "Why didn't the gods protect the sacred pools from the frogs? The Nile from turning to blood? Why would they destroy what we dedicate to them? They sure aren't telling us anything and don't respond to our inquiries. A just god would at least tell us what we did wrong. We're always dedicated and loyal to them. Becoming more dedicated and loyal isn't helping, so that can't be it. Dancing in front of them and dressing them up isn't working either."

He stopped, overwhelmed with emotion, and gazed at the priests, who silently waited for him to continue. Denouncing the gods was not his plan—at least not yet.

"I didn't mean to harm the bull, but I had to know. I wanted to hear from Ra, but I did it wrong, and I'm sorry." He dropped his head in shame.

His father put a hand on Seti's knee. "Seti."

"Just take me to Pharaoh. Get this over with."

Instead of annoyance, the priests looked at him with pity.

After a moment of silence, Sebeki spoke up. "Perhaps we can stall due to the plague. And don't respond until Pharaoh inquires again."

The others nodded.

Seti's head shot up. "Why? What's the purpose of prolonging it?"

"Because Pharaoh's mood will improve the better he feels. It will be to your advantage if we wait," his father told him.

Seti rolled his eyes. "I don't care anymore. My life is ruined already. What difference is it going to make whether he's in a good mood or not?"

"Seti, I care. You're my son."

Seti stood and grabbed the jar and bowl. "I'm done. Come get me when you're ready to go."

"Seti."

Seti left the room, whipping the curtain shut behind him. His bare feet squeaked on the marble floor, echoing in the empty corridor.

The reflection staring back at Seti in the polished bronze looked like a mummy ready for burial. He applied the final linen strip to his neck before snapping the gold cuffs over the cloth on his arms. He left his splotchy face uncovered. It nearly glowed red, like a raw sunburn that had peeled prematurely. His skin radiated heat. The thin layer of oil he smeared over his face refreshed him, but he was careful not to overdo it. His hair had grown long enough that he could almost run his fingers through it. Though layered with oil, it was the only remnant of the old Seti.

He added oil to Chewy's underbelly and legs while the horse studied him, Seti's defeated feelings reflected in the equine eyes. Over a month ago, his impending marriage to a beautiful dancer and near completion of his scribal training promised a bright future. Girls loved him and would do anything he asked. His mother bragged about her older son, the future priest.

What happened?

Though blessed with favor from the gods, he had given no thought to those less fortunate. He was a cocky, selfish child who paid no attention to the slaves at the pyramid or in his own household.

"Oh, Chewy. Why am I like this? Why do I care who my wife dances for? Why do I listen to the gibberish of slaves? Why can't I be like the other priests?"

What's better, a handsome brat who has everything but no self-awareness, or a hideous but thoughtful man who has nothing?

What priest didn't want the pleasure of dancers and priestesses? But he wasn't like the priests. He wasn't even like other Egyptian men who kept a chasm between themselves and their slaves. Though late, his compassion for Eliza was genuine. The desire to befriend Hoshea came from his heart. Seti was losing himself.

Chewy snorted and swatted his tail at him, bringing a much-needed smile.

"Tomorrow I will stand before Pharaoh, so don't wait up for me. I might not come back. I'll leave the door open a crack, and if I don't return by sundown, you are free. Sound fair?"

Chewy bobbed his head, and Seti hugged him tight.

Chapter 15

Seti lay curled in bed, mind reeling, when his father burst into his room and tossed a tunic at him. "It's time."

He jumped up and slipped the tunic over his head while his father paced. Ameneten wore a long cotton robe that dragged across the floor, his entire body covered except his bandaged arms. A leather strap, tied in a knot at the waist, gathered the extra fabric in front.

Seti followed him quietly through the temple. Upon entering the foyer, he came face-to-face with the dancers. Lumeri stopped mid-step when their eyes met. All twenty-five girls glistened in oil, but none were permitted to wear bandages. Seti dropped his gaze, refusing to let her affect him. Sebeki and Kipuri, dressed like his father and with sandals over their bandaged feet, joined them as they hurried across the foyer. How foolish Seti must look, like a mummy wearing a tunic. His wrapped feet slipped on the polished floor, and he swatted at a loose bandage flopping from his rear end, falling further behind the others.

At the bottom of the steps, a four-person litter topped with a reed canopy rested on the ground, its Minoan carriers bowing beside it. The four sat on two benches facing each other, Seti and his father facing the rear. Seti gazed pensively at the temple. Would this be his last glimpse of it? He swallowed hard and suppressed the urge to jump from the litter, dash up those steps, grab Chewy, and disappear forever. Like a chapter in his life coming to a close, the temple shrank behind them as they rode away.

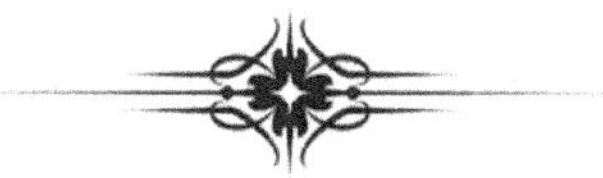

"God has spoken." Moshe poked his head into the room. "I'll be leaving shortly. Those who desire to come, be ready, and don't delay me."

His head disappeared, and the door shut. Eliza, Rahel, and Miera dropped their game of sticks and stones and locked eyes before jumping to their feet. "Wait!"

They dashed down the stairs to the shop, only to find the place empty. None of the Egyptian workers had returned since the boils erupted, leaving the place a heaping mess of mixed linen piles, scraps, and tools. The girls stumbled over each other at the bottom of the steps before racing out the front door. Moshe stood in the middle of the road with Aharon. Both their wives stood nearby, and Miriam gestured for the girls to hurry. The marketplace remained a mess of food, tables, and trash, as if an invading army had swept through and left everything behind but the civilians. The only signs of life were the eight of them.

Miera bounced around the men like an excited young goat. Eliza reached to pull her away, but she evaded her grasp.

"Miera!" Eliza hissed. "Leave them alone!"

Moshe and Aharon sauntered down the street, Aharon's staff thumping on the road.

At the first pause in their conversation, Miera cut in. "What's it going to be this time?"

Moshe and Aharon turned to her, eyebrows raised.

"You'll find out when I announce it," Moshe said as they continued to march ahead.

"Is it going to be the last one? Is Pharaoh going to give in this time?"

"Is it worse than the farm animals dying?"

"Are people going to die?"

"What about Goshen?"

"Why will this be our only chance to come with you? What about the next time? And the one after that?" Miera peppered them with questions while dodging Eliza's snatching hand.

Moshe stopped, eyes wide. "Why this time? You tell me why you're coming."

"I don't know. I guess because my sister asked you?"

"Alright, then. Please, now, no more questions."

Miera paused both her questions and her bouncing long enough for Eliza to clamp her hand over her sister's mouth. She shook her head, cheeks burning. She would have asked Moshe those very questions. Though embarrassing, her sister's lack of decorum came to be useful at times. When freed, Miera skipped ahead while Eliza remained behind and grabbed Rahel's arm, heart pounding. This was it. They were going to the palace.

As the litter approached the outer courtyard, six guards opened the gate, no questions asked. Sebeki and Kipuri acknowledged them with a nod as they passed. Upon entering the colonnade, the crunch of gravel gave way to the smooth quietness of polished granite. A canopy of stone shaded the road all the way to the palace, supported by pillars staggered on each side. Intricate carvings in the pillars depicted the history of previous dynasties.

Seti clung to the arm of the litter as they were jostled past a myriad of avenues, archways, stone houses, and flowered gardens. Well-manicured grass stretched up the hills to the granite fence running parallel to the road—the same fence Seti and Sabu had spied from weeks before. Seti scanned the length of it, hoping to find Sabu. But Sabu would be on the farms.

Seti never did say goodbye to his friend, having fled when the boils erupted. What progress had Sabu and Hoshea made? No word had reached him about the harvests or the slaves from the Ameneten pyramid.

The patterned road had once fascinated Seti. Now he paid it no heed and watched the gate fade in the distance. Once past that second gate, they'd be beyond the great wall, entering the inner courtyard.

As before, six guards opened the gate with nothing but a nod from the priests. They passed through the six-foot-thick stone wall separating the two courtyards and surrounding the palace. Seti's chest tightened, and his pulse hammered. There was no turning back now. The sun stung his eyes, forcing them shut. He inhaled slowly, exhaled, then opened them and looked at his father for the first time since leaving the temple. Ameneten sat like a carved image, staring blankly ahead, his hand gripping the rail.

Two limestone lions, as tall as the Great Wall, stood on either side of the road, guarding the gate they had entered. Their onyx eyes seemed to converge on Seti as he rode away from them, sending a chill up his spine.

Giant quartz statues of various gods dotted the courtyard, all facing east. Around them, smaller statues in submissive poses emulated the proper order of nature.

Around the side of the palace, Seti caught a glimpse of the marbled buildings where Pharaoh's family remained tucked away in seclusion. The quay at the Nile wrapped around them, private barges parked along the sides.

A pair of Cushite guards, with gold rings in their noses and ivory staffs in hand, flanked the litter. Dressed in leather military kilts with long flint daggers at their waists, they escorted the group in silence. More guards paced the top of the wall, armed with spears and bows. Besides the litter and guards, not a soul could be seen.

The litter halted at the bottom of the palace steps. The carriers lowered them and bowed their faces to the ground. Seti's heart raced as he stepped off in silence. He paused, wiped the sweat from his hands on his tunic, and tilted his head back to gaze upon the palace. Its immensity and grandeur mocked him, dehumanizing him to the size of a dung beetle, but one with no favor. His insides churned, and the back of his throat burned with acid. Seti swallowed and followed his father.

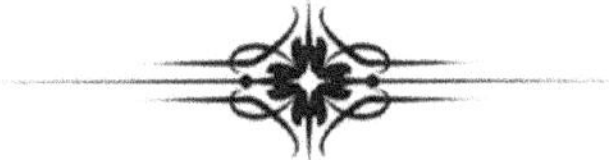

"Where's the Api bull?" Pharaoh asked when they entered the throne room.

He leaned uncomfortably to the side of the throne, surrounded by women with giant tamarisk fans. Their natural blonde hair and light skin suggested they were from the north. Pharaoh's golden throne, inlaid with emeralds, rubies, and carnelian, was so enormous it made him appear amusingly small. Six marble steps, lined with imported plants, led to a dais where the throne sat. On either side stood identical pink granite lions with green marble frogs at their feet. A mottled gray cat yawned at the bottom step.

Hapnir, the vizier, stood behind the throne, decked in a mother-of-pearl collar laced with gold, staring through kohled eyes and nursing a steamy drink.

Seti and the priests bowed. Pharaoh flicked his hand, they stood, and the three priests stepped behind Seti, as if to hand him over.

"I am sorry. We did not bring the bull," Sebeki answered.

"Why not?" Pharaoh demanded. "I asked for the Api bull. I am not in any sort of condition to go to the temple."

"My lord, the bull died in the plague."

Seti winced at Kipuri's curt words.

Pharaoh sat up at once, hand closing around his golden scepter. "It's dead? How could the Api bull die? What about the others?"

"Just the sacred bull."

Pharaoh's already red face deepened to a burgundy. He took a deep breath and studied the four men, eyes resting on Seti. With forced calmness, he asked, "Tell me, how is it that the Api bull was the only sacred animal that caught the plague? I sent word to have them locked up and protected. Did you not receive that message?"

Sebeki's gulp was audible. "We received the message, my lord."

The room went silent for what seemed like an eternity. Then Pharaoh asked, "What happened?"

Seti's father stepped forward beside Seti. "My lord, my son—he took the bull into the field to consult Ptah and Ra. He had a crisis of faith and attempted it on his own. He was not aware of the lockdown or the plague. He fell asleep in the field, and when he woke, the bull was dead."

Shame and stupidity engulfed Seti as he cast his eyes on the marble floor, feeling the heat emitting from his father's body. He kept his head down as Pharaoh squirmed on the throne.

"You took the Api bull out of the stable and fell asleep in the field?" Pharaoh's voice pierced the silence and echoed off the marble walls. He gripped both armrests with his bandaged hands.

A guard entered from a side door. "My lord?"

Pharaoh waved off the guard with his scepter, rising from the throne. "How does the son of my highest priest allow the sacred bull to die over a crisis of faith?"

Heat rose to Seti's cheeks. His father trembled beside

him.

"An entire night passed, and no one noticed the bull was missing? Do you not have guards in the stable at night? This boy just grabs the bull and leaves the stable with it? How does this happen?"

The women froze mid-motion.

"We don't have guards—" his father started.

"You don't have guards for the sacred animals? They house the gods! Do you see the state Egypt is in? I can blame Moshe for all that's happened in my kingdom except this. This is your fault." He aimed his scepter at Seti like a spear.

"I didn't kill it on purpose." Seti's voice broke.

"You didn't kill it on purpose?" Pharaoh descended several steps, eyeing Seti with malice. "There's a strict protocol for removing a sacred animal from the stable. You were aware of the procedure, were you not? Yet you chose to do it your way. Did you make the bull distinguishable from the other livestock?"

Kipuri stepped forward, hands clasped behind him. "No, he did not, my lord. The bull was unadorned."

"So you didn't kill it on purpose. Yet you took it from the stable without following protocol. How is that not on purpose? How did you think the plague was supposed to know that this was Ptah and not just a bull?"

"My lord?" the guard said again, inching a step into the throne room.

"Do not interrupt me!" Pharaoh's bark sent the guard scurrying to the side door. "Tell me, what did you think when you found the stable locked? It was locked, wasn't it?"

"The gate was closed but not locked, my lord," Kipuri said.

"It wasn't locked?" Must Pharaoh repeat everything?

"No, my lord. But it was closed. And it was late at night when he took the bull out, my lord. He brought his horse in but took the bull while we were asleep."

Exasperated, Seti turned to Kipuri. "Can I defend

myself?"

"First of all, kill the horse," Pharaoh said.

Seti spun back to Pharaoh, his breath catching.

"A horse is a small price to pay for a prophetic bull. Feed it to the crocodiles."

"Let me explain—" Seti started.

"But the life of a man is an even smaller price to pay for such a god. Kill him too, right here on my steps. Then send the body with the horse." Pharaoh pointed at the step he stood on.

A spear-toting guard stepped forward from behind the women.

"No!" Ameneten's hands shot to his mouth.

"Wait—" Seti glanced at his trembling father and fought to keep his knees from buckling.

Ameneten dropped to the floor, head bowed, hands extended in front of him. "Pharaoh, please. I beg you to hear our proposal."

The breath left Seti's lungs at the sight of his father prostrate on the floor.

"And what do you propose, Ameneten?"

All eyes turned toward Seti's father. He lifted his head just high enough to speak. "We have discussed the issue and agreed on what we hope will be a suitable punishment." His voice trembled despite his obvious attempt to hide it. "In the past, when the Api bull dies, a search is made for its successor. Ptah is without a dwelling place until we find one and consecrate it. We thought it best to allow Seti to assemble a team and search for a replacement. His priestly heritage, scribal studies, and inheritance are forfeit, transferring to my second son, Kabelo."

Pharaoh descended the remainder of the steps and marched to Seti, who held his breath and forced himself not to step back. He locked eyes with Pharaoh's.

"That's what you came up with?" Pharaoh's face stopped inches from Seti's.

"Ye-yes, my lord."

"No." Pharaoh's steely, impassive voice vibrated every hair on Seti's body.

"My lord—" his father started.

"No. This boy's life for the bull, along with his horse. Ameneten will assemble the team to find the new bull. This is preposterous. The boy dies, and Ameneten is stripped of his title and heritage for producing such an irresponsible, hideous flaw in Egyptian society. Mark this as the end of the Ameneten priestly—"

"Pharaoh." The voice was deep and commanding.

Pharaoh's back straightened, and his eyes bulged, but he didn't turn. Behind him, a man stood on the far side of the throne room.

Seti's heart caught in his throat. Moshe.

And he wasn't alone. The group crossed the floor toward them.

Pharaoh slowly turned to face Moshe.

As Seti's focus shifted to Moshe's followers, his eyes widened. Eliza. Mouth dry, he whispered her name. She was radiant. As lovely as a spring morning. She followed behind Moshe and Aharon, her gaze taking in the columns and painted tiles of the room. Her scar had faded to a light pink, no longer flaming red as he remembered. Her skin glowed, and her hips peeked from under her tunic. She must be eating well. Had his family not fed her enough?

The heaviness of the past few weeks lifted, replaced with angst and butterflies. The urge to run to her, to take her in his arms, overwhelmed him. He'd tell her everything and hold her face in his hands and kiss the scar away. She was free now.

Free to love him.

Eliza stared at the vast, ornate expanse of the throne room, nearly bumping into Aharon when he halted. She had heard shouting while still in the corridor, but now the room was silent. Everyone focused on the figure in the center of the room, and Eliza stepped out from behind Aharon to get a better look. The man stood motionless, eyes ablaze and mouth set in a firm line.

Pharaoh was wrapped head to toe in linen strips. A brilliant blue tunic trimmed with intricate gold stitching barely covered his muscular form, while a sheer gold cape encircled him. His arm cuffs, bracelets, and jeweled collar lay over the bandages. A tall headdress with golden horns, beaded with carnelian, lapis lazuli, and rubies, adorned his bald head. Even in his thirties, Pharaoh was known for his boyish good looks. With his stunning stance against the backdrop of muraled walls and a carnelian-laced marble floor, his magnificence was marred by boils that ravaged his face.

Behind him, Ameneten rose from a prostrate position, and Eliza drew in a sharp breath. What was he doing here? Normally calm and in control, he now appeared frazzled and shaken. Someone next to him stepped forward. Seti? He caught her eye, and her heart fluttered, a gasp escaping her mouth. She fought the instinct to jump behind Aharon and hide as usual. Instead, she remained still and dug her fingernails into her palms to check if she was dreaming.

Seti's stare bore into her as if trying to say something. Like the priests near him, linen wraps covered his body, but he only wore a simple tunic over them. Thick eyebrows framed his eyes. Though he stood tall, there was something vulnerable about him she didn't recognize. Then, it dawned on her. Pharaoh's angry words were directed at him.

"Rahel," Eliza whispered.

Rahel gripped Eliza's and Tzipporah's hands, mouth wide. The girl looked as if she might float to the ceiling or pass out.

"Moshe." Pharaoh switched to a deceptively relaxed pose and tilted his head. "I see you brought an audience this time. Your family?"

Moshe opened his mouth, but Aharon broke in, pointing at Seti. "Isn't that one of the boys who threw rocks at us?"

Seti shifted his stance as everyone turned to him. His father stepped back in horror.

Pharaoh turned to Seti in shock. "You threw rocks at Moshe?"

"Well," Seti mumbled, "yes, but that was before all this started."

While his father buried his head in his hands, the other priests turned away.

Letting out a chuckle, Pharaoh passed a glance toward his vizier. "This keeps getting better."

Eliza's mind swirled. Seti threw rocks at Moshe? And he's admitting it?

"Where's the other one?" Moshe asked.

Seti shrugged, head still down.

"Eliza," Miera whispered. "It's—"

"Shhhh!" Eliza's heart pounded.

Pharaoh faced Moshe. "I don't think I have smiled once since you've returned. Until now."

"I have received word from God." Moshe's voice was low and sharp.

Pharaoh's smile vanished at once, and he took a deep breath. "Haven't you done enough, Moshe? Don't you see what you're doing to my people? My land?"

"This is what Yahweh, the God of the Hebrews says: 'Let my people go, so that they may worship Me. Otherwise,

I will send all My plagues against you, your officials, and your people, so that you may know that there is no one like Me in all creation. For by this time, I could have stretched out my hand and struck you and your people with a plague to wipe you off the earth. But I have raised you up for this very purpose, that I might display My power to you, and that My name might be proclaimed throughout the earth. Still, you lord it over My people and refuse to let them go.'"

Moshe's voice echoed off the walls, commanding the room. "'Behold, at this time tomorrow, I will rain down the worst hail that has ever fallen on Egypt. So, give orders now to shelter your livestock and everything you have in the field. Every man or beast not brought inside will die when the hail comes down upon them.'"

"There's no livestock left anyway," Pharaoh stated, unmoved.

All eyes turned to Pharaoh—except for Eliza and Seti. They stared at each other, or to be precise, he stared her down, making her squirm. What was Seti doing? Why was he here?

"What do you want me to say?" Pharaoh spread his hands to both the Egyptians and the Hebrews.

"I will be waiting for your answer." Moshe pivoted and pushed past his companions toward the door. Aharon followed, his staff tapping the floor, with the women and Miera trailing behind. But Eliza didn't move. She couldn't. Rahel tugged at her hand, but she pulled away.

Eliza looked to Pharaoh. Fear for her life and anguish for Seti warred within her. *Say something!*

"Eliza," Rahel whispered, grasping Eliza's arm.

"Do you have something to say too?" Pharaoh asked.

She shook her head and retreated. After one last look at Seti, she turned her back and ran for the side door.

The door slammed, and then Eliza and Rahel raced after the others down the broad hall toward the entrance.

"Is that it?" Eliza cried.

Everyone stopped and turned.

"That's it? Aren't you going to wait for his response? We just got here!" she yelled.

"No." Moshe narrowed his eyes. "I came to deliver God's word. It's what He instructed me to do. I allowed you to accompany me as an observer, not to make googly eyes at troublemaking youths!"

Eliza clamped her mouth shut and fell back a step. She had angered the Prince of Egypt.

Moshe marched on, taking long strides. The women struggled to keep up.

A woman and three children wearing bejeweled collars of royalty peered at them from a balcony overlooking the broad hall. A courtier stopped to watch them pass. Two guards revealed themselves, following in the shadows with spears at their sides. Rahel grabbed Eliza's arm, gaining her attention.

"What was that?" Rahel whispered as they hurried.

"What?"

"That priest. The one who threw the rocks. You two couldn't take your eyes off each other."

"Oh?" Eliza spied another guard lurking behind a pillar.

"Eliza!" Rahel hissed. "You know what I'm talking about."

"Shhhh!"

Miera slowed and walked backward in front of them. "That was Seti and his abba!"

Eliza grabbed the girl's shoulders and shook her. "Shut up!"

Eyes widening, Miera raised her hands in defeat. Eliza let go and hurried past her. Fear and anger surged through her veins—fear for Seti and anger at her powerlessness to save him.

Moshe and Aharon nodded at the guards holding open the large doors. The group hurried down the steps to the patterned road, passing an ornamented litter resting on the ground between four carriers who sat, waiting.

Head spinning, Eliza glanced over her shoulder, tempted to run back up the steps. Seti was in trouble with Pharaoh. He recognized her and wouldn't stop staring, his gaze kind and intimidating at the same time. He was trying to tell her something.

"When we return," Rahel whispered. "You're telling me what happened in there."

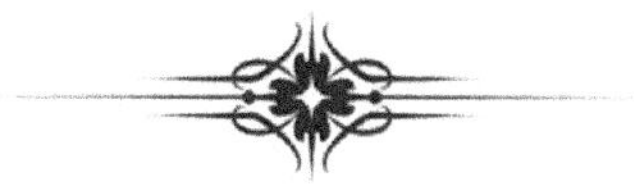

"What are you going to do?" Kipuri asked Pharaoh once the door shut.

Pharaoh's gaze lingered on the exit, brows furrowed, fingers tracing the gold etchings on his scepter. He turned to the priests and Seti, exacerbation in his eyes. After rolling his head back with a throaty moan, he flicked his hand at the priests and ascended the steps to the throne. "Get out of my sight."

Seti started for the door when Pharaoh shouted, "You!"

Freezing mid-step, Seti closed his eyes, waiting for a spear to enter his back.

"As for you," Pharaoh said. "Find the next Api bull as your father proposed. But since I'm allowing you to live, your horse will be forfeit. I want it here tonight. His life shall be given."

Seti was about to protest but held his tongue, not wanting to worsen his fate. He hurried toward the door, not only to escape Pharaoh's wrath, but to catch which direction Eliza headed.

"As you wish. Thank you for sparing his life," his father said behind him.

Chapter 16

"What was that about, Seti?" his father demanded on the ride back to the temple.

Seti didn't answer. He faced the rear, eyeing the guards that followed through the inner courtyard. At any moment, Pharaoh could change his mind, and the guards would pounce on him.

His father wouldn't let up. "You threw rocks at Moshe?"

"It was Sabu," Seti muttered, fixated on what looked like a drawn bow on a balcony.

"I don't care if it was Sabu! You were with him. What were you thinking?"

Kipuri and Sebeki inched away, looking elsewhere.

"It doesn't matter anymore," Seti said, refusing to take his eyes from the guards. "Even so, you can thank Aharon for pointing it out. It's probably what saved me."

His father sat back with a sigh. Seti didn't move, despite his father's glare.

"What am I going to do with you, Seti?"

"Exactly as you said you would." Seti didn't have time for this. He had to warn Sabu and Hoshea of the coming storm. Chewy must stay hidden. And, most of all, he couldn't let the sweet image of Eliza fade from his mind.

"Well, when we get back," Ameneten swiped the sweat

from his forehead, "we're taking Chewy to the palace."

At this, Seti returned his father's glare but held his tongue. His father had lost control of his life, his heritage, and had almost lost his son. Obeying Pharaoh would save him and Seti, but Moshe's declaration nullified everything. "Pharaoh's not getting Chewy."

Sebeki shifted in his seat.

"Seti." His father's voice was stern. "Be thankful Pharaoh didn't have you speared. The horse is the least of our concerns."

"No. I'm not letting Pharaoh or anyone else get Chewy."

Ameneten took a deep breath and said through clenched teeth, "When we get back, you will ready Chewy, and we're going back to the palace."

Seti gripped the ivory rail. He braced himself and said with forced calmness, "Did you not hear Moshe? Forget about the Api bull and Pharaoh. Everything that's happened is because Pharaoh won't comply with the Hebrew God. We face destruction by the worst hailstorm in our history. Yet, your biggest concern is pleasing Pharaoh."

His father didn't answer.

Seti continued. "Moshe's God could have killed us all with a single plague and wiped out the entire nation, but He didn't. Why? Because He's warning us. And you can't see it, Jt. We are stuck in the crosshairs of a war between gods. His God doesn't want to kill us, but we will be held responsible for how we respond. He's making a point, and if we don't comply, we'll die."

Kipuri and Sebeki faced him, eyes wide. His father stared. "What makes you think that?"

"Why am I the only one here who understands this?" Seti asked in disbelief. "Did any of you listen to what Moshe said? I was distracted, yet I understood. Moshe is speaking on behalf of his God. This isn't Moshe punishing us. Or *our* gods. His God proclaimed He raised up Pharaoh for this purpose, and that He will display His power over him. That's why Pharaoh won't listen. The Hebrew God isn't finished displaying His power yet. Pharaoh is a son of the gods, right? The spirits of Isis and Osiris are in him. This is a war between gods, and the Hebrew God wants us to witness it. Moshe's God wants His people to see it and follow Him. His God's destroying everything that gives witness to our gods. And if we get in the way, we'll die too."

Did Seti help the Hebrew God by taking the Api bull out during the plague? A chill shot through him at the thought. But what god needed human help?

The three priests stared, dumbstruck.

"And your main concern is pleasing Pharaoh." Seti sat back in his seat and crossed his arms, looking away.

They finished the ride in silence. He had to find Sabu and Hoshea. They should have finished harvesting Sabu's field by now. Seti had given Sabu the names of those praying in the temple the other day, but it was up to him to locate them.

Moshe said the hailstorm would start tomorrow morning. He didn't give Pharaoh a chance to barter or negotiate; he simply said he'd be waiting for a response. That meant he'd be staying nearby, and so would Eliza and her sister—if they stayed with Moshe.

There was no denying his feelings for Eliza now. Her strength radiated beauty. The scar testified to her love for her sister and a willingness to accept what she deserved. Egyptians didn't form relationships with their Hebrew slaves—such a thing was unthinkable. Priests were strictly forbidden from it. But Seti was no longer destined for the priesthood, and Eliza was no longer a slave. He'd been so stuck on himself that he never noticed the girl working under his roof, living in an outhouse. Fool. He had to find her.

At the temple, Seti sprang from the litter and flew up the steps. He grabbed oats and a jug of water from the kitchen and dashed to the room where he'd left Chewy. After dropping the oats on the bed, Seti wrapped his arms around Chewy's neck in a tight hug.

"I'm sorry, Chewy. Don't worry, no one's going to get you. I promise." The room reeked of manure and urine. Clumps of hair scattered along the floor like tumbleweeds. "Soon, I'll take you for a walk and a run. I'm sorry I had to keep you here."

"Seti!" His father's voice sounded from outside the window. Seti peered down at his father, climbing the hill to the front of the temple. He must have thought Chewy was still in the stable.

"Don't worry. I'll be back," Seti whispered and kissed Chewy's nose.

He left the room, gently shut the door, and darted down the winding steps to the first floor as his father entered the foyer.

"Seti, let's go. Where's Chewy?" Ameneten demanded.

Seti opened his mouth to protest when his father interrupted. "Let's go. I don't need Pharaoh's guards coming after us. And Pharaoh might change his mind if we delay. I checked the stable. Where's the horse?"

His father had the key to the stable?

"You didn't see him?" Seti asked. "That's where I left him."

"He's not there. Did you hide him?"

"Well, wouldn't you hide me?" Seti asked.

His father did a double-take at the question. "That's different."

"No—"

"Seti, where is he?" His father's voice rose to a shrill, and Seti's eyes widened.

"In the stable, last I saw."

Still singing, the choir watched from where they stood. Stragglers stopped praying and sat up to look. His father was losing control.

"You're coming with me." His father grabbed Seti's arm, startling him, and yanked him toward the entrance. They descended the steps and headed around to the hill. Above, Chewy's head stuck out the window, watching. Seti gulped and hoped Chewy would pull his head back inside. If his father looked up, it was over.

"As soon as the storm is over, you'll make your announcement about the bull, and we'll start preparing for the viewing ceremony. The people are asking questions. I'm done lying for you."

"When did you lie for me?"

His father's behavior was so uncharacteristic that shame coursed through Seti's veins. He didn't fight his father's manhandling or dare say anything else. Things were about to get worse.

Ameneten unlocked the stable, and together they lifted the crossbar. The doors creaked open, noon sunlight spilling across the straw-strewn floor. The stream gurgled at their feet.

"Where is he?" Ameneten demanded.

Seti followed a couple steps behind and stopped. The sacred animals were stalled against the north wall, ten horse stalls lined the south wall, and storage closets and food bins lined the east wall. Beyond that, a larger room housed the chariots, ornaments, and dressings.

"You said he was here. I don't see him." His father searched the stalls.

"I hid him in the back," Seti lied. He squeezed his eyes shut at the thought of his father's face when he'd learn the truth.

"By the chariots?"

"Yes."

His father marched to the back room, disappearing in the dark. Seti grabbed a set of reins from the wall and harnessed the nearest horse. By the time his father emerged from the back, Seti had led the horse outside.

"What are you doing?"

Seti shut the doors, avoiding his father's face.

"Seti!"

"I have to warn Sabu and Hoshea." He pulled the crossbar down and secured it with a large rock. "I'm sorry, Jt. You'll be safe in there."

His father shouted in protest and shook the doors to no avail.

Seti mounted the horse. He had never ridden a horse other than Chewy and was unsure how to handle one he didn't know. He stroked the mane gingerly as they rode up the hill. Halfway to the top, Seti slapped the reins, and the animal bolted, forcing Seti to grab his mane. He caught his breath, gave a nervous chuckle, and gripped the horse tightly with his legs as they sprinted toward the farms of On.

Fields lined the east side of the Nile, separating On from Goshen farther north.

Ahead, the pastures behind Sabu's house had been completely harvested. Seti stopped the horse at the small brick house and jumped from it, stumbling to the ground.

"Sabu!" He struggled to his feet and raced up the walkway to the door. No one answered. He returned to the horse, heaved himself onto its back, and headed down the road.

Private farms, yet to be reaped, lined the gravel road. Not a soul was outside. Shielding his eyes from the sun, Seti searched up and down the road to the horizon but saw no one.

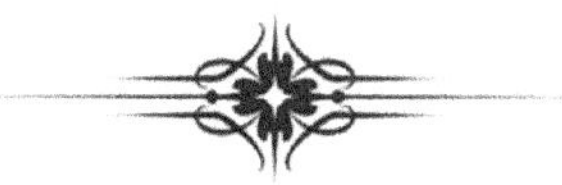

After reaching the marketplace, Moshe and the group stopped in front of the linen shop before parting ways.

"Stay in the shop until the storm is over. If the

Egyptians return to work, I expect you to as well until Pharaoh allows us to leave," Aharon instructed them.

"Yes, thank you for letting us come," Rahel replied.

Moshe eyed Eliza with disdain before turning away. Eliza gave Aharon a nod but kept her face from Moshe. She had made a fool of herself at the palace. Hugging herself tightly, she stood to the side as the women wished the girls goodnight before heading to another building.

When the girls entered the shop, Rahel slammed the door and demanded, "Tell me. Who was that?"

"That was Seti. He's the one who saved her when she was whipped," Miera answered for her.

"Miera." Eliza rolled her eyes.

"What?" Rahel's gaze darted between Miera and Eliza. "You never told me about this. He saved you? What happened? Who is he?"

Eliza sat on a nearby bench, her fingers touching her scar. It no longer hurt unless pressure was applied. She had not told Rahel or anyone else the full story.

Miera opened her mouth to speak, but Eliza held up her hand. "I was due to receive twenty-five lashes, but Seti stepped between his ima and me after five."

"Wait—his ima? Twenty-five?"

"We worked for his family. I put the frog guts in his ima's stew. It was either the twenty-five lashes or Miera and I go to the brick fields. So, I chose the lashes. And as it was happening, he—he just stepped in and shielded me."

Rahel sat across from her, concern written on her face.

Eliza welled up with tears. "Then his ima banished him from their home. Because of me." Her voice quivered.

"Eliza has been secretly fond of him for years." Miera took a seat beside her sister.

Was it that obvious?

"Why didn't you tell me?" Rahel's gentle voice eased Eliza's trembling heart.

Eliza shook her head. "I was embarrassed. I didn't

want him to get into more trouble. He's studying to be a priest, and I didn't want anybody knowing I had feelings for an Egyptian priest. That's absurd. Forbidden."

"Everyone saw what he did," Miera said.

"Only those who were there."

"Well, the way he stared at you in the palace, I think he's fond of you too." A faint smile etched Rahel's lips.

"He can't be. It will ruin him!" Eliza clenched her fists.

Rahel stared, her hand on top of Eliza's. "Something tells me he's already in trouble. And I don't think it's because of you."

"I hope not."

"He's a troublemaker anyway," Miera said.

"No, he's not." Eliza shook her head.

A moment of silence passed.

"I wish you had told me, Eliza. I'm your best friend. I care about you. I would tell you if it were me," Rahel said.

"I know. I'm sorry. Truly." Tears streamed down her cheeks. There was no fighting them now, and it felt good to get them out.

Rahel smiled. "I mean, he is handsome."

Eliza giggled between sniffles and wiped her nose with the back of her hand. Even with a red face and wrapped in linen strips, Seti was still as handsome as ever. His dark hair had grown back around his angular face. Thick eyebrows framed gentle brown eyes. He inherited his father's towering stance and broad shoulders.

When Lumeri came around, Seti would shift from arrogance and obnoxiousness to a gentle protector, his energies directed toward her well-being. The transformation fascinated Eliza. Even before Lumeri, there had always been a lucky girl he'd make the "switch" for. Eliza learned quickly what she wanted in a man.

But it wasn't just that. He distinguished himself from other young men—strong drink or sensual pleasures didn't rule his heart. Instead, he found contentment in the quiet peace of a sparkling night sky, the mystery of an open scroll, a sweet melody of strings and lutes, and a deep devotion to the gods he loved.

She rested her head against the wall and closed her eyes, wishing she had said something at the palace. Words to keep her there longer, to help him. But the shock of seeing him had silenced her as usual. He had called it the "scared little kitten" act.

"I don't think I'll ever see him again." Her whisper carried despair.

"Moshe doesn't like him," Miera said. "Seti's not that nice anyway. He just barks orders."

Eliza shook her head.

"Well, I understand. If somebody threw rocks at you, would you like them?" Rahel asked before turning to Eliza. "I can't believe you're in love!"

"I'm not in love," Eliza said.

"Look at you! Right now, you're daydreaming about him. You're in love. You used to tease me all the time about my love for Hoshea. Now here you are." Rahel laughed.

"Yeah, maybe I am, I guess." Eliza shot Rahel a tentative smile. "But it's futile. I'll never see him again. We're going to Canaan soon, and he'll be a priest in a few years. To Egyptian gods."

"Well, my feelings for Hoshea are futile too. He's way older than me and hates me."

Eliza sighed. She couldn't have imagined anyone dominating her thoughts the way Seti did.

Precious time slipped by as Seti searched for the pyramid slaves. How long before someone discovered his father missing? Or found him in the stable? The plan was to warn Sabu and Hoshea and return to free his father before anyone found out. Though his father would have mercy on him, others wouldn't. If discovered, Seti would be accused of stealing the horse, disobeying Pharaoh, and imprisoning a priest. The ambition he had set out with had long faded, and a cloud of hopelessness hung over him. The longer he roamed the streets, the more questions and doubts about his fate flooded his mind.

While most Egyptians nursed their boils indoors, a few painfully toiled at their crops, leaving the city unusually quiet. Evening had settled in by the time he spotted the large group in the distance. A surge of energy jolted Seti, and he spurred the horse to a sprint.

A small mud-brick house and a half-built stable fronted a widespread pasture. At the far end, several rows of slaves worked the field. One line of men branched off from the harvesters, stretching to the stable. While those at the front cut barley with sickles, others bundled the stalks and passed them down the line to be stacked in the empty stalls. They worked as systematically as they had on the pyramid.

As Seti approached, he assessed their rapid progress, amazed at their efficiency. An uplifting tune rumbled across the field, causing him to pause. Singing. Sweaty, laboring men sang joyfully in the hot sun. Did they do this often?

"Come to check on us?"

Seti snapped out of his bewilderment and glanced around.

In the stable near two neatly stacked walls of barley bundles, Hoshea stood, every bit of the strapping commander that he was. He wiped sweat from his brow, panting in the dry heat, eyes on Seti.

In one fluid motion, Seti leaped from the horse, beaming.

"My lord?" Hoshea asked, catching a bundle tossed to him.

Seti spread his hands and gazed at the slaves once

more. "It's incredible."

A grin crossed Hoshea's face as he tossed the barley bundle on top of the working pile. He raised his eyebrows at Seti.

"What are they singing?" Seti asked.

Before Hoshea could answer, the back door of the house slammed. Sabu followed a blistered, elderly man down the stone steps. Both carried twine and empty sacks. It was the man from the temple—the one whose show of grief pierced Seti's heart. Though feeble and scabbed, he moved with a bounce in his step as he hurried into the field. Newfound hope spilled from Seti in joyful laughter. He was making a difference.

"Seti!" Sabu jumped from the steps and ran to him.

Feet skipping, Seti hurried to meet Sabu, and the two collided. He lifted him off the ground in a constricting hug, pinning his arms to his sides.

"Easy! Easy, Seti!" Sabu squeaked in a pained whisper.

After releasing his friend, Seti looked him over. "You look terrible."

Sabu wore nothing but a loincloth. If not for the blisters and boils, he'd blend in with the slaves. Dirt caked his bare feet and sunburned calves, crusting the open blisters. Had he been working alongside them?

Ignoring him, Sabu hissed as he tugged the remainder of a loosened scab from his arm. "Look what you did."

Nothing anchored Seti's appreciation for him like the familiar jabs between old friends, but it was the selfless toil for strangers etched into Sabu's battered body that cemented a respect long overdue. Seti swallowed his rising emotion and handed Sabu his bag. "Oil everything first so the strips stay on without sticking to the wounds. It prevents drying and keeps them clean."

Sabu pulled the jar from the bag and chuckled. He looked at Seti. "You have no idea how glad I am to see you."

"Same."

"Hoshea told—"

"We can talk later." Seti turned to Hoshea. "We're out of time."

"Don't worry, we'll be done before nightfall," Sabu said. "But Hoshea—"

"Listen." Seti shot a glance toward the pristine sky as if expecting clouds to roll in at any moment. "I was in the palace when Moshe arrived."

Hoshea dropped a barley bundle and faced Seti, eyes wide.

"You were in the palace?" He and Sabu asked at the same time.

"I'll tell you all about it later. But Moshe announced the next plague. His God is sending a hailstorm tomorrow morning that will kill everything outside. You have to find shelter. All of you. And make sure the crops are under a roof. He specifically told Pharaoh to send officials to warn everyone."

"Really?" Sabu's sweaty brow knitted. "Why would their God send a storm to kill but warn us beforehand?"

"He's not out to kill the people. He's destroying everything that our gods represent. If we get in the way, we'll be destroyed also."

"Are you sure? I feel like He wants us dead." Sabu pulled another scab from his arm.

"But you're not dead." Clamping his mouth shut, Hoshea dipped his head in a hasty bow.

Sabu ignored him. "We've finished harvesting my fields, and three others besides this one."

That was five families saved. Seti nodded toward Sabu. "I stopped at your house and saw the barley stacked against the wall. If it's left out, all that work will be for nothing."

"You stopped at my house?"

"I was looking for you, Sabu."

"So we have to go back and put it in the stable."

"Whatever you can do before morning."

Hoshea stepped forward. "There's only one farm without a stable. We can secure both before nightfall if we split up."

Seti suppressed the urge to hug him. He ran a hand over his hair, overwhelmed with gratitude. The man never failed to impress.

"Sabu and I can run to town and get refreshments." The words escaped Seti's mouth without thinking. There was no food in town. And they didn't have time. Or money.

Hoshea shrugged. "We've been drinking from the irrigation streams, and the owners fed us. They might not be able to help, but they've been gracious."

Drawing in a breath, Seti inwardly thanked Osiris before he caught himself. Why would Osiris hurt his people, ignore the harvests, but nourish the slaves? He shook his head and refocused. Time was running out. "Good. I can't stay long. My jt's been locked in the temple stable since early this afternoon."

"What?" Sabu's eyes widened, and he covered a smile with his hand.

Seti ran a hand over his hair again. There was so much to tell but no time. He hated to leave Sabu not knowing if he'd see him again. "I'll tell you later. So much has happened. But it's going to take me till nightfall to get back. Meet me on My Mesa after the storm. I don't know how long it'll last." He turned to Hoshea. "Ride out the storm somewhere, then take the men back to the pyramid."

Hoshea bowed.

How had he not known Hoshea after all these years? And now, like with Eliza, it was too late. He bit his lip and cleared his throat. "I'm sorry I hadn't made the effort to know you earlier, Hoshea."

Hoshea straightened, the corner of his mouth lifting into a slight smile. "We shall meet again."

"I don't know about that. You'll be leaving soon."

"Well then." A hint of surprise lifted Hoshea's voice. He gave a slight bow. "You have left a lasting impression on me as well."

Seti's heart tugged at him, and he swallowed. He turned to the horse, not daring to let the slave see his surfacing emotions. Regret for his past blindness. Wasted time. A wasted life.

"Where's Chewy?" Sabu nodded toward the horse.

"Hidden." Seti's voice caught in his throat. He couldn't face either of them. He quickly mounted and turned the horse toward the road. "I'll see you at My Mesa."

He didn't want to leave. Didn't want to go back to that temple. With the joyous tune at his back, he sighed and hurried back to his father.

The last sliver of the sun had disappeared below the horizon by the time Seti reached the temple stable. As he approached, it became apparent that the door's crossbar was not secured. Maybe he was just looking at it from a bad angle. He jumped from the horse and ran to the stable door. The rock used to secure it now lay on the ground. A chill shot up his spine. He had been caught. His heart pounded against his chest, and he placed his forehead against the door to gather his thoughts. Now what? After a moment, he locked eyes with the horse. Seti could run. But he'd promised his father he wouldn't.

"Seti?" His father straightened as Seti opened the curtain to the pool room.

Seti stopped, at a loss of words. His father, Sebecki, Kipuri, Asmuri, Ipuur, and Amoshe lounged in the purification pool, their linen strips piled in an oily heap on the ledge. While they regarded him with indifference, his father's eyes penetrated deep within him. Did they not know?

Seti didn't move.

"You and I are going to have a word when I get out." His father's voice was grave.

The others looked from Seti to his father and back to Seti again.

Seti acknowledged him with a slight bow, pulled the curtain shut, and left.

Seti waited on the windowsill of his room. The sky had darkened to a deep blue, and the first stars popped into view. He had never experienced a storm before. Where were the clouds?

The door opened, and his father entered, wrapped in a towel. He shut the door and raised a face hardened for battle. Seti nodded, climbed down, and slowly sat on the end of the bed, ready for his lashing. His father remained standing.

"I swam through the stream under the stable gate, Seti, if you're wondering how I got out."

Seti was stunned. He hadn't thought of that.

"I hope you returned the horse."

"I have, but the door's locked. I tied him to the tree."

His father stepped closer, arms crossed. He dropped his gaze to the floor.

"I'm sorry." Seti's voice cracked. "I had to do it. I needed a horse, and I needed to warn Sabu."

The betrayal on his father's face stung. His father had covered for him, not saying a word to the other priests. Nothing Seti could say would alleviate the pain he'd caused.

His father gazed at Seti. "What are you hiding from me, Seti?"

"What do you mean?"

"You said you needed to warn Sabu and Hoshea. What's going on?"

That was in the stable. Seti had blurted Hoshea's name when shutting his father in. No more lies. "I recruited the pyramid slaves to harvest the fields and put Sabu in charge."

"You removed the slaves from the pyramid?" Ameneten's voice rose a notch, as if the stake Seti had plunged into his heart twisted.

Seti winced but couldn't back down. Not now. "The pyramid can wait a few days. There are more pressing issues." Why couldn't his father be thankful for the harvests?

"I don't believe this." Hands clawing at his blistered, bald head, his father turned away.

"They will return. I told them to finish up and seek shelter."

"Seti—"

"Jt, listen. You know the farmers lost their livestock in the plague. It's the middle of harvest season. The crops will die, and people will lose their income. The farmers can't harvest without their livestock. I sat in the foyer last week and saw the devastation on their faces. They were crying, begging the gods. We have the means to help them, and I couldn't ignore that. Jt, even Sabu was at a loss. His sisters and Nala were trying to reap it all by hand. They depend on their crops."

"They should depend on the gods, not the crop."

"And the gods used me to help them."

"Pharaoh will have my head. It's the gods that want the pyramids done. Souls are waiting on us!"

"Pharaoh doesn't have to know. What does he care about our pyramid anyway? Besides, he's not interested in helping, or he would have had the fields harvested himself."

His father sat beside him, hands on his knees. He shook his head.

"Did he send officials to warn the cities about the storm?" Seti asked. "I didn't see anyone while I was out. No one I talked to knew about it. What's Pharaoh doing?"

"You were doing all this without my knowledge? Behind my back?"

Seti wasn't getting through to him. "You said the pyramids come first. I was going to have them back before you returned."

After a moment of silence, his father stood. "Chewy must go to the palace. Pharaoh wants him there tonight. He's going to send men here to get him, and they might take you as well. He had mercy on you, Seti, and yet you disobeyed him."

"I'm not giving him Chewy."

"I'm not giving him you!"

"It doesn't matter, Jt. We are the least of his worries. The hailstorm is coming, and he will beg Moshe to stop it. But it won't be the end. More plagues will come until Pharaoh lets the Hebrews go."

His father threw up his hands. "What am I supposed to do then? You have any more bright ideas?"

Seti stood and met his father's gaze. "Don't do anything. If Pharaoh wants me, he'll come and get me. If he wants Chewy, he can come for him, but neither of us is going to Pharaoh."

"The bull's ceremonies and your announcement are coming up. You have to find the new bull. You can't stay in this temple forever."

It couldn't have been a worse time for mourning ceremonies. Yet only a small window remained before the body had to be entombed. "I know. And if I ever find the new Api bull, I'll breed him, so we never have to search again."

His father blinked. "What?"

"You'd think that for such a rare animal we would have bred him by now. Set him up with a black cow. We'd always have a bull on hand for Ptah."

Jaw set, his father shook his head.

Seti grasped his shoulders. "Jt, my future wife left me for a god who doesn't care for his people. The Hebrew God used me to save Eliza, and now she's free. I'm banished from home and my studies, I lost my inheritance and my heritage, my name will forever be tarnished. What am I to do? Let

Pharaoh have me. I have brought shame on our family. At least I will die knowing I helped people."

The color drained from his father's face.

Seti let go of him. "I wasted my life chasing after gods who only want to be served. We are slaves. Seeing you work like you do for them, and they don't even respond—I don't want that. The Hebrew God cares for his people. He fights for them and loves them. Our gods don't love."

"We have to serve them. It's our role. It's what keeps the Maat. Order." His father's words sounded flat and empty.

"Why should a god need help? Doesn't that make him weak? I don't know how long Hoshea has been working for you, but he's a remarkable man. And I watched how the slaves work together. It's fascinating, Jt. I never paid attention to them before. I never cared. Just a few months ago, if I'd seen all those farmers crying at the foot of the gods in the foyer, I would have said the same thing as you. I would have never noticed them. In the five years Eliza worked for us, I never once talked to her. I wasted so much time! Now she's gone, and I'll probably never meet another girl like her." The words and feelings that had built up inside now freed, he turned away.

"Seti, the Hebrew God has a hold of your heart."

He spun back to his father. "And is that such a bad thing? I didn't like it at first, but now I'm glad."

The grief and resignation on his father's face shattered Seti's heart. "I—I don't know what I'm supposed to say to that."

What did he expect his father to say? Seti sat, a pain in his chest growing with the realization that his relationship with his father would never again be the same. The loss was unbearable, but Seti could never go back. Not after all he'd seen. Not after Eliza, or Hoshea. "I know one thing."

His father looked at him.

"You have to get more mules for the pyramid slaves. Give them what they need to work. You need to take care of them."

With a huff, his father shook his head and hounded toward the door.

"Jt." Seti shot to his feet, not willing to let him go.

"I've heard enough, Seti. I'm done listening. I have to leave." His father left the room, shutting the door behind him.

Seti dropped to the bed. Perhaps he should have saved that last part for another time. What if Moshe went away after his God stopped the storm? All would go back to normal, right? No, nothing would return to normal. The damage had been done, and the end result would be either a heart of stone or of flesh.

Chapter 17

A rumble of thunder jolted Eliza awake. The dormitory above the linen building was quiet. She sat up on her mat and peered out the window. Gray clouds blanketed the sky, hiding the pale light of the usually bright Egyptian dawn. A cool wind lifted the curls from her face. Refreshing, though chilling. This was it. Her stomach tightened, and she glanced around for Miera or Rahel.

She was alone. She jumped from the mat and dashed down the stairs.

The side door to the loading room flapped open in the breeze. Rahel, Miera, and two Hebrew women stood in the road, faces lifted skyward. Hebrews and the few Egyptians who returned to work lurked in the doorways of their tents, booths, and buildings, watching the mountainous clouds dominate the sky. A shadow befell the nation. God had turned His face away.

A thunderbolt cracked so near it sent Rahel and Miera screaming to Eliza's side, crouching, hands over their ears. Her parents' and brothers' faces flashed through Eliza's mind as she locked eyes with Miera.

Rahel laughed nervously beside her.

"Where are Moshe and Aharon?" Eliza asked.

Both shook their heads. The men wouldn't have returned to Goshen without them, would they? Regret pinged at Eliza's heart for not fleeing there earlier. The three girls had warned neighbors of the coming storm the night before, hoping they would spread the word.

Another lightning bolt and crash of thunder startled the growing crowd, bringing more screams. A heavy sheet of rain hit Eliza's face, and she gasped, closing her eyes. She swept the water away, laughing apprehensively. While Miera bolted for the linen building, Eliza joined hands with Rahel and faced the sky, letting the downpour soak them. The abrasive raindrops stung like the grainy wind of a dust storm. A defiant laugh escaped Rahel's lips before a strong wind swept them off their feet, tossing them onto the ground.

Lightning struck something nearby, and Rahel screamed, while Eliza covered her face and curled into a ball in the muddy road. They didn't wait for the next strike. They jumped to their feet and fled into the linen building. Eliza slammed the door shut and hurried to the window just as a vendor tent rolled by. The rain and wind muffled her shouts to Rahel.

Rahel joined her at the window, clutching her arm. The rolling tent switched directions and came at them with a vengeance, sweeping into the air and twisting in on itself before crashing against the side of the building. The girls jumped back in alarm. More tents tumbled by. A gust of wind shot through the window, knocking them to the floor. Before they could get up, a cold torrent of rain slapped their faces.

Eliza shielded her face. "Cover the window!"

"No. Get out of here!"

With waterlogged hair whipping in every direction, Eliza crawled toward the main room with Rahel at her heels. Miera darted by in a blur.

A clap of thunder shook the walls. Eliza paused and braced herself for the roof to collapse.

"This is crazy!" Rahel screamed.

They reached the main room and pushed the door shut.

Eliza leaned against it, panting. She wiped her face with her hand. With each lightning strike, the lone window on the far side illuminated the room. Horizontal rain poured in, soaking everything. Empty tables slid across the floor. Clothing, tools, and linen spun in a vortex in the middle of the room.

The door burst open, and Eliza fell forward. Two Hebrew women raced inside, followed by three Egyptians, dripping water. They pressed the door shut.

"I want to go home now," Miera cried.

"I've never seen anything like this," one of the Egyptian women gasped before closing her eyes and murmuring spells of protection.

Lightning lit the room, forcing them to shield their eyes.

"Fire!" Miera cried.

Eliza blinked, her vision slow to return. "It's not fire."

"I can't see!"

"Wait, I'm coming," Eliza struggled to make out her sister's cries over the shouts of the women and the noise of rain and thunder. "Cover your eyes!"

"We should have gone home!" Miera's voice wailed from a pile of linen against the east wall, and Eliza crawled toward her.

The drumming of raindrops shifted to a fierce hammering, and the shouting stopped. Eliza lifted her gaze to the ceiling.

"What's happening?" Miera yelled after a moment.

"The gods are stoning us!" someone cried.

Eliza's heart leaped into her throat at the thought.

The door swung open, and two men stumbled in, slamming it shut.

"Eliza!" Miera's contorted face peered out from the linen pile.

Eliza dove into the heap and grabbed her sister, pulling her close. Rahel joined them. The men raced about the room, dragging tables to the walls. They flipped them onto their sides and covered the women with one and the girls with another before ducking behind a third.

Miera covered her ears and cried into Eliza's chest. Indignation coursed through Eliza's veins, rendering her motionless, staring. The storm was nothing like she had imagined. The Lord was destroying everything. Where were her brothers and parents? And Seti? What about those caught unaware in the fields? Would God kill His own people? Goshen offered refuge but not to those who couldn't make it there.

More stragglers burst through the door. How many others had tried to seek shelter but couldn't find any? Stoned by the God of Israel.

Scared, shivering, wet bodies crouched behind the tables lining the north and east walls. Dirt shaken loose from the ceiling landed on Eliza. She searched for cracks in the ceiling with each flash of lightning. The second floor of the building only covered the loading room. They'd either be beaten to death by hail or crushed by the collapsing building.

Miera's grip tightened with each peal of thunder. Rahel leaned against her, face buried in her knees. Hail the size of figs slashed through the window and ricocheted off the walls and tables, bouncing across the floor. Eliza closed her eyes. *Please God, don't kill my family. Please relent.*

He didn't relent. The storm raged at a steady pace into the evening. The yelling had long since ceased, and Eliza's anger had faded into exhaustion, but sleep was impossible. Her stomach rumbled in hunger, her muscles ached from the constant tension, and the hard, wet floor made her backside hurt. Helplessness and abandonment weighed on her soul, God's promise to deliver them all but forgotten. Death awaited in many forms: washed away by the flooding Nile, beaten by hail, crushed beneath collapsing walls, poisoned by contaminated water, or wasted by starvation.

"Eliza? Eliza? Wake up. It's over."

Eliza blinked at the closeness of her sister's face.

"It's over," Miera repeated.

Tables scraped across the stone floor as the others dared to move. Except for a few mumbles from the men, all were silent. Eliza gently pushed Rahel back and glanced around. Sun rays danced across the water-laden floor and peeked through newly formed cracks in the ceiling. But the roof had held up. Linen, tools, baskets, and weaving machines lay scattered throughout the room. After the deafening roar of hail and thunder, her ears rang in the odd silence.

The girls kicked the table away and stood, gingerly moving their stiff joints. One of the men yanked open the door to the loading room, letting more water pour in around their bare feet. Was this what it felt like when Noah emerged from the ark? With her hand shielding her eyes, Eliza stepped outside.

Though several tents plastered against the wall of the linen shop, everything else was gone. The tables, wooden booths, and merchandise—nowhere to be seen. Trees had been stripped bare.

A creeping dread gripped Eliza at the eerie stillness as she scanned for survivors. She sloshed toward the street, Miera on her heels. The mud-brick buildings remained erect but sparse and empty with nothing between them. Moshe and Aharon had to be near. How did they travel to the palace during the storm?

A horse, soaked and lifeless, lay in the street, but it wasn't alone. Cats, birds, and vermin killed during the storm mixed with corpses from previous plagues, some floating, others bunched in piles.

Nausea flamed up her throat. Did God have no mercy? Warning or not, this was heinous. But the sky's beauty contrasted the battered landscape.

The setting sun chased the dark clouds east. Despite the

danger they held, the fluffy layered clouds glowed pink and red along their edges, a lovely image Eliza had never seen before. Wasn't that just like God to follow something horrible with something beautiful?

Seti awoke, soaked, and chilled. He had weathered the storm attempting to calm Chewy, not wanting the priests to hear him. But there was no calming his horse in the unfamiliar violence of the storm, and he had eventually collapsed against the wall, shielding himself with the woven blanket against the pelting hail.

He now joined Chewy at the window and marveled at the sun's rays illuminating the dark blue clouds in the distance. But despite their wonder, they were only a backdrop to the real beauty. Brilliant colors spanned across the sky in an arched band from north to south, taking his breath away.

Seti dashed from the room to find a better view. The colors stretched in a display only the gods could produce. Did this mean the Egyptian gods had won? Maybe the great and powerful Hebrew God wasn't so powerful after all. Moshe said his God would be the one to stop the storm. If the gods had won, then the entire crisis was over. But if the Hebrew God had won, then He truly did command the sky.

Seti leaped down the winding staircase to the foyer and raced to the steps outside. Dead animals, trash, and building materials littered the waterlogged road. The aftermath of the battle of the gods.

The phenomenon in the sky should be recorded. It resembled the colored glares on the temple's glass baubles when the sun hit them just right. Its beauty rivaled the sunsets and night skies. Was this a known event or a sign of a new era? Then, like a dream, the colors faded. Seti bolted down the road in a desperate attempt to reach it, his bare feet slapping in the water. But the faster he ran, the faster the colors withered away.

Seti halted, bent over in defeat, while he struggled to catch his breath. The clouds remained, but the colored arch had vanished.

Eliza emerged from an empty brick building the next morning. No Moshe. No Aharon. No women. Her sister huddled on a rock up the street, crying into her knees. The water flowed around the rock toward the Nile as the light breeze carried a new, putrid stench. Whoever had weathered the storm in the marketplace was gone, leaving it empty and devoid of everything but dead animals, water, and tangled tents. A committee of vultures circled above.

"Anything?" Rahel called from the rooftop of the building across the street.

"Nobody's here!"

"I'm here," a little voice answered.

Eliza spun to the neighboring building. Two young boys peeked out a window. One appeared to be around Miera's age, the other much younger, his thumb tucked in his mouth.

"Who are you looking for?" the older boy asked.

"We're searching for Moshe. His family. Anyone."

"We're looking for food," the younger one added, thumb muffling his words.

The older boy nodded toward some overturned tables nearby. "We hoped there was some left."

"Nothing's left. Everything was blown away," Eliza replied.

"There's wine in here."

"Wine?" Miera jumped from the rock and bounded toward them. "We haven't had anything to drink all day."

Eliza eyed the boys. By their dirty white tunics and unkempt hair, they were clearly domestic slaves. "What brings you two to the marketplace?"

"Hunger."

"What about your masters?"

"They let us go. We were headed home but got hungry."

Miera crashed into the building and leaned through the window where the boys had spoken from. "They let you go?"

Eliza glanced at Rahel on the roof. "What do you mean they let you go?"

"I don't know. They just told us to go. We're going to Goshen. See?" The tall one pointed down the road.

Confused, Eliza ran to the middle of Marketplace Road to view City Street.

A long procession of slaves traveled north, filling the main road that connected Goshen, the marketplace, On, and Menf. Was this it? Was Pharaoh letting them go?

Rahel squealed and disappeared from the roof. She then bounced off the doorstep and took off in a mad dash toward the slaves.

"You didn't know?" one of the boys asked after watching Rahel.

Eliza stood dumbfounded. Miera snatched her hand and pulled. "Come on, let's go!"

Forget searching for Moshe and Aharon. It was time to go home. She and Miera raced after Rahel, leaving the boys behind. The only thing better than freedom would be finding her brothers and parents alive and well. She wouldn't leave Egypt without them.

The street was packed. Young domestic slaves in their dirty tunics mixed with older project and government slaves wearing only loincloths and the men who worked on the brick farms. They crowded the street as far as Eliza could see. They didn't trudge or drag their feet but marched with a bounce to their step. Cheerful chatter and a lively song reached Eliza's ears.

The girls stopped at the edge of the street. Children skipped around them like a stream of water rounding a rock. Heart in her throat, Eliza scanned the crowd for her family or anyone she recognized. Miera squeezed her hand in anticipation. No Egyptians chased after them. The devastation from the hailstorm and the other plagues must have been too much. It appeared the Egyptians had let them go, whether Pharaoh gave them permission or not.

Eliza considered joining the march when Adam broke away from a group of men and grabbed Miera. She squealed as he lifted her into a tight hug and pulled Eliza into his embrace.

"You made it," Eliza gasped into his shoulder.

"Yes, and so did you."

"Oh, Adam, we have so much to tell you." Tears soaked Miera's cheeks.

"Where's Zechariah? Ima and Abba?" Eliza asked.

"Zechariah's coming. I haven't seen Ima or Abba yet. They might be ahead."

He put Miera down but kept her hand in his. "Come on. We'll meet them at home."

The hailstorm meant no scribal studies that morning, and with the priests and scribes preoccupied with the aftermath, Seti had the library to himself. Determined to find answers about the mysterious arch, he gathered as many scrolls as he could hold before retreating to his room.

He paused at the doorway. This would be a good time to research the Api bull. A record for every previous sacred animal—their life, death, dedication, and tomb—was kept in each temple's library.

Scrolls already spilling out of his arms, he shook his head at the thought of adding more and continued through the corridor.

He spread the scrolls across the floor of his room and placed his sandals, jars, the oil lamp, and his woven bag on the corners to hold them open. Seti carefully crawled over them, scrutinizing every symbol. He left the room once for a snack and to feed Chewy but spent the remainder of the afternoon meticulously reading and deciphering. A tiny colored arch in the corner of a scroll caught his eye, though there was no indication of what it was. Seti sighed.

He leaned against the bed and rested his head in his hands, elbows on his knees. The Menf temple library rarely had what he wanted. The oldest records were kept in Giza, but there was no way he'd be allowed there now.

He gazed at the clear blue sky out the window. If Egypt had no information on the arch, then Moshe must know something. Moshe. How Seti would love to sit and converse with the man. He returned his head to his hands and closed his eyes.

Eliza's almond-shaped eyes sparkled as she grinned up at him. He wrapped his arms around her and returned the smile. How could he not? She wore the same braids piled on her head as when he caught her in the stable. His fingers wove into the loose curls at the nape of her neck. She smelled like a roast on a cookstove. Though he held her close enough to kiss her forehead, something stopped him.

She lifted her face to his. "Don't worry, Seti, you're safe with me."

Seti's eyes shot open. A dream. No! It was so real. He

closed his eyes but couldn't go back. Only the memory lingered.

He pushed himself up from the floor, a scroll stuck to his face. He pulled it off and drew his knees to his chest, replaying the dream. *"Don't worry, Seti, you're safe with me."* Finding information on the arch paled in comparison to his desire to be with Eliza.

"His horse was in here."

Seti's mind snapped to the present. Kipuri's voice came from outside. Seti sprang to his feet and ran to the window. The priest and two armed guards locked the stable door. They had come for Chewy. Or Seti. He backed away from the window. Even after the storm and all its devastation, Pharaoh still wanted Chewy. Perhaps Pharaoh anticipated another plague and felt the need to deal with this before things got worse. Or the storm left Pharaoh wanting the bull, renewing his anger. Whatever it was, Seti had not anticipated it.

Did his father know they had come for him? Heart pounding, Seti slipped on his sandals, grabbed his bag, scrambled over his bed, and ran for Chewy's room. He burst through the door and jumped onto the bed. He bounced and landed on Chewy's back but slid off and hit the floor hard with a thud. The horse snorted and inched away. The last application of oil had outlasted the storm. Seti rose and rubbed his tailbone. He tossed a heavy blanket on Chewy's back and then mounted with care.

He guided Chewy down the hall toward the stairs. Adrenaline coursed through his veins, and he held back the urge to run. Chewy's hooves clicked on the winding stairs as they descended. Seti stayed low, clear of the sloping ceiling.

Upon reaching the main floor, he kicked the horse into a mad dash across the foyer, sending dancers and worshippers screaming and lunging out of their way. Kipuri and the men had reached the top of the temple steps when Seti flew past them. Chewy cleared the steps with ease and, upon reaching the road below, reared up on his hind legs with an invigorated whinny. Clinging to his mane, Seti glanced behind at the shouting men. Kipuri's reddened face blazed with fury.

"Go, Chewy!"

Seti took the back roads toward On.

Sabu's house stood out against the flattened fields and darkening sky. After ensuring he wasn't followed, Seti led Chewy to the back of Sabu's stable and slipped behind stacks of flax and barley. Nimrod, tethered to the front corner, raised his head at the sight of them, his stall overflowing with barley bundles.

With a tired sigh, Seti knelt and leaned against the barley. Other than Nimrod's snorts, the place was silent. No night bugs, birds, cats, or even wind. His pulse slowed in the quiet, and he took a sobering breath.

The pretty image of Eliza flashed through his mind. Her sparkling eyes and soft voice. She was out there somewhere. Free. And here he was, hiding in a stable behind his horse. How ironic. The Hebrew God was having His way with him, vindicating her. And she deserved every bit of it. Eliza's God loved her. He could do whatever He wanted with Seti, if that's what it meant for Eliza to be free and justice to be served.

The adrenaline seeped away, leaving him weak and slumped over with sadness. He had done nothing right by her, except setting her free. She had been an easy target for jokes and ridicule—entertainment for him and his friends. He cringed at the thought. He'd been so awful. No wonder she always hid. Was it because of the teasing? Or was she afraid of him?

He thumped his head against the barley bundles, wishing they weren't so soft, regretting running like a fool. He should have confronted Kipuri. Chewy would still be safe. But because he acted in haste, they were now fugitives, and his presence in the stable endangered Sabu's family.

Exhausted, he closed his eyes and willed himself to dream of Eliza again. It was the perfect escape—a spark of joy in a sea of sadness.

"Sabu, there's another horse in the stable!" a woman shouted.

Seti's eyes shot open after being asleep. Chewy had been spotted. He peered over the barley as Sabu hopped down the steps and moving toward him.

"Where?"

"In the back, behind the barley."

When Sabu rounded the corner, he startled. "Seti?"

"Sabu." Seti went to Sabu and embraced him.

"How long have you been here?" Sabu asked.

"Not long," Seti lied.

"You look like you've been sleeping."

"I haven't."

"You're hiding." Nala joined them. She tucked a loose strand of black hair behind her ear and raised a brow, one hand holding a shawl closed around her shoulders.

"No." Seti shook his head, eyes darting to Chewy.

Sabu squinted. "I'm not stupid, Seti. You're a terrible liar. We were supposed to meet at the mesa later. What's going on?"

"Come in the house. I'll fix you something to eat," Nala said.

Seti nodded, stomach gurgling at the mention of food.

Sabu's sisters and mother slept in the back room. The household must have been headed to bed when Nala spotted Chewy. He pressed his lips together and sat on a soft rug at the table, regretting the inconvenience to them.

Sabu placed a small lantern on the table between them, filling the three-room single-floor home with a soft orange glow. Two cups of barley beer were set before them.

Nala broke the loaf of bread in the dark and set a plate of leftover crocodile meat in front of him. It had been sitting out but still emanated a savory, broiled aroma. "We already ate. Crocodile is all we have left until we get the barley and flax threshed."

"Croc is wonderful." Seti grabbed the slab of rubbery, warm meat and tore a chunk off with his teeth. Between bites, he filled his mouth with bread, then washed it down with beer.

"The hail didn't harm the wheat, thankfully," Sabu said. "I was worried we'd lose it, but it's still going strong. I think we'll be alright for now."

Seti smiled and nodded, unable to form words with his mouth full. He wiped his mouth with his bandaged arm when he finished and sat back against the wall, his hand resting on his stomach.

Sabu also leaned against the wall, arms crossed. "Now tell me why you're hiding in my stable, what happened at the palace, and about your jt."

"There's a lot to tell."

"You two catch up. I'm going to bed." Nala kissed her husband on the cheek.

Before she left, Seti thanked her for the meal.

He recounted the events at the palace, beginning with Pharaoh's demands and his encounter with Moshe. He told how Aharon remembered them throwing rocks and that it may have saved him from certain death, then went on to explain how he hid Chewy in the temple, stole the horse, and locked his father in the stable. By the time Seti finished with the guards and Kipuri searching for him, the oil lamp was nearly dry, illuminating only their faces, as they leaned toward it.

"I don't think those were guards, Seti," Sabu said. "They were probably from Pharaoh's army. He doesn't send palace guards out like that."

"That's even worse. I should have stayed and pretended I didn't know where Chewy was. If they were to take me, then so be it. But I panicked and ran." Seti hit the table with his fist.

Sabu glanced toward the curtained doorway to the back room before reminding Seti to lower his voice. "Pharaoh would have you killed if they returned with you."

"It would be better than this! What if they take my parents or Kabelo to get to me?"

"You better not wake anybody up." Sabu reached over to smack Seti in the temple, but Seti dodged the blow.

"I know. Sorry," Seti whispered.

"I heard that during the storm, Pharaoh promised Moshe he'd let them all go. But when the storm stopped, he changed his mind. He's irrational right now."

"Where'd you hear that?"

"In the city. I think you should lie low until everything blows over. Pharaoh will simmer down."

"There are going to be more plagues, Sabu." Seti leaned into the light again. "Nothing will simmer down. It's like birth pangs—they'll get more intense and frequent until the Hebrews are allowed to leave."

Sabu shifted on the floor. "Are you sure?"

"The hailstorm was the seventh plague. Seventh. It's not going to stop until Moshe's God gets what He wants."

How would Sabu react if Seti said he believed Moshe? And if he believed Moshe, then he'd have to believe that the Hebrew God won the battle in the sky. Seti rested his face in his palm. Was it really a battle between gods or just the weather? The constant questioning exhausted him. He fought to keep his eyes open.

"Pharaoh's being stubborn," Sabu said. "He's the son of Isis, so he thinks if he holds out long enough, the Hebrew god will give in."

"And destroy Egypt in the process."

Seti's body diverted its remaining energy to the food

in his stomach. He burped and slumped forward. "I need to sleep."

Sabu led him to the roof. Perfect. Seti hadn't slept on a roof patio since moving to the villa. Sabu's prized pomegranate trees lay dead and leafless from the hail, the canopy and sleeping mat long gone. He laid out a dry mat for Seti before leaving him alone.

Seti sprawled on the mat. There was no gazing at the stars tonight. He let his eyelids have their way and slept.

Chapter 18

At the sound of rickety chariot wheels on gravel, Seti approached the roof edge. A full army lined the road in front of Sabu's house. Archers, spearmen, foot soldiers, and chariots as far as the eye could see stood waiting. The commander spoke with Sabu, whose back was to the house. Sabu then turned and pointed to Seti, and the eyes of the commander locked with Seti's. The commander raised his scepter, and the army charged.

Seti's eyes popped open. He shuddered, the mat beneath him soaked in sweat. The heat baked the linen wraps to his skin. Raising a hand, he blocked the scorching sun from his eyes and forced his pounding heart to slow. The voices of Sabu and Nala reached his ears. He lay still, listening, but the words were muffled by the bustle of activity below and the snorting horses. Seti heard his name and sat up, pushing the knit blanket aside. The putrid air brought back the events of the day before. He had run from the temple after promising his father he wouldn't. He and Chewy had become fugitives.

He yawned and peered over the ledge of the roof. Sabu fumbled as he untied Nimrod.

"Where are you going?" Seti called.

Sabu's head jerked up.

Seti's dream came back clear as day, and his muscles tensed. He narrowed his eyes. At this time of day, Sabu should be in the field, not hitching his horse. He never left his house this early.

"I, well, I—"

"Where, Sabu?" The hair on the back of his neck stood up at Sabu's nervous reaction. Would his best friend turn him in? Or was Seti losing his mind?

Sabu straightened. "I'm going to your pyramid. I told Hoshea I'd meet him there after the storm. Afterward, I planned to go to the mesa, but now you're here."

The pyramid? "What words are you having with Hoshea?"

Sabu stepped from the shadow of the stable and shielded his eyes. "Why don't you come with me?"

Seti scoffed and turned away. *Since when do I need to be invited to my own pyramid?* He slipped on his sandals, grabbed his woven bag, and hurried down the steps.

When he reached the stable, Sabu had already fastened his chariot to Nimrod. A leather sack lay in the bottom. Without taking his eyes from Sabu, Seti fetched Chewy and mounted. Silently, he followed.

As they kept to the edge of On, an eerie emptiness stilled the air. Slaves were nowhere to be seen. Either Pharaoh had let them go, or they fled to Goshen to ride out the storm. Hoshea might not even be at the pyramid.

The once neat piles of sun-dried carcasses were now strewn all over, rotting flesh soaked and bloated once again. A fresh odor of death filled the air and poisoned the flooded streets. Like the weary, blistered faces of its citizens, the nation was unrecognizable.

Seti kept a watchful eye on Sabu. His friend had spent a considerable amount of time with Hoshea, perhaps developing a friendship, and now he visited him at his leisure?

Occasionally, Sabu peeked his way. Seti had never

asked how he weathered the storm or anything about the harvests or managing the slaves. They didn't have much time to talk the day they met in the field, and last night the conversation centered around Seti's ordeals. Seti turned his face in shame. He'd hit something if he could. Break something. If Sabu wanted to turn him in, he had good reason to.

The ride to the pyramid took longer than usual without racing. Sabu's leisurely pace seemed intentional. To torture Seti's patience? Or to urge him to talk? Nope. Sabu wasn't going to win this one. Seti wouldn't say a word, not even to hasten him. If Sabu wanted to meander, so be it. Seti laid his head on Chewy's neck and groaned.

They passed the first pyramid. Not a single worker anywhere. The Ameneten pyramid was next, but still too far away to see if the slaves continued to work. If they didn't, he wouldn't be surprised. They might as well flee while they had the chance. He would. A small part of him hoped they had left just to spite Sabu.

His heart fell when hundreds of laboring bodies came into focus. What were these crazy slaves doing? He turned to Sabu, mouth open, but said nothing. He'd be a fool to not know the intentions of his own slaves.

Hoshea met them at the entrance to the tunnel, two-thirds of the way up the pyramid. He waited for Seti to dismount and Sabu to step from his chariot before bowing.

"You don't have to bow before him. He's not in charge anymore." Seti nodded toward Sabu. "That was only while you harvested the farms."

Sabu flashed him a scowl before handing Hoshea the leather sack from the bottom of his chariot. After opening it, Hoshea peered inside and pulled out a chunk of beef and bread. His face lit with surprise.

A grin crossed Sabu's face. "It's a goodbye gift."

Seti's mouth hung open. "Where'd you get that? I thought all you had left was dried crocodile."

"I was saving it to celebrate the harvest but decided to give it to Hoshea instead for saving my crop."

"*I* saved your crop!"

Sabu had made him look like a fool. He knew Seti wouldn't have anything to give. Seeing the shocked faces staring at him, Seti straightened and regained his composure. "I see you two are friends now."

"Well, we did spend the last five days together." Aggravation riddled Sabu's tone. "And had a lot of interesting conversations."

"I bet."

Hoshea stuffed the items into the sack and handed it back to Sabu.

"No, keep it." Sabu thrust the sack at Hoshea but kept his gaze on Seti.

"It's not worth it if it's going to make him jealous," Hoshea said.

"I'm not jealous!"

"You're acting like it!" Sabu shot back.

Hoshea stepped back, both hands up. "Thank you, but no thank you."

"You weren't supposed to become friends!" Seti stepped toward Sabu. "He's my slave!"

"Since when did you care about your slaves? Oh yeah, you're in love with one, and now Hoshea—"

Seti pounced on Sabu, knocking him to the ground. The beef and bread toppled from the sack at Hoshea's feet. The frustration and uncertainty of the past few weeks exploded in a series of blows to Sabu's face.

Seti roared insults as he straddled Sabu, both fists swinging.

Sabu rolled his weight, and Seti dropped beside him. They struggled until he pinned Seti to the ground with his knee, railing blows on his face. Seti screamed incoherently and grabbed Sabu's wrists, pushing him away. A headbutt from Sabu dazed Seti, blurring his vision. Sabu ripped his wrists free and smacked Seti across the chin. Bucking and kicking, Seti dislodged him. After wiping blood from his face with his forearm, he tackled Sabu, punched him in the nose, and kneed him in the stomach. A cross swing slammed into Sabu's head, splattering the pyramid bricks with blood.

Hoshea backed away from the spit and blood splatter. "I never thought I'd see the day when two Egyptians fought over me. You have the attention of everybody here."

Pausing mid-punch and gasping for breath, Seti scanned their surroundings, while Sabu used the respite to wipe the blood from his face.

Rows and rows of staring slaves quickly returned to work like nothing had happened. Halfway up the pyramid, five soldiers approached in chariots.

Seti jumped to his feet and backed away from the ledge. He glanced around for somewhere to hide, but he had already been seen. Nimrod and Chewy stood in full view.

"What? You're done already?" Sabu spat.

Seti sent Sabu a fiery glare. He tried to speak, but his voice caught. He searched high and wide for an escape route. The path ended at the tunnel. The tunnel ended in the chamber.

Sabu sat up. After spotting the soldiers, he returned Seti's glare. "You don't think—"

Seti didn't know what to think. Had they been followed? Had Sabu tipped them off? "I have to go." He jumped onto Chewy's back.

"Seti—" Sabu yelled.

Seti held up his hand, stopping Sabu. The only escape route was down, head-on into them. He was about to descend when Hoshea jumped in front of Chewy. "Seti, listen!"

Seti blinked at Hoshea's use of his name.

"Go that way." Hoshea pointed to a narrow foot path that split from the main path and wrapped around the side of the pyramid. "I'll slow them down."

With a nod, Seti put his heels into Chewy's sides.

"Take the city route! I'll meet you," Sabu yelled as he hobbled to his chariot.

The implications of Sabu's words were clear. Seti carefully led Chewy up the narrow path and around to the south side of the pyramid. It was too narrow for a horse, and Chewy's hooves slipped on the bricks.

"Careful, Chewy."

The world spun. He gripped the reins as the trail blurred, his head still foggy from the fight. Chewy slipped. Seti's heart leaped into his throat. He swallowed and took a deep breath as Chewy regained his footing. Why did Hoshea send him this way? The trail led up, not down.

He had no choice but to continue. Chewy couldn't turn around. They rounded the west side and then the north and approached the east side again. At this rate, they'd end up trapped at the top.

He halted Chewy before reaching the east side in full view of the soldiers. The tunnel entrance was a good fifteen cubits below. The soldiers ascended toward it, whipping their horses in a frenzy, scattering the slaves off the path.

Sabu charged, and Seti's breath caught in his throat. He'd be killed. He hadn't betrayed him after all. As Nimrod plowed ahead, four of the soldiers pulled their chariots to a halt, moving out of the way, but the last sped on. Nimrod and the approaching horse skidded, swinging both chariots forward. The wooden wheels and sides of the two chariots shattered when they collided, ejecting Sabu and the soldier.

Seti covered his mouth, refraining from screaming out loud.

The remaining four, after watching their comrade go down, continued up the path.

"Go, Chewy!"

Seti forced Chewy off the path and onto the bricks. He had to get off this pyramid. Chewy placed one wobbly hoof in front of the other. It was steeper than Seti had thought. He sucked in a breath through his nostrils as he slid onto

Chewy's neck. He gripped the mane and squeezed his legs, head spinning. Bits of rock and stone broke free. The last thing he needed was to roll down the side of the pyramid with his horse.

"Master!" A Hebrew poked his head over the north corner. "What are you doing? You're supposed to go this way."

Seti exhaled and gladly eased Chewy backward but stopped at what sounded like a war cry. Hoshea stood on top of the pyramid, hands in the air. Three rows of slaves near him dropped the rocks they held. The stones tumbled toward the approaching soldiers, picking up speed as they went. Hebrews below staggered their positions as the rocks bounced past and crashed into the soldiers, flipping chariots and pulling the horses down. Sabu ducked beneath his broken chariot as the stones pummeled it.

"Master, now!" The Hebrew reached for the reins and pulled.

Another path branched off the north end, switch-backing downward. Seti thanked the slave and hurried down.

Once on the ground, he drove Chewy into On. Thanks to Hoshea and Sabu, he gained good headway. They galloped through the empty streets between pyramids and turned toward the grain fields, short-cutting to City Street, where he finally dared to check behind. Two soldiers trailed him. Where had they come from? Chewy bolted, veering onto Marketplace Road.

The marketplace between Menf and On lay deserted, as though a siege had befallen the area. No workers, no shoppers, and the only animals were dead—no one to come between Seti and his pursuers. Flies swarmed the decaying produce and the abandoned meat market, which looked as if it still suffered from the fly plague.

A slack in Chewy's stride signaled fatigue. With a nudge, Seti urged him back to a full sprint. They turned onto the shipment road that led to the Nile, weaving between stables and empty brick buildings. A putrid smell assaulted Seti's nose as Chewy splashed through the flooded street.

He looked back. One soldier remained. Where'd the other go? Seti turned his gaze forward, and the missing soldier appeared ahead, having gone around the linen building. Seti swerved off the road between two stables piled high with dead livestock and headed in the opposite direction.

The water, carcasses, and debris slowed the chariots, giving Seti an advantage.

He veered off the road toward the inner city, reaching a winding, narrow lane flanked by taverns and small worship houses of faceless northern gods. Drunken civilians stumbled in the street and hollered as he raced by. He aimed for the inner-city residential zone. Chewy slowed again, but Seti urged him on. Rest would come later.

The road, congested with mud-brick houses topped with grass thatches haphazardly scattered and stacked, wove and wound as though it had been added after the houses were built. Each corner provided a surprise. Household items littered the street, hazards for chariots but jumping hurdles for Chewy. Startled pedestrians flung their hands in the air and leaped aside. The two soldiers kept pace, taking alternate routes as Seti emerged from alleyways and corners.

They climbed the hill toward the villa neighborhood, reaching dry land. Only the wealthy afforded dry homes during the annual inundation of the Nile. Despite the lack of flooding up here, it lay as windblown and death-ridden as the rest of Egypt.

The two soldiers didn't let up, though they lagged a good distance back. Once out of the water, and their path free of obstacles, they gained ground quickly. But Seti had a plan. The main road switch-backed up a steep hill before leveling out, with stone villas of various sizes lining both sides.

Seti cut across the switchbacks, forcing Chewy straight up the hillside. One soldier's cumbersome chariot struggled to follow, while the other kept to the road.

"Almost there."

Cramped muscles tightened in Seti's legs, making it difficult to maintain his hold. After he reached level ground, Seti pulled up, attempting to stretch his legs, but the sound of screams and a crash caught his attention. Several bystanders had barely dodged the two soldiers as they thundered by, coming up behind him—again closing the gap.

With a groan, Seti kicked Chewy to full speed. He turned onto a cobblestone walkway that connected the side streets. The chariot wheels rattled and clattered behind him. If this didn't wreck them, there was one thing left.

After two more walkways failed to disable the chariots, Seti returned to the main road that circled the neighborhood atop the hill. Up ahead lay the reason Sabu had directed him to take the city route: The S-Turn. If this succeeded, Seti was sure to rename it the Sabu-Turn. The residential road veered sharply, forcing those at high speeds to slow or shoot through the hedges and over the side. On a horse it was perfect, but not so much for a chariot. Chewy slowed, his hide lathered from the run.

The crack of the soldiers' whips signaled their ignorance of the ledge. Chewy recognized the turn and gained speed with no cue from Seti. Seti leaned forward as they reached the curve, and Chewy rounded it with ease.

After the curve, Seti steered Chewy behind a house to watch as the soldiers barreled on. The first chariot flipped over the hedges, hurling the driver off and down the steep drop-off while his horse slowed to a stop. The second pulled back hard, but it was too late. The chariot flipped, he clung to it, and skimmed across the top of the hedges, coming to a rest bloodied and scraped.

Seti blew air through his cheeks and pushed Chewy onward. The bloodied soldier could still continue his pursuit.

He flew by his empty house and passed the clearing Eliza had led him to. Nothing remained but dirt and a few flattened weeds. My Mesa wasn't much further.

Turning down a street perpendicular to his, he continued until reaching the path he had found years ago. It led into a grove of acacia and sycamore trees that ran along the outskirts of the neighborhood.

The path cut across the grove and broke out into a sandy field of weeds and patches of grass. The field ended at the steep limestone cliff overlooking Menf to the south, the four pyramids, and the southern section of On. Seti believed it was once a city-sized limestone mesa, not unlike the one from which the Sphinx had been carved, with one side sinking into the earth, buried under On, and the other side jutting out at an angle facing south. A mesa, cursed by the gods to be buried for some unknown reason, but halted midway because of the picturesque cliffside. It was a theory, at least, one Seti preferred over Sabu's sensical proclamation that it was never a mesa but just a boring old cliff. Regardless, the name Seti gave it stuck.

Most of the trees had been stripped bare, except for those in the center, where they grew denser. Not wanting to lead anyone to his spot, Seti turned off the trail toward a stream.

He dismounted Chewy, collapsing when he hit the ground, and rolled down the bank into the water. He trembled, legs frozen in a riding position, like a corpse before mummification. The cool water soaked his bandages and soothed his aching muscles. *"Mesas don't have streams, you imbecile"*. Sabu's words sank deep in his heart as Seti replayed the image of Sabu crashing into the soldier.

Chewy lurched into the water and drank.

Bare branches swayed with the breeze above Seti, the blue sky as a backdrop. He almost thanked Osiris but stopped short. The god had nothing to do with his escape.

Seti peeked over the edge of the trail after struggling to stand. No soldier. No Sabu. The grove was empty. Would Sabu make it? What if he was seriously hurt?

He sat up and unwrapped the wet bandages from his body, not having changed them since the purification pool. The oil had long since dried, and the strips were stained. He gritted his teeth as the top layer of blisters tore off with them, despite being wet. The air stung the raw spots, but the cold water eased the pain. He lay on his back and let the water rush over him, cleansing his wounds. The stream looked and smelled clean. There weren't any dead animals in it, at least from what he could see.

The trickling sound of the water rushing over stones and roots calmed his nerves, and he closed his eyes. His head pounded from Sabu's blows.

Chewy snorted, startling Seti. Someone was near. Rising from the water, he put a calming hand on Chewy's flank and glimpsed Sabu riding Nimrod bareback toward the field. His bandages had also been removed. Seti's heart leaped into his throat, and he almost called out to his friend, but someone could be following. Once Sabu left the grove, Seti mounted Chewy and followed.

Sabu did a double-take after glancing back at Seti. "You made it!"

With an awkward laugh, Seti sped up beside his friend. "I've been waiting for you all day. Did you get stuck at the S-Turn again?"

A lopsided smile from Sabu suggested their friendship remained intact, and a heaviness lifted from Seti's conscience.

At the edge of the mesa, they dismounted and embraced.

Sabu winced. "Careful. I have battle wounds." Red gashes and purple bruises covered his body. A large gash crossed his back.

"Looks like the blister plague all over again." Seti slapped him hard on the back, causing Sabu to yelp and jump aside. He punched Seti's shoulder in retaliation before sitting on the ledge.

"Ow! Alright, you got me." Seti rubbed his arm and joined him. He eyed Sabu's black and blue face before turning away, the guilt eating at him like a thousand hungry dog flies.

Sabu flashed another smile. "You look worse."

Seti's right eye had swelled slightly. The fight with Sabu only added to his growing list of foolish moves. He seemed to be on a roll. Sabu had not only endured the soldiers and falling rocks for him, but lost his chariot as well, something he wouldn't be able to replace. "Wreck the chariot?"

Staring straight ahead with a far-off look in his eyes, Sabu said, "It was a cheap old thing, handed down to me by some spoiled priestly boy anyway." He turned to Seti and winked.

Seti bit his lip. "The S-Turn saved my life, Sabu. I'm thinking of renaming it."

"Really?"

"Yes, but keep the 'S.' How does the Sabu-Turn sound?"

Sabu shook his head with a chuckle.

"I mean it. I'm sorry. You deserve a monument. A pyramid. You can have my chariot. I distrusted you without reason."

"Well, it does pay to be your friend."

He gave Sabu a playful push. "Seriously though, I don't know what's wrong with me. Turns out I don't handle pressure as well as I thought. I turned on you. Turned on my jt. I'm questioning everything I've been taught. And I'm starving. Do you still have that meat?"

"I'd lose it too if the son of Isis wanted me dead."

Seti's eyes widened. He hadn't thought of it that way. He rolled a stone between his fingers, the weight of his situation growing heavier with each passing moment.

"I left the meat at the pyramid."

What was he thinking, asking for that? It was Hoshea's. Seti stared at the sores on his legs, ashamed of how his emotions and stomach overpowered him. He tossed the stone.

They put their legs together and compared sores. After joking about how ugly they had both become, Sabu asked, "So what are you going to do? Where will you go?"

"I don't know. I guess I'll lie low like you said. Wait and see. Maybe hide out in the woods."

The prospect of hiding in the grove sounded pathetic. Desperate. Seti always had a place to stay. Plenty of friends. But he was now a danger to anyone who'd help him.

After a moment of silence, Sabu said, "Hoshea and his team are leaving for Goshen. He told me he'd wait one more day for your jt, and that was yesterday. I think they're the last to go."

Images of Eliza, Moshe, and Hoshea played in Seti's mind. He blew out a long, slow breath as he buried them. "Once Hoshea's gone, I can hide in the pyramid."

"And Chewy? I don't think you'd fit a horse in there."

Seti shook his head. "I'm due to announce that I killed the Api bull. They were getting ready for the procession before we went to the palace. And Pharaoh will be waiting. I promised my jt I wouldn't run. It's so stupid and unfair. Ptah should find his own bull. I wasn't even aware of the plague!"

"Do you want to run?"

"No. I want my life back. I want Egypt back, before all this happened. I want my mwt and Kabelo. Jt."

"Lumeri?"

"No," Seti said with disgust. Lumeri was the last person he wanted. His old life provided stability. Wealth. Enriched learning and a connection to the gods. But he now only wanted one woman—Eliza.

His shoulders slumped. The setting sun painted the sky

in oranges and reds. Such a sight would normally lift his spirits, telling him Ra was in control. How could the sun be so beautiful and not be a god?

He remembered the colorful arch from the day before. "I saw something new. Something I've never seen before."

"What has the son of Ameneten never seen before?"

"After the storm, I saw a colorful arch in the sky to the east. A band of colors across the entire sky. I've never seen anything like it."

"A rainbow? I saw that too."

"You know what it is? How?"

"It's a rainbow." Sabu shrugged. "Hoshea told me."

Seti stiffened, jealousy heating his veins. "Did he tell you where it came from?"

"He said it comes whenever it rains and the sun's out. Basically, when a storm is on its way out. Usually in the east, but not always. I attributed it to Ra, but he corrected me."

"It's not Ra?"

"He said that every culture has a theory, but it's from when the Hebrew God flooded the Earth. After the flood, his God promised He'd never flood it again. The rainbow is a reminder of His promise."

The Hebrew God and His promises. This time with reassurance that He was a God of His word. A fighter, defender, and promise keeper. This God loved His people.

Fascination replaced jealousy. "Did he say anything else?"

"Hoshea? Yes, about this whole thing his God's doing to Egypt, and that it's going to end soon. He doesn't know when, but soon. Then he said something weird: his God let them grow in Egypt like a baby in the womb, developing them into a nation."

Their conversation the night before came to mind. "Then why punish the womb?"

"I asked him that. He said it's not so much about the people of Egypt, but their gods. And the Hebrews are His children. Something strange like that. But He wants everyone to know who He is, that He is the God of all gods. And He's vying for the Hebrews' love."

"Like a love story." Seti watched the sun disappear beyond the horizon. "Like two men fighting over the same girl." That would make the Hebrew God the lover, not the father.

"Sort of. I think."

"Moshe said at the palace that his God could easily use one plague to wipe out Egypt but chose not to because He wants us to know that He is God."

"Makes sense." Sabu sat back, leaning on his hands.

"The Hebrew God's showing off."

They locked eyes. Did Sabu think the same thing? That he secretly wanted to be the girl in the middle? Seti dared not ask. Or maybe he was so used to being someone important that he couldn't take being a nobody. Was that his problem?

"Are they really that special? The Hebrews, I mean, to fight over like that?" Sabu asked.

Eliza and her shining eyes came to mind. Then Hoshea and Moshe. "What do you think?"

"If they are so special, does that mean we aren't?"

"I don't know. Does it have to be either/or?" Eliza was special, and now she was gone. Everything he wanted he couldn't have.

"I wish I had more time with Hoshea." Sabu let out a long, heavy sigh.

Seti had had plenty of time but failed to recognize Hoshea's value.

When Sabu rose to leave, they hugged. "Until the next plague?"

"Until the next plague." Sabu flashed his signature lopsided smile.

As Seti watched his friend depart, he couldn't help but wonder if he'd ever see him again. Sabu looked painfully pathetic, riding Nimrod bareback in such bad shape, and Seti hoped he'd stop by his house and take his chariot. An overwhelming sense of loneliness swept over him, and he hugged Chewy's warm body, facing the grove. If anyone deserved a friendship with Hoshea, it was Sabu.

Chapter 19

Chewy lurched to his feet, and Seti's head hit the hard ground with a thud.

"Chew—"

Locusts! The crawling boils in his dreams were locusts. They burrowed into his hair and whizzed under his tunic. He jumped to his feet and swatted at them. How did he not wake up earlier? The sand moved with locusts—as if frogs, gnats, or flies hadn't been enough. Though the sores on his skin were unaffected, Seti squirmed and slapped as the vexatious insects flew into every orifice.

How early was it? Through the clouds of flying insects, the outline of Menf could barely be made out. The morning east wind pushed the locusts across the land like a giant sandstorm.

After he cleared them from Chewy, Seti mounted and headed for the grove. Why would the Hebrew God send locusts, of all things? This meant Moshe had to be near the palace…and Eliza might be with him. It would be too risky to enter the city. But then again, what soldier would search for him in the middle of a plague?

Seti left the mesa and took the back roads through On toward Menf. The temple seemed the best place to go. His father and the other priests would have finished their monthly duties and gone home, replaced by a new round of priests. Plus, it housed places to hide, and plenty of food. His stomach begged for breakfast.

As Chewy's hooves crunched the insects on the gravel road, the implications of the plague became clear. The locusts would finish off the wheat and the spelt—what the storm hadn't gotten. Everything green would be devoured.

Farmers would watch helplessly as their livelihoods disappeared before their eyes, and Seti could do nothing to help them this time.

This would be Egypt's first famine. For the past four generations, Neper, the god of grain, kept a surplus of crops in constant supply, rotating through the storehouses. Every nation endured routine famines that drove them to Egypt, desperate for help. In exchange for food and provisions, Egypt gained its goods and land. Together with the god Hapi's annual inundation of the Nile, Neper's crops kept Egypt at the top of the world—as long as the people kept the principles of Maat. Until now.

Anger burned through Seti's bones as he gazed upon the land. Neper had failed them, as had all the gods. How necessary was this? Were the Hebrews so stubborn that they still didn't believe His power? Seti was convinced and now wanted nothing to do with them or their God. He flinched at the thought.

Seti hid with Chewy on an embankment along the stream behind the Menf temple. The dim outline of the sun settled on the horizon, but he stayed hidden despite his stomach aching. Chewy grew restless beside him with nothing to munch on. The locusts piled into layers on the ground but avoided the stream to keep their wings dry.

Sleep evaded him in the wet dirt. He'd sleep and dream of Eliza the rest of his days if he could. He'd have to resign himself to seeing her only in his dreams. Her people would leave, and she'd go with them. He wouldn't dare think of holding her back.

The sacred animals remained inside the stable with the stable priest. An unfamiliar man came out at sunset and locked the doors. The new rotation of priests had taken over. His father would be cleansing himself one last time in the pools before heading home. The moon rose in the east, and soon the new priests would sleep.

Seti waded along the stream toward the temple, pulling Chewy beside him. Though the foyer stayed open, the doors to the corridors and priestly chambers had been locked at sundown. He stopped Chewy alongside the temple below the kitchen. Standing on his back, Seti swiped locusts from the windowsill. He pulled himself up and over and dropped into the kitchen, squishing more of the loathsome insects that had settled on the cool marble floor.

"Stay here, Chewy. I'll be right back."

With sandals in hand, he paused to listen for movement. Satisfied with the silence, he grabbed a container of bread, a jar of water, and oats sealed in a silver bowl, safe from the locusts. With the bread slung over his shoulder and his woven bag stuffed to the brim, he grabbed an oil lamp and tiptoed down the dark hall toward the foyer, swiping a clear path with his bare feet.

Seti unlocked the door to the foyer, slipped his bag into the doorframe so it wouldn't shut behind him, and peered out. The god-statues had been removed, though several destitute farmers remained, mumbling prayers in the moonlight. Among the swirling locusts, their shadowy forms faced the empty wall. Seti sighed. Their desperate prayers meant nothing to the gods.

He hurried outside.

Returning with his horse, their feet crunched against the locusts, and the mumble of prayers paused momentarily before continuing again. Seti hurried to the back hall, grabbed his bag, and gently shut and locked the door. Then he led Chewy up the winding steps to the living quarters on the third floor.

Unsure which rooms were in use, Seti tiptoed to the far end of the hall, where it was sure to be empty.

"I'm sorry we have to come back here." He opened the door to the last room, but Chewy hesitated. Seti went in first and pulled his steed inside. "This time, I'll stay with you."

He brushed the locusts off the bed, sat cross-legged, and pulled the food and water from the bag before laying out the oats for Chewy. They ate silently in the dark. After Seti chased the bread with a swallow of water, his belly calmed to a quiet gurgle, not fully satisfied. The moon lit the room enough to see the movement on the floor and walls. Locusts everywhere. Seti pulled the bed linen over his head and curled into a ball. The air buzzed all night. He closed his eyes, willing himself to sleep.

Chapter 20

Moshe had called for the men of Goshen to meet on this eighth day of Aviv to discuss the last plague, triggering rumors of leaving Egypt. Eliza couldn't bear being left out of such crucial information. In the guise of taking the two lambs for a walk, she and Rahel hiked up the enormous hill bordering Avaris. On the other side, men crammed the valley from all over Goshen, including Eliza's father.

She stared past the rolling hills on the horizon, her mind wandering. By this time, Ameneten would have returned home from his work in the temple. Life proved quieter with him at home, for he kept Huya preoccupied. Eliza caught herself counting the days until his return out of habit. It didn't matter now. She'd never see Huya—or any of them—again.

Word had spread that God sent locusts over the face of Egypt to finish off what the hailstorm had left behind. Seti would survive. His father was above such problems.

Wasn't he?

His distressed face at the palace flashed before her eyes.

A cheer erupted from the gathering below, startling Eliza from her wandering thoughts. Moshe and Aharon stood on a platform in the middle of the valley where their voices carried over the audience, but Eliza was too far away to hear. Aharon raised his hands, and the crowd quieted.

Either Moshe or Aharon said something, and within seconds, the crowd cheered again. The girls leaned forward as if to close the distance.

Eliza shook her head. "We need to get closer."

"We're close enough. Maybe if you don't talk, I can hear."

The next announcement clearly came from Moshe, but his words were indistinguishable.

"Alright, a little closer."

They moved halfway down the hill and stopped at two large acacia trees standing side by side, separated by a large boulder—a small oasis in the blazing sun. Leaving the lambs in the swaying grass, they climbed onto the boulder. After another round of cheering and applause, the girls leaned forward, cupping their ears.

"I still can't hear them." Frustration clouded Eliza's concentration. She was about to jump down and sneak into the gathering when Rahel grabbed her arm.

"Shhh!"

They listened again. Nothing.

Moshe shuffled about on the platform, hands animated, but the wind swept his voice away.

"I hear something." Rahel waved her hand at Eliza.

Eliza gave up and rested her chin in her palm. It was no use. Maybe her father would fill her in when he returned.

"Hey girls!" Hoshea popped up behind them.

They both started, and Rahel screamed, lost her balance, and slid off the front of the rock.

Obnoxious laughter erupted from Hoshea as he hoisted himself up and plopped down beside Eliza. He looked at Rahel and shook his head. Rahel stood, gawking, her hand on her heart.

Eliza froze. Never had she been so close to such a handsome, burly man. Though Seti sat close the night before her whipping, he wasn't this close. She'd move away, but that meant getting off the rock, which would be obvious. His pungent body odor reached her nostrils, and her eyes widened. She exchanged a nervous look with Rahel. Laughter threatened to burst from her, though she'd rather shrink into a crevice in the rock.

"She's a funny one." Hoshea nodded toward Rahel before adjusting his position, bumping Eliza's hip. "What are you doing here?"

She tensed, staring at Rahel, whose mouth hung open.

Rahel raised her eyebrows, motioning for her to speak.

"Wondering what you're doing here," Eliza squeaked.

His eyes bore into her, and she leaned away.

When it dawned on her that he was studying her scar, she turned and frowned at him, but it didn't dissuade his stare or the look of concern in his eyes. No longer intimidated, she fought the urge to push him off.

"What's going on?" she demanded.

"Well," he finally looked away. "You see, there's a dilemma, and it involves you."

"Me?"

"Yes, you. I've learned there's more to the frog story than you're letting on. You know, the whole whipped-in-the-face thing?"

Eliza's heart galloped. Rahel shook her head. No one else knew except the children who witnessed it.

Hoshea squinted at the gathering below before turning to Eliza. "I learned some interesting things. Like you were supposed to get twenty-five lashes but only received five."

She looked away, cheeks heating.

"But somebody stepped in and saved you. Seti, son of Ameneten."

After ripping a blade of grass from a crevice in the rock, Eliza twisted it between her fingers.

"Right?"

"Yes."

"Well, you're not the only one who worked for

Ameneten."

That got her attention.

"I was assigned to their pyramid."

She glanced at Rahel, but Rahel stared at him wide-eyed.

"I was under the impression you were due five lashes, including one in the face. And so, they have quite the reputation among us at the pyramid."

She busied herself with the blade of grass.

"But," Hoshea went on, "come to find out, the Ameneten family aren't all that bad, are they?"

Eliza nodded, struggling between defensiveness and shame. "No, they're not."

"Now, I imagine you're quite grateful Seti helped you."

"Yes." She'd never forget.

"Well, Seti has gotten himself into trouble with Pharaoh, and I think I know how you can help him. He's accused of killing the Api bull during the livestock plague, an act that incurred a death sentence."

"What?" Her eyes widened, and fear engulfed her heart. *That's why he and his father were at the palace.*

"The only way he lives is if he finds another bull to replace the one he killed."

The breath left her lungs. That would be impossible. Why would Hoshea tell her this if she couldn't save Seti? "How?"

"There just so happens to be a farmer nearby who breeds black bulls with white triangles on their foreheads and split tails. You can guess what he does with them."

She blinked. Was it that easy? But her heart sank. "I have nothing to give for a bull. No money. Nothing. Bulls are expensive." Did he think her family was rich?

Hoshea smacked himself in the forehead as if the realization had just struck him. "Wow, that's too bad, Eliza. Yes, bulls are expensive, especially such rare ones. It's too bad you don't have any money or anything he would need." He paused dramatically. "Except there is one thing the farmer doesn't have and desperately needs."

Eliza narrowed her eyes. "I have nothing, Hoshea."

Hoshea turned his gaze to the two lambs munching on grass a few paces away. "Moshe said every family needs to offer a blemish-free year-old male lamb. Not everybody has lambs, especially a farmer who only raises cattle. The lambs must be ready by the tenth and offered before leaving for the promised land. That man must be desperate. He has a family." He stuffed a wadded piece of cloth into Eliza's lap. "I don't know what to do with this. Maybe Adam can figure it out."

"Adam?" Eliza was about to open the cloth when Hoshea jumped from the rock, landing on his feet.

He pointed across the valley. "His farm is just beyond that hill."

Before he took off down the hill, he added, "By the way, you might want to tell your family what really happened."

Eliza stood. "Wait! Who told you this?"

Hoshea hesitated. He looked toward the horizon then back at her. "Sabu. He gave me that map too."

"Sabu?"

He gave a tight nod and bounced down the hill toward the gathering, taking his manly odor with him. The crowd in the valley began to disperse, signaling the end of the meeting.

Eliza's stomach knotted with a sense of urgency as Hoshea disappeared into the sea of men. The lambs were blemish-free and male. One-year-old twins. How did he know?

"Where'd you get those lambs, Eliza?" Rahel's voice interrupted her thoughts.

"I don't know. They were given to me." Eliza was stunned. Her family would need one. The other, she could trade for the bull.

"What's that?" Rahel pointed to the cloth clenched in her fist.

Eliza opened her hand. Rahel watched as she unraveled the cloth.

"It's a map." She flipped it around.

"To the farm?"

Small green squiggly lines filled the center of the picture with two words printed on one side and what looked like a single road, a grove of scribbled trees, and a blue wavy line on the other side.

"What is it?" Rahel climbed up beside Eliza and scrutinized the map.

"It looks like the map is to that spot." Eliza pointed to the two words.

"What does Adam have to do with it?" Rahel asked, referring to Eliza's brother.

"I don't know. He knows the alphabet. Maybe Hoshea meant that Adam could read it."

Rahel pointed to a square at the far end of the road. "That looks like a house."

"I have no idea what this is." Why would Sabu give Hoshea a map? And how did Sabu even know him? So many questions. Eliza folded the cloth in frustration and stuffed it in a small pocket in her tunic. "We have to get to that farm."

"You're going?"

She jumped from the rock, landed on her feet, and turned to Rahel. "That man needs a lamb."

Rahel smiled. "And you need a bull."

Seti peeked from beneath the bedsheet. The locusts were gone. Chewy stood at the window, hanging his head out. Alarmed, Seti leaped from the bed and grabbed the reins, pulling him back.

He hadn't slept that long since before the plagues. The bed linen lifted from a west wind that blew into the room, the only sound in the eerie silence after his ears had grown accustomed to the buzzing. Pharaoh must have begged Moshe to send the locusts away, but not before they destroyed everything. The pastures and fields behind the temple lay dead and brown. Nothing green remained.

Stomach aching with hollowness and mouth parched, Seti settled back on the bed. He'd have to wait until nightfall to sneak out. More soldiers might have been sent for him, especially after yesterday's violent chase. The new priests were bound to know about the bull. If he showed his face, he'd be expected to make the announcement.

The announcement concerning the dead Api bull would devastate the already defeated people. The procession would slosh through the murky waters of the streets, heralded by loud mourners, dancers, and every priest from this side of Egypt. Its mummified corpse would be displayed on a ceramic cart, dressed and crowned, with Seti standing over it, proclaiming how he carelessly destroyed the nation's only remaining hope.

All of Egypt would be after him.

Seti covered his face, hands trembling. Even though he'd promised his father—the greatest Ameneten since his Father of Old—that he wouldn't run, he'd had no other choice. Tears welled in his eyes. This final twist of the dagger in his father's heart would kill him. His father would either watch him die at the hands of Pharaoh or face the shame of his runaway, disobedient son and the fall of their heritage. Not only had he shattered the hope of the people, but he had destroyed his family.

Seti peered at Chewy through a blur of tears. Moshe fled to Midian years before and survived. They might welcome Seti…if they didn't worship Ptah.

He made his choice. He'd raid the kitchen in the middle of the night and be gone before morning. The debilitating pain encompassing him wouldn't compare to what his father would suffer.

Eliza and Rahel stopped to rest on top of the hill opposite Avaris. Wooden stables dotted the green pastures below as far as the next range of hills.

A small brick house surrounded by a wooden fence rested where the hill met level ground. Cows and bulls meandered in the enclosed area, but a small group of jet-black bovines gathered in a corner near the stable. Five total. The Ameneten house had several figurines of the Api bull, but Eliza had never seen a live one.

A stout man entered the house. Eliza had spotted him earlier when he left the gathering and ascended the hill.

"That's them." Rahel pointed to the bulls in the corner.

"And that's the owner."

Rahel stood. "We're going to have to drag one of those bulls up here."

"I'll figure out a way."

"Then what?"

"I don't know. Take it to the Ameneten house?" Eliza stood and grabbed the lambs' twine leashes.

"Maybe you could ask one of your brothers to go with you. Seti's family might make you stay if you go alone."

Though unlikely, it was still a possibility. She might have to deliver it to the temple in Menf, since Seti had been banished from home. Wherever he stayed, the bull belonged to the temple. She had never been there and didn't know the way.

There was no point in knocking on the man's door only

to find out the bulls didn't meet the requirements. When they reached flat ground, Eliza went straight for them, climbing over the fence and into the yard. Rahel followed.

The three adults and two calves gathered by the well. Their shiny ebony hides were broken by a white triangle on their foreheads, the tell-tale sign of an Api bull. Each had a split tail, another sign. They looked exactly like the polished figurines on Huya's mantel. The man had obviously bred them for this reason.

"I think these are them." Eliza moved between them, checking the little ones.

"But they must have the scarab lump under their tongue."

"I'm not prying open any mouths."

Twin boys toddled out of the front door and dashed to the girls with squeals and laughter, as if they'd never seen another human until now. Eliza knelt to greet them at eye level.

"Can I help you?" The man stepped from the house. Suspicion clouded his bearded face and questioning eyes.

Eliza stiffened.

"Let me talk," Rahel whispered.

If Eliza were Moshe, Rahel would be Aharon.

Rahel stepped past the boys. "Just admiring your cattle."

The man's eyes darted from Eliza to Rahel, then to the boys as they chased after one of the lambs. The other lamb chomped on grass, oblivious to the rambunctious tots.

"Indeed, they are rare. Egyptians worship this breed. I plan on taking them to Canaan. I wouldn't want those people getting their hands on these."

"I'd like one," Rahel stated.

Eliza's mouth dropped, having expected more small talk.

"They're not for sale."

"I heard you need a lamb." Rahel got right to the point.

Eliza remained by the cattle and watched as Rahel joined the two boys near the lambs, who settled together near the fence. Twin lambs and twin boys sat in the grass. She knelt and whispered something.

The man neared them, hands on his hips.

Rahel looked up at the man. "Twins?"

"Yes, they are twins."

His eyes narrowed, and he stepped toward her. Eliza caught her breath when he reached out for Rahel but stopped at the sound of a baby crying in the house.

Rahel gave one twine leash to the nearest toddler and whispered something in his ear before patting his head.

"Can we keep it?" the child asked.

Eliza's eyebrows rose. Good idea!

The baby's cries distracted the man, and he hesitated.

Rahel knelt by the other child. "Did you know that these lambs are twins too? And boys, just like you and your brother." She stroked the lamb's head. "Look how perfect they are. God makes such amazing creatures, doesn't He? I mean, even if it had a blemish, it would still be perfect, but these have no blemishes. They are a rare find and worth quite a lot, probably more than those big black bulls. What would you name this one?"

"I don't know."

The man growled. "It's not getting a name. We're only keeping it for four days."

Rahel stood. "So, it's settled?"

"We get to keep it?" the child squealed.

His father ignored him. "What are you going to do with the bull?"

"What are you going to do with the lamb?" Rahel asked.

"We are commanded to offer a lamb, not a bull."

"And you don't have what you need to heed that command. Isn't this God's provision? He wouldn't command you to make an offering without giving you the means to follow through. How accountable would you be if you refused His means and then failed His command?"

He ran a hand down his beard, eyeing the boys.

"Everyone in Goshen seeks these lambs." Rahel nodded toward one. "Those who don't have one will pay handsomely. You can't get them from Egypt. God is literally handing you a lamb for a price not nearly its worth. We were lucky enough to have twins—one to spare. It won't hurt us to give one away."

How does she do it? Eliza would be lost without Rahel.

The man teetered. "Those bulls and cows are worth a lot, especially to Egyptians."

"But to Israelites? To God? Once we leave Egypt, those cattle will be equal to any other. God knows about them." Rahel shifted her weight and crossed her arms. "Why do you even have these? Do you really want to bring idols with you?"

"You're going to sell it to the Egyptians."

"Not sell. But what does it matter? The bull will live and be worshipped. If you take it with you, its fate is death, slaughtered for food and clothing, maybe an offering. By making the trade, you will save his life and yours."

Was he hesitant because he idolized these bulls? Eliza's mind spun. He might as well stay in Egypt.

The baby's wails grew louder, and the man glanced at the house and back at the lamb. "Take them then. Take them all. Give me the lamb and take all five. I have several figurines in the house. Take them too."

Eliza's eyes widened, astonished.

"Burn the figurines. I only want the cattle. They'll be worshipped in Egypt and their safety guaranteed, as will yours." Rahel didn't look the least surprised at her success.

He went to the house and returned with a rope and tied a length around each adult's neck. The little ones would follow. "Two adult females, one male. The calves are male and female."

Rahel took the leash from the boys and handed it to their father. "You're doing the right thing."

He knelt over the lamb, examining it while the boys ran circles around him, filled with joy for their new pet.

Rahel held the ropes of two of the bovines while Eliza grabbed the other and the twine to the remaining lamb, fighting the urge to join the boys in their dance.

She gazed at the lamb staying behind. "Sorry, little lamb." A sacrifice for Seti. "You will be given to God as an act of worship." She petted the white triangular spot on the bull's forehead. "And you're going to be worshipped as a god."

She and Rahel thanked the owner. He stood with a sigh and nodded before hurrying into the house.

"Five! They'll never be without a bull again," Eliza squealed.

"You can thank God for that. If this doesn't redeem your friend, nothing will."

Dragging the cattle up the farmer's hill, into the valley, and then up the Avaris hill proved more difficult than anticipated and took too long for Eliza's liking. Evening had come and gone when the girls went their separate ways, and Eliza took the reins of all five cattle. She found her family and two houseguests at the fire beside the house. The houseguests had arrived the day before, having no home in Goshen since they had been palace slaves.

She left the animals tied to a tree in front of the house but took the lamb with her to the fire. The aroma of freshly baked cinnamon cakes hit her nose, and she stopped short of showing herself. Another supper missed. Her family chatted with quiet laughter, unaware of her presence. She had played different scenarios of her approach in her head on the way back, but now her mind went blank.

"Where have you been?" her father asked. He sat

across the circle, facing her.

The quiet chatter stopped. It appeared the twins were already in bed, but the others turned. Their curious eyes glowed in the flickering light.

Eliza stepped out from the shadows, the lamb at her side.

"I was making a business transaction." She had hoped to eat first and answer questions later.

"A what?" Miera giggled.

"I'd like to eat first," she stammered.

Her father's eyes narrowed. He nodded toward the lamb nestled at her feet. "Where's the other one?"

"The other lamb's missing!" Miera shouted, making Eliza wince.

There was no way around it. "I sold it."

"You what?"

"Let me explain." Eliza sat on a rock, her designated spot, and fumbled with the twine in her lap.

Adam leaned forward. "Sold it to who?"

"Why?" her mother asked.

"For how much?" Zechariah asked.

Her father raised his hand to stop the others and said with forced calmness, "We need the lamb this week. As an offering before Pharaoh lets us go."

Pharaoh hadn't let them go? "You need one per family. One. We have this one. The man I sold it to didn't have any."

He leaned back against a disabled cart, arms crossed over his chest. "How do you know about the offering?"

"What offering?" Adam's gaze bounced between his father and sister.

Eliza studied him. Her father hadn't told them what the meeting was about.

"For the last plague." Her father's eyes didn't leave Eliza. "Each family has to make an offering of a year-old lamb on the last night. Then Moshe will lead us out of Egypt. The lamb must be consecrated by the tenth and offered on the fourteenth."

"That's it?" Adam narrowed his eyes. "We waited for Eliza to return for you to tell us that?" All eyes turned to him. "That's what the meeting was about?"

"Moshe has very specific instructions on how to offer the lamb," her father said.

"And how to prepare to leave," her mother chimed in.

Her mother and father exchanged glances, and her father uncrossed his arms. He opened his mouth to continue when Zechariah spoke. "What did you sell it for?"

Disappointed the attention had turned back to her, Eliza straightened. "That's what I have to explain." Everyone waited. "I didn't tell the whole truth about what happened when I was whipped."

Miera jumped from her log. "Oh, can I tell it?"

"No, Miera." She wished Miera had gone to bed too. "No."

"What do you mean? What does that have to do with the lamb?" her father asked.

"Listen." She drew in a deep breath. "I was supposed to get twenty-five lashes, but I only got five because Seti stopped his ima from continuing. She was the one with the whip, and Seti's her oldest son. The whip struck him when he stepped in to make her stop. Then he untied me and told Miera and me to leave. His ima banished him from ever returning home." The sting on her back returned, and Eliza shivered, remembering the moment she realized Seti had saved her.

"Seti?" Zechariah asked.

"So," she continued, "I don't know where he went, but he's in trouble with Pharaoh, accused of killing the Api bull during the livestock plague. Pharaoh will kill him unless he finds a replacement for the bull, but they are so rare..." She faltered at their stares.

Horror spread across her father's face.

Zechariah's head tilted to the side, deep in thought.

Then the questions came at once from all sides.

"Wait—"

"The Amenetens?"

"Your master's son? Set you free?"

"Is the frog part true?"

"Twenty-five?"

"Why would he set you free?"

Her father's hand shot into the air, and they quieted. He stood, glowering across the fire at Eliza. "What does his trouble with Pharaoh have to do with you?"

"I found one. An Api bull. Five, actually. And I traded the lamb for them, because the owner needed one. And I can free Seti as he did for me. He can present them to Pharaoh in exchange for his life."

Zechariah sat forward. "You're kidding."

"Eliza!" her mother replied in shock.

"I was there. I saw the whole thing," Miera announced.

Adam narrowed his eyes at Miera. "You knew?"

"She made me keep it a secret, because she didn't want anyone knowing she's in love with an Egyptian."

"Miera!" Eliza jumped to her feet. Multiple voices rang out at once.

"This can't be true."

"Eliza!"

"No!"

"I knew it." Eliza's hands balled into fists. She threw the twine to the ground. "I knew you'd all react like this. That's why I kept it a secret."

"I was going to beat the breath out of those boys before leaving Egypt," Adam said.

Eliza gasped. "You wouldn't! You know nothing about them."

"You should beat the breath out of their ima," Miera told him.

"Miera, shut up!" Tears spilled from Eliza's eyes.

"Alright, calm down," her father patted the air.

"You're a fool."

"Shut up, Adam!" Eliza's voice rang above the others.

"Eliza, that's enough!"

She couldn't remember the last time her father raised his voice at her, and it shook her to the core. She held her breath and locked eyes with him, trembling.

Her father huffed, the others clamped their mouths shut, and Miera sat. He took a deep breath. "Where are the bulls?"

Heart pounding and eyes blurred with tears, Eliza stomped to the front, grabbed the rope, and returned with the cattle. Her mother gasped at the sight, Miera laughed, and her father buried his head in his hands.

Adam remained on his rock, arms crossed, unfazed by the large black animals that had joined the family at the fire. "You're in love with an Egyptian?"

Ignoring him, Eliza met the calculated regard of her father.

"How does a Hebrew fall in love with an Egyptian?" Adam wouldn't stop.

Zechariah petted one of the calves. "We should just keep them all."

"If he killed the Api bull, he should be punished," her mother said.

Her father's voice came low and riddled with accusation. "You're trying to cover for him."

Before Eliza could answer, the others spoke all at once.

"Why would he kill the Api bull?"

"Sounds like a rotten family."

"But he saved her."

"Are you in contact with him? How do you know about this?" Her father's voice boomed over the rest.

"No," Eliza trembled. "I have no idea where he is. Hoshea told me. He worked for them on the pyramid."

"Hoshea?" Adam straightened at the mention of his friend and mentor.

"They know each other. He told me how to save Seti and where to find the bulls."

"When did he tell you this?"

"Earlier today. Rahel and I followed Abba to the meeting and ran into Hoshea. He gave me this." She pulled out the white cloth, unfolding it.

"Hoshea worked for the same family as you?" Adam asked.

"Yes. I didn't know either until he told me." Her voice calmed.

"I can't believe I'm hearing this. And my biggest fear was you falling in love with a Danite," her father said.

After a moment of silence, Eliza said with conviction, "I'm not asking for permission. I'm taking them to Egypt. I'm telling you now because I want you to know the truth."

Fire blazed in her father's eyes. As the animals shuffled in the searing silence, Eliza fought the impulse to grab them and run. She rarely saw her father, let alone made him angry. Seti's life depended on her. Her father would forgive.

But his searing gaze pinned her in place. "Adam, Zechariah, you will go with your sister. Leave tomorrow morning. I want you back before nightfall. Take those animals straight to the temple in Menf."

Eliza held her breath.

Adam cut his father a look of disdain.

"You're afraid she might get attacked?" Miera asked.

"No. I'm afraid if she sees him again, she won't come back."

"I will be back," Eliza promised.

"This will be interesting," Zechariah muttered.

Chapter 21

It was still dark when Seti woke, and it took a minute to reorient himself. He had shoved the bed against the door to keep anyone from entering. After devising his plan to flee Egypt like a coward, he had fallen asleep. He hadn't dreamed, unless this was a dream, more likely a nightmare. Unfortunately, Chewy's rhythmic breathing told him it wasn't.

Seti sat up.

"Chewy?" His voice sounded far away, muffled, as if his ears were covered.

Chewy snorted. The blackness of the room made Seti question whether the window was on the opposite wall. That was the old room. No, both rooms. Maybe clouds were blocking the moon. Even so, it shouldn't be this dark. He'd wait a little longer before escaping; perhaps the moon would come out.

Too excited to sleep, her mind reeling with ideas, Eliza crawled off her mat before the sun rose. She couldn't remember the last time she had woken up so early—

willingly. She shook her brothers awake then crept down the steps to the kitchen, halting on the bottom step. Her father sat at the table, staring out the open door at the cattle. An oil lamp burned dimly on the table.

He turned. "You're up early."

"I couldn't sleep."

"I forgot to tell you, Moshe's back in On. This darkness is from God. You will need this lamp."

Eliza blinked.

"It's the ninth plague from God, Eliza. You will be delivering the animals in the dark."

She looked to the window. "How long will it last?"

"We don't know," he replied. "It's complete and utter darkness outside of Goshen. We have light in our homes, but the Egyptians don't even have that. Your oil lamp will be the only light."

"What?"

"Go wake your brothers."

Eliza's father followed her and her brothers outside onto the front porch. Zechariah yawned, and Adam sighed heavily, but Eliza's heart galloped in her chest. She found the rope to the adult bovine in the dirt and skipped around it to the porch. Her father handed Adam the oil lamp from the table then gave Zechariah and Eliza lamps of their own.

"The neighbors provided the extra lamps. You will be the only ones in all of Egypt with light. They're in total darkness."

All three nodded. Eliza grinned.

"Adam, Zechariah, make sure she doesn't come too close to him. And if he puts his hands on her, you have my permission to do whatever it takes to subdue him."

Eliza rolled her eyes, and Zechariah snickered under his breath.

"And if we get arrested?" Adam asked.

"Then I will come get you."

"You can't be serious, Abba," Eliza said, elation turning to defensiveness.

Adam stretched. "Remember, we're still slaves to Pharaoh."

"You know what I mean, Adam. All three of you had better be back before nightfall."

"None of us are coming back if we lay our hands on him," Adam said.

Zechariah rested his chin in his palm. "And how do we know when it's nightfall?"

Eliza turned to Adam. "Then how did you think you were going to beat him up before we left Egypt? Or were you just antagonizing me?"

"Listen up!"

All three straightened and faced their father.

He pointed at Eliza. "I'm only doing this so you won't run off on your own. I could have sold them while you slept—"

"No!" Eliza cried.

"Then get these animals out of here and be back as soon as possible. All of you."

"Yes, Abba," Adam and Zechariah muttered.

Eliza closed her gaping mouth and spun away from her father. The thought of losing the cattle sent chills down her spine. The indifference her family showed toward Seti—the very one who set her and Miera free—choked her with sadness.

Windows glowed with oil lamps as if night had just come upon them. It would take three hours to walk to On, a little longer to reach the palace. Menf lay just beyond the palace, and Zechariah knew where to find the temple. They took City Street south.

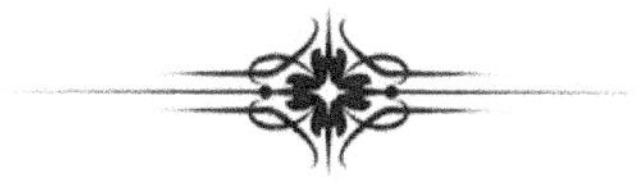

A loud thud against the door jerked Seti awake.

"That's a wall!" a voice yelled from the other side.

"No, it's a door," a muffled voice argued.

"We're at the end of the hall. Turn around," the first voice said.

Another thud sounded farther away.

"That was my head!"

"Curse Moshe's God! He's rendered us blind. Where'd you go?"

"I'm right here, you dog!"

"Keep going."

Seti's muscles tensed as he listened, holding his breath, willing them to go away. The voices faded, leaving Seti in silence. Either his room was pitch black, or he was blind too. Another plague from Moshe.

He sat up, trepidation pumping through him. How long would they be blind?

"Chewy?"

A shuffle of hooves sounded near the bed, and Seti sighed. He waved his hand in front of his face but saw nothing. It would be impossible to flee Egypt now. But then again, who would find him if no one could see him?

"No," he moaned. "Please, Hebrew God. Have mercy on us."

Why would the Hebrew God hear him? He was worthless to Him.

The oil lamp. He searched the bed for his woven bag. Finding it, he pulled out the lamp and tried to light it to no avail. There was oil—his fingers were wet with it. He wiped them on the blanket and tried again. Nothing.

Maybe it was already lit, though it wasn't warm. His

breathing intensified. How long would this last? All the other plagues had been temporary.

Seti crept off the bed and felt along the wall for the window on the opposite wall. The cool breeze struck his face, and he paused, letting it refresh his lungs in the stuffy room. The trickling of the stream below solidified his fears. The Hebrew God had blinded Egypt.

He waved his hand in the air but leaned forward too far, catching the windowsill before he'd fall. Heart racing, he backed away and bumped into Chewy. The horse stirred, and Seti stumbled backward. Not able to grab anything, he hit the floor hard and knocked his head on the frame of the bed.

"Ow."

Then it dawned on him. They weren't blinded. This was against Ra. Ra was either defeated by the Hebrew God, was hiding, or worse—he didn't exist. Ra, the most powerful god. Seti's earlier idea that Ra and the Hebrew God were one and the same had been proven false.

He leaned against the bed, his legs outstretched. If Pharaoh gives in, then the curse would be removed. But the chances of that were next to none, even with Ra's absence. How many plagues must they endure? The locusts had left only a day or two ago, depending on how long Seti had slept. He took a deep breath. This wasn't the end for Egypt. The darkness would lift, but what would be next?

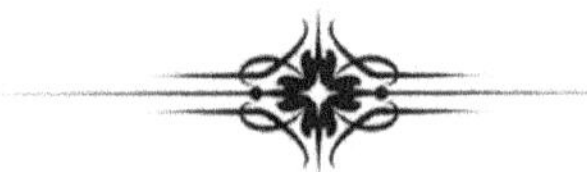

The streets were empty. The stables were empty. The sky was empty. It wasn't long after leaving Goshen that Eliza had lost sight of the moon and stars.

Having grown accustomed to Goshen's clean air, the wretched smell of death shocked Eliza's senses, hitting her so suddenly her eyes watered. They were surrounded by death in every sense of the word. Eliza's throat constricted at first, but a few deep breaths kept panic at bay.

The darkness was too oppressive. She couldn't tell where the houses were. They stepped over dead livestock and frogs, branches, and merchandise scattered over the road. Eliza had never seen City Street so lifeless, not even at night. It was as if the citizens got up and ran, leaving everything behind. The eerie stillness sent chills through her body.

Despite the overwhelming heaviness, she wasn't afraid—not because of the presence of her brothers, but because of the presence of God. The oil lamps proved it. One would think their light would go out after leaving Goshen. But it didn't. The little oil they started with continued to burn.

Three hours into their walk, Adam, Zechariah, and Eliza passed Palace Road. Menf was just ahead. Adam led the way with the adult bull. Zechariah and Eliza led the cows while the two calves followed.

Eliza caught up to Adam and handed him the map. "Hoshea said you might know what this means."

Adam handed Eliza his lamp while he opened the wrinkled cloth and examined it. "He gave this to you?"

"Yes, and he said he doesn't know anything about it, just that Sabu gave it to him. I don't know if it leads to Seti, the temple, or the farm."

"I wonder why he didn't give it to me?"

"You were in Avaris. I was at the valley field. Probably because he saw me first, or it has something to do with Seti."

"Still."

A thought struck her. "I know why. Because he wanted me to tell you the truth about the lashes, not him. It was my secret."

Adam sighed. "It's written in Egyptian."

"You know Egyptian script, don't you?"

"Not really."

Eliza reached for the map, but Adam swung it out of reach.

"If you can't read it, give it back."

"Hold on!" Adam halted, studying it once more.

Eliza stopped beside him, hands on her hips.

Adam pointed at the two words in the corner. "The first letter of both words is M."

"Menf?" She reached for the map again, but Adam turned away.

"I don't think Hoshea drew this. He wouldn't have written in Egyptian. I don't think he even knows how to write in Hebrew," he said.

"He said it came from Sabu, Seti's friend."

"But why would he give it to Hoshea? And then Hoshea give it to you?"

"Maybe you should ask him when you get back." Eliza bounced in front of him, attempting to snatch it.

"Oh, I will." He grinned and handed it to her.

She scowled and shoved the map into her pocket. Deep down, she missed his teasing, but she couldn't let him see that. His comment about beating up the Ameneten boys still stung.

She squinted and gazed into the darkness but saw nothing. Would Seti be at the temple? Awake? She yearned to see him one last time before leaving. To see his face when they arrived with the bull. The last time she had seen him, he was wrapped like a mummy and at the mercy of Pharaoh. Was he even alive? What if she was too late? Panic rose inside her. It had been over a week since she'd last seen him. Anything could have happened in that time.

Another hour passed. Eliza's feet ached despite her hard-earned calluses. Zechariah had taken the lead when they entered Menf. Unable to make out the buildings or structures, they kept to the middle of the street until he tripped over a step.

He held the lamp high, illuminating a set of granite steps. "This is it."

Eliza's heart sped. Was he here? She followed her brother up the stairs, leading the bovine and calves close behind. The darkness was so thick, the temple couldn't be seen, though it stood right in front of her. Zechariah kept the light on the steps. Eventually, the steps ended, and the floor turned to marble. While Eliza marveled at the smooth marble reflecting a dim glow, Zechariah moved ahead, the cow's hooves clicking on the floor.

"We're going inside," Zechariah announced, passing a pillar.

Eliza hurried to catch up. Though she could see his light, she didn't want to fall too far behind in the dark.

She gazed upward. If Ameneten wasn't here, then why would Seti be?

"Seti!" Eliza yelled, her voice echoing off the stone walls.

Adam's hand clamped over her mouth. "Are you crazy?"

He let go of her, and she turned to face him.

What was he so afraid of?

"Shhh! Just because we can't see anybody doesn't mean nobody's here," he whispered.

Zechariah halted. "Find somewhere to tie them up. Let's get out of here."

Adam came forward and snatched the rope from her hand. He tied the three ropes together around a pillar. The little ones moved in beside their mother.

"Now, let's go," Adam said after he finished.

Eliza spun around, looking for doors or windows, but there was nothing to see. She wasn't ready to leave yet. She had to see Seti. She looked at Zechariah. If she ran, they wouldn't be able to find her. Surely her family wouldn't leave Goshen without her.

"Eliza," Adam demanded from the steps.

"Wait." Zechariah ran to the bulls.

"What are you doing?" Adam asked.

"We have to leave a note. When they discover the cattle, I want them to know they're from us and not from their gods."

"We have no papyrus."

Eliza's eyes lit up. "Good idea!" She tore a piece of her tunic.

"Eliza!" Adam ran to her.

She shot her hand out to block him and hissed, "You told me to be quiet and now you're yelling."

He reached out to grab the cloth scrap, but she snatched it away and darted toward Zechariah. "We needed something to write on."

The small piece of dirty white cloth resembled the one the map had been drawn on. She spread it out on the floor near the bovine.

"You might as well give them your entire tunic," Adam spat.

"Shut up."

"Adam, you know how to write," Zechariah said.

"Not in Egyptian."

"Then write it in Hebrew."

Adam sighed as he got on his knees on the floor. He dipped his finger into his lamp oil and spelled out in Hebrew: "To Seti." The letter could barely be seen against the white background.

"Now, say who it's from," Zechariah told him.

"Wait," Eliza stopped him. "You can't say my name. They know who I am."

"I thought you wanted them to know."

"Yes, from a Hebrew, but not me. I want only him to know it's from me. I didn't tell anyone he saved me because I didn't want him to get into more trouble than he was already in. It can't point back to me. But I want him to know that I was here."

"What?" Zechariah wrinkled his nose.

Adam sat on his heels and looked at her. "How are you going to do that?"

Eliza shook her head.

"Does he have a nickname for you?"

Eliza thought a moment. He didn't call her anything but Eliza. Except once. "Scared little kitten."

Her brothers stared at her, dumbstruck.

"That's what he calls you?" Adam asked.

"No, he calls me Eliza. He doesn't have a nickname for me, he just called me that once."

"He picks on you?" Adam asked.

"No! He was mad at me."

"He was mad at you?" Adam's eyes widened. Then he shook his head. "It doesn't sound like he shares the same feelings as you."

"That was before I got whipped. I was too shy around him, and he caught on to it." She could hear how stupid she sounded. They weren't going to believe her, no matter what. In their eyes, she would always be their dumb sister.

"Wait," Zechariah said. "Have you two ever held a real conversation?"

"Once."

"Once?"

"Once."

"He's messing with your head," Adam said.

"Well," Zechariah stuck the lamp in her face. "You do realize that he only saved you out of pity, and now you think there is something between you two? Again, why are we doing this?"

"We should have just let the Egyptians deal with their own and stayed out of it," Adam said.

"Just shut up and write it!" There was no way she could explain to them the way Seti had looked at her at the palace.

Something was there. She knew it.

"So…this sounds extremely stupid," Adam said as he wrote, "From Scared Little Kitten." He sat back on his heels again, admiring his handiwork. "I can't believe I'm doing this."

"You have a weird taste in men," Zechariah said.

Adam stood. "Sounds more like a little girl crush to me."

After snatching up the note, Eliza looped it over the rope around the cow's neck. The three of them stood back, gazing at it. Adam shook his head in disbelief, Zechariah laughed, and Eliza smiled.

"Wait till they see that," Zechariah said.

"Good, now let's get out of here," Adam said.

"Who's out there?" a burly voice called from inside the temple.

They froze, and Adam clamped his hand over Eliza's mouth. She grabbed his wrist, attempting to free herself. If Seti were here, she had to know.

Zechariah turned to her and put a finger to his lips.

"I heard someone. Who's out there?" The voice didn't sound familiar.

"We're leaving," Adam whispered in her ear.

Zechariah nodded and picked up the lamp.

Now was her chance to find out about Seti. But Adam wouldn't let go.

"We're leaving," he whispered again. "I'm going to let go, but if one peep comes out of you, I'm tearing apart that map and you'll never find him again." He reached into her pocket and pulled out the map.

Heat flared in her cheeks as ire pushed her beyond reason. Never had she been so furious with him.

Zechariah disappeared behind them. Adam slowly let up on the pressure until she could turn around. She faced him and glared before lunging for the map. He stumbled backward but caught her wrist before she dared to run. If she snatched the map from him and disappeared into the darkness and waited for light, their father would blame him.

"I heard voices," the voice repeated.

"Where?" another asked.

"Outside. But they won't answer. Listen."

"Shhh." Adam pulled Eliza forward to whisper in her ear. "I know what you're thinking. No tricks on my watch. All three of us are returning home, just as promised."

Zechariah had only walked a few paces ahead before his lamp dimmed to a nearly imperceptible glowing ball. Adam tugged at her wrist, and she reluctantly followed.

She would get that map. She'd find out where it led. And she was coming back.

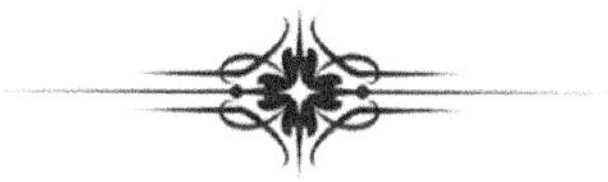

Seti's eyes opened to nothingness. At some point, he had returned to bed. How long had it been? He pulled his knees to his chest and tucked the sheet under his chin. This plague would be temporary like the others, right? What if Pharaoh gave in, but the Hebrew God decided to punish them indefinitely? They'd never see the sun again. If the Hebrew God had His way with Egypt, He'd destroy them all. It'd be the grand finale of plagues. The Egyptians would be made an example for the rest of the world.

Chewy's breathing kept Seti's awareness in check. If the Hebrew God took away sound as well, there'd be no telling what was real and what wasn't. The silence was so deafening, he wished the fumbling priests would come back. Or even the thunder from the hailstorm.

Perhaps the Egyptian gods had deserted them. If so, people would cry out for their return like jilted lovers. Eventually, they'd give up, alone and confused, without knowing what they did wrong.

Though Seti was at fault for killing the Api bull, he didn't think he'd upset the gods before that. Did the priests? Maybe they skipped something in their rituals that set off this cascade of events. No, Seti knew the answer but struggled to accept it. He clawed at his head, questions flooding his mind and mingling with the sounds of his breath.

This would be a great time to sleep.

"Give me one more dream of her."

He replayed the earlier dream of Eliza, keeping it at the forefront of his mind. Unlike the smile on her face when she laughed as they walked up the road, the smile in the dream revealed a sweet gentleness, timid but tender. It gave Eliza's words a certainty that he was safe with her. Unintimidated, she held his gaze, and he cherished it. But why did she smell like roast beef?

Was it a glimpse into the future, a wistful longing, or nothing?

Lumeri's taunting face replaced Eliza's. *You're acting like a little boy.*

Sabu's laughter filled his head. *What does the son of Ameneten not know?*

His ideas and fantasies were a bore to those around him, making him different. It set him apart, not only from the average Egyptian, but also from the priests. He didn't want to share his wife with them or their gods. Strong drink had never appealed. He acted like a stupid child. His mother rejected him.

Seti turned in the bed, tears filling his eyes. He wiped them with his hand and whipped them against the wall, wanting to scream. The festering within him spiraled out of control, darkness seeping into his heart.

"It's just darkness. Never bothered me before. It will be over soon." He wanted so badly to go home to his family. He clawed and pulled at his hair.

"Stop!" He stuffed his hands beneath him.

His father's words echoed in his ears: *The Hebrew God has gotten a hold of your heart.*

"Why? Why would you do this to me?" What would the Hebrew God want with him? Seti was nothing to the Egyptian gods and nothing to the Hebrew God. Only a tool to set Eliza and her sister free.

Sabu and Hoshea helped him escape. His father tried to save him, but Seti betrayed him. Pharaoh and the priests were coming for him. He'd either die at the hands of Pharaoh or out in the desert.

What did he think would happen if he fled? He had never learned to farm, hunt, or fish and would probably starve. Building a shelter was out of the question, as he had no carpentry skills. His knowledge of reading and writing would be useless outside of Egypt. Moshe had survived, but Seti didn't have the Hebrew God protecting him.

He groaned.

Think about Eliza.

For five years, she had worked for his family, and he had done everything he could to make a mockery of her— teasing her in front of his friends, making her look stupid, and forcing her to do extra work if he thought she was slacking.

Think harder.

Her beautiful smile and sparkling eyes when he placed the net over her head. The sure, soft voice she used when talking about her God. How the moonlight bathed the perfect features of her face. She chose the whipping to keep her sister from being transferred to the brick farms. So brave and noble—the opposite of him.

This isn't working. The darkness was too strong.

Seti jerked awake. Did he fall asleep? He hadn't dreamed. Or was he still sleeping? He listened for Chewy's breathing. Instead, a familiar buzzing filled the silence. Gnats!

Just like in the pyramid, the drone grew louder, filling

the room.

The god-statues from Giza appeared before him, glowing gray and floating above him. Seti was about to sit up when three spirits spewed from their mouths like vomit. They glowered at him with white eyes, hovering.

Seti sank into the mattress, eyes widening. They dropped in unison, pushing on his chest. He yelled, but no sound came. His lungs ached, ready to burst under their weight. He swatted frantically, pushing them away, his hands swallowed up by the darkness.

Their eyes turned black, personified in white silhouettes. They were going to snuff out his life and take his spirit. He turned his head to the side, his hands covering his face.

"No," he whispered, then his eyes rolled back.

Chewy snorted, and Seti woke. Was that a nightmare? His chest heaved, but the spirits and buzzing were gone. He had been sleeping. Seti took in a deep breath, slowing his breathing. The darkness continued, complete and binding.

Something hard hit the wall next to him, and he recoiled. Chewy whinnied and snorted.

"I know, buddy," Seti said. "It's messing with me too."

Chewy's tail hit Seti's face, and his hooves clattered on the floor. Seti pinned himself against the door. Chewy was going berserk.

"Chewy, stop!"

Wood cracked beside him, and the bed moved. Chewy struck the wall with a bang.

Seti froze, afraid to move.

"Whoa!" He covered his face with his arms.

"It's okay." He whistled, but Chewy didn't respond.

After finding his bag on the bed, Seti pulled out the last of the oats and tossed them into the darkness, hoping to pacify Chewy, but the snorting and stomping continued.

Chewy was in a full-blown panic. The bed rattled against the wall.

"God, don't let me die yet," Seti whispered, unsure which god he pleaded with.

What a terrible way to die, but he'd die soon regardless. He ran his fingers through his hair and winced when his fingers touched the bump on the back of his head. It felt like forever ago when he hit his head.

"Chewy, here boy." Seti reached out to find the reins but thought better of it. There was no calming Chewy.

Afraid to move, Seti closed his eyes.

"Seti? Seti, open the door!"

Seti slumped over the end of the bed. Sunlight cut through his eyelids, and he shielded them with his hand. The bed jolted when the door moved.

"Seti, I know you're in there!" It was his father.

Seti sat up, his head spinning. Chewy stood calmly near the window. The room was in ruins—manure everywhere, holes punched through the walls. Seti's bag lay near the window, and his shattered lamp spread across the floor in pieces.

He jumped from the bed and pulled it to the middle of the room. The door flew open, and his father toppled in, crashing to the floor. Seti ran to help him up.

"Seti." His father grasped Seti's arms, eyes wet with tears.

Seti pulled him to his feet, and they embraced. Tears ran from Seti's eyes onto his father's shoulder. He quickly wiped them away.

His father held him at arm's length. "Are you well?"

"Yes, you?"

"I am."

They hugged again.

"Just to be clear," Seti's voice cracked, "it was dark

everywhere, right?"

"The whole nation."

"That's what I thought."

Ameneten looked him over. He wrinkled his nose at the stench of the room.

"How did you find me?" Seti rubbed his palms on his tunic.

"The others heard Chewy last night. As soon as the sun came out, they got me."

Of course. All knew where he was now. He had planned to run. Had he lost his chance? Parting with his father again would be unbearable, but his fate hung in the air.

"How long has it been?" Seti asked.

"I don't know. I heard three or four days. I don't even know what day it is." Ameneten gave a nervous chuckle.

"That was the worst night of my life." Seti dropped his gaze.

His father gave the room a once-over before saying, "Seti, there's something you need to see."

Seti lifted his head. "What?"

Ameneten motioned to the door. "Go ahead, I'll grab Chewy."

"No—"

But his father held up a hand and nodded toward the door. Seti hesitantly grabbed his bag from the floor and shuffled from the room, followed by his father and Chewy.

"The foyer," Ameneten directed.

They descended the winding stairs to the private hall. At the front, Seti pushed open the door to the foyer. A group of priests and dancers huddled together near a pillar by the steps. Other than them, the place was empty. Not even the god-statues were out.

Seti's mind raced. *It's a trick. They're going to turn me in.*

The group grew quiet, and Lumeri stepped aside,

staring at Seti. Behind her, a giant black bull lifted its head. Could it be?

The others stepped away, revealing three adult cattle and two calves. Seti stopped in his tracks, eyes wide, unsure if he was seeing things. He glanced back at his father, who entered the foyer with Chewy, giving Seti a nod.

Seti ran to the cattle. He touched the white triangle on one of their foreheads, tracing the outline in disbelief. He grabbed the bull's snout, opened its mouth, and peered inside for the scarab bump that resembled the beetle. Sure enough, it was there.

"Five of them." He laughed as he examined the others.

Silence filled the foyer as he rounded behind the bovines, taking the ends of the tails in his hand, feeling the hair in his fingers. How? He continued around each one until spotting the dirty white cloth stuck in one of the collars.

Written in Hebrew: "To Seti, From Scared Little Kitten."

The breath left his lungs.

"Who's Scared Little Kitten?" his father asked, standing behind him with arms crossed and brow raised.

How was he to answer? Where did Eliza get these? How did she know? The only people who knew were the priests and Sabu. Did his mother know? Kabelo? Did Eliza go to his house?

"Seti?" his father urged.

"I don't know," Seti choked.

He reread the words written in oil, bringing the cloth to the sunlight to make sure.

"We found these animals this morning," one of the priests said. "You don't know who left them here?"

"No." Seti's voice shook. If he could be a good liar just once, let it be now. "Maybe the gods answered my prayers. Maybe I found favor with them." He looked at the priests. "And you. They heard your cries."

The three priests glanced at each other and nodded. But

his father didn't move. Seti stared at the note, aware of his father's eyes drilling into him. Ameneten could see right through his lies.

"What does it say, Seti?" Lumeri's voice broke into his thoughts.

Turning to her, he answered, "Like I said, it must be the favor of the gods."

She tilted her head. Her long, dark hair, grazing her shoulders, had lost its shine, and the boils had dulled her once-glowing skin.

Then the words left his mouth. "How are the gods treating you?"

She huffed and turned away. Satisfied with her reaction, Seti untied the rope from the pillar. He snatched the note and stuffed it into his bag, then faced his father.

"I think you should present them to Pharaoh." His father's words came slow and careful.

"I think so too," Seti said.

He led the cattle down the steps, the calves following. Unable to satisfy his father's questioning gaze, he dared not look back. "Scared Little Kitten" was Eliza. He had called her that only once, and she remembered. What a ridiculous thing to call her.

The thoughts that had run rampant in his head during the past three or four horrible, dark nights would haunt him forever. Though the darkness had an influence, they still rang true.

He didn't deserve these animals. She had saved him from certain death, yet instead of relief, shame washed over him. Seeing her one last time would be an answer to his prayers—to ask her why and how, to apologize for the way he had treated her.

Perhaps finding a replacement Api bull was payback for helping her, but she owed him nothing. Rescuing her had been the least he could do.

He paused and waited for Chewy to catch up, then

grabbed the reins with one hand while leading the cattle toward the palace.

The gate to the outer courtyard was shut in the early dawn light, though it should have opened at sunrise. A lone guard leaned against it, arms crossed, clearly not bothered by the complaining townsfolk. Upon seeing Seti approach with the cattle, he opened the gate without a word.

The outer courtyard had been stripped of its lush green grass. Only dirt remained. Stone houses sat dull and lifeless, sparring fields now mud pits, and the streets of dressed stones now littered with debris, giving the place a haunted appearance.

An Ethiopian foot soldier accompanied Seti, leading him in silence. The cattle seemed to lend Seti a sense of authority among the guards. Their staring eyes made it clear, as did the way they ensured nothing interrupted his procession. Even the few stationed along the walls paused to watch.

The inner courtyard wasn't as impenetrable as Seti was led to believe, its grandeur snatched away like it had all been an illusion. The stone statues stood bare and filthy, their luster dulled by layers of dirt and dust. Sand filled every crevice of the intricate designs and inscriptions on the columns in the colonnade, now riddled with chips and cracks from the storm. They looked centuries old.

The palace, typically bustling with carriers, travelers, and those seeking the face of Pharaoh, appeared abandoned, the throne sitting empty and forgotten.

The soldier scowled and said in a heavy accent, "Wait here. Pharaoh wasn't expecting visitors, but I will tell him you have arrived."

Seti nodded, masking his surprise that Pharaoh would come out of his private quarters for him. No, but for an Api bull he would. It might rejuvenate his fight against Moshe's

God. What other disasters awaited Egypt because the Api bull would give him hope?

The private sector of the enormous palace stretched to the Nile. How long would it take to find Pharaoh? But word of the bull's arrival would spread. Seti's mouth grew dry, and his heart pounded as the wait dragged on. He had arrived with the confidence of freedom, but how far-fetched was that? Pharaoh could still demand Chewy's life. Or his.

At last, a side door opened, and Pharaoh's face poked around it. Seti blinked, making sure his eyes weren't playing tricks on him. Pharaoh disappeared, and seconds later, he marched through the door with his shoulders back, wearing the ceremonial horned headdress. He eyed Seti as he climbed the steps and sat on his throne, fanning his dull, red tunic over the sides. The linen strips, gold cape, and jeweled collar were absent.

Seti rolled his shoulders and waited as Pharaoh pulled a gold belt plated with rubies, onyx, and lapis lazuli from behind a cushion. After fastening it around his waist, he secured matching arm cuffs. His royal splendor contrasted his sickly appearance, but at the sight of the cattle, a light sparked in his eyes.

He straightened and fixed his gaze on Seti, who fumbled under his stare before dropping into a bow.

Pharaoh rose from the throne and descended the six steps toward the bovines. "Five of them. Remarkable!"

Seti held his breath, face to the floor.

The cattle stirred as Pharaoh inspected them, opening each mouth. He nodded his approval and stepped in front of Seti. "Rise."

Standing, Seti kept his gaze downcast.

"Where did you find these?"

Seti cleared his throat. "They were given to me, my lord."

Pharaoh's brow raised. "Given to you?"

"Yes. They were left in the foyer in the Menf temple

and discovered when the sun rose this morning. They had a note addressed to me."

His wrinkled brow lifted higher. "Do you have the note with you?"

"No, my lord."

He narrowed his eyes, and Seti's heart thumped against his chest.

Pharaoh stroked the snout of the cow but kept his eyes on Seti. "So the gods have smiled upon you and not me?"

"I-I don't consider it favoring me, my lord. They smile upon you."

"Right, but the note was addressed to you."

"Yes, with instructions to present them to you, my lord. I believe someone wants us reconciled."

Pharaoh barked a sarcastic laugh, startling Seti. "That someone being a god? Ptah?"

Seti nodded, his voice trembling as he responded, "We have been praying and prostrating ourselves for favor from the gods. Perhaps this is a sign that things will turn around."

Was that moisture in Pharaoh's eyes? He moved toward the cattle, and Seti drew in a deep breath, glad for the increased space between them.

"We can breed them. How could this be?"

Seti stilled, quite sure it had nothing to do with the gods and everything to do with Eliza.

With a grunt of approval, Pharaoh examined the animals once more before stepping near Seti and whispering in his ear, "You haven't given me your horse like I demanded."

Seti struggled to slow his pulse under Pharaoh's hot breath. "You told me to find another Api bull. Now you'll never be without."

Palace guards lurked in the shadows behind pillars, giving something for Seti to focus on as Pharaoh breathed in his ear. Chills ran up his spine, and he half expected a spear to pierce his flesh at any moment, despite not seeing any weapons on Pharaoh.

"What do you want from me, Seti, son of Ameneten?"

With masked calmness, Seti answered, "The gods want us reconciled. I think if we are, it will please them."

Pharaoh swallowed, and Seti heard it loud and clear. "I will free you and your horse. But you will not work under me. You are not fit to be a priest." He moved in front of Seti.

"I realize that, my lord." Seti lowered his gaze once again.

Pharaoh studied him. "Your brother will continue with your inheritance."

"Yes, my lord."

"You will never return to the temple again."

"It will be as you say, my lord."

"Look at me," Pharaoh demanded.

Seti raised his head and met Pharaoh's regard, realizing he had used those exact words and tone with Eliza.

After a moment of studying Seti's face, Pharaoh turned. "The procession and your announcement regarding the previous Api bull still stand. If Ptah doesn't accept the new bull, I'll know you are lying, and I will require both yours and your jt's heads."

"Yes, my lord."

Without giving Seti another look, Pharaoh flicked his hand.

Seti snatched Chewy's reins and hurried for the exit, not daring to exhale until he reached the bottom step outside the palace.

He hugged his horse. "We're free, Chewy." But Pharaoh's threat hung, Ptah didn't exist to accept the new bull. Seti mounted Chewy and raced toward the gates.

Chapter 22

"Wake up. There's work to do." Eliza's father yanked the thin flax sheet off the boys.

Eliza turned away from the bright window, shielding her eyes with her hand. The much-awaited sun had taken forever to come back. She squinted at her father as he stepped over his sleeping family, pulling off blankets and sheets.

Miera sat up beside Eliza, smiling at the window.

"Ima's preparing food for the journey. Eliza and Miera, you two will go into Egypt and collect gold and silver. But not far, not to the Ameneten house." He eyed Eliza. "Adam and Zechariah, you need to help in the pastures. Gather the equipment and animals. We need as many carts and wagons as possible. We leave in two days."

Zechariah squinted through tired eyes. "What? For sure this time?"

"For sure this time." A large grin spread across her father's worn face, lifting the sides of his beard.

Miera cheered, and the twins stirred beside her.

"Gold and silver?" Eliza asked.

"Moshe said to go into the towns and ask for gold and silver. He said the people will give it to us," he answered.

"Really?" The boys exchanged looks of amazement.

"That's what he said. Miera, make sure she doesn't go

back to that house. Go with Rahel if you want. Stay on the outskirts, away from On."

"Yes, sir."

The twins crawled across Eliza, tugging at the knots in her hair, and woke the lamb sleeping at her head.

"We're going to be rich!" Miera tossed hay into the air.

Her father headed to the door. "I'm not sure it's for us to keep, so don't get too excited."

Zechariah sat up. "I want gold."

"No. I need your help. We only have two days."

The siblings scrambled out of bed with vigor, but Eliza didn't move. Setting foot in that terrible nation would only make her yearn for Seti. She had meandered about in the dark for three days, fretting over him. He'd discover the bovine this morning—if he was still alive.

Adam tossed a handful of hay toward her. He pulled the map from his pocket and waved it before her eyes. "Looks like I'll be hanging on to this for a little longer."

What use did it serve now? The sun had risen, and time was running out. If the map was to Seti, then she had served its purpose already and saved him from Pharaoh.

The aroma of warm, unleavened, huckleberry and blueberry bread filled the house. A bowl of rolls sat on the table near the door.

Eliza surveyed the fresh bread before studying her mother. "What are you doing?"

Her mother wiped her sweaty brow with her arm, hands caked in dough, but she wouldn't look at Eliza. "I packed the kneading trough already. Other than that, I'm preparing for the trip." She nodded toward the rolls.

The rolls were the last of the leavened dough. There wouldn't be much left to eat on their final days in Egypt.

"Maybe we should save them."

Her mother sighed and finally gazed at her daughter. Unlike the rest of the family, there was no joy in her eyes.

"Is something wrong, Ima?"

Her mother forced a smile. "Yes, just tired. I woke early this morning. There's much work to do, and the darkness robbed us of time."

"Do you want me to stay and help?"

"No. Get the jewelry from the Egyptians. Anything they give you. Our houseguests will help around here as soon as they wake up."

"Did the sun rise in Egypt, too?" Miera asked, sniffing the air.

"The sun greeted the whole world, Miera." Eliza gave her sister a small shove.

Miera nodded, grabbed a roll, and dashed for the door.

Her mother always rose early in the morning to make breakfast when they were home. This shouldn't be stressful. Maybe the darkness had weighed on her. Though three days was a long time, Eliza enjoyed spending the hours stargazing in the fields with Rahel. The lights of campfires and lanterns had given Avaris an enchanting feel.

She and Miera met Rahel on City Street with empty baskets. To Eliza's astonishment, the street was filled with women and children excitedly bouncing around, baskets, buckets, and bags hanging from their arms.

"Moshe and Aharon were at the house of Nun again last night," Rahel said as they shuffled down the street with the crowd. "But I heard they're returning to the palace one last time."

"I thought Pharaoh was letting us go, that the darkness was the last plague," Eliza wondered out loud.

"There must be one more."

"So, we haven't officially been set free yet? And we're to go into Egypt to ask for silver and gold?"

"I guess." Rahel shrugged.

Then what's the last plague? If only she could have heard what was said at the meeting. Her mother must know more than she was letting on. A sinking feeling drained what little energy Eliza had.

She glanced at Rahel. "Were you spying on the Nun household?"

"Who, me?"

"How did you find out? Abba said nothing about this."

"I was looking for Hoshea, but he wasn't there. I heard Moshe talking about going into Egypt, and that Pharaoh hasn't let us go yet."

"Rahel." Eliza shook her head. Her friend had to have done this in the dark.

Rahel shrugged. "He thinks I'm funny."

"Moshé?" Eliza asked.

"No, dimwit! Hoshea, remember?"

Hoshea had to know more about the map, as did Sabu. He wouldn't have told her how to save Seti if he were already dead.

"Maybe he thinks I'm cute. Cute and funny, same thing, right?" Rahel asked.

"Animals are cute, not people," Miera commented.

"No, people can be cute."

Eliza patted her sister's frizzy head. "Did you name that little lamb yet?"

"I don't know. I wanted to call it Whitehead, but it's going to die soon anyway."

"Whitehead? So creative," Rahel said sarcastically.

Eliza smiled. "I think he's serving a special purpose. We're offering him on our last day in Egypt. He deserves a name."

"Then Whitehead it is!"

The light conversation was sweet, but Eliza's thoughts lingered on Seti. If he was still alive, he'd hopefully be free of his troubles by now, and she could move on with a satisfied conscience.

On lay three hours away, and it would be a gold mine with its prominent residents, like the Amenetens. The girls turned down a lonely side street dotted with Egyptian farms while the rest of the crowd continued toward On and Menf.

Eliza peered over her shoulder at the crowd. She could make it to the Ameneten home and back before evening if she hurried, but Seti wouldn't be home anyway. She should be thankful for the opportunity to repay him for saving her. Now more than ever, it was important to please her father and obey.

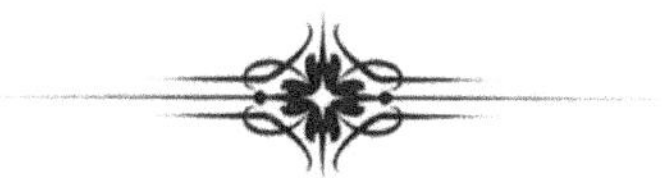

The last time Seti had spoken with Sabu was the night before the locust plague on the mesa. The joy of not having to flee Egypt built to a crescendo as Seti hurried to Sabu's house to tell him but wilted at the sight of the empty stable. Even the flax and barley were gone. He must be at the threshing square. Seti ran up the steps to the house and knocked. No answer. Odd—the women wouldn't have gone with him. No matter, he'd go to the threshing square. He mounted Chewy and steered him toward the city.

He longed to go home. What would his mother say if he returned, even if only to exchange a few words with his father? Perhaps, if she saw him, she'd want him to stay. It had been too long since he'd seen her or Kabelo, and he missed them.

It was a miracle Pharaoh hadn't kept Seti prisoner until the bull's acceptance was secured, whatever that entailed. If Ptah really did exist, he may have left the bull when the plagues started, and that would explain why he didn't protect it. Seti's father needed to be warned.

Chewy halted at City Street, jolting Seti from his thoughts. A wooden cart with two oxen blocked the road. Hebrews filled the streets, going from house to house. They hadn't left Egypt yet. This could only mean that more plagues awaited Egypt.

Seti inched closer to the cart. Clothing, jewels, trinkets,

dishes, wigs, and many more expensive items filled it to the brim. A Hebrew woman stood nearby, wearing a seashell choker and trinkets on her arms. She shot him a scowl, and he quickly backed away. Egyptians ventured out of their homes and mingled with the slaves, but no one worked.

Two Hebrew girls strolled along the edge of the street, and Seti blocked their way with Chewy. They stopped and peered up at him in wonder.

He cleared his throat. "What's happening?"

"Moshe said we are to ask for gold and silver from the Egyptians. Do you have any?"

Seti's eyes widened. "What?"

"Do you have gold or silver?" One of the girls pointed to the gold cuffs on his arms.

Seti looked at his cuffs. "No." He never removed them. They were heirlooms from his Father of Old.

"But Moshe said—"

"And I said no. You're not getting these." With a snap of the reins, Chewy moved away. This was absurd.

"Hey!" Seti shouted at a group of Hebrew boys.

Necklaces, beaded headdresses, wigs, and dyed capes adorned not just them, but everybody. People were actually relinquishing their valuables.

Seti eyed the red and gold tunic that one of the boys wore. "What's everyone doing? What's happening?"

"Moshe says you have to give us your gold and silver."

"Just the gold and silver?"

"What do you have?" one of the boys asked.

"Nothing."

"Yes, you do. What about those gold cuffs?" He pointed.

Seti should have removed them. Their eyes flashed like ravenous lions, ready to pounce. He was not getting off Chewy. A tall girl approached wearing a jeweled headband and leather sandals fastened with turquoise baubles. She carried a basket filled with silver cups, jewelry, and utensils.

She glowered at him with an expression he couldn't read.

A boy with a nose ring placed his hands on his hips and nodded at Seti. "Your gold, sir."

Their God had sent them to plunder the Egyptians.

Seti shook his head. "Did Pharaoh free you?"

"One more plague."

One more plague? It made sense. Plunder Egypt first, then destroy it. The grand finale. Seti drew a breath. "Did he tell you what the final plague would be?"

"The death of the firstborn," another said.

Seti bit his tongue. "Firstborn of what?"

"The firstborn of all of Egypt must die." The boy's smile lifted his nose-ring as he regarded Seti with amusement.

A wave of hot air hit Seti's face, and his muscles weakened. "People? You mean—" he gulped. "Egyptians?"

Nose-ring boy laughed. "Everybody."

Seti's vision blurred, and their smiling faces spun in circles. Laughter filled his ears. Seti rubbed his eyes with hands as heavy as lead. His life had just been given back, and now this. He grasped the reins to keep from falling.

"If he falls, I get the cuffs," someone said.

"Forget him. See how he's shaking? He knows he's going to die."

The words bounced off Seti's ears with no meaning, like a dream. A dream. With all his strength, Seti straightened and asked, "Eliza?"

"Who?"

"Eliza, the Hebrew girl. Big, curly hair. Scar—" His mind fogged, grasping for something distinguishable about her. "Have you seen her?"

"Frog Girl?" the girl in the sandals asked.

They call her Frog Girl? It had to be her. "Where is she?"

"Do I look like her keeper?" Nose-ring boy chuckled and turned away.

"Do you know anything about her?" Seti yelled after him.

Another boy tossed a bracelet in the air and responded as he caught it. "Just that she's Frog Girl."

The answers offered little relief to Seti's rising panic.

The girl with the headband remained after the others had left. "I saw her in Goshen."

That didn't help. She offered him a hopeful smile before running after them.

He had to focus. Find Sabu. Find his father. Find Eliza. He removed the gold cuffs and stuffed them into his bag before another confrontation arose. But the last plague. What did the firstborn mean to such a God? Revenge for drowning the babies eighty years ago? But that had been all male babies, not just the firstborn.

This was it. Pain makes a heart vulnerable, and it would break Pharaoh. His firstborn would die. The Hebrew God had planned it this way. If the previous plagues hadn't convinced the world who the one true God was, this last one would.

Seti rode in a daze as Chewy trotted toward the threshing square. It didn't matter anymore that Pharaoh had lifted the target from his head. Or that he had found a replacement for the Api bull. It didn't even matter if Ptah accepted it or not. The Hebrew God would have their heads before Pharaoh would. Like the pyramid gods coming for his soul that one night, the Hebrew God slowly sucked Seti's life before finally taking it. There would be nothing left of him for the afterlife.

The public square lay just outside On near the Nile. Two rows of three threshing floors spread across the top of a large hill where a strong wind blew. The use of the floors required a tax on the final product.

During harvests, farmers would line the gravel road leading up the hill, sometimes for weeks, waiting their turn. Laughter and celebration would fill the nights as long as they waited. Afterward, the temple bustled with gracious farmers paying homage to the gods.

But the hill lay empty when Seti and Chewy climbed it, the place barren except for one threshing floor toward the end. Two old men toiled together, wearing nothing but loincloths. The hot breeze offered no relief in the afternoon sun. Their barley spread across the floor in a mess while bundles lay stacked in a pile nearby.

Not finding Sabu, Seti slumped on Chewy and started to turn back when one of the men hollered at him. He sighed and collected himself before approaching them.

A hairy little man stared wide-eyed at Seti.

Seti opened his mouth to speak, but nothing came out. Panic rose in his chest again. He dropped from Chewy and found himself on his knees, leaning on his hands. His stomach heaved, and bile burned his throat.

One of the men rushed over, but Seti held up his hand, stopping him.

His fingers dug into the dirt. *Pour it on your head. Tear your tunic.* He sat back on his heels. No, he couldn't give in to grief yet. His throat burned and made breathing difficult. He clutched his chest, gasping for air, hyperventilating. Talking himself down only made it worse. This was it. The last plague.

A bald, withered old man came at Seti with a bucket and hurled water at him.

Seti fell onto his rear, drenched. He ran a hand down his face and breathed deeply. "Thank you."

Neither man moved.

"I'm...I'm..." Seti said. "Thank you."

"You sure?" the bald one asked.

Seti nodded and forced a smile.

"You're the son of Ameneten!"

Standing, Seti wiped mud from his tunic.

"You saved our crops. It was you who sent the slaves." The man flung himself at Seti, embracing him. "I can't begin to say how grateful I am. It was right before the storm; they were going to be destroyed. We lost all our animals and wheat and everything else, but this should get us through to next season. I don't know how to repay you."

Seti struggled away. "It's fine." He gathered his composure. "I'm looking for Sabu. He oversaw the slaves who saved your farm. I thought he'd be here."

The men exchanged glances. "Nobody has been here but us. I imagine more will come now that Ra has returned. There were a few here when the darkness hit but nobody familiar."

Seti's heart fell. Maybe Sabu was on his way but took a different road. He'd be using Nimrod to transport the bundles and may have to make a few trips.

"Is there anything we can do to help you?" the hairy man asked.

Seti's thoughts jumbled together, swirling as if in a whirlwind. He shook his head and mumbled, "I have no place to stay."

"You're more than welcome to stay with us. How long do you need?"

"I don't know. Not long." With the speed of the most recent plagues, the last one should hit soon, like birth pangs.

"We'll be headed back once we're finished. If you give us a hand, we'd finish faster."

Seti nodded, rubbing the bump on the back of his head. "I've never threshed before." Sabu would show up soon, and keeping busy would help him not lose his mind again.

The bald man tossed him a flail. "It's easier with oxen, but this is all we have. I'll teach you."

Seti examined the flail. How hard could it be? The man pushed his flail across the barley, grinding it down, using his weight. It crushed the straw into pieces, and the grain piled beneath it.

It looked daunting, but Seti followed suit. It didn't take much skill.

"There you go!" The hairy man clapped his hands.

Seti flashed him a half smile, but his head spun. When was the last time he drank?

"We do this until all the grain is separated from the straw. Then we'll use the shovels to toss it into the air. The wind will blow the straw to the side, and the grain will fall. It'll have to be sifted, but the women can do that at home. Your horse can feed on the straw if he likes."

Seti nodded and wiped the sweat from his brow. "Do you have more water?"

"Yes, of course!" The hairy man rushed for their supplies near the stone wall that edged the floor.

The water cooled and relieved Seti's dry throat, and he drank all they gave him.

They flailed until late evening. The old men moved with ease, but Seti grew weak and exhausted. Racing Chewy with Sabu had been the only physical work he'd ever done, but he refused to stop until they did.

At nightfall, the men nestled into the loose straw and pulled out a loaf of stale bread and beer, sharing it with Seti. He sat to the side and slugged the beer, slathered his bread with grape jam, folded the pieces into a sandwich, and ate six sandwiches before the bread ran out.

"When's the last time you ate, boy?" the bald man asked.

"I don't know." Seti shrugged and emptied his beer bowl. "Before the darkness?" He leaned against the stone wall, watching the stars appear one after another. Never had he been so grateful to see those stars. Of course, never had he thought he'd lose them either.

The men talked quietly, and Chewy ate his fill before joining Seti near the side wall. Sabu never showed.

Seti woke to the scraping of flails against rock and dirt. They had let him sleep. The sun barely broke the horizon.

He sat up, brushing the straw from his hair.

A couple more days of flailing, and they'd start winnowing—tossing the straw into the wind. He didn't have a couple more days. He had to see his father.

Both Seti and his father were going to die.

He'd find his father, warn him, then return to help the men finish. They had fed him and Chewy; they deserved his help. The irony of being well-fed before his impending doom wasn't lost on him.

Eliza rested her cheek in one hand at the table, absentmindedly tracing the drawings on the map with the other. Adam had left it there the day before, when she and Miera had gone back into Egypt, evidently assuming she wouldn't try anything with so little time left and under her mother's watchful eye. But her mother paid her little heed, rushing about the house like a madwoman. Ruby-speckled gold bangles decorated Eliza's forearms, and jewels piled on the table.

The little house was in shambles, and her mother was even more frazzled than the day before. Eliza couldn't remember accumulating so many useless items. Most of what they possessed had been passed down from their ancestors before becoming slaves.

Her mother dried her hands on her tunic. "Eliza, we need more water. Make yourself useful and go to the well."

Eliza sighed, grabbed two clay basins from the floor, and headed out. Sheep stood in the firepit behind her house. Livestock of every kind crowded the yards in between wagons, which had carts stacked inside them. She shook her head. They would need to be unstacked to load them.

Hopefully, that would be the boys' job.

She paused and surveyed her surroundings. Every day revealed new surprises, things she never dreamed of—gatherings with music, laughter with her family, three straight days of darkness, and Api bulls on a Hebrew farm. That didn't begin to describe the surprises in Egypt. A sense of unity and pride filled the air in Goshen. The people were many yet worked as one.

She hauled a small cart from a pile and placed the basins inside. Once on the street, she turned to gaze at her house but could barely see it above the carts and wagons. It was quite the sight, enough to make her chuckle. She tucked a reminder in the back of her mind to sketch the scene before they left. Adam would have to teach her to write while they traveled. There was too much to leave to memory. The great Israelite exodus would be passed down for generations by word of mouth, but not her specific experience.

In one more day, they would leave Egypt. Forever.

Chapter 23

Seti lay in the hay and covered himself with a dirty flax sheet, the only thing resembling a blanket in the outhouse. Eliza had slept here. No wonder she stank. A small window provided little light or air circulation, and Seti sneezed. Egyptian homes were stuffy, but this was unbearable.

With his hands folded over his chest, his gaze wandered over the mud-brick walls and straw ceiling. Wasps buzzed around a nest hanging in the corner. He couldn't straighten his legs. How did she sleep in this mess without complaining? He sneezed again and attempted to wipe his wet hand on the hay when he felt something solid. His fingers closed around a leathery object. Lumeri's sandal.

The other sandal lay nearby. Either Eliza or her sister must have stolen them. But they hadn't been in the outhouse since that fateful morning. What other treasures lay hidden in here? After a thorough search and finding nothing, the sandals joined his arm cuffs in his woven bag.

He returned to staring at the ceiling, this time with a mischievous grin. What would Eliza want with Lumeri's sandals? Lumeri's father had brought them from his sailing adventures in the north—leather with blue pearls, exotic even to Egyptians.

A neighing horse and chariot wheels woke Seti from

his nap. Father. He jumped up and peered out the window. Ameneten unharnessed his horse in the stable. How many times had Eliza watched Seti come home in the middle of the night? Or his make-out sessions with various girls in the wee hours? He pushed the thought away and stumbled out the door as his father emerged from the stable.

The two stopped, locking eyes.

"Seti."

Seti straightened, his forehead dripping with sweat. He'd wasted time thinking about Eliza instead of rehearsing how to break the news of his father's impending death.

"Jt."

A grin replaced his father's bewildered expression, and he marched over and flung his arm around his son. "Come in for supper, and you can tell me everything."

Seti wrung his hands and glanced at the house. "But—"

"Your mwt can tolerate you for one meal, I think."

Seti closed his mouth and let his father lead him up the stone walkway.

"There you are!" Rahel's voice broke into Eliza's daydreaming at the well. She had been waiting in line for nearly an hour.

Rahel emerged from a herd of cattle. "I found Hoshea!"

Eliza straightened. She had given up on deciphering the map. Saving Seti from Pharaoh was the most she could do, but what if it was all for nothing and he had been killed? Hoshea might at least know if Seti still lived. She glanced at the well. Water would have to wait. Who knew when they'd find Hoshea again?

Leaving the wagon and basins behind, she broke into a run after Rahel.

Rahel ran ahead toward her own street where several carts blocked the road. A couple of young men harnessed oxen to the carts while others loaded them with Egyptian goods brought out from nearby houses. Hoshea stood in one of the carts, stacking the treasures.

"Hoshea!" Rahel screamed. "Hoshea!"

He lifted his head and jumped from the cart.

Eliza pulled the map from her pocket as she ran, scrunching it in her fist. The men paused at Rahel's screams. She skidded on the gravel, fell, and landed at Hoshea's feet, her legs tangled with his. Eliza slid to a stop before crashing into him, the map in hand.

"What's wrong?" Hoshea asked.

Eliza panted and held the map up to his face. "Is Seti still alive? And Adam couldn't read the map. What did Sabu say about it?"

Hoshea exhaled and put his hands on his hips. He looked at Rahel. "You were screaming like somebody died."

Eliza dropped her hand. "You'd know if Pharaoh killed him, right?"

Hoshea sighed and tilted his head. He lowered his voice. "Did you do the thing with the bull?"

"Yes. We delivered them to the temple."

He smiled with satisfaction. "I wouldn't have had you deliver them if Pharaoh had killed him."

"But he could have had him killed right before or afterward, before they found the cattle."

"In the dark?" Hoshea laughed. "I don't think so. And all Sabu said about the map was that it was about Seti. I assumed it was where to take the bull."

"So, it leads to Seti?"

"That's what I would presume. Sabu didn't say much. He was in a hurry. He was hoping I'd do something with it, but I couldn't."

"What does it say?" She shoved the map in his face again.

Hoshea shifted his weight. "I can't read, remember? I thought Adam could read it. We are leaving in the morning. There's nothing you can do now. Besides, you must be in your house by this evening."

"What do you mean?"

"When we slay the lambs. We have to put the blood on the sides and tops of the door frames, and you can't leave the house after that."

She returned the map to her pocket. "What? Why?"

He furrowed his brow. "You don't know?"

Something about the way he asked made her stomach twist into knots. "No."

Rahel stared at Hoshea wide-eyed from where she sat on the ground. He grabbed her hand, helping her to her feet, and she winked at Eliza.

He returned his attention to Eliza, concern in his eyes. "Your abba has to put the lamb's blood on the door mantel for when God comes at midnight and slays every firstborn who isn't in a house marked with the blood. You can't go outside. And the lamb has to be roasted, not boiled. And—"

"The firstborn of Egypt?"

"Yes, including us Israelites. Only the blood on the door will keep us safe. Your abba didn't tell you?"

It explained her mother's behavior over the past couple of days, as well as Adam's questioning them the night of the meeting. Her parents kept it from him. "No."

If Seti was alive, he wouldn't be for long. Her heart pounded, and she stepped back, putting a hand on her chest.

She turned to run, but Hoshea grabbed her arm. "You aren't going after Seti, are you?"

Eliza's mouth dropped open, but her throat closed.

"You don't have time," he said.

She yanked her arm free, but he caught hold of her again.

"Listen, Eliza! You don't have time. You did what you could for him." The urgency in his voice sent chills through her body, and tears streamed down her cheeks.

"My parents…they didn't tell us." They either didn't want Adam to know or feared Eliza would try to save Seti. They were right. She broke free of Hoshea's grasp and darted out of his reach.

"Eliza!" He lunged forward, but Rahel wrapped her arms around him.

Eliza sprinted around the carts and down the street. Rahel wouldn't be able to hold him for long. He'd either come after her or go to her parents. Map balled in her fist, she raced home.

Miera sat out front, milking a cow. Eliza halted on her street upon seeing her. She couldn't go home. There was no way her family would let her save Seti. And Hoshea would catch up any moment.

She'd find Seti, bring him home, and hide him in the house, under the protection of the lamb's blood. It was just after noon. She could make it.

After weaving between houses, she took the neighboring road toward City Street.

At City Street, she paused as a sharp cramp stung her side. A horse would make this easier, but the only animals around were livestock. It would take three hours to reach Seti's house on foot, less if she ran.

Seti sat on his hands at the family table while Huya set a plate of lentils and bread before him. She smiled, waiting for his reaction to her attempt at dinner. He gave her a slight nod of approval but looked away. Her pustuled face broke his heart. Kabelo's eyes flicked between Seti and Huya, while he masked a smile with a mouth full of warm bread.

Paying no attention to the food, Ameneten said, "Seti, tell your mwt what Pharaoh told you."

Seti focused on his lentils. "He said I was free to go. And Chewy. But the inheritance still belongs to Kabelo, and I cannot become a priest anymore."

"Good." Kabelo sat beside him.

A good wrestle with his brother would cement Kabelo's memory of Seti—the rogue firstborn, marked for death by the Hebrew God. They hadn't wrestled in years.

"You cannot become a priest anymore?" Huya sat across from him. "You brought him a replacement for the Api bull, didn't you? He should have freed you as well as given back your future."

Seti lifted his eyes. "I was still reckless, Mwt. I'll take what I can get."

"You could have bartered with him," Ameneten said. "After all, you supplied five perfect cattle, not one. You can make your announcement at the procession and reassure the world that you not only provided the bull, but now Pharaoh can breed them."

"I didn't want to push my luck. He's already distressed."

"Perfect time to barter—when a man's desperate."

"We're talking about Pharaoh, not a man."

Ameneten's head shot up, and his bread hit the plate. "Seti, you'd make a great priest. You're the best student and take your work seriously. You need to reconsider."

"There's nothing to consider. Pharaoh has already decided. It's not up to me." Why did Seti have to defend himself in his own home? But this wasn't his home anymore.

"Seti, your jt wants what's best," Huya said.

Of all people for those words to come from. Seti shot her a look of disdain. "If Ptah doesn't accept the bull, Pharaoh will have both mine and Jt's heads. I am in no place to barter. Besides, Ptah—" Seti paused before dropping his suspicions that Ptah didn't exist.

Huya and Kabelo's mouths dropped open.

Ameneten didn't flinch. "I figured as much. That's why you wait until after the anointing of the new Api bull. Talk about perfect timing." He picked up his bread.

No more subtleties, get to the point. Seti closed his eyes and inhaled. "I don't want to be a priest anymore."

Huya stood abruptly, jarring the table with her knee. "What are you saying?"

"It's over, Mwt. I no longer trust in the gods. They've failed us against the Hebrew God because they couldn't or wouldn't stand up to Him. Either way, they're cowards. My heart is not with them."

The three stared, eyes wide.

After a moment, Huya said, "I can't believe I'm hearing this."

"I knew this was going to happen." Ameneten pointed at Seti with his tongs. "I told you, Huya. Seti, this is why I was worried about you. The Hebrew God has got you under His spell—"

"Spell? More like our gods are under His spell. Pharaoh, too!"

"Seti!"

Seti glared, the stake in his heart twisting. This was a mistake. He should go back to the threshing floor. The men were waiting.

"Jt." He rose from his cushion. "I have to tell you. There's one more plague. The Hebrew God will kill every firstborn of Egypt. It will be what compels Pharaoh to release the Hebrews. We're going to die."

Silence sharpened the tension in the room.

"Where did you hear this?" Ameneten asked.

"The Hebrew children told me the other day when they were collecting jewelry. Moshe told them what the last plague would be."

"Hebrew children?"

The stake twisted more. "You don't believe me. I know they are children—and Hebrew—but I believe them. Everything their God has said He'd do has come to pass. You said pain softens the heart enough to be influenced by outside factors, right? This is what gets Pharaoh."

"This isn't Moshe talking, it's children."

"I still believe them."

"Even if it's true. What do you want me to do?"

That was a good question. Seti thought a moment while the others waited. "Maybe," he shifted his feet, "maybe get Pharaoh to let them go before this happens."

"When is this supposed to happen?"

"I don't know." Seti should have asked the children. "Soon. They were packing up, collecting gold and silver. They're plundering our nation before their God destroys us."

"What?" Kabelo asked.

"I thought they were already freed." Huya's eyes darted between her husband and son.

"And, if nine curses didn't convince Pharaoh, how do you think I will?" Ameneten asked in exasperation.

"I don't know!" Seti grabbed his hair in frustration, defeat washing over him.

"It's about the land, Seti," Ameneten went on. "The plagues have all been about the land. Remember? Why would the Hebrew God suddenly now come after the people?"

"I don't know. Maybe because we killed the babies?"

"It's possible, if their God is so vengeful."

"Of course it's possible. We brought this on ourselves," Seti said.

"And how would I stop that?"

"I don't know!" He was getting nowhere.

Seti gave up and grabbed his bag, filling it with bread from the table.

"Are you leaving?" Ameneten asked.

"I have to find Sabu," Seti replied, voice trembling.

Huya leaned forward, a hand on her hip. "What's wrong with you, Seti? Look at you!"

He looked at her scrunched face. "Did Sabu stop by here?"

"No."

"Eliza?"

Silence.

Huya blinked rapidly before asking, "Why would she stop here?"

"I don't know. Maybe she was looking for silver or gold."

"Even if she did," Huya lifted her chin, "I wouldn't give her any."

Seti rolled his eyes and stormed out the door, his father trailing behind him. "Where are you going?"

Halting on the stone walkway, Seti turned. "Jt, I love you. I'm sorry for everything I've done. I'm sorry I failed you. But I must find Sabu. Coming here was a mistake."

His father's mouth dropped open before he shook his head, lowering his gaze. "I'll be at the temple tonight. I'll talk with the priests about this new plague. Perhaps they have heard something. Maybe there's more to it, something that can be done."

"I don't know how much time we have," Seti said. "I'm sorry, Jt."

He hurried to the stable and grabbed Chewy, glancing at the house one last time as he passed. He had to get to the mesa.

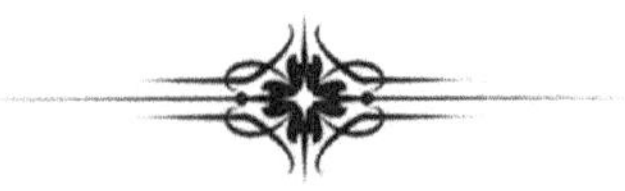

Eliza paused on the empty street, studying the map. The house drawn on it had to be Seti's. She knew how to get there—no need for a map. She swallowed and took one last look behind. No one had come after her—yet. The city of On lay just over the horizon. She picked up her pace.

The adrenaline had long since faded, and doubts began to creep in. Hoshea's concerned voice rang in her head, calling her name. Why would he tell her about the Api bull but stop her from saving Seti from the final plague? What if she were making the biggest mistake of her life?

What if Miera was right, that Seti really was just a troublemaker? But she had spent five years with him. It wasn't like him to cause trouble, except when on his chariot. Her brother's words haunted her: Seti had saved her out of pity. Was that all it had been? She could be fooling herself— falling in love with an idea, a fantasy.

But the way he had stared at her at the palace and held her gaze—that was not a look of pity, but one of longing she had never seen before. She held onto that. He was worth saving. Worth incurring her father's wrath and risking her life for. She couldn't live with herself if she didn't try.

She prayed for God to consider him. God would decide what to do with him if he came back with her. The blood would save him, not Goshen, nor being Hebrew.

On lay in ruins when Eliza arrived, worse than she remembered. The all-too-familiar smell of rotted flesh greeted her, as if sadistically welcoming her back. The ground had dried up, but the sun still cooked the corpses.

In all of Egypt, one Hebrew walked alone.

Even from inside the barren grove, it was apparent that the mesa was empty. Seti checked behind him before nudging Chewy into a run across the field. Rage surged through his veins, charging his pulse into his throat and heating his face. Where was Sabu? Not a note or sign anywhere to indicate he had been there. Seti leaped from Chewy before coming to a full stop and ran to the ledge.

He drew in a breath as stones tumbled down the rocky slope. He'd kill himself before the Hebrew God could claim his life and soul. Would he? It'd be a violent, painful death. Better than a death at the hand of the Hebrew God?

His father didn't believe him, and his mother could not care less. The Egyptian gods had abandoned him. And now Sabu?

The unfinished pyramids lay beyond the city, their tips peeking from a green haze that had settled over the land. The evening sun cooked his shoulders.

"Curse you, Ra!" Seti shook his fist at the sun. "Yes, it's for real this time. I'm cursing you. You and Osiris. And Ptah. All of you! You cowards!"

He grabbed a stone and threw it with all his might, then hurled another toward the pyramids. "I did nothing wrong! Nothing!" He stared into the distance, catching his breath.

"I hate you!"

His feet teetered the ledge, legs trembling. The Egyptian gods abandoned their own people. The Hebrew God would never do such a thing.

Seti turned toward Chewy but tripped over his feet and fell to his knees on the limestone.

The rage left him instantly, his shoulders slumped, and he closed his eyes. A wave of resignation washed over him, sending his face to the ground. His chest heaved as tears poured into the dirt. He grasped the sand, and with trembling hands, poured it over his head.

The familiar neighborhood sparked a surge of energy in Eliza's exhausted muscles as she reached the villas atop the hill. She had arrived. The mud and straw houses lay in heaps, but the villas, made of brick, had weathered the storm. Few people lurked about in the stench of thousands of dead animals that hung thick in the air.

Eliza showed a man on the street the map and asked him to interpret it, but he couldn't read. Neither could the next. Had Seti drawn it? If so, the house would be his. If it was Sabu's, she was doomed. She didn't have time to search the whole city.

She skipped at the sight of the Ameneten house, not having seen it since that fateful morning. Her heart raced. What if his family detained her? She paused at the stable. Seti's horse and chariot were gone. Eliza stepped back, hand on her chest, as if the breath and hope had been sucked from her. He'd been banished. Why'd she think to even come here? His family might know where he went.

Please, God. Eliza climbed up the walkway with measured steps, took a deep breath, and knocked. No answer. She pounded. The door opened, and Kabelo poked his head out.

"Is Seti here?" she croaked, throat burning with trepidation.

"No."

His head disappeared, and the door started to shut, but she stuck her foot in the way. It went over the side of her foot, scraping her. She winced.

He peeked out again, first at her foot, then at her.

"I need you to read this for me." She held up the map.

He scanned it and shrugged. "It says 'My Mesa.'"

"What does that mean?"

"How would I know?"

"Scared Little Kitten?" Ameneten's voice came from behind Kabelo. He pulled the door open wider.

Instinct told her to run, but she didn't move. She dared to look her former master in the eyes. "What is '*My Mesa*?'"

"Are you Scared Little Kitten?" he demanded.

She hesitated. He knew. "Where's Seti?"

"Answer my question."

Kabelo shifted out from between them.

Eliza pulled the bracelets off her wrists and held them out. "You can have these if you tell me where he is."

Undeterred, Ameneten studied her with such intensity that she stepped back, ready to bolt, until he said, "He went searching for Sabu."

Tears filled her eyes, and she turned away, dropping the bracelets.

"Is it true?" Ameneten asked.

Eliza paused.

"The last curse. That the firstborn will die?"

She faced him. "Yes, it's true. And I can save him, but I need to find him."

He stared, mouth agape, eyes dull and vacant as if God had struck him right there in front of her.

Eliza held her breath, waiting.

He inhaled heavily, shifting his gaze to the ground, and Eliza let her breath out.

"I told you, he went to look for his friend. He can't be far. He left only a little while ago."

"The temple?" She prayed he didn't go there.

"No. He's banished from there."

A silent plea flashed in Ameneten's eyes before he shut the door.

Eliza stared at the door, stepping back. She was on her own. With no choice but to assume the house on the map was Seti's, she had to take the chance. If there wasn't a grove like the one shown on the map, she'd turn around and go home.

She hurried down the steps and to the road. After one last glance at the stable and house, Eliza ran.

Her secret prayer spot was no longer distinguishable from the rest of the bare field. The locusts had eaten everything. A desperate prayer escaped her mouth as she passed, going farther down the road than she had ever been.

"Let me find him."

Her breath caught when she came to the leafless grove and a branching road, exactly as drawn on the map. A trail entering the grove lay ahead.

"Oh, God! Oh, God, thank you," she whispered, finding hoofprints at the trailhead. "Please let it be him."

She balled the map in her fist and darted down the path, through a mixture of wet and dry sand. A stream trickled nearby where she knelt to drink, then returned to the trail. According to the map, there was a field and then My Mesa.

Sweat beaded on her forehead from the journey—or nerves—she wasn't sure which. Would he be appalled at her stink again? What if he rejected her?

As the barren trees gave way to a sandy field, Eliza caught sight of Chewy in the distance and halted, nearly falling flat on her face. Seti lay on the ground, on his back. A hand shot to her mouth at the thought of being too late. No, Hoshea said midnight. She took a deep breath and hastened her pace.

She stopped a few paces away from Seti and covered her mouth to stifle her panting, when Chewy lifted his head. Seti lay before her, arms outstretched, eyes closed, and speaking calmly.

"Aren't I worth saving?" Seti asked into the wind.

A strong breeze whipped sand over him, stinging his wounds.

"Take me, God of the Hebrews, and do what you want with me. You've destroyed all that I am and all that I believed. Just what you wanted. I am yours."

The wind howled, but the lightning strike, poisonous snake bite, or evil spirit appearing to steal his soul never came. Not a lion, please don't let it be a lion! But nothing happened. Not even an answering voice.

He opened his eyes and gazed at the deep blue sky. A heaviness of disappointment settled in his chest, pushing out a drawn-out sigh. Did the Hebrew God even hear him?

Shielding his eyes with his hand, Seti turned to Chewy, and his heart stopped. Eliza stood across from him.

Seti jumped to his feet, not believing his eyes. Tears streaked her dirty face, and long curls hung from the wrap on her head, blowing in the wind.

"Eliza?"

"Seti?" Her voice trembled but soothed his heart like a gentle strum of a harp.

It wasn't his imagination. He fought the urge to take her into his arms.

"Seti, you are worth saving." Another tear ran down her cheek like a droplet on a porcelain vase.

How long had she been standing there? Long enough to hear his pathetic plea? She was alone. No horse, no friend, no sister. The sun illuminated her perfect skin and highlighted the tears on her cheeks.

"Seti, if you want to live, you must come with me." She visibly shook.

He struggled to keep from embracing her. "What are you doing here? You're supposed to be leaving."

"All the firstborns will die. I came to save you."

He gulped. "I know I'm going to die. I'm okay with it. It's okay." Nothing mattered anymore but to calm her. To lightly brush the hair from her face and hold her. He stepped close enough to touch her.

She shook her head.

"How did you get here?" he asked. "What happened? Is someone after you?"

"No."

"Then why are you here?"

"I came here to save you, but it's too late. We won't

make it." She appeared on the edge of hysterics.

What was wrong with this girl? "Eliza, you need to tell me what's going on, so I can help you."

"No, you can't. We have to be back by this evening. We won't make it. It's too far."

Seti glanced at the setting sun, then at Chewy, then grasped her shoulders. Her eyes widened. "It's okay," he said with forced calmness. "We have time. We have Chewy. He can run fast." His hands slid down her arms, and he took hold of her hands.

A glimmer of hope sparked in her eyes as she looked toward Chewy.

"Tell me what to do, where to go. If you can save me, then let's go," he said.

She nodded.

"We can do this."

"I'm sorry." She turned away.

"For what?"

"I don't know," she whispered.

He smiled. "Scared Little Kitten."

Her eyes sparkled when they met his.

He squeezed her hands. If it were up to him, he'd never let her go again. "You don't have to apologize. I should be apologizing to you. I should have never called you that."

Her gaze dropped.

"I never knew you. Still don't. I let you get away. I wasted all those years—"

"Seti," she said, and his heart skipped at the sound of his name on her lips. "I knew you were worth saving long before you set me free."

Heat rushed to his face. The world spun, and his legs weakened. But he snapped out of it when Eliza pulled away.

She ran to Chewy and placed both hands on him, standing on her toes.

Dumbfounded, he followed.

"I've never ridden a horse before," Eliza said in a small

voice.

Seti regained his composure. "That's alright. I'll do the work. You just hang on." His eyes wandered over her until they caught sight of the faded scars on her back, peeking out from under her dirty tunic. He looked away in shame.

With a deep breath, he knelt and cupped his hands.

She crinkled her brow.

"Step in," he said.

She placed a foot into his hands, and he boosted her, hurling her onto Chewy. She landed awkwardly, legs dangling over the side.

"Are you sure about this?" he asked, watching her struggle into a sitting position.

"Yes, we don't have much time."

He climbed onto Chewy in front of her and grabbed the reins. Chills shot through him at her nearness, her touch. "Hang on." He hadn't ever ridden a horse with someone else.

Her arms awkwardly encircled his waist.

Chewy jerked forward, and Eliza gasped, her grip tightening around him. She pressed herself against him. A nervous chuckle escaped his throat at the sensations warming his body. Never had he felt so self-conscious and tingly at the same time. He had come to this field alone, but now he was leaving with Eliza holding on to him. Her God hadn't killed him, but he might as well be in the afterlife. This was too good to be true.

"Eliza, I'm sorry I was so mean to you," he began as Chewy trotted. "And I called you Scared Little Kitten. That was awful. I'm sorry you had to sleep in the outhouse. That's no place for someone like you. Eliza—"

"I know this horse can go faster."

Nodding, he pressed his lips together. "Alright, Chewy. You heard her." He snapped the reins, and Chewy broke into a gallop.

Her breath hitched, and he smiled, glancing over his shoulder. Was this the last time he'd set foot on the mesa? If

it meant leaving with Eliza, that would be fine with him.
"Goshen!" Eliza yelled.

Chapter 24

Entering Goshen felt like emerging from the hot, dark tunnels beneath Giza, except cooler. Different shades of green greeted Seti and Eliza from every direction. Long grass swayed in fields of rolling hills. Giant sycamores and acacias speckled the land. The moon illuminated a clear, crisp sky, and night bugs sang as Chewy passed beneath trees—their song, along with the braying of livestock, a symphony to Seti's ears.

Not only did the breeze soothe his skin with a sense of cleanliness, but a fragrance of lilacs and grass filled his nostrils. Seti inhaled deeply through his nose. Though it had only been a couple of months, it felt like a lifetime.

Eliza directed them away from City Street, just inside Goshen toward a small town she called Avaris.

"We're almost there." The fear etching her voice suggested they weren't safe yet. Her grip on him didn't relax. Crossing into Goshen wasn't the answer.

They followed the gravel road into a neighborhood of mud and brick homes packed tightly together, livestock filling the narrow spaces between them. Carts and wagons had been parked in the streets, overflowing with belongings. Bags and crates littered the yards.

Despite the abundance of life, not a person was in sight.

The crimson door mantels of each house drew Seti's curiosity. Stomach knotting with dread, he opened his mouth to ask Eliza about it when her arm shot to the left.

"Turn there."

As Seti steered Chewy, the first people they'd seen since entering Goshen came into view, sitting on the doorstep of a two-story brick house. The door hung ajar behind them, the only house without blood on it. Their faces lifted as Chewy approached.

Eliza's sister beamed, but the others—two lanky boys, a set of toddler twin girls, and an older couple—openly scowled. Even the toddlers. She had an entire family? Of course she did. Seti shook his head. Sweat dripped from his hands as he gripped the reins and swallowed a large lump.

The group stood, glares zeroing in on him.

Eliza jumped from Chewy before he came to a full stop. Seti dismounted, and Eliza grabbed his hand. "Come with me."

The family parted as she pulled him up the step. She led him inside while the others followed in complete silence. Two young adults sat at a table in the main room. Their eyes lifted and widened at Seti's entrance.

Everyone had gathered around the table except the older man, who remained outside.

"You're late, Eliza." The older woman cut Seti a look before turning her wet, puffy eyes to her daughter.

Eliza pressed her lips together. Her sister dashed out the door, and the twins attempted to follow, but one of the boys grabbed them and steered them to the table. The other one shut the door.

"Ima," Eliza's voice came loud and overly confident. "This is Seti. The one who freed me and Miera."

The glares didn't ease up.

"Seti, this is my ima, Sarah. Those are my brothers, Adam and Zechariah. You already know Miera, who went outside. And the two little ones are my twin sisters. Those two are guests rooming with us until we leave."

Seti nodded at each introduction and forced a smile that no one returned.

Her mother motioned everyone to sit.

Eliza squeezed his hand before letting go and plopped onto the hard floor, crossing her legs under the table. Seti sat awkwardly beside her. Not a cushion in sight. Not even a rug. Bags and sacks lined the walls and countertops. Several staffs and rods leaned against the inside wall by the door. Most of her family wore cloaks, as if prepared to leave at any moment.

A clay plate with unleavened bread sat in the middle of the table. Beside it was a small jar of oil, a plate of bitter herbs, and a bowl of shriveled lentils. Nothing looked fresh. They were going to eat? Now?

The front door slammed, and Miera entered, face wet with tears.

"It is done." She squeezed in beside Seti.

After all this time, Seti had never learned her name. Why was she crying?

The brothers folded their hands meticulously on the table, clearly enjoying his squirm under their penetrating stares. He looked everywhere but at them, wishing for something to distract them.

The door burst open, and Eliza's father entered with blood on his hands. He wiped them on a rag and donned a cloak from a hook on the wall, his gaze kept low.

With wide eyes, Seti struggled to hide his curiosity as he watched the man drag in a small cart containing a dead lamb. He grabbed a hyssop branch from beside the door, dipped it into the pooling blood in the cart, and painted the outside mantel with it. Then, leaving the hyssop outside, he shut the door and took the cart to a fire in the other room. He placed the lamb on a rack over the hearth, roasting it.

The family stared in silence until the man stepped into the kitchen and pointed at the door. "No one is to go outside.”

“Abba,” Eliza said, her voice unnaturally sweet after his stern words. “This is Seti.” She gestured toward him. “Seti, my abba. His name is Jeremiah.”

The man was the epitome of Hebrew manhood. With a full, scraggly beard and bushy gray eyebrows, he moved with purpose, though with a slight limp. His broad shoulders attested to the strength and authority he carried over the family. The dynamics weren’t much different from Seti’s family.

Seti swallowed a lump in his throat. “Nice to meet you.”

Her father’s eyes rested on Eliza but gave Seti no acknowledgment. He went straight to the lamb in the other room.

A solemn hush settled over the table like a thick haze. Aside from the crackling fire and her father’s shuffling footsteps, the only sound was Miera’s muffled whimpering. Eliza sat motionless, and Seti fumbled with his hands, trying to ignore the glares directed at him.

Adam, the taller boy with a hint of stubble on his chin, finally spoke, “How’d you like the gift?” His tone dripped with contempt.

No one answered, and it took Seti a moment to realize the question was directed at him. “Gift?”

“The cattle.”

The Api bull! Seti bit the inside of his cheek. “They were from you? The note said Scared—”

“Scared Little Kitten. You know who that is, right?” Adam leaned forward.

Seti glanced at Eliza, who kept her head lowered.

“Yes. How—”

“It was Eliza’s idea. She felt the need to pay your debt.”

“We brought them through the darkness. Eliza traded one of our lambs for them,” the younger brother, Zechariah, said. He couldn't be much younger than Kabelo. With a full head of curls and big brown eyes, he was the male version of Eliza.

Seti reached for Eliza's hand, overcome with compassion, but she sat on them. "Eliza?"

She nodded, hair hiding her face.

"She didn't tell you?" Zechariah asked, amusement flickering in his eyes.

"We haven't had much of a chance to talk yet." Seti turned back to Adam. "The bull saved my life. Pharaoh would have killed me if I hadn't found a replacement for the Api bull. When I delivered them to Pharaoh, he lifted the sentence from me and Chewy—"

"Chewy?" Adam interrupted.

"My horse. Because I had hidden my horse in the temple stable when I took the bull out."

Adam tilted his head. "Why would you kill the Api bull?"

They were going to interrogate him now? "It was an accident. I didn't know about the plague. I wanted answers from Ra and fell asleep in the field. When I awoke, the bull was dead."

At this, Eliza lifted her head.

"Did Ra respond?" Zechariah asked.

"No."

Zechariah smirked, and Adam raised a brow. Seti shrank under their gaze, the target of their mockery.

To his relief, Eliza's father stormed into the room with a tray of burnt meat. Miera gasped in horror as he slapped the tray on the table, startling the twins.

"Eat," he said, taking a seat beside his wife.

He offered a quick blessing to their God before a slew of hands grabbed at the meat and unleavened bread. Seti didn't dare move until everyone had served themselves.

As the sound of teeth gnawing on over-cooked meat filled the room, Eliza's father announced, "Here's what's going to happen. Nobody is to go through that door. The blood is what protects Adam."

Seti froze mid-bite. Adam's head jerked up, as if surprised.

Her father continued, "The Lord will come at midnight and slay the firstborn of any household without blood on the door—man and animal. Moshe is in On waiting for Pharaoh's summons, which won't happen until after his son dies. Then Pharaoh will give us permission to leave. We go at first light and meet Moshe on City Street. He'll lead us from there. There will be no returning to this house. This will be the only opportunity to leave…"

The man's voice faded as the realization dawned on Seti that the only thing protecting him was the blood on the doorframe. Would God kill his own people?

The Hebrew God was consecrating the firstborn, Egyptian and Hebrew alike, to Himself, the lamb serving as a sacrifice in their place. It wasn't just about the slaughter of Hebrew babies eighty years ago, but about a sovereign and holy God of gods. And yet, He provided a way of escape, an act of mercy.

Seti's father would die at midnight. If only he could warn him, find a lamb, and put its blood on their door. But it was too late. A crushing sorrow seized his chest, and his bread dropped to the table, uneaten.

The implications of her father's words pummeled Seti, his mind a jumbled whirlwind—the Hebrew God's mercy and wrath, the pending death of his father, and Eliza's saving grace. She sacrificed a lamb to atone for the Api bull. That act cleansed his sin in a way no purification pool could. And she risked the wrath of her family, maybe even her God, to bring him under the protection of the lamb's blood.

He wouldn't go home after this, no. He'd follow her wherever she went.

After they ate, Eliza led him to the side room where the remainder of the lamb had burned to ash. The room was completely empty—no furniture, no cushions. Not even boxes or crates. Smoke billowed through a hole in the ceiling. They sat on the hard ground beside each other, Seti cross-legged, Eliza on her knees.

She spoke for the first time since introducing him. "Is Chewy the firstborn?"

He hadn't thought about Chewy. He glanced around for a window. "I don't know." They had left Chewy out front.

Her hand touched his, drawing his attention. "Don't go out there."

Miera entered, her solemn gaze on the carcass in the fire. "That's Whitehead. We ate Whitehead."

"Whitehead?" Seti asked.

"The lamb." Miera pulled the head wrap from Eliza's head.

"Hey!"

Ignoring her sister's protests, she yanked Eliza's hair. "God's coming at midnight."

"I know! Go away."

"Eliza, stop moving!" Miera pulled again, eyes wet with tears. "Let me do this for you."

Eliza shot her a look but slumped her shoulders in resignation when she met Miera's gaze.

Confused at the curious exchange, Seti's nerves eased up. The two had lived under his roof for so long yet felt like strangers to him. Eliza looked away from him with a shy smile while Miera braided her hair.

Lumeri's sandals came to mind, and he snatched the woven bag off his shoulder and pulled them out.

"I found these in the outhouse." He held them out to Eliza.

Her eyes widened. "Those are Lumeri's."

"You can have them."

"My feet are too big. Miera wanted them."

"Here." He motioned for Miera to stick out her foot.

Miera beamed. Seti slipped the sandals on her feet and tied the leather straps around her ankles. She squealed and dashed around the room before racing to the kitchen and up the stairs.

Eliza's eyes shone. "That was very kind of you. She hasn't had a pair of sandals in a long time."

"What about you?" Seti asked.

Eliza shook her head.

"I'll have to find some for you then." He moved his hand to touch hers when Miera bounded down the steps and danced around them.

Seti chuckled, cherishing the rare moment of joy.

She bounced away after piling the braids on Eliza's head, leaving out a few small curls to frame her face. Except for the fire, the house darkened. Eliza's parents remained at the kitchen table. Her brothers took the twins upstairs to bed, and the boarders followed.

Orange firelight danced across Eliza's small, round face. A love for her that Seti had never known filled his heart, and a fluttering warmth spread through his chest as he reached for her cheek.

Her breath caught as he moved the stray hairs from her face, gently touching the light pink scar stretching from eye to chin. She closed her eyes as he traced her scar.

"Does it hurt?" he asked softly.

"Not anymore."

He held his hand under her chin. "I'm so sorry for that."

Her gaze locked onto his, and time stopped. He fought the urge to take her face in his hands and kiss her—to erase all the pain he and his family had caused. He wanted to love her, to hold her, to protect her. She was an original, like no other. She had saved him.

"How did you know about the bull?" he asked, voice cracking.

"Hoshea told me."

Hoshea?

"And you came in the dark to deliver them to the temple?"

She nodded, swallowing. "Were you there?"

"I was. Those were the worst few days of my life. I wish you had come to my rescue then."

She smiled, and his heart skipped.

He angled his head. "Why'd you come for me, Eliza?"

Dropping her gaze, she shrugged. "You know."

He tilted her chin up again and searched her eyes. She said he was worth saving long before he set her free. Why? "How did you know where to find me?"

She pulled a wrinkled cloth from her pocket and handed it to him. "Hoshea gave it to me. He said Sabu gave it to him."

Sabu? Sadness engulfed him as Seti opened the cloth, revealing a hand-drawn map. Sabu's sloppy handwriting spelled My Mesa. His best friend. He'd never see him again.

"It wasn't just me, Seti," Eliza whispered. "It was Hoshea. And Sabu."

It was her God. Seti wasn't a tool after all. The Hebrew God had chosen him long before Seti gave himself to Him, long before the first plague. Their God wanted him. His stomach knotted.

The wind howled, and the animals stirred outside. The low voices in the kitchen fell silent. Eliza's father shifted awkwardly at the table, leaning against the wall, the light from the lamp glowing in his eyes while her mother ran up the steps.

It was time.

Seti stood and went into the kitchen. He pulled a thin curtain from the window just enough to peek outside. An oil lamp sat on the porch, providing enough light to see Chewy stirring. He gripped the curtain.

Let me see you.

Eliza's words flashed in his mind—that sometimes her

God would manifest in a way humanity could comprehend Him. That is, if He wanted to be seen.

The fire in the oil lamp flickered in the breeze like a storm blowing in.

Show yourself.

Eliza stepped beside him and gently lifted his hand from the curtain.

Hands trembling, he wrapped his arms around her shoulders and clasped them together behind her neck to keep them still.

She gazed into his eyes. "Seti."

Her sweet voice drew his gaze from the window, but a longing stirred within him, a sudden desire to see the Hebrew God.

"Don't worry, Seti," she whispered. "You're safe with me."

His mouth dropped open as the dream came back, and he laughed, butterflies taking flight in his chest.

A loud squeal from outside stopped his heart. A human-shaped shadow, brandishing a sword, hovered a few paces away.

The air left Seti's lungs as he stared at the silhouette. It stilled, as if locking eyes with him—the lamb's blood the only thing between them. Then, as quickly as he could blink, it was gone. The fire in the lamp snuffed out. Seti gasped and pinned himself against the wall.

Eliza's hands shot to her mouth.

Seti let out a breath. "I think I saw Him."

His legs gave out, and he slid to the floor, swiping at the cascading tears, but they came too fast. Images of his father flashed through his mind: laughing, smiling, even screaming obscenities. His father was dead.

Seti grasped his knees, then his hair, then the dirt covering the rock floor. His chest heaved, and he couldn't catch his breath.

Eliza knelt and grabbed his hands, holding them as

they trembled beyond control.

He buried his face in his knees, letting the tears fall, his shoulders convulsing.

After the commotion of animals outside had settled, Eliza's father stood and left the room.

A distant wailing pierced the eerie night, and Seti straightened. His face had been buried in his knees for what seemed to be hours. The lamp on the table had been relit and provided the only light in the house, its tiny flame unmoving, as if all of Goshen had stilled to listen.

The dark nights in the temple flooded Seti's mind, and he shuddered. Eliza's head rested on his shoulder, grounding him.

He gently lifted her head. "Eliza?"

Her eyes opened a slit, lashes fluttering. A shy smile crossed her face, and Seti fought the urge to kiss her.

He moved the hair from her eyes. "I'm still here."

"Yes, you are," she whispered. Her eyes darted to the empty spot where her father had sat.

Seti scooted in front of her and took her hands in his. He looked her directly in the eyes and stated with earnest, "I'm coming with you."

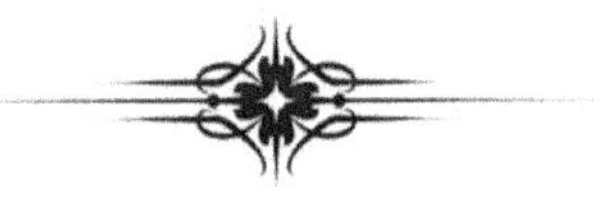

Eliza blinked. She hadn't thought about that. The last thing she had ever considered was him leaving Egypt with her.

She glanced at their hands. His strong hands held hers so gently, like she had seen him do with Lumeri.

"Eliza," he whispered. "You heard me on the mesa. I can't go back. I gave myself to your God, and He took me and saved me. He did so for a reason. Everything you said that one night is true. After all He's done, I can't go back. I don't want to. I want to be with you, your family, and Hoshea. I want to honor your God."

Her mouth fell open, and tears spilled from her eyes.

"Why are you crying now?"

"I don't know," she whispered. "I—I wasn't expecting that, I guess."

"Me neither." He smiled. "But I know I don't want to live without you."

"No." She shook her head. "Don't say that. It's not right."

"Why?" His eyes widened. "I mean, if your God doesn't want me traveling with your family, then fine, I'll find Hoshea or follow behind. But I would rather go with you. How could I not after all you've done? After everything that's happened?"

God had heard her pathetic little prayer.

His dimples appeared just for her. His eyes were so gentle, his touch so soft. Seti—who preferred beautiful, graceful, delicate girls and cared nothing for the Hebrew God—now sat in her parents' house in Avaris, wanting to honor her God, holding the hands of clumsy, dirty, and definitely not delicate Eliza. Telling her he didn't want to live without her.

She took a deep breath. "I don't know how this is going to work."

He squeezed her hands and smiled. "I don't know either. But we'll figure it out together."

The Hebrews packed in silence, a solemn fear settling over Goshen. The beauty of the sunrise seemed inappropriate for the situation. Seti's mother had lost her husband and firstborn. The two farmers must have assumed him dead by now. And where was Sabu? He tried to shake them all from his mind as he helped Adam and Zechariah load the last wagon.

Jeremiah, Eliza's father, hollered from inside the house, shaking Seti from his thoughts. Shouting followed, and Eliza's voice rose to a pitch that froze him solid. He had never heard her yell. And this wasn't just yelling, it was a full-fledged argument.

Zechariah paused, eyeing Seti. Adam stood tall, blocking the way to the front of the house. Her father must have ordered her brothers to take him outside, away from Eliza. He dropped the harness to the oxen, pushed past Adam, marched around front, but stopped short at the sight of the dried blood on the door frame.

The boys followed.

Heart pounding, Seti opened the door.

Eliza and her father faced off in the kitchen, her mother and Miera huddled by the stairway.

"You've saved him twice." Her father leveled her with a hard glare. "It's time for him to leave."

"The only way he's leaving is with us."

"He's not coming! You got what you wanted. He's alive, now obey me for once."

"If he doesn't go, then I won't either!" The fierceness in Eliza's eyes contrasted with the tears pouring down her cheeks.

"Eliza!" her mother yelled in horror.

Cowering on the steps, Miera covered her ears. "All of you, please stop."

"You barely know him!" her father shouted.

"I barely know you!"

Her father flinched, and Seti gulped.

Her mother reached for her. "Eliza—"

"I've only seen you maybe once a year." Eliza's voice leveled, if only for a second. "I've protected Miera like you wanted. I've cared for her and myself most of my life. Now you think you can take over as if you've been around all these years? I'm sixteen."

As her father drew in a breath, his hands balled into fists. "You're still my daughter. And I will not have you running around with—with him!" His arm stretched toward Seti.

All eyes turned to Seti, and he stepped back. He had to say something.

Eliza's eyes remained on her father. "I don't care. He has submitted to God, and God accepted him. He spared him."

"He's an Egyptian."

Seti tore his bag off his shoulder and dug out the gold cuffs. He slammed them on the table. The room went silent. "There. Consider me a Hebrew now."

One of the brothers smirked.

With eyes ablaze, Eliza's father brandished a jagged flint dagger from his cloak. Everyone gasped.

Seti froze.

"You really want to be one of us?" her father hissed through gritted teeth.

"Abba, wait." Eliza reached to stop him, but he blocked her with his hand.

"Let's see how serious you are, Son of Set." He stepped toward Seti, who backed into the brothers. "If you really want to be one of us, then you must be circumcised."

Eliza's hands covered her gaping mouth.

Seti's gaze darted between her and the knife, heart pounding. "I—I am."

"Like a Hebrew! Not that partial half-snip hack-job you call circumcision."

"Abba—"

Her father silenced her with a look of venom. "You said he's committed to our God?" He glared at Seti. "You're not going anywhere with her unless you're circumcised first."

Hands in the air, Seti stepped back in resignation. "If

that's what it takes."

Her father grabbed his arm like a vise, spun him around, and shoved him between Adam and Zechariah, out the door.

After shutting the door, Adam turned toward Eliza, eyes as big as saucers. Miera wrapped her arms around Eliza. No one else moved.

The urge to run after Seti jolted Eliza forward, but she forced her feet to stop and wiped her eyes dry. Her father spoke the truth. God required it of all His people, a physical sign of the covenant between God and Avraham for the inclusion of males into the Hebrew faith.

After a few moments, her father returned, alone. He entered the kitchen and wiped his hands on the rag. "I wasn't expecting him to go through with it."

"Did he?" Zechariah asked.

"He did." He nodded toward Eliza. "I left him by the fire pit. You might want to leave him alone for a while, though he could use some wine."

"There's some on the table." Adam pointed to a wineskin.

Grabbing it, Eliza rushed out the door and around to the side of the house. Seti sat beside the fire pit, covered with her father's cloak. He leaned against a log, legs sprawled. She knelt beside him, hands trembling as she presented the wineskin.

"It's official now," Seti said quietly, a half-grin on his pale face. He took the wineskin and guzzled.

Aware of her family's prying eyes, Eliza stared, mouth agape, though she desperately wanted to hold him.

"Don't worry about me." He shifted positions and

winced. "I just won't be able to ride Chewy for a few days."

"I can't believe you allowed my father to circumcise you."

"Me neither."

She dropped her gaze. "You didn't do that just to please him, did you?"

"Eliza!" her father called, leaning against the side of the house. "Leave him alone."

With a reassuring smile, Seti nodded toward him.

Eliza stood, wiped the dirt from her tunic, then went to her father. She flung her arms around him and buried her face in his chest. "I'm so sorry, Abba. I've been terrible to you."

Her father gently lifted her chin, his eyes smiling down at her. "You make my hair turn gray." He kissed her forehead. "And you're the first of four daughters. God help me."

She smiled, wiping the tears from her eyes. She hated crying.

Adam and Zechariah emerged from the house, peering at Seti.

"Get the oxen." Her father turned to go inside. "Time to go."

"That's him?" Rahel asked, gazing at the pitiful Egyptian crammed into the front of the wagon, facing the rear.

Seti's head bobbed, arms on his knees, wineskin dangling from his hands, the hood of her father's cloak shadowing his eyes. The family joined others from Avaris on City Street, headed east. Two oxen pulled the wagon. Zechariah fell behind, leading Chewy by the reins.

"Don't you remember from the palace?" Eliza asked. They strolled behind the wagon amid the crowd.

"He looks different not wrapped in linen."

"He's the handsomest, most beautiful man I've ever set eyes on," Eliza gushed.

"Listen to you." Rahel threw an arm around Eliza's shoulders. "You're starting to sound like me."

After hours of walking in the morning sun, the caravan came to a rippling halt.

"Moshe must be announcing something," Eliza said over the rambunctious children, crying babies, and voices singing and hollering.

"Let me guess, you want to find out?"

"You know I hate being left out." Eliza glanced around for Miera, finding her lagging behind, a twin hanging on each hand. Her mother carried a neighbor's baby, chatting with a group of women. Eliza was free to go. With an excited wave, she grabbed Rahel's hand, and they darted toward the front. The Hebrews were finally free.

Chapter 25

Seti woke from his stupor to darkness. Families surrounded him, trekking through the sand in a daze or quiet conversation. Babies slept in their mothers' slings, and young children slept on animals or in carts. Those who could stay awake toted large sacks on their backs. Three boys a few paces back locked eyes with him and turned away, whispering.

Eliza was nowhere to be seen. Her mother towed a small cart and gave him a warm smile that made Seti shy away. She offered him a date from the woven sack looped around her neck. The sweet, sugary taste contrasted sharply with the bland unleavened bread in the sack beside him. It wasn't enough to satisfy his hunger, but their food was limited.

"How are you feeling?" Sarah asked.

"Well." His face warmed as he mumbled between bites. Water to wash the bread down would be nice, but he didn't dare ask. His head spun from the wine, though nothing like earlier. "Where's Eliza?"

"She and Rahel went looking for Moshe. I wouldn't worry too much about her. She knows how to find you."

He nodded and straightened his stiff legs. Flat desert stretched into the darkness. How long had he been asleep? A full moon hung high in the sky, yet the peoples' shadows were cast behind them, and their faces glowed a deep orange.

Seti turned, craning his neck. A pillar of fire swirled ahead in the distance, like a dust- devil made of fire. He rubbed his eyes. Was this another Hebrew natural phenomenon like the rainbow?

"That, Seti, is the manifestation of God. He is showing us where to go," Sarah said, a sparkle in her eyes.

"He's a fire?"

"He's whatever He wants to be. He's everywhere, and yet He's there, leading the way and lighting our path."

She spoke like Eliza. Seti shifted his gaze from the fire to her, then back to the fire. A peculiar people with a peculiar God.

He's everywhere, yet He's there. How was that possible? Unlike when Seti looked at Ra, his eyes focused effortlessly on the Fire Pillar. This God had manifested in a way that was safe for the human eye, provided warmth in the cool desert night, and light to pierce the darkness. He is there, but He's everywhere. Did that mean He was in Egypt as well? Was He in Egypt with His people before Moshe came? He had to be. He formed them in the womb. He raised up Moshe. He raised up Pharaoh.

Did the Hebrew God raise up Seti?

He had to get a better look at this fire. He located Chewy being led by someone he didn't recognize. Seti rose, stretched his legs, and carefully stepped down from the cart. He took Chewy's reins, hoisted himself up, and winced.

Clamping his eyes shut, he tightened his mouth against the throbbing pain in his groin. Curiosity outweighed good sense. He rode away from the main group to gauge its vastness and get a better look at the Fire ahead.

The majority of the multitude traveled in a line, cutting across the plain as if on an invisible road, but many had scattered outward, following at a distance. When Hoshea had told Sabu that God had built a nation, he wasn't kidding.

Seti slapped the reins, and Chewy broke into a run,

shooting pains through his loins. He groaned and gritted his teeth. Dry desert air blasted his face and whipped his cloak. Exhilaration surged through his veins, the pain fading into oblivion.

"To the fire, Chewy!" he yelled into the wind.

They blasted past the Avaris group, quickly moving up the assembly with ease.

The head of the congregation came into view, but the Fire Pillar moved farther away the closer he got, much like the rainbow had. Seti's heart fell. The Hebrew God wouldn't let him get close. Seti swallowed a sigh and slowed Chewy into a canter. The flames wound upward as if pulled by the wind. Colors undulated inside, like a tangled rainbow. Transfixed, Seti let Chewy take the lead.

"Let me see you," he whispered, longing to meet this God who saved him.

Pain reignited in his groin, and he lost his balance. He grasped onto Chewy, groaning. Chewy slowed, and Seti rested his face on the horse's neck, taking deep breaths. He closed his eyes in resignation.

As the pain subsided, Seti opened his eyes, not daring to move. At the front of the congregation, several carts led by oxen carried caskets as if in a ceremonious procession. Seti sat up. Ahead of the carts, Moshe and Aharon walked in a small group, leading the Hebrew nation. He steered Chewy toward them, studying the twelve caskets. Unlike Egyptian caskets, these were carved from limestone, unadorned. No pictures. No words.

Guarded glares settled on Seti as he approached, and children cowered.

"Don't worry," he announced with a courteous wave. "I mean no harm. I was circumcised the other day."

"Seti?" A familiar voice called from the crowd.

Hoshea emerged from a small group of men, eyes wide

and glowing.

"Hoshea!" Seti leaped from Chewy and stumbled to his knees, gritting his teeth. Hoshea laughed as Seti regained his composure. "I was recently circumcised."

"And you're riding a horse?"

"Not the wisest decision I've ever made." Seti straightened and stretched his back.

Hoshea embraced him. "I can't believe it. You're alive!"

"I am." Seti's voice muffled under Hoshea's embrace.

After releasing Seti, Hoshea looked him over. "What are you doing here?"

"Eliza came for me. She said you helped her."

"I tried to stop her."

Seti did a double-take. "You did?"

"She learned about the firstborn that morning and took off running."

Seti wiped his sweaty palms on his tunic. She had fled Goshen to save him? "And the cattle? She said you helped with that."

"Cattle?"

"The Api bull."

"More than one?" Hoshea asked.

"Five. She and her brothers brought them to the temple."

"All five? I only told her about the bull."

Strolling beside Hoshea, Seti filled him in on everything that had happened since parting on the pyramid. It felt like ages ago. From the terrible nights in the temple, Eliza's daring rescue, to her father's words at the meal before the final plague.

Seti stopped, grabbing Hoshea's arm. "When your God came to kill the firstborn, I saw Him. I looked out the window, and He was there with a sword, looking right at me."

Hoshea's mouth parted, his gaze locked onto Seti's.

"That wasn't God, Seti. That was the Angel of Death sent by God. Nobody can look upon the face of God and live."

"But—" Seti pointed at the Fire Pillar.

"That's not God either. It's a manifestation of Him."

"How do you know the Angel of Death isn't Him?"

They continued walking, and Hoshea dropped his gaze. "It's possible. Maybe that's how the firstborn died, by seeing Him. But Moshe called it the Angel of Death, not God. I don't think they are one and the same."

How could Hoshea not know? He seemed to know everything about his God. Seti bit his lip.

The oxen groaned when the cart they pulled hit a rough gravel patch, and the wheels cracked under the weight.

"Who are in these caskets?"

Hoshea smiled. "They're the first of the Hebrews to come to Egypt when a famine struck the land. The sons of the patriarch Yaakov."

Seti smirked. "Egypt doesn't have famines." Until now.

Hoshea shot Seti a puzzled look. "Didn't you learn history?"

He relayed the story of Yoseph, the eleventh son of the patriarch Yaakov. He was the firstborn of Yaakov's favorite wife, Rahel. His brothers were jealous because of the favoritism shown to him by their father and sold him into slavery in Egypt, telling Yaakov he had died. God used Yoseph to prosper Egypt during the famine. When his brothers came seeking aid, Yoseph housed them in Goshen. He's the reason Egypt's storehouses remained full each year. Not Neper, not Hapi, not Osiris.

How could this have not been in Seti's studies? Egypt and the pharaohs were notorious for recording only favorable facts about themselves and their empire. One wouldn't dare credit Egypt's salvation to a Hebrew.

"Did Yoseph go by a different name?"

"He did. I don't recall what it was. Paneah?" Hoshea's

gaze drifted to the open sky before continuing. "These twelve will be buried in Avraham's cave in Canaan, the land we're headed to." He flashed Seti a fervent look. "The land God promised to Avraham's descendants."

"Avraham?" The name was familiar.

"Do you remember, Seti, when I told you about the covenant? About returning there in four hundred years, and that Israel would be a blessing to all the nations of the world?"

Seti stopped in his tracks. Hoshea had explained the covenant while they were in the Ameneten pyramid—in pitch darkness when Seti had hidden his true identity.

Hoshea smiled.

Seti gulped. "You knew?"

"Seti." Hoshea shook his head in amusement. "First, you and Sabu left your horses at the entrance of the tunnel, but you two were nowhere to be found. Then, when I tripped, you spoke Egyptian first. You didn't switch to Hebrew until I revealed I was a slave. I didn't have anyone on my team with the name you gave me, Ezekiel—that's a rare name. Remember when you were looking for the team leader, and I said you should know the names of those you entrust with responsibility?"

Fool. Seti's cheeks heated with embarrassment. "And what you said about my family, that we whip our slaves in their faces."

"Well, it was the truth. I thought I'd give you a taste of how you were perceived."

Anger and shame washed over Seti, and he fought the urge to leave. To go somewhere he could be alone. To ride Chewy at full speed, despite the pain. The Hebrews knew him, and he would never outrun the taint of his family's shame.

"Seti," Hoshea's voice became unexpectedly gentle. "I knew something was different about you when we met in that tunnel. You were hiding. Amenetens don't hide. You were defensive. I wasn't aware of the whole story until I talked with Sabu. Otherwise, I wouldn't have led Eliza to the Api bull."

Different. The word grated on him. His insecurities would follow him into the promised land.

"You defended one of our own, and I will defend anyone who defends one of us. Eliza is the sister of my friend. Your actions didn't go unnoticed."

Instead of sharing Hoshea's conviction, Seti withered, walking beside such a wise man. How was he to respond? Even Hoshea had noticed something peculiar about him. Was it the Hebrew God who made him different? When he defended Eliza, it brought him shame among the Egyptians but honor among the Hebrews, according to Hoshea.

Seti pressed his lips together and eyed the otherworldly fire looming in the distance, knowing he'd never get close.

But God had drawn him to the front of the procession, to the caskets, and to Hoshea. God didn't want him in Egypt.

"I need to find Eliza," he muttered.

"Before you go," Hoshea said. "There's one more thing."

Seti looked at him.

"Moshe calls me Yehoshua. You can call me that, too, if you want. I thought I'd let you know."

"God saves?" Seti asked, remembering his Hebrew.

Hoshea's grin grew so big his beard lifted. "I don't tell many people. And I don't know why he chose to call me that, but I felt compelled to tell you."

"Me?" Why would Hoshea reveal this? And to Seti of all people. Hoshea helped save Seti, if anything, but Moshe didn't know that. "Okay, Yehoshua."

Hoshea stuffed his hands in his cloak pockets. "And your name means 'Son of Set.'"

Seti smirked. What was the point?

"Son of Seth. And Seth means 'Appointed One,'" Hoshea said.

"Sometimes we call Set 'Seth.'"

"Seth was the first patriarch of God's people. Through him will come the promised seed of the woman, the future savior of mankind. Do you know what I'm talking about?"

Eliza spoke of this "seed" but vaguely. Was Hoshea saying he was the seed? "You're the prophesied one?"

Hoshea laughed heartily, and Seti smiled.

"No, I'm not. He has yet to come, but when He does, we will know. But think about your name and the meaning of 'Seth', not the Egyptian god. God changed Avram's name to Avraham by adding a 'ha' sound. As you learn more, the significance will become apparent, and it might change you too."

Seti furrowed his brow. Either Hoshea was being cryptic, or he only spewed words to raise Seti's spirits.

Why would Moshe call him 'Yehoshua'? Did Moshe see something in him? And did Hoshea see something in Seti?

Eliza had clearly underestimated the distance to the front of the congregation. Seti flew by on Chewy a while ago, oblivious as usual to how he stood out, probably searching out Moshe too. But there was no way she'd make it to the front in one day. Giving up, she decided to wait out in the open for Seti to return.

As Seti came bounding back on Chewy, she and Rahel waved their arms to get his attention. Thankfully, the Fire Pillar gave enough light. His face lit up with a toothy grin as he slowed and bent, hand extended.

"Come with me!" he yelled as he neared her.

Eliza skipped toward him, heart aflutter. That beautiful smile of his gleamed for her. She peered over her shoulder at Rahel.

"Don't worry about me." Rahel gestured with her hand as she followed. "You two turtle doves go on. I'll head back."

"Oh, Rahel. It's so far back. We'll come back for you."

"I only have room for one," Seti said, his hand reaching for Eliza.

"Go ahead!" Rahel laughed.

Eliza shot her a worried look but grabbed Seti's hand, and he hoisted her up behind him. Rahel's eyes widened as she shook her head in disbelief.

"Hang on," Seti said.

She wrapped her sweaty palms around him and pressed against his back. His cloak smelled like her father. But his warmth and strength gave her a sense of safety she hadn't felt since the last time she rode with him.

Seti stopped Chewy halfway up a barren hill hidden in the darkness of the night. They had roamed beyond the light of the Fire Pillar, into the shadows where nobody would see them. He dismounted and gazed at the Fire Pillar in the distance before turning to Eliza.

"You going to let me help you down this time?"

Eliza gave a shy smile and slipped off Chewy's back into Seti's arms. She braced herself as she landed, grasping both his arms. Her cheeks warmed, and she looked away. They were in the dark, away from everyone. Alone.

He let go except for her hand. "Look." He led her further up the hill.

She followed behind with a timidness so obvious that he stopped and turned to look at her.

"You can trust me," he said with a squeeze of her hand.

She nodded, biting her bottom lip. He narrowed his eyes but continued pulling her along until he finally sat on the stony ground amid the tall dune grass. Eliza swallowed and sat beside him. It must not have been close enough to satisfy him because his arm came around her shoulder and pulled her in close.

"Look. It's like a sunset." His free hand swept over the view below. "And you can see everyone. Look. The birth of a new nation, Eliza. All in one view. Under the eye of God."

The Fire Pillar illuminated an endless stream of people on the move. It cast them aglow—from Moshe all the way back to the Avaris group. If such a magnificent people could be seen all at once, Seti would find a way.

He gazed at her, his gentle eyes and dimpled smile disarming her. She had become his treasure, his precious metal. She had surpassed Lumeri in his heart. He left his home to be with her and her God. His God.

Not long ago, she had wished to be the one under his arm, gazing at the sunset, listening as he spoke of his adventures. She was a slave then, a nothing, with no future. But now she sat with him, gazing at this strange Pillar of Fire, listening as he told of how he had found Hoshea and the caskets of the twelve patriarchs. God had regarded her and set before her a future of marriage and a home.

345

If you enjoyed Eliza and Seti's story, this is only the beginning. God hadn't put on an elaborate show of power just to convince the world who He is and to bring His people to a new land. He wants more for His people than that. This book has, in fact, only set the stage for what's next. Follow the love story between Seti and Eliza and between God and His people in the sequel, as they venture into the unknown.

Thank you for reading my first novel!
Please leave a review on Amazon or Goodreads.

Visit my website AshmoresWildernessBooks.com for more on God's great love story for His people as well as the story of how this book came to be.

ABOUT THE AUTHOR

EJ is a wife, mother, and nurse, with a passion for young believers who are searching for answers about God. Whether it be what God wants, who He is, or why He does some of the things He does, she seeks to use ordinary, relatable characters to illustrate God's unwavering faithfulness and devotion even to those who feel unworthy or invisible.